Wild Montana Sky

DEBRA HOLLAND

The characters and events portrayed in this book are fictitious. Any similarity to real persons, living or dead, is coincidental and not intended by the author.

Printed in the United States of America.

Published by Montlake Romance
P.O. Box 400818
Las Vegas, NV 89140

ISBN-13: 9781612184661
ISBN-10: 1612184669

This Book Is Dedicated To:

MIKE SAMPLES
The young cowboy who inspired this story
and thus changed my life.

JAMES GLENNON
(1942–2006)
Emmy-winning cinematographer and
director of photography for *Deadwood*,
who loved this book enough to try
to bring it to Hollywood.

JOHN DENVER
(1943–1997)
In thanks for all the music and for the song
"Wild Montana Skies," which inspired my title.

Acknowledgments

This was my first book, and a lot of people helped me on the journey. Many thanks go to:

Louella Nelson, writing teacher extraordinaire.

My first critique group: Alexis Montgomery, Diane Dallape, Brenda Barrie, Linda Nusser, Erika Burkhalter, Janis Thereault, and Judy Lewis.

Authors who read chapters or the whole book and gave feedback: Jill Marie Landis, Linda Prine, Robin Lee Hatcher, Linda McLaughlin, Elda Minger, and Kathleen Givens.

My first agent, Bob Tabian, and my second agent, Kelly Mortimer, who both made contributions.

Geoff Nichols of Black Sabbath, for creating the sound track to the book.

My aunt, Hedy Codner, and friend, Kim Beckley, who helped with edits.

My uncle, Larry Codner, who helped with anything to do with guns in the book.

Romance Writers of America, especially my local chapter, Orange County.

Delle Jacobs, who designed the beautiful covers for the series.

The Wet Noodle Posse, for their ongoing friendship and support.

CHAPTER ONE

Boston, 1893

Laurence married!

Elizabeth Hamilton leaned against the blue-and-gold-papered wall of the entry hall and stared in shock at the telegram from her brother. Her vision blurred into dark whirls. She tried to breathe deeply lest she faint into a heap on the tiled floor, but with her lungs constricted by more than the tight lacings of her corset, she could only gasp for air.

Katie, the parlor maid, rushed forward, putting a steadying hand under Elizabeth's elbow.

"Are you all right, Miss Hamilton?"

Elizabeth glanced at the anxious face of the maid and tried to pull herself together enough to dredge normal words from the maelstrom of her feelings. "I'm fine. Just a little faint." She strove for a semblance of calm. "I need to sit down."

Leaning on Katie, Elizabeth crossed the hall into the parlor. She sank into her favorite blue velvet wing chair, slumped against the cushions, and closed her eyes.

"Should I bring your smelling salts, Miss Hamilton?"

Opening her eyes, Elizabeth shook her head. "I don't have smelling salts. I've never needed them."

"I could borrow Cook's?"

"No, thank you." Elizabeth tried to smile. "I'll be fine."

Katie's indecision flickered in her brown eyes. She twisted her hands in her white ruffled apron. "I know it's not my place to ask, Miss Hamilton, but is it bad news about Mr. Hamilton? Should I send for anyone?"

"Actually, it's good news. I was just taken by surprise." Elizabeth was too shaken to care if she broke protocol by not first sharing the news with the housekeeper. "My brother has married."

Katie drew in a hissing breath through her teeth. "Mr. Hamilton married?" The puzzled look on the maid's face reflected Elizabeth's own confused feelings. She looked again at the telegram in her hand.

MARRIED GENIA BAXTER. ARRIVE HOME TWO WEEKS.

"We'll have a new mistress." The girl covered her mouth, then dropped her hand. "Everything's going to change," she whispered.

Yes, everything.

Elizabeth tried to give her a reassuring smile. "We have a well-run household, Katie. I'm sure the new Mrs. Hamilton will make very few changes." She waved her hand at the door. "I'm feeling better, thank you. You may go."

The lump of pain lodged in Elizabeth's throat belied her casual words to the maid. She'd no idea her brother had been courting anyone. Now suddenly he was married! And without inviting his own sister to the wedding. Hurt and betrayal burned through her chest. She stood up and balled her hands into fists, crushed the telegram, then threw it into the fireplace.

Unable to sit still, Elizabeth paced the room, trailing her fingers across the blue-and-silver striped wallpaper. When she had redecorated the parlor, she'd resisted the current fashion for darker shades of red. Instead, she'd spent many hours searching for soothing blues, which were a more personal statement of her tastes.

She had deluded herself into thinking this day would never come—that her brother would never marry, and she'd always serve as the mistress of his house and hostess for his business affairs. Yet at times she'd sensed the emptiness in his heart, hidden beneath a stiff exterior and demanding business and social life, and wished he could find a congenial life companion.

She glanced up at the portrait of Laurence and herself, painted twelve years ago, at the start of her first season. Callers always admired the picture of the tall, blond-haired, blue-eyed siblings. A much younger Elizabeth, dressed in the white silk and lace gown she'd worn to her debutante ball, sat in front of her brother. Laurence, in formal evening clothes, stood behind Elizabeth with his hand protectively on her shoulder.

Hope threaded through her hurt. Perhaps in Laurence's bride she'd find a true sister to fill the empty place in her heart caused by her best friend's marriage and move to Montana. Even though they'd been separated for ten years, she missed Pamela so much. How wonderful to have a close confidant once again—someone to help banish the loneliness trailing after her like a phantom.

A vision of Elizabeth's personal ghost slipped into her mind. Tall and handsome, with laughing brown eyes and a playful grin—Richard, her beloved fiancé...The fingers of her right hand crept up to her chest—a familiar gesture—to clasp the gold locket containing his picture. If Richard had lived, he'd be teasing her now with outrageous descriptions of Laurence's wife. In her laughter, she'd forget her pain. Of course, if he'd lived, this wouldn't be an issue.

Somehow, after his death, eleven years had slipped by. Although she'd had offers, no one had measured up to Richard, and she refused to marry any man she didn't love. Besides, her brother had always said he needed her.

Tears welled in her eyes. "I hope, Laurence," she told the portrait, "you've found the kind of love Richard and I had."

❋ ❋ ❋

Katie burst through the door of Elizabeth's parlor. "They're here, Miss Hamilton!"

"Thank you, Katie."

"Yes, Miss Hamilton." The maid left the room.

Excited in spite of all her fears, Elizabeth set down her book of poetry and took a steadying breath. Then she rose and walked into the hall, determined to show her brother and his new wife a proper welcome.

Her brother stood with his arm around a petite, dark-haired woman dressed in gray with black lace trim. At first glance, Genia appeared younger than Elizabeth had expected, only twenty-two or twenty-three. Her big brown eyes, with dark lashes and brows, gazed frankly at Elizabeth. Her nose had a pert tilt. She smiled, revealing a slight overbite.

"Here she is." Laurence gestured with his free hand toward Elizabeth. "Genia, my dear, this is your new sister." He bowed and spoke with a gallantry Elizabeth had never before seen him display. "Elizabeth, I'd like you to meet my lovely bride, Genia."

Elizabeth barely had time to register the astonishing change in her reserved brother. He seemed so animated—so happy. Her heart lightened in response. She smoothed an imaginary wrinkle out of her green silk dress and crossed the few steps to give her new sister-in-law a kiss on the cheek.

"Welcome, Genia. I've been looking forward to meeting you."

"Dearest Elizabeth! Laurence has told me so much about you."

"I wish I could say the same," Elizabeth murmured, with a wry glance at Laurence that he didn't acknowledge. Instead, he beamed at his new bride.

"You're so pretty, Elizabeth," Genia bubbled. "Why, I'd never have taken you for a spinster."

Spinster. The word hit Elizabeth like a slap across her face. Was that how people would see her now—as a twenty-nine-year-old dried-up old maid? She repressed a shudder. Was that how she'd come to see herself? *No, never.* She'd known a deep and abiding love. When Genia knew her better, she'd understand.

Genia gushed on. "I can't believe we're finally here, although we've had a wonderful honeymoon. Haven't we, dear?" she asked with a coy glance up at her new husband.

Color rose up Laurence's throat, and a small sound escaped him. Apparently choked with emotion, he could only nod.

A polite smile straining the corners of her mouth, Elizabeth asked, "Why don't you let me show you to your room so you may refresh yourself?" Then, ashamed that she might seem unwelcoming, she tried to infuse more warmth into her voice. "Or would you like tea?"

"Oh, tea, please," Genia said.

"Then let's go into the parlor." Elizabeth turned to lead the way, but before she could move, Genia stepped ahead of her. "You don't need to show me the way, dear Elizabeth. Laurence has described the house so well, I believe I already know it."

A disturbed feeling settled in Elizabeth's stomach. She followed in Genia's wake, Laurence trailing behind her.

"Oh, what a beautiful room," Genia cried. She walked over and seated herself in Elizabeth's favorite chair, then pulled off her gloves. "It's similar to my parlor in New York, except I used red, which is so-o-o stylish."

"Red is popular in Boston too," Elizabeth said.

Elizabeth watched Laurence settle on the blue velvet sofa. In spite of Genia's distressing behavior, Elizabeth knew she must give her the benefit of the doubt. Perhaps her new sister-in-law was nervous.

"Several of our friends have used red to superb advantage," Elizabeth added, "as you will see when you make calls with me."

"Dear Laurence has promised to introduce me to all the best people," Genia said, with a fond glance at her husband.

There was an awkward pause. "Let me ring for tea." Elizabeth tinkled a tiny silver bell. She seated herself in a small straight-backed chair across from Genia, giving her a chance to study her new sister-in-law.

Genia was pretty, rather than beautiful, and had an air of vivacity about her. No wonder her normally staid brother looked captivated.

Katie entered the room in response to the bell.

Elizabeth gestured toward the woman. "Genia, this is Katie, our parlor maid."

Katie bobbed a slight curtsy toward Genia.

"Katie, this is Mrs. Hamilton."

Genia gave the maid a gracious nod.

"Will you please tell Cook we'd like some tea?" Elizabeth asked.

"Yes, Miss Hamilton," replied Katie, turning to leave.

"I'm sure Laurence has described our servants as thoroughly as he's described our home," Elizabeth said, "but I'll still introduce them to you."

"Yes, he has," Genia replied with a laugh. "I had to tease him because he was rather vague on their positions and duties. Isn't it just like a man to not pay attention to housekeeping?"

"They've no need to." Elizabeth gave her brother an ironic glance.

Genia fluttered her hand toward her heart. "It was difficult to give my servants their notice. It so distressed me that dearest Laurence said I might keep any who wished to move to Boston."

"Dearest Laurence" beamed at his wife, and she smiled at him before continuing. "They'll remain with the house until it sells, and then any who haven't found new employment will pack up my furniture and other possessions and accompany them here."

"Here," echoed Elizabeth, trying not to sound as dismayed as she felt. "All your furniture?"

"Oh, not everything. There are some pieces from my late husband's parents. Dark and dreary old things, which I've never liked, but Henry insisted on keeping. I was glad to give those to Henry's sister. Everything else I couldn't possibly part with. Dear Laurence assured me there would be ample room."

Her brother nodded his agreement.

With a constriction in her throat, Elizabeth recalled the pleasure she'd taken in decorating her home. She swallowed down a lump of pain and anger. How could her brother have told Genia she could bring everything…even the servants? The only way there would be room in the house for Genia's furniture would be to move theirs to the attic. Unless Genia was planning to move Elizabeth to the attic…or maybe out onto the street!

To turn her mind from such ridiculous imaginings, Elizabeth changed the subject. "When did your first husband pass away?"

"Six months ago."

Genia wasn't even out of mourning! Elizabeth hoped the shock didn't show on her face.

"I know it's too soon to wed again, but dear Laurence swept me off my feet. And he wouldn't wait a single moment longer."

What will people think? Shame knotted Elizabeth's stomach and sent heat rising to her face.

Genia sent Laurence a tender smile. "I knew it would be difficult to leave New York." She shrugged. "But when you fall in love, nothing else matters."

Katie's entrance with the tea tray allowed Elizabeth a moment to compose herself. Seeing the laden tray, Elizabeth seized upon a safer topic of conversation. "Cook has been baking for several days in anticipation of your arrival."

"It looks wonderful." Genia's tone of voice said the opposite.

"Her plum cake is quite a favorite. My friends continually beg for the recipe, but she refuses to divulge it."

Elizabeth reached for the rose-patterned tea service; the familiar aroma of tea promised to sooth the fear jumbled inside her.

"My dear Elizabeth, you must let me pour." Genia grasped the teapot before Elizabeth could reach it. "I refuse to be treated as a guest."

Elizabeth pulled back her hand, hiding her distress behind a polite social smile. "Of course, you must pour, Genia. I take one spoon of sugar, and Laurence takes—"

"Laurence takes two," interrupted Genia in a syrupy tone. She poured him a cup and spooned sugar into it. "I too have a recipe for plum cake. It was my grandmother's."

"Oh."

"Laurence told me it's a favorite of his. I'll give my recipe to the cook for her to make from now on." Handing her new husband the cup and saucer, she smiled at him. "Here you are, dearest."

Laurence smiled. "Thank you." He fell silent, seeming content to let the two women, or rather Genia, do all the talking.

As her new sister-in-law chattered on about plans for redecorating the house, Elizabeth's head began to ache. Although Genia included her in the plans, it was only a token gesture.

A wave of resentment flushed Elizabeth's cheeks. She'd worked hard in the last week to reach an attitude of surrender and compliance about her new position. Dozens of times she'd pictured scenes where she gracefully handed the reins of the household over to its new mistress, but it had never occurred to her they would be wrenched from her hands under the guise of charm.

Elizabeth stopped attending to Genia, nodding when it seemed appropriate, but was more concerned with hiding her anger and hurt. *I'm not going to let her suspect she's upset me.*

Genia's voice jerked Elizabeth out of her thoughts. "Elizabeth!"

Elizabeth glanced up. "Oh—yes?"

Genia's pinched look of disapproval said she didn't like being ignored. "Laurence and I should have a party to celebrate our marriage. I know we shouldn't hold a ball until I'm out of mourning, but a dinner party should be acceptable."

"Perhaps in two weeks, after you've settled in."

"I'm so looking forward to meeting your friends, although I must tell you that I do know many people in Boston already. My friend Helen Lloyd—do you know her? She has the most dashing brother! You'll have to meet him."

"No, I don't believe I've made their acquaintance."

Genia gave her a conspiratorial smile. "My friends consider me the best matchmaker of our set. I've helped many marriages along. Even some women who hadn't a hope."

How dare the woman insinuate I'm on the shelf.

Elizabeth took the deepest breath her corset would allow. The gloves were off. Turning to Laurence, she matched Genia's sweet tone. "We'll have to introduce dear Genia to Miss Weston, won't we, Laurence? She's been trying to find a husband for years."

Laurence nodded in agreement, apparently not understanding the undercurrents. Elizabeth couldn't believe he could remain so oblivious. Could he not see the barbs beneath Genia's sweet behavior? For his sake, she hoped he'd never feel them.

Elizabeth's headache worsened. Finally, they finished the interminable tea.

"Would you like me to show you to your room, Genia? I'm sure you must be tired after your journey."

"That's not necessary. You'll find I'm always full of energy and rarely need to rest. Besides, I'd rather my dear Laurence show me my new home."

"In that case, I'll leave you two alone." Elizabeth stood and offered a faint smile. "I think I'll go lie down."

She hurried to her room and rang the bell for her personal maid. Grasping one of the bedposts, she rested her forehead against the smooth carved wood and closed her eyes. When she heard Josie's knock, she straightened.

"Come in."

She kept her face averted in an effort to hide her feelings. "Josie, please help me undress."

Holding back tears while Josie unfastened the long row of pearl buttons down the back of her dress, Elizabeth focused on the rose-patterned wallpaper until her vision blurred. Josie's chattering about the glimpses the servants had caught of the new Mrs. Hamilton only worsened the pounding in her head. Finally, the maid noticed Elizabeth's mood.

"Are you well, Miss Hamilton?"

"I've a headache," Elizabeth said, pressing her hands to her aching forehead. She dredged up a smile to combat the look of concern on Josie's plump, freckled face. "Please draw the curtains and see that I'm not disturbed until it's time to dress for dinner."

As soon as the door closed, Elizabeth turned the key in the lock. She'd never before locked her door, but she wanted to ensure that Genia's house inspection didn't include her room.

She crawled into bed, nestling under the pink flowered covering, wishing she could find oblivion in sleep. But there was no comfort to be found. She curled up around a lavender-scented pillow, clutching it to her with one hand, while the other hand balled around her locket.

The suppressed feelings of the last two weeks burst forth, and she let loose the sobs she'd been holding back. She had no more hopeful words to bolster her spirits. Reality was worse than anything Elizabeth had imagined, and she dreaded what the future held for her.

Pamela. The name brushed across her mind like the touch of an angel's wing.

At the thought of her best friend, she eased her grip on the tear-soaked pillow. After Pamela married and moved to Montana, the two women engaged in faithful correspondence. Only in her letters to Pamela would Elizabeth let down her reserve and pour out her feelings. Elizabeth might live in the East and Pamela in the West, but their hearts remained connected regardless of the miles between them.

Shoving the coverlet aside, she slid out of bed. With a few watery sniffs, she made her way over to her writing desk, sat down, and pulled out her stationery.

The act of putting pen to paper released a new flood of tears. Sentences gushed out almost more quickly than her fingers could write. Her usually perfect copperplate handwriting slanted and squished its way across the paper.

Teardrops splashed on the page, forming miniature pools, the ink rising to the surface before feathering across the letters. As she wrote, the constriction in her chest ceased, and the rush of words slowed.

Elizabeth sniffed and signed the letter. As she scrawled Pamela's address, one last tear dropped, blurring a word. But when she blotted the script, the writing still remained legible enough to send.

She flexed the fingers of her hand, working out the cramps. The storm of emotion had passed, leaving her drained and exhausted, but calmer somehow. But would it be enough to help her face life with Genia?

CHAPTER TWO

Sweetwater Springs, Montana

Nick Sanders gripped the raccoon-skin overcoat closer to his chest with one leather-gloved hand, while the other hand guided his horse around a large mud hole. Although the spring thaw had finally arrived, the brisk Montana wind nipped through the layers of clothing, chilling his body to ice. With every step, his Appaloosa, Freckles, kicked up muck. The mud splashed his chaps and clung to the horse's legs.

At the outskirts of Sweetwater Springs, he reined in, thankful to be riding, not walking, through town. A murky quagmire spanned the main street. A few half-buried boards linked the false-fronted stores. For several years there had been a debate about building wooden sidewalks, but so far, nothing had been done. If it were up to him, he'd vote for sidewalks—hell, he'd even help build 'em.

When he reached the train station, Nick dismounted, grimacing as his boots sank six inches into the mire. With a grunt, he pulled one foot free, then the other, looped the reins around the depot rail, and slogged through the last few feet to the relative safety of the wooden stairs. He knocked the worst of the mud from his boots, then stepped onto the platform and hurried into the yellow-and-brown building.

Nick pushed open the door, wrinkling his nose at the stale air. But he didn't stop until he reached the cast-iron stove in the corner. He yanked off his gloves, then held out his hands to the welcome warmth.

Behind the counter next to the stove, the stationmaster huddled beneath several tattered wool scarves and a faded red Indian blanket.

Nick nodded. "Afternoon, Jack."

"Nick." His gray hair standing out in a bushy halo, the squat stationmaster bobbed his head toward the shelves behind him. "My rheumatism's painin' me somethin' fierce today. You'll have to get yer mail yerself."

Wooden crates, stacked behind the counter and labeled with faded black letters, identified all of the Sweetwater Springs inhabitants who regularly received mail. Jack relegated the occasional letters or packages to a plain box on the floor.

Reluctantly, Nick moved away from the stove, went behind Jack to scoop up the catalogues and a few envelopes from the wooden crate labeled Carter Ranch, and scooted back to the stove. The heat felt good, so he took his time while he paged through the mail. Most looked like business correspondence for John Carter. There was a letter for Nick from Great-Aunt Agnes, and Miz Carter's father had written again, but it was the last envelope that caught his attention.

Many a time he'd picked up letters sent from Pamela Carter's dearest friend in Boston, Miss Elizabeth Hamilton. He called to mind the portrait of Elizabeth and Pamela, painted right before Pamela's wedding, that hung in the parlor of the ranch house. Miz Carter had told him the picture was a good likeness of blonde, blue-eyed Elizabeth. The portrait always drew him. He snuck peeks at the Boston beauty whenever he was in the parlor.

So he was intimately familiar with the exquisitely formed copperplate writing scrolling across the expensive stationery Elizabeth used. But this time the usually perfect words straggled in slanted lines across the envelope. The watermark that marred the word "Mrs." could have been made by rain, but Nick doubted it. He ran his finger over the blotched letters.

Not a raindrop, but a tear.

The hand holding the letter tightened at the thought. A strange gut instinct told him Elizabeth Hamilton needed help, and the need tugged with such force, he could barely resist its pull. If she lived nearby, he'd mount his horse and ride to the rescue. But what could he do? She lived on the other side of the country, and he didn't even know her.

Nick shook his head in frustration and tucked the letter inside his shirt, next to his skin. He pulled a small canvas sack from his pocket and dropped the other mail inside.

Still mesmerized by the need emanating from the missive, he pulled on his gloves, tilted his hat to the stationmaster, and stalked out the door. He wanted to head back to the ranch straightaway to get the letter into Miz Carter's hands, but he still had to collect Mark and Sara Carter from school.

Once outside the station, he could see children pouring out the door and down the steps of the white frame schoolhouse, the boys laughing and shoving each other, the girls in more sedate bunches. Some stopped to loiter under the large oak next to the building, while others scattered off. It should only take a minute for the Carter children to get their ponies from the livery stable, and they could all head home.

As he rode closer, he spotted Sara holding the hand of an unfamiliar woman and clutching a book and doll to her chest. He assumed she must be the new schoolteacher who'd arrived in town sometime after Christmas. He hadn't had a chance to meet her because the ranch had been snowed in for weeks, and the children had taken their lessons with their mother.

Sara caught sight of him, dropped the teacher's hand, and waved so hard the brown braids dangling beneath her red knitted cap bounced on her shoulders. He stifled a sigh. He hated talking to strangers, especially females, but didn't see a way out of it. For politeness' sake, he'd have to make another dismount into the mud.

He slid off his horse, careful not to splash the woman or children.

"Nick, Nick," Sara shrilled, her smile so big he could see the wide gap where she'd just lost her two front baby teeth. "This is our teacher, Miss Stanton."

"Ma'am." Nick touched his hat. The teacher was a pretty little thing, her shiny brown hair rolled into a sleek bun, and the gray of her eyes matching the wool coat she wore. Those eyes sparkled up at him in a way that gave him an uneasy feeling in his stomach and dried up any words he might've said.

"I'm pleased to meet you, Mr. Sanders. The children have been telling me all about you. I gather you're their best friend."

"Reckon so."

Mark Carter strolled over, pretending to ignore his sister. Out of the corner of his eye, Nick noted the mischievous look on Mark's face. He reached over to place a restraining hand on the boy's shoulder, too late to stop the scuffling elbow he'd sent toward Sara.

Sara's book and rag doll flew from her arms into the mud. "Catherine," she wailed, shoving her brother. In resisting, he stepped on her doll, pushing it into the muck.

Nick grabbed Mark, squeezing his shoulder to stop any further attacks. "What kind of behavior is this? You apologize to Miss Stanton and your sister."

Mark hung his head. "Sorry, ma'am."

Miss Stanton nodded.

"And your sister."

Mark hesitated.

Nick sent him a stern look.

"Sorry, Sara."

Nick turned Mark in the direction of the stables and gave him a gentle shove. "You go get saddled up."

"Good-bye, Miss Stanton." Mark's mischievous grin reappeared, then he scampered off.

Sara ignored her brother and stared down at her doll, its embroidered face so buried only the yellow yarn braids trailed free.

Nick stooped to pick it up, but before his hand touched the muddy red gingham dress, a memory punched him so hard he had to resist snatching back his hand.

Marcy's doll.

He tried to swallow down the unexpected lump of pain that jumped into his throat, threatening to choke him.

The wagon accident had killed his parents and little sister while he'd remained safely at a friend's house. He'd insisted on riding out to view the death site and seen the wagon smashed against the rocks by the bank of the snowmelt-swollen river. He refused to believe the truth, until his sister's rag doll, buried in the mire next to a deeper indentation, made the nightmare all too real.

Nick remembered holding that rag body cradled to his chest as he cried for what seemed like hours in gut-twisting torment, followed by a wave of shame for the unmanly tears. He'd angrily tossed the doll into the river and watched as the blood-red dress filled like a sail and floated away.

Nick grabbed the leg of Sara's doll and pulled it free. Holding the doll dangling by the leg, he handed it to Sara.

"Nick." Sara's tone protested his handling of her baby. She snatched it away from him.

"Wait," he ordered. Glad of the excuse to turn his back and hide his feelings, he strode to his horse, opened the saddlebag, and pulled out a gunnysack. "Put Catherine and your book in here. We'll clean them up at home."

Sara complied.

"Now," Nick said. "Go get your pony. And no more fighting with your brother."

Sara wrinkled her nose at him, then turned to her teacher. "I'll see you tomorrow, Miss Stanton."

"Don't forget to study those spelling words, Sara."

"Yes, Miss Stanton."

"You should get in out of the cold, ma'am." Nick wanted to escape. He needed time to settle down his thoughts.

"Oh, I don't mind." Her smile showed straight teeth. "It's nice to stand. I've been doing a lot of sitting on a hard chair."

He sent a sidelong glance to the stable. No sight of the children.

"Sara told me your mama used to be the teacher in this very school."

He nodded. "Yes, ma'am."

"I'm honored to be following in her footsteps, Mr. Sanders."

The pleasant memory of his mother sent warmth through the chill in his heart and loosened his tongue. "Just call me Nick, Miss Stanton. Anytime someone calls me Mr. Sanders it makes me look around for my pa."

"Very well, *Nick*. If you'll call me Harriet."

"No, ma'am. I couldn't do that, you being the schoolteacher and all." With a feeling of relief, he saw Mark and Sara lead their ponies out of the stable. "Here come the children." He touched a forefinger to the brim of his hat. "I'd best be goin'."

Nick mounted and headed toward the livery stable. He sensed Miss Stanton remained outside, watching him ride away. He resisted scrunching his shoulder blades together and instead urged Freckles into a trot.

He reached up to check the placement of Elizabeth's letter. As the paper crackled against his skin, the schoolteacher and uncomfortable feelings faded from his mind.

"Come on, you two," he called to the children. "We've a long, cold ride, but there's a hot fire and warm soup awaitin' us."

Mark and Sara kneed their ponies into a trot. Still holding his hand over the letter, feeling Elizabeth's need sear through his skin, Nick signaled Freckles to follow.

❋ ❋ ❋

The letter continued to burn against his heart, and Nick longed to turn it over to Miz Carter. Mark and Sara riding their ponies held him to a slower pace. By the time Nick and the children arrived at the ranch, their numb fingers could barely clutch the reins.

Nick dismounted and hobbled a few stiff steps to the barn door. Pulling it open, he beckoned the children to lead their ponies inside before following with Freckles. Blinking several times to adjust his eyes to the darkened interior, he stepped into the barn, grateful to be out of the chill wind. The children quietly unsaddled their ponies and started grooming them.

He longed for the warmth of the indoors, but Freckles needed his attention. It would take more than an urgent letter from Boston to make him abandon the needs of his horse.

With a flurry of blue wool skirts, Pamela Carter entered the barn. "There you are, my dears." A blue-and-brown knitted shawl hung haphazardly around her shoulders as if just tossed on. Tendrils of brown hair slipped from a knot on the top of her head and curled around her plump face. Hurrying into the pony's stall, she hugged Sara. "You feel so cold, my darling. Are you all right?"

"Yes, Mama. But look." She pulled the rag doll out of the sack and dangled its limp, muddy body in front of her mother. "Mark pushed me and made me drop her. Then he stepped on her face."

"Oh, dear. Mark, you know better than to push your sister." Pamela shook her head and turned back to her daughter. "Why did you bring Catherine to school?"

"I wanted to show Mildred the new dress you'd made for her."

"You know school's no place for toys. From now on Catherine stays at home." Pamela kissed Sara's forehead, then walked into the other stall to stand next to Mark. "You're going to help me wash up Catherine until she's clean as can be. Understand?"

"Yes, ma'am."

"Good." Pamela ruffled Mark's hair. "Annie's made cookies in honor of your first day back to school."

Mark and Sara whooped simultaneously.

"When you're finished with the horses, you can each have *one* cookie. Just don't spoil your dinner."

Nick waited until the children had finished and returned to the house. Before Miz Carter followed, he slipped the letter from underneath his shirt and handed it to her. "It's from Miss Hamilton. I think something's wrong."

Pamela's brown eyes darkened with worry. "What makes you say that?"

How can I tell her it's just a feeling? "Look at the envelope."

She reached for the letter, backed toward the nearest hay bale, and sat down. Glancing at the writing, she tore the envelope open and scanned the letter.

"She's not ill, thank God, and no one has died." Pamela relaxed her rigid posture. "Her brother, Laurence, who everyone thought was a confirmed bachelor, has married unexpectedly. I can't believe it." She shook her head. "Poor Elizabeth."

"Why's that bad news?" Nick asked.

"Laurence's marriage will certainly change things for her." Pamela gave another sad sigh. "Apparently his new wife isn't very kind."

Nick frowned. In a protective urge, his fingers brushed the side of his coat covering his gun. Realizing his gesture, he jerked his hand back and laced his fingers behind his back.

He couldn't understand his strange reaction to this woman's plight. But then again, he'd always felt an attraction to Elizabeth's portrait. He didn't have to interact with a painting, not like with a real woman. She was safe—a Boston beauty, as far above him as an angel.

"Can't she live with someone else?"

Pamela shook her head. "There *is* no one else. And she certainly couldn't live alone. That's not done in Boston."

"It's a shame she never found someone to marry." Strange how those words tugged at his heart.

Pamela gave the letter a thoughtful glance. "Maybe she will now. It's really her only solution." Her finger traced the tear stains on the paper. "She was crying when she wrote this." Pamela's eyes filled with tears threatening to spill. "I hate that she's so unhappy, and I'm not there to help."

Nick leaned closer and awkwardly patted her shoulder. "You should invite Miss Hamilton here."

Pamela's tears vanished, replaced by her eager smile. She bounced off the hay bale. "What a lovely idea."

He took a hasty step backward.

"I'm sure John won't mind. I'll ask when he comes in." She whirled around and almost tripped over her skirt in her haste, then hurried out of the barn.

Nick shook his head in wonder. *What have I opened my mouth and gotten myself into? I can't say more than two sentences to a woman without fidgeting.*

When he thought of Elizabeth Hamilton living at the ranch, where he could see her every day, he didn't know whether to kick up his heels like a spring colt or saddle up and ride away to the next state.

CHAPTER THREE

"Good morning, Miss Hamilton."

Josie's cheerful greeting woke Elizabeth from a light doze. The maid poured hot water from a pitcher into the porcelain washbasin, then sprinkled in a few dried rose petals. "Will you be getting up and going down to breakfast?"

Elizabeth turned her face away from Josie. "Why don't you just bring me some tea?"

"That will be the fifth time this week, Miss Hamilton."

Elizabeth ignored the reproach in Josie's voice.

"Why don't I draw the curtains? The sun is shining, and it's a beautiful day out." Without waiting for a response, Josie pulled back the blue velvet draperies.

Elizabeth winced, turning her face away from the sudden light, and pulling the covers up to her neck.

"Miss Hamilton, you've got to start eating, or I'll be taking your dresses in."

Elizabeth wanted to shut out Josie's concerned voice, but knew she was right.

I need to get out of bed and face this situation, she scolded herself.

But all she wanted to do was drift back to sleep.

I can't keep hiding.

Reluctantly she climbed out of bed and walked over to the washstand. A look in the mirror told her she really had lost weight.

The purple smudges under her eyes didn't disappear when she splashed the rose-scented water on her face.

What have I been doing to myself?

She dried her face with a linen hand towel, annoyed at her own weakness of character.

It's time to confront my brother and force him to see what he and Genia are doing to upset my life.

❋ ❋ ❋

When Elizabeth entered the dining room, she saw her brother sitting at the mahogany table. "Good morning, Laurence."

He nodded. Standing, he held out a chair for her, then moved to the sideboard to serve himself.

Elizabeth poured tea out of the silver teapot into the rose-patterned teacups. The delicate Dresden breakfast service had belonged to her grandmother and had always been a favorite of Elizabeth's. Soon perhaps they might be eating off something entirely different. She couldn't bear the thought.

Elizabeth helped herself to a piece of toast, frowning as she watched Laurence fill his plate. The fishy smell of kippers, for which he had acquired a taste while on a business trip to England, turned her stomach.

"Genia was tired this morning, and I insisted she stay in bed," Laurence remarked, pushing eggs onto his fork. "She and I have been so busy with these wedding visits. She's looking forward to some peace and quiet after they're over. She has so much she'd like to do with you."

What might that be? Elizabeth sipped her tea and tried to look interested.

"I'm glad she loves Boston," her brother continued. "I was worried about her leaving her familiar life in New York."

Elizabeth reached for the silver butter dish and slowly buttered her toast. "She seems happy, and she certainly is full of plans."

Genia always has so much energy." Marvel showed on his face. "I'm sure when you come to know her, you will admire her as much as I do."

"I would have welcomed a chance to make her acquaintance before your marriage." Elizabeth put the toast in her mouth and bit down hard.

Laurence finished chewing before he answered. "Genia wanted to invite you for a visit, but I knew you'd like the surprise."

"Knew I'd..." Elizabeth dropped the toast on her plate. The bite she'd just taken formed a hard ball in her throat. The hurt of her brother's words pounded in her heart and spread to her stomach.

He seemed oblivious to the effect his words had on her.

She swallowed enough to speak. "Laurence, I enjoy the surprise of an unexpected gift." She strove to keep the edge out of her voice. "An unexpected sister-in-law is entirely different."

Laurence shifted in his chair and moved his hand toward the newspaper, but after he glanced at her face, his hand stilled.

"This is a happy change for you," she said. "However, it's different for me." Her voice rose. "This has always been *our* home. *I* was the mistress of this house. Now it's yours and Genia's. Did you stop to consider *my* feelings at all?"

His left hand played with the edges of his newspaper. "I thought you'd be pleased. I know how much you've missed Pamela. I thought Genia would provide you with the close female companionship you've been lacking."

I wanted that too. But you chose a woman I couldn't abide. And I know the feeling's mutual.

Rage rose in her. Elizabeth had a nightmarish vision of standing up and throwing her teacup and toast in his face, all the while screaming like a shrew at the top of her lungs.

Instead, she reached out a shaky hand for her cup. The simple act of bringing it to her lips and swallowing the warm tea calmed her, allowing her to think. She could point out to him, sentence by painful sentence, exactly how his marriage had affected her, but what would that accomplish? The deed was done.

Elizabeth wouldn't allow her shoulders to slump in despair, so she sat erect, protecting the pain in her heart. To share her feelings of betrayal and sadness would only humiliate her further. She would distress Laurence, but nothing would change. He might even share her feelings with Genia, and that would be intolerable.

He's married to Genia, and that's that. I must accustom myself to the situation.

Pulling the last vestiges of pride around her like a cloak, Elizabeth held her head high. "I *have* missed Pamela," she said in a quiet voice.

Laurence looked relieved. "I'm sure Genia and you will become just as close." He patronized her with a thin smile, then hid behind his paper.

Genia fluttered into the room, waving a letter. "My mother will arrive in two days," she caroled. "It will be so lovely to have her here in my new home. Don't you agree, dearest?" She dropped a kiss on Laurence's forehead.

He looked up from the paper, smiled, nodded, then began reading again.

Genia took a seat, reached for the teapot, and poured herself a cup. "But I'm concerned with where I'll put her."

"The blue guest room is our best."

Genia grimaced. "My mother's a light sleeper. She needs absolute quiet. The two nicest guest rooms overlook the street."

Elizabeth sipped her tea. "The garden room, then. It's quiet."

"Oh, no. That would never do. Pink gives my mother a headache. As for the other…it's so pokey. Hardly fit for a maid. Don't you agree, dearest?"

Laurence didn't look up. "Hmm."

Elizabeth got a sick feeling in her stomach. Genia couldn't possibly be angling for her to give up her bedroom?

"Elizabeth, would you mind? It's only for a few weeks. And I know you'll adore my mother. All my friends do."

Silence stretched out. She couldn't make herself acquiesce.

Genia appealed to the paper. "Don't you think that's a good idea, dearest?"

Laurence cleared his throat, but didn't lower the paper. "I'm sure Elizabeth would be glad to help your mother."

Elizabeth stared at the back of the newspaper in despair. If anything, this breakfast conversation had made her feel worse, not better. She could no longer make excuses for her brother's selfishness and lack of concern for her feelings. She needed to stop worrying about his marriage. He and Genia deserved each other.

Somehow, some way, I need to find a way out of this situation.

❋ ❋ ❋

Elizabeth stuffed one last quilt into the already overflowing wooden crate on her parlor floor. Another packed crate, one of dozens the Ladies' Aid Society would send to missions in China, stood nearby. As she slipped a small blonde doll into the folds of the quilt, she smiled.

Some black-haired, almond-eyed Chinese girl will love this doll. I wish I could see her face light up when she finds it.

The mission boxes were Elizabeth's favorite charitable endeavor. Not only did she enjoy collecting clothing, blankets, and medical supplies for orphans, she loved the happy memories associated with the task.

As girls, she and Pamela had helped their mothers pack the boxes. They'd always slipped in a few toys as a surprise for the Chinese orphans, and Elizabeth continued to keep up the tradition.

Today the mission work had proved a good distraction. As she packed, her vivid memories kept her from feeling alone. It seemed as if Mother, Pamela, and her dear Richard worked alongside her.

Over the last unhappy weeks, Elizabeth had often found her thoughts drifting from fears of the future to past memories. Especially to Richard, the man she had loved and come so close to marrying.

At the thought of him, a smile flitted across her face. In the weeks before they packed mission boxes, Richard always solicited money from his male friends. He turned most of the funds over to Elizabeth, but with the rest, he bought some of the special presents she and Pamela hid in the boxes.

With the last painted doll tucked away, Elizabeth struggled to fit the wooden lid onto the crate. She really shouldn't have packed them so full, but she couldn't resist putting in the extras. One more smash of the blanket did the trick. The lid snugged into its groove.

Dusting off her hands, she relaxed back into her favorite chair, the one Genia seemed determined to usurp. Noticing Genia had placed the Oriental vase on the table in the wrong spot, she defiantly pushed it back six inches.

She lifted the gold locket resting on her bosom and ran a finger over the flower of seed pearls on the front. Snapping the cover open, she studied the photograph of Richard. Her imagination gave life to his warm brown eyes and the wayward lock of dark hair falling across his brow. Although a good likeness, the photograph didn't catch the laughter that had so often lit up his face.

Richard had given the necklace to Elizabeth on her eighteenth birthday, a few months before they'd become engaged, and she seldom took it off. Bringing the locket to her lips, she kissed his face, and for the thousandth time silently asked his picture why he had died. How different her life would have been—

A knock on the parlor door interrupted Elizabeth's solitary musings. She snapped the locket closed.

"Come in."

Katie entered the room, her starched black skirt rustling. "A Mr. Sanders is here to see you, Miss Hamilton."

"Mr. Sanders?" Elizabeth rummaged through her memory. The name sounded vaguely familiar, but she didn't recall knowing a Mr. Sanders. "Did he state his business?"

"He mentioned knowing Mrs. Carter."

"Pamela?" Elizabeth jerked upright in her chair, her heart lightening in excitement. "Show him into the parlor." Now she remembered. Nick Sanders was one of the cowboys who worked for John Carter. Whatever was he doing in Boston?

❋ ❋ ❋

Nick glanced around the blue-and-gold entryway, taking in everything—from the sweeping marble staircase to the intricately carved wooden ceilings and the massive crystal chandelier hanging overhead. The silence of the room settled on his shoulders. The starched cotton shirt he wore under his Sunday suit scraped against his newly scrubbed skin, sandpaper rubbing off the thin veneer of refinement. So much for trying to gloss up a simple cowboy.

Trepidation tightened his stomach muscles. Until he stood in the oppressive opulence of the Hamilton mansion, he hadn't known what he was up against. He dug his boot heels into the black-and-white marble floor, lest his feet up and carry him out the door. Right now, he'd rather face a grizzly bear than tackle Elizabeth Hamilton with his errand.

In the days since Miz Carter had received Elizabeth's letter, a flame had burned in his heart. The need to pluck Miss Hamilton right out of her distressing circumstances and ride off with her to Montana had caused him a ceaseless ache.

When John Carter had bought a fancy new stud from a breeder near Boston, he'd suggested Nick travel east to pick up the horse. Nick had demurred, until Pamela asked him to fetch Elizabeth at the same time. Then he'd snapped at the idea like a trout after a fly. Nick half smiled, remembering the astonishment on John's face. Carter had no idea how sweetly his wife had baited the hook.

But now, seeing the mansion she lived in...The fire inside him flickered. Worry gnawed through his thoughts. While living with the Carter family, Elizabeth would receive all the love and respect she deserved. However, the ranch itself, with its passel of cowboys, grit, and farm smells, might not be a setting in which she'd shine. Could she adjust from upper-class Boston to life on a ranch?

They'd soon find out. His mission was to bring her west. His fingers tightened around the letter he'd brought from Miz Carter.

The maid returned. "Miss Hamilton will receive you."

She turned and Nick followed her, his boots thudding on the marble floor, disturbing the heavy stillness of the house. His discomfort increased. He hadn't seen anyone in Boston wearing cowboy boots.

The maid ushered him into a plush parlor, with gray-blue velvet chairs set against papered walls striped in blue and silver. At the sight of Elizabeth Hamilton, all his previous concerns flew out of his mind.

She was dressed in green, the color of new leaves, with her burnished blonde hair pulled back in a simple knot. Her blue eyes, more azure than the sky back home, turned in inquiry toward him. The color of her surroundings suited her. Nick had never seen a more elegant woman.

Damn, she's beautiful.

His tongue froze like lake water in a Montana winter, and his greeting died on his lips.

❋ ❋ ❋

Elizabeth heard his footsteps, slow and deliberate, before she saw him. He stepped into the room, holding a wide-brimmed black hat in his hands. She hadn't known what a Montana cowboy would look like, but she certainly hadn't expected the handsome young man in a black suit whose brown hair waved to the tops of his shoulders. He stood about three inches taller than her and had dark-lashed green eyes, a nose with a slight bump as if it had been broken at one time, and a strong jawline.

"Miss Elizabeth Hamilton?" As he looked her over with unabashed appreciation glinting in his eyes, the last syllables of her name trailed away.

Elizabeth suppressed a smile. Although used to admiring glances from gentlemen, she'd never had her appearance render a man speechless. He seemed five or six years younger than she, and she didn't want to hurt his feelings. Besides, the idea of an attractive man having that look in his eyes for her touched a place in her heart that had been cold for a long time.

"Mr. Sanders?"

The sound of her voice appeared to bring the man back to earth. "Nick Sanders, ma'am. I work for the Carters on their ranch in Montana."

"Yes, Mr. Sanders; Pamela has written to me about you."

He smiled, showing straight white teeth.

Elizabeth caught her breath at the way the smile blazed his green eyes to jade fire.

"I suppose you're wondering why I'm here." The tanned skin around his eyes crinkled with apparent amusement. "Miz Carter sent me to fetch you to the ranch."

"Fetch me to the ranch?"

"Yes, ma'am. Miz Carter wants you to come out for a visit. Maybe even make your home in Montana." He held out a letter. "This explains everything."

Elizabeth reached for the letter. Her fingers brushed his, sending tingling warmth up her arm. Her response startled her.

Oddly nervous, she glanced down at the envelope. Indeed, it was Pamela's familiar handwriting.

"I have to go to the Foster Horse Farm and pick up a stud for John. I'll be back in four days' time. If it's all right with you, we can leave then."

Leave? I can't leave. Whatever would I do in Montana?

Elizabeth snuck a peek at him though lowered lashes. And she certainly wouldn't be traveling with this cowboy—even if he was an attractive man. *Especially* not since he was an attractive man. Elizabeth shook her head. "I couldn't possibly travel to Montana with you."

As if trying to see into her thoughts, he shot her a penetrating look. "Is it that you won't go to Montana, ma'am? Or that you don't want to go to Montana with *me*?"

Disconcerted at how he read her mind, she took a step back; heat flooded her cheeks. His direct manner brought her up short, and for a moment she wondered what to say. She'd better send this man on his way.

With a rustling of taffeta underskirts, Genia entered the room, the scent of violet trailing in her wake. "Elizabeth, I was informed we have a caller." When she saw Nick, she raised her eyebrows. Her critical gaze rested on his long hair, then slid down to his boots. "I don't believe we've met, Mr....?"

"Sanders, ma'am. Nick Sanders." He nodded.

Genia's nostrils pinched together. "Mr. Sanders." She gave him only the faintest inclination of her head.

Elizabeth's stomach tightened in embarrassment at her sister-in-law's lack of graciousness. How dare Genia treat a gentleman caller in such a way, no matter if he was a young cowboy. Elizabeth stepped forward, gesturing. "Mr. Sanders, this is my brother's new wife, Genia Hamilton."

"Pleased to meet you, ma'am."

Genia seated herself in Elizabeth's chair, smoothed her gray silk skirt, and lifted the gold and diamond watch pinned to the bosom of her dress, pointedly checking the time. "I haven't had a chance to meet all my dear sister-in-law's...*friends*."

The inflection in Genia's voice raised Elizabeth's hackles, and she changed her mind about sending the man away. "Won't you join us for tea, Mr. Sanders? We can all become better acquainted."

Genia cleared her throat.

Nick rocked his weight back. "No, thank you, ma'am. I'd best be goin'."

"Very well, then."

"I'll stop back in four days to see if you've changed your mind—"

"—Oh." Genia's hand fluttered. "That wouldn't be a good day to call. We're giving a party that evening."

Elizabeth drew in her breath at Genia's rudeness. "Actually," she said smoothly, "it would be a perfect day to call on us. In fact, I'd like you to attend our dinner party as my guest. It will give us an opportunity to discuss your proposal further."

Genia gasped.

Elizabeth suppressed a smile at the pop-eyed look on her sister-in-law's face.

Reluctance, and perhaps shyness, lurked in his eyes.

"There won't be many people," Elizabeth urged. "Mrs. Hamilton is still in mourning." She sent him her sunniest smile. "Please say you'll come."

"I'm not a man with a lot of experience at fancy partygoin', Miss Hamilton," he said, his gaze intent on her. "However, I can't rightly turn down such a cordial invitation."

"Excellent." Seeing the glow in his green eyes sent a shiver feathering down Elizabeth's spine. *Why did he look at her that way? And why did it have such an effect on her?*

Genia sighed in frustration, and Elizabeth knew she'd better get Mr. Sanders out of the house before her sister-in-law said or did anything even more ill-mannered. Knowing Genia, she might even go so far as to rescind the invitation. "Let me see you to the door, Mr. Sanders."

He inclined his head toward Genia. "Good day, ma'am."

Genia gave him a stiff parting nod.

To make up for Genia's coolness, Elizabeth tucked her hand around his upper arm.

He flexed his elbow in response, leading her to the door.

The feel of the hard muscle moving under her hand brought a flush of heat to her body. *Do all the men in Montana have...?* Elizabeth pulled back her thoughts. She obviously wasn't accustomed to such an outdoorsy type of man.

They walked into the entryway; their footsteps tapped on the tile floor.

"I must apologize for my sister-in-law's treatment of you, Mr. Sanders." She hesitated. "She's new to Boston and is perhaps still unsettled by the changes in her life."

Understanding shone in his eyes. "There's no need to apologize, Miss Hamilton," he said, his tone quiet. "It must be difficult for you, her bein' here." He briefly touched the hand she'd laid on his arm. "Thank you for welcoming me."

Elizabeth's throat closed. There'd been so little kindness in her life lately. She lifted her chin, determined to bid him a composed good-bye. When the door had shut behind him, she sagged against the door frame, tipping her head against the smooth wood. She shut her eyes, letting the unfamiliar feelings of caring and hope seep into the frozen places of her heart.

Like one of the heroes in the dime novels of the West, Mr. Nick Sanders had ridden into her life, offering to rescue her from her unhappy situation. In just a few minutes, his admiration, kindness, and handsome presence had lightened the bleakness of her days.

Should I consider his offer?

* * *

Nick strode away from the Hamilton mansion, mentally berating himself. Crossing the cobblestone street, he dodged a slow-moving buggy. What did he know about fancy Boston parties? He'd be as out of place as a trout in the horse pasture.

But I've given my word.

He'd just have to bite the bullet and get through the evening as best he could. If he stayed quiet and carefully watched everyone else, he shouldn't make too many social blunders. Besides, he didn't care what Genia Hamilton thought of him. Only Elizabeth's opinion mattered.

Ever since he'd seen her portrait, Nick had dreamed about meeting Elizabeth Hamilton. But the reality had been more wonderful and awful than any of his imaginings. When he'd looked into her lovely blue eyes, his throat had constricted, and he'd experienced the strangest sensation of not being able to utter a sound. If it had been up to him, he would have stood and stared at her all afternoon.

Although he'd resisted an instinctive ducking of his head and shuffling of his feet—remnants of the shyness that had plagued him since his family had died—he hadn't been able to prevent the heat rising in his face. Hopefully she hadn't noticed.

At the memory, his face flushed again, and he inhaled a deep breath of the sea-scented air. Thankfully, no one was around to see him acting like a boy in puppy love. If the ranch hands saw him now, he'd never hear the end of their teasing. But then again, if he persuaded Elizabeth to come to Montana, when the men caught sight of her, they'd probably have a similar lasso-around-the-tongue response.

* * *

Inside the safety of her room, Elizabeth sank into the chair by her dressing table. She traced a finger over her name written on the envelope in Pamela's careful penmanship.

When they were debutantes, Pamela had been the one everyone thought would end up an old maid, not popular Elizabeth. Then John Carter, an older rancher from Montana, had traveled from the West on business and to find a wife. He had been canny enough to see Pamela's loving heart beneath her plain exterior. With the good wishes of Pamela's relieved family, he'd conducted a whirlwind courtship. The new Mrs. Carter returned home with her husband when he finished his time in Boston. Elizabeth missed her dearly.

In Pamela's letters, she wrote about the many ways her husband continued to cherish her and how she loved her life in Montana. Pamela had three children now: nine-year-old Mark, seven-year-old Sara, and three-year-old Lizzy, Elizabeth's godchild.

She always eagerly awaited news of them. It wasn't the same as knowing them herself, but the letters brought them closer.

With sudden impatience, she tore open Pamela's letter. The words of commiseration in the first sentences caused her to release the breath she hadn't even been aware she'd been holding.

Elizabeth smiled at Pamela's idyllic description of life on the ranch. But the final paragraph jerked her upright, her heart pounding like a kettledrum.

> *I've been playing matchmaker for you, Beth. The man who owns the bank in Sweetwater Springs, Caleb Cabot Livingston, is handsome and intelligent. He is related to the Boston Cabots and was educated there. He is one of our most eligible bachelors. John and I don't know him very well, but he has always seemed charming and personable. I've mentioned you might visit, and he expressed eagerness to make your acquaintance. I'm sure, my beautiful Beth, you will quite captivate him.*

Elizabeth couldn't believe it—a wealthy bachelor, eastern-educated and attractive, who just happened to own the bank in Sweetwater Springs, Montana.

A pang twanged at her heart and pulled down the corners of her mouth. She cupped her locket, opening the case, and touched it to her lips. This man could never be her beloved Richard. She gazed at the picture for a few more minutes before snapping the locket shut.

But maybe? How lovely it would be to be courted by a western man of means and breeding. Her heart lifted at the thought.

CHAPTER FOUR

Elizabeth watched Genia's mother descend the last few stairs to the entryway. Lucinda Simmons had arrived in Boston for the newlyweds' first formal dinner party. For the past two days, Mrs. Simmons had made everyone's life miserable, especially Elizabeth's. After a few hours of her company, Laurence had escaped to his office, and had seldom emerged, leaving the burden of entertaining Mrs. Simmons to Genia and Elizabeth.

Mrs. Simmons reached the landing. Eying Elizabeth's gown, she said, "Pink, my dear Elizabeth? It's such a youthful color."

"I agree, dear Mrs. Simmons." Elizabeth matched the older woman's sugary tones. "When I was a debutante, I had so many pink dresses that Laurence teased me when I wore a different color." She held out a fold of her silk-satin Worth gown. "Even now I love the rose colors. So flattering to the complexion; wouldn't you agree?"

Mrs. Simmons's mottled cheeks flushed a deeper hue. "After a certain age, one shouldn't wear such low-cut dresses." This time her tone had dropped the sugar and held only pure starch.

Elizabeth straightened her shoulders. She knew she had a womanly bosom. Over the years she had seen enough appreciative male glances slide downward. Not like Genia's meager endowment or Mrs. Simmons's ample lace-covered pigeon breast, straining above a waist even a tightly laced corset could not make trim.

"Yes, time does take its toll on a woman's body," Elizabeth agreed. "Thank goodness one can always wear dark colors and use lace to cover up."

Mrs. Simmons's bosom huffed up even more. Before she could respond, Genia stepped in. "Mother, did I tell you I'm eager for Elizabeth to meet Mr. Lloyd? He'll be quite captivated by her."

Elizabeth shrugged inwardly. Her thoughts slid to the handsome cowboy she'd rashly invited. If this Lloyd fellow proved to be too much of a bore, she could spend time with Nick Sanders. At least he could tell her more about Pamela and life on the ranch. Maybe he even knew Caleb Livingston...

A dreamy smile started across her face. But the cross frown leveled at her by Lucinda Simmons brought Elizabeth back to the ordeal before her.

Laurence, elegant in black evening clothes, joined them. "You ladies look lovely." He bowed gallantly, bending to kiss Genia's cheek.

She flushed with apparent pleasure and tucked her hand in the crook of his arm. Elizabeth had to admit Genia looked her best tonight in purple lace over a lavender silk underdress.

Laurence seemed to think so. He positively beamed at his wife. "Your first party here, my darling. Are you ready?"

"Of course, my dear."

"Yes, my Genia does look beautiful," gushed Mrs. Simmons. "And those diamonds, my dear Laurence, are positively splendid on her." She threw a malicious smirk at Elizabeth.

Laurence nodded, giving Elizabeth an uncomfortable glance. She sent him a reassuring smile in return, although her heart wasn't in it. Ever since her mother had died, Elizabeth had worn the heirloom Hamilton diamonds on special occasions, and she'd come to think of them as her own. But as the male heir, Laurence was the real owner of the diamonds, so Genia had every right to them now. Elizabeth had kept the less ornate diamond necklace and earrings bequeathed to her by her mother.

Tonight, however, she wore the pearls her parents had given her for her debutante party. She touched the pearls at her throat and ran her fingers down the silky strand. Wearing them always reminded her of her parents, and tonight she needed the support of their memory.

Genia had invited twenty guests for dinner. Except for the Lloyds and Nick Sanders, all were friends of Laurence and Elizabeth. Genia had spent several weeks planning the party, never once asking for Elizabeth's assistance.

Elizabeth had made her own preparations for the evening. She'd spent days accustoming herself to her new role. Inside she felt prepared for the changes in her position; outwardly she determined to look her best. She'd ordered a becoming new gown from her favorite dressmaker, and her upswept curls and interwoven braids had taken Josie an hour to arrange.

Earlier, she'd checked the place cards on the dining room table, wanting to know in advance where Genia had seated her. When the time came for everyone to move into the room, Elizabeth wanted no hesitation, no bumbling for her position. No curious eyes must see what Laurence's marriage had cost her.

The distant sound of the doorknocker prompted the four to hasten into the drawing room, used only for formal occasions. Elizabeth had decorated it in sumptuous green and gold. Floor-length emerald velvet curtains, lined with gold silk, were swagged with tasseled golden ropes. Soon, one of the maids would draw the curtains across the windows to shut out the descending night.

The same velvet covered the two sofas where the older women would sit. The gentlemen preferred the matching green leather armchairs. The less comfortable Hepplewhite chairs rested along the walls, reserved for the latecomers.

Elizabeth's piano stood in the corner, draped in a gold fabric with green leaves that matched the cushions on the chairs. She usually kept the piano uncovered, but tonight it sat shrouded and silent. Genia had declared she didn't want music after dinner.

Vice Admiral Harding arrived first. Long retired from active service, he'd been a close friend of Elizabeth's grandfather, and he was Laurence's godfather. Having been ill for several weeks, he'd not yet met Genia.

Laurence stepped forward, hand extended. "Uncle Edward, I'm so glad you're feeling better. I'd like you to meet my wife, Genia." Laurence had to raise his voice so the hard-of-hearing vice admiral would hear him. "And her mother, Mrs. Simmons."

"Delighted, my dear boy, delighted." He beamed at the ladies. Turning from them, he leaned over to kiss Elizabeth's cheek. "My dear Elizabeth, as pretty as ever. Will I have the pleasure of hearing you play tonight?"

She smiled fondly at the old man. A true music lover, the vice admiral always sat right next to her piano so he would hear every note.

"I'm sure you'll enjoy my daughter's playing," interjected Mrs. Simmons. "She has studied under some of the finest teachers in New York."

"Mama," Genia said in an undertone. "No music, remember?" Louder, she said, "I'm afraid I haven't planned for music tonight, sir."

He looked disappointed. "Another time, perhaps."

"Now, Genia," said her mother, "you could play a few songs. You know, those two you do so well."

Laurence joined in. "Yes, my dear, a little music would be most enjoyable."

Genia wound her arm through her husband's and smiled at the vice admiral. "Being a newlywed has kept me so very busy, I'm afraid I haven't practiced in weeks. Maybe next time we'll have a musical evening."

With amusement, Elizabeth watched Mrs. Simmons's subsequent attempts at conversation with the vice admiral. He obviously couldn't hear most of what she said, but since he nodded amiably, the woman didn't even notice. The vice admiral was a good choice of dinner partner for Mrs. Simmons; she couldn't do much damage to him.

Genia had also placed her mother beside shy Jacob Culver. If balked by her attempts at conversation with the vice admiral, Mrs. Simmons would turn her attentions to Mr. Culver, annihilating the poor man.

Gregory and Sylvia Markham arrived in a flurry. Sylvia, her plump figure encased in seafoam-green silk, with emeralds dripping from her neck and wrists, headed straight for Elizabeth.

Elizabeth smiled in welcome.

"Elizabeth, how are you?" Sylvia clasped Elizabeth's hands, kissed her cheek, then stood back and surveyed her. She said, sotto voce, "You're pale. What has that girl been doing to you?"

A longtime friend of Elizabeth, Sylvia had been the only person to express her opinion of Laurence's hasty marriage. She'd disliked Genia from their first meeting and sympathized with Elizabeth's position.

"And you've lost weight," Sylvia continued without pausing. "You're too thin. Maybe *I* should acquire a disagreeable sister-in-law…although after five children…" She leaned closer, touching her stomach and whispering, "and another on the way…"

"Sylvia!" Her friend's preoccupation with her growing brood of children was legendary. "How wonderful." Elizabeth squeezed her hand. "I had begun to worry," she teased. "The twins are almost three. I was wondering what you would do without babies."

The two women chatted about Sylvia's children. While one part of Elizabeth's mind engaged in the conversation, another part observed the new arrivals. How strange she felt not standing beside Laurence to greet the guests and welcome them to their home. In spite of Sylvia's efforts to distract her with stories about her oldest son's antics in school, Elizabeth's unsettled feeling grew stronger.

Maybe when Nick Sanders arrived, he'd help divert her from her unhappiness. "One of Pamela's ranch hands arrived in Boston, and I invited him to join us tonight."

"Pamela's ranch hand?"

Elizabeth gave her an impish smile. "Nick Sanders. He's quite handsome, and Genia was nasty to him." She playfully shrugged her shoulders. "You should have seen the look on her face when I invited him."

Both women laughed.

"Actually, he was quite kind. I'll introduce you."

"But of course." Sylvia's eyes twinkled. "It's been a long time since I've seen you look mischievous. Since this cowboy's responsible, I can't wait to meet him."

Five people unknown to Elizabeth entered the room. "I do believe the Lloyds have arrived," Elizabeth whispered. "They recently moved here from New York. Miss Lloyd is one of Genia's best friends, and she believes Mr. Michael Lloyd will do for me."

Both women covertly studied Michael Lloyd, a handsome man of medium height. His sandy-colored hair glinted in the glow of the gaslight. Pale blue eyes scrutinized his surroundings with patent condescension.

"I don't know, Elizabeth," said Sylvia. "I suppose he is attractive, but I know you prefer men with dark hair and eyes."

"Yes, but haven't you heard? I'm on my last hopes. I should be willing to fall at the feet of any halfway suitable male."

Sylvia rolled her eyes and shook her head.

Across the room, Genia beckoned to Elizabeth.

"I'm being summoned. It's time to meet *the man.*" She lifted an eyebrow at Sylvia in ironic farewell and moved to Genia's side.

"I want you to meet my dear friends," Genia said, tucking her hand around Elizabeth's elbow in a show of sisterly affection. "Mr. and Mrs. Lloyd, Mr. Michael Lloyd, Miss Helen Lloyd, and Miss Grace Lloyd, this is my new sister, Elizabeth Hamilton."

"I'm delighted to meet you all," Elizabeth said, with her best social smile. "Genia has spoken so highly of you."

More guests entered the room, and Genia moved forward to greet them. Michael Lloyd remained next to Elizabeth. His gaze dropped to her bosom before lifting to linger on her face. "I'm very glad to meet *you*, Miss Hamilton," he said with heavy-handed gallantry. "Genia told me so much about you; however, she didn't do justice to your beauty."

Elizabeth stifled an inward sigh. *What a bore.*

Seeming to sense her displeasure, he switched to a more innocuous subject. "Do you ever visit New York, Miss Hamilton?"

"It's been several years since I was last there."

Mrs. Peterson, the wife of one of Laurence's business associates, dodged between them. "Miss Hamilton, how nice to see you again." She directed a curious glance at Mr. Lloyd.

"Mrs. Peterson, I don't believe you've met Mr. Lloyd," said Elizabeth. "He's one of my sister-in-law's friends. He previously lived in New York."

"Oh. Do you know..."

Saved by Mrs. Peterson. She'll ask him about everyone she knows in New York.

Elizabeth excused herself and looked around the room for Sylvia.

"I wonder," said a female voice behind her, full of malice, "how Miss Hamilton is taking her brother's marriage? Probably not at all well. She isn't the high-and-mighty hostess anymore."

Elizabeth glanced over her shoulder. On the other side of a large potted palm, two wives of Laurence's business associates traded gossip, apparently unaware she stood only four feet away. "The new Mrs. Hamilton is such a dear thing," the other woman said. "I'm sure Miss Hamilton adores her."

Elizabeth stood rooted to the spot. *Adore Genia!*

"Miss Hamilton has become quite the spinster. One didn't notice it so much before, but now...tsk, tsk."

"It's too bad she never married. Now she's an old maid. But she'll soon be an aunt. After all, that's the next best thing to having one's own children."

The horror of those words uprooted her. *Spinster. Old maid.* Her knees shook, and she crossed the room searching for a safe harbor. *There. Nick Sanders.* He must have arrived while she spoke to Mr. Lloyd. *Thank God.* He'd be unaware of the undercurrents rippling through the room.

Even through her distress, Elizabeth noticed how handsome the cowboy looked. Long wavy hair, tucked behind his ears, just brushed his shoulders. The green in the patterned waistcoat worn under his black suit emphasized the color of his eyes. She hoped Laurence and Genia had given him a polite, if not warm, welcome.

He turned his head, and his gaze met hers. The admiration in his eyes worked like a balm to her wounded spirits. *Old maid, indeed.* At least this *young* man thought otherwise. As she reached his side, the dinner bell rang.

"May I escort you in to dinner?" He extended an arm to her. She smiled and tucked her hand into the crook of his arm.

Nick didn't move for a moment, his gaze traveling over her flushed face. "Something's upset you."

The concern in his voice brought a lump to her throat. This stranger, who'd barely met her, had noticed her feelings. She tried to swallow. How different from her own brother…

Nick must have seen the answer in her eyes. With a swift glance around the room, he laid his hand over hers. "I guess a dinner party's not the place to talk about it."

Feeling heartened by the touch of his hand on hers, Elizabeth managed a slight smile. "We'd better go to dinner."

Entering the dining room, Elizabeth paused and took a deep breath. This would be the first party since her parents' deaths where she would not sit as the hostess at the foot of the table.

She directed Nick to her chair and let him pull it out. She nodded, murmured her thanks, and sat down.

The familiar room embraced her, and she relaxed. Genia hadn't made her mark here yet. Candlelight blazed from crystal chandeliers over the long table draped in heavy white linen, while gaslight shone from the sconces on the wall. The Georgian silver, engraved with the Hamilton crest, which her great-grandfather had brought from England, shone in the flickering light.

Her own preference for blue was apparent in the royal-blue velvet curtains pulled across the windows and the blue-and-gold flowered chair cushions embroidered by her grandmother. The room looked beautiful, as always. *I'm the one who's different.*

"Miss Hamilton," said a simpering female voice. "I do believe you're sitting in my chair."

"What—?" Elizabeth looked up in confusion. Grace Lloyd stood next to her, pointing to the place card. Elizabeth's gaze followed her finger. The calligraphed name leaped out at her: Miss Grace Lloyd.

What happened? This was my seat. Where is my place card? She rose to her feet, her heart racing. "I'm so sorry," she murmured with a distracted smile. "I must not have been paying attention."

By this time most of the guests had found their proper seats, and Elizabeth knew curious gazes rested upon her. Trying not to look as flustered as she felt, she moved along the table, checking the place cards. Heat raced through her body, and her breath came in quick, quiet gasps. Where was her seat? Time stretched. It was taking forever to find it. Now all eyes were upon her. Embarrassment flushed her face.

Across the table, Nick met her eyes. He half rose to help her.

"Over here." Lucinda Simmons waved to her, and for one foolish moment, Elizabeth experienced a rush of gratitude.

Mrs. Simmons gave her a malicious smile and pointed to an empty place. In an undertone audible to several people, she said, "I moved you next to young Mr. Lloyd. He's so eligible."

Elizabeth's face tightened. She forced a polite smile in return and, crossing to the empty chair, slid into her seat. She took great care in unfolding her napkin.

Nick, seated across the table, next to Sylvia, communicated encouragement with a smile and a slight nod.

She couldn't smile back. Nor could she bear to look at Sylvia. She knew her friend's eyes would be full of compassion, or even pity, that would overset Elizabeth's fragile composure.

Movement to her left drew her attention. Mr. Lloyd picked up his napkin, shook out the linen and placed it in his lap. He glanced around the room, his gaze coming to rest on a large oil painting of a clipper ship in full sail upon a stormy sea. Two other paintings, one of bustling Boston harbor, and another of surf smashing on a rocky beach, evidently also caught his notice.

"What interesting paintings, Miss Hamilton," he said. "It's rather unusual to hang seascapes in the dining room. One usually just sees boring still lifes of mounds of fruit or dead fowl. These are quite good. Do you know the artist?"

By this time, Elizabeth had recovered her outer self-possession. With his compliments, her tight muscles further relaxed. "Actually, I painted them."

"My dear Miss Hamilton, I'm impressed. Usually ladies never graduate from watercolors."

Across the table, she could see Nick listening to their conversation. "I enjoy watercolors as well," she said. "However, here you see the best results of my oil painting stage."

"I'd like to see the rest of your work." He looked down her dress, and his voice lowered. "I consider myself quite a connoisseur of art, Miss Hamilton. Or may I call you Elizabeth? After all, our sisters are close friends."

The warmth she had felt at his compliment dissolved. "I haven't painted in several years, Mr. Lloyd," she said with cool emphasis on his name. "I've been much too busy."

"That's too bad. Such talent must not wither away. Now that your brother's married, you'll be free to resume your painting... Although perhaps other things might claim your attention." His hand slid over her knee.

Elizabeth shifted away from his touch. *Repulsive man.*

In her attempts to speak with the vice admiral, Mrs. Simmons's voice boomed down the length of the table. "I've been telling my daughter she really *must* commence with the decorating of this house. Her furniture should be here in a few weeks. She has everything in the latest style. Her home in New York was quite, quite beautiful...very much admired...and I'm sure she'll make this one just as lovely."

Startled glances flitted Elizabeth's way. The clink of silver on china stilled. Listeners paused with forks suspended in air. Her stomach tightened, but she pretended not to hear Mrs. Simmons's remarks.

"Oh, I don't know," Michael Lloyd said to Mrs. Simmons. "I rather like the present decor, especially these paintings."

Genia leaned forward; the Hamilton diamonds around her neck sparkled in the candlelight. "Then, my dear Michael, you must have them. Come for the pictures in a few weeks. My own will have arrived by then."

Elizabeth stifled a gasp at Genia's effrontery. How dare her sister-in-law give her paintings away! She looked up the table to Laurence, but he was deep in discussion with his dinner partner and oblivious to his wife's manipulations.

Sylvia flashed a concerned look at Elizabeth, then down along the diners to Genia. "Mrs. Hamilton, perhaps you don't realize Elizabeth painted these."

"Did she? Elizabeth, I had no idea you painted. You don't mind, do you? My paintings are by some of New York's *premier* artists. You'll love them. And I'm sure you don't want your paintings just sitting in the attic collecting dust."

More covert glances shot Elizabeth's way. She didn't know whether to get up and slap the smug look off Genia's face or slide under the table and not emerge until the last guest had left. Of course she didn't want to part with her paintings. But Genia had put her in such a humiliating position by publicly offering them to Mr. Lloyd that she couldn't let the woman's audacity go unanswered.

She was formulating a firm rejoinder when Nick came to her rescue.

"Actually, Miz Carter once told me that Miss Hamilton had promised her any paintings she wanted to part with. Therefore, I believe Miz Carter has prior claim." His steady green gaze pinned Genia to her chair.

Genia shifted in seeming discomfort. "Well, of course, but it would be quite an undertaking to package all those paintings and ship them out to her ranch."

"I'll be glad to take them back with me. I'm sure Miz Carter will enjoy them."

With an acknowledgment of his head, Mr. Lloyd conceded the paintings.

Sylvia leaned closer to Nick. Although she kept her voice low, Elizabeth still heard her say, "Well done, Mr. Sanders."

Now that the confrontation had passed, Elizabeth's anger receded, leaving her shaky. She looked down at her lap, twisting the linen napkin. She couldn't bear to see the pity or curiosity on their faces. Her throat burned, and her eyes stung with unshed tears.

She fought the urge to flee from the table, fling open the front doors, and run into the street. And she wouldn't stop. She'd never stop. She'd run—frantically, breathlessly, until she collapsed.

She looked up and met Nick's eyes. The support she saw in his green gaze caused her to stiffen her spine. Oh, no, she wouldn't. She'd never give Genia that satisfaction.

She'd survive this party. She'd get through the next hour with a minimum amount of conversation and, since her stomach was tied in a knot, an even smaller amount of food. Then she only had to endure time alone with the ladies while the men enjoyed their port. Another hour when the men joined the ladies for tea, then the evening would be over. She could escape to the sanctuary of her room.

The party would be over, but sometime tomorrow Elizabeth would still have to emerge. Her life stretched out before her. Long days of boredom, punctuated by endless humiliations. She'd tried, truly tried, to adjust to Laurence's marriage. Had Genia been kind and understanding, surely she would have succeeded. Now she knew the task to be impossible.

Across the table, Nick's green eyes met hers. The compassion and understanding in them almost made her weep.

In that moment, she made her decision. She'd go west with him. She could no longer bear to live in Boston. The western banker floated through her thoughts. And maybe there'd be a new man.

Sudden hope lifted her gray spirits. As soon as this party was over, she'd start packing.

* * *

Elizabeth slowly descended the broad marble staircase. Her gloved hand trailed along the smooth mahogany banister, then tightened at the memory of her childhood slides down the straight length. She remembered how her heart had raced in a combination of excitement and fear as she sailed down the railing—not unlike her current feelings.

Laurence was the only one who knew about her mischievous behavior. Sometimes, when she knew he was home, she would perch on the banister waiting for him to enter the foyer. As he crossed the hall she would release her grip, hoping to take him by surprise. But halfway down her giggles always gave her away. When she reached the bottom he'd catch her in his strong arms, whirling her around until they were both breathless with laughter. "Fly away, little bird," he'd tease. "Someday you're going to grow too big for me."

Elizabeth sighed. *Were we really that young and playful? When had Laurence become so stodgy?*

It must have been after their parents had died, and he'd had to take over the business.

Below her, Laurence paced the entry, stopping to take out his gold pocket watch and check the time. He glanced up and saw her. "Ah, there you are." He lost his worried frown. "There's not much time, Elizabeth. The carriage is waiting. Your trunks are already loaded. You know we told that Sanders fellow you'd be early." His frown returned. "I don't know where Genia is."

Elizabeth continued her measured descent. The skirt of her blue woolen dress trailed behind her. It might be a long time, if ever, before she trod these stairs again. She wouldn't be hurried.

Some of her feelings must have shown on her face, for Laurence stepped forward. In a rare show of emotion, he took her hand to guide her down the last two steps.

For a moment, she flashed back to when it was just them—before Genia.

True concern shone in his eyes. *This* was the brother she had always loved. "It's not too late to change your mind," he said.

Tears sprang to her eyes. *It is too late, Laurence.* Unable to manage a reply, she squeezed his hand.

He patted her arm. "I shall miss you, my dear sister."

"Thank you, Laurence. I shall miss you too."

Petticoats rustled in the landing above. "There you are, my dears." Genia's voice sang out like a knife slicing between them.

Laurence dropped Elizabeth's hand. He glanced up at Genia, a look of reproof on his face, the first she'd ever seen directed at his wife.

"You almost missed Elizabeth's departure, Genia," he chided.

"Martha took forever to do my hair." Genia patted her coiffed dark curls and glided down the stairway. Her eyes assessed Elizabeth's appearance. "Elizabeth, my dear, how clever of you to wear an old traveling outfit." Genia continued down the last three steps, complacently smoothing the dark-green silk morning dress that had arrived from the dressmaker earlier in the week. "It may not be in style here, but those westerners will be impressed."

"I doubt that," Elizabeth said, her tone wry. She grasped a fold of her dress and held it out. "After four days of traveling, I won't be in any condition to impress anyone. Not even my traveling coat will protect this dress from the dirt and cinders of the train. I'm sure I'll have to throw it away."

"Such an adventure. I'm sure you'll have a wonderful time." Genia pulled a lace handkerchief from beneath the cuff of her sleeve and dabbed daintily at her eyes. She glanced up at her husband. "This is so sad. We'll miss her, won't we, Laurence?"

"We shall indeed." This time his voice held the approving tone he usually used with his wife.

Elizabeth knew there were no tears behind that handkerchief. The two women had not become closer in the last few days. Only her eminent departure kept the uncomfortable situation from becoming even more strained. She suspected the minute Elizabeth left the house, Genia might pick up her skirts and dance a jig.

That picture of her sister-in-law banished the last of Elizabeth's melancholy. She couldn't wait to get away from Genia. She accepted her sister-in-law's insincere kiss on her cheek, and then a heartfelt one from her brother.

"Remember," Laurence said, his voice gruff, "you always have a home with us."

"I'll remember. Good-bye." Without a backward glance, Elizabeth turned and walked out the door toward the waiting carriage.

CHAPTER FIVE

A thin stream of tobacco juice narrowly missed the brass spittoon, landing with a *splat* on the wooden floor of the train. Elizabeth closed her eyes in disgust, but the lack of vision didn't help. She could still hear the sound of spitting and the *ping* the juice made when it landed in the spittoon, or the *plop* as it hit the floor.

Her closed eyes spared her the sight of the old man sitting across the aisle with his wild gray hair and dirty clothes. But only holding her nose would shut out the odor of a body that hadn't been washed since long before boarding the train.

She'd been dismayed when he chose the seat across from her and had wondered how he could afford a first-class ticket. Now she didn't dare meet his eyes because he'd already offered a gap-toothed grin that he seemed to expect her to acknowledge. Instead, she focused her gaze out the window.

The excitement of her adventure had faded. *If I had known what it would be like, I wouldn't have come.* The words had become a refrain, running through her head to the accompaniment of the rackety train wheels. *I'll go mad if this journey isn't over soon.*

After four days of traveling Elizabeth felt stiff, exhausted, and grimy. She desperately needed a bath and a long sleep in a comfortable bed. She abhorred the lack of privacy and hated making a toilette behind closed curtains in a swaying, cramped space.

She'd barely seen Nick. He stayed in the stock car with the golden stallion, Midas. Sometimes he'd check on Elizabeth during the train's brief stops, but they never had much time for conversation because he had to take the opportunity to exercise the horse.

She was lucky she had her thoughts for company. Most of the trip she'd spent thinking or dozing. She had few regrets about leaving the people in Boston, but gazing out the window as the ever-changing landscape rushed by, she found herself remembering the places in Boston that she might never see again, especially the ocean. In her mind, she had revisited her favorites, imprinting them on her heart.

Exhaustion and impatience to arrive flooded her. Between the noise of the train and the snores of her fellow passengers, Elizabeth had slept very little. Her eyes felt gritty from the dust and lack of sleep.

Soon it would be over…

❋ ❋ ❋

"Sweetwater Springs! Sweetwater Springs!" The conductor's voice interrupted her light doze.

Elizabeth jerked herself upright. *Thank God, we've finally arrived.* Keeping her face averted from the man across the aisle, she smoothed the linen duster protecting her dress.

With its whistle blowing amid billowing steam and a *whoosh* of brakes, the train pulled into the small station at Sweetwater Springs. She stifled a sigh of disappointment. The town looked similar to dozens of others she'd seen on her journey—a broad dirt street flanked by false-fronted wooden buildings. She'd hoped for something larger.

A woman carrying a basket and wearing a sunbonnet and plain brown dress crossed the street, trailed by a mangy yellow dog. She entered the only brick building in sight, leaving the dog behind on the porch. Cobb's Mercantile, painted in large letters on the plate glass window, proclaimed the name of the shop.

Three old men had planted themselves on a bench on the side of the depot platform as if they'd nothing more important to do than sit and gossip all day. They eyed the train, scrutinizing the disembarking passengers. No doubt Elizabeth would be the next subject of their speculation.

She gathered her possessions together, rose from her seat at the back of the carriage, and walked down the aisle. The conductor followed with her baggage. Squeezing by her, he stepped down from the train. He set her carpetbag, satchel, and hatboxes on the landing, then turned to help her down.

She thanked him and inhaled a deep breath of crisp, clean air. What a relief to not have to smell the soot from the engine and the unpleasant odors of her fellow passengers. At last she stood on firm ground! She took several steps, reeling slightly like a sailor just off a ship.

Suddenly Nick appeared, sliding a hand underneath her elbow. "Steady there, Miss Hamilton." His green eyes twinkled down at her.

A surge of gratitude swept through her. Such a kind man—a familiar face in a strange new world.

"I've given Midas over to Jed," he said, lifting his chin in the direction of a thin, beaky-faced man with a protruding Adam's apple. "John sent him with the carriage. I'll see to your things, then we can be on our way to the ranch."

Elizabeth pointed to the trunks and the wooden crate containing her paintings, which had been unloaded onto the railroad platform beside her carpetbag, satchel, and hatboxes. "There are my trunks." She glanced around the depot. "Perhaps we can find a porter to help you carry them."

Nick's mouth quirked into a smile. He walked over to the trunks, then grasped the handles of the first one. With a swift jerk, he lifted it up and strode in the direction of a nearby carriage.

"Wait! It's too heavy," Elizabeth called after him.

Nick kept right on walking until he reached the carriage and deposited the trunk on the rack in the back. When he returned to her side, he smiled at her. "Not much bigger than a hay bale, Miss Hamilton."

Before Elizabeth could respond, Nick stooped down, lifted the second trunk, and carried it to the carriage. In tired bemusement, Elizabeth watched Nick's broad shoulders and the muscles moving beneath his faded striped shirt. She felt a stirring in her breast and wondered at the unexpected feeling.

From this view, she could see how his light brown hair curled below his hat and over his collar. With a smile, she remembered the swashbuckling heroes in the forbidden novels she and Pamela used to read in secret. How they had swooned over those stories, their hearts beating rapidly in their not-yet-blossoming chests. Did Pamela ever remember those books when she looked at Nick?

He placed the second trunk on the back of the carriage and returned for Elizabeth's trio of hatboxes, satchel, and carpetbag. Still thinking about Nick and her childhood fantasies, she trailed after him. He turned and caught her speculative stare. A flustered look flashed across his face, answering the warmth rising in her body. Did he suspect her thoughts?

To cover her embarrassment, she glanced at the pair of chestnut-colored horses hitched to the carriage. The nearest horse tossed its head, then turned to assess her. Something seemed different about the harness. It took her a few seconds to realize the animal wasn't wearing blinders.

Of course, she thought. There was no traffic to distract them.

Elizabeth had never petted a carriage horse, but something about these two made her forget proper behavior. She stroked the lustrous chestnut hide of the nearest one.

"That's Sandy."

"She's beautiful." Elizabeth turned away from the horse and realized the carriage was the very one John had purchased in Boston when he married Pamela.

The shiny black body and dismantled wheels had traveled in the baggage car of the train the Carters had taken west, to be reassembled in Montana. The original paint was no longer as glossy, and the once-bright yellow wheels had faded, but to Elizabeth its familiarity felt comforting.

"All aboard!" The conductor's call swiveled her glance back toward the train station. A tall man, dressed in a gray broadcloth suit, dashed up the steps of the depot. *How nice to see a man correctly attired. At least some western men had proper sartorial taste.* Then she glimpsed his face—that dear, beloved face—and for the second time in her life, Elizabeth almost fainted.

The blood drained from her head into her pounding heart. The edges of her vision blurred. As if to stop him, she reached out a shaking hand, then watched helplessly as the man with Richard's face boarded the train.

Elizabeth grabbed her locket, and her knees buckled. Before she could fall, strong arms grasped her elbows. She swayed against Nick.

"Miss Hamilton, are you ill?" Anxious green eyes scrutinized her face. His arm tightened around her. "You're pale."

With a rush of steam and churning wheels, the train pulled away from the station, stealing the vision of Richard from her. Her mind gasped. Who was he? In a minute, the train had vanished, and only a lifetime of rigid training in ladylike deportment kept her from totally collapsing.

Waves of weakness washed over her, but Nick held her firmly against his side. "Let's get you into the carriage," he said.

As Nick guided her toward the conveyance, she allowed herself to lean on his arm. It had been so long since a man had been this attentive. Not since Richard…

A memory of her beloved fiancé, laughing as he clasped her in his arms, taunted her, only to be supplanted by the vision of him on his deathbed…the loving words of farewell she'd whispered in his ear…the tears she'd dropped on his still face as she'd given him a final kiss. She'd imagined reuniting with him in heaven, but never in her wildest dreams had she thought she'd see an image of him on earth, much less boarding a train in Montana.

* * *

Nick mounted Midas, gathered the reins, and with a nudge of his heels, started down the road to the ranch. The horse jumped sideways and jerked at the reins, working the kinks of the journey out of his body. "Easy, boy," Nick crooned.

Behind him, he could hear Jed start up the horses and the rumble of the carriage as it moved. His stomach felt as if he'd swallowed a bucking bronco. He needed time to think about what he'd just experienced.

Having his arms around Elizabeth had felt so right. He shook his head. He just wished it hadn't been because she felt ill. If only he had another excuse to hold her. He smiled to himself. He'd just have to look for opportunities, or maybe make them…

When he remembered her reaction to his carrying her trunk, his grin widened. While the trunks looked about the size of a hay bale, they'd actually been much heavier. But after his smart remark to her, he had to make carrying the darn chests look easy! His foolish pride was going to make him pay tomorrow. Ranch work made for sore muscles, but never before had he earned any from showing off for a beautiful lady.

He hoped she'd take to life on the ranch. He remembered some of Miz Carter's initial impressions of the ranch. Of course, when she'd arrived, there'd been no woman living in the big house since John Carter's mama had died. The ranch hands might be good with animals, but not with housekeeping.

Although most of the men had lived in the bunkhouse, the house had still become dilapidated and none too neat. And even though he and John bathed regularly, the men…Well, they managed a couple of dips in the river in the summertime.

He and John were used to it—just more farm smells—but one twitch of Miz Carter's nose had been enough to change the men's habits. They'd joined the ritual of regular Saturday night baths. Miz Carter had set into a whirl of cleaning, decorating, and planting. Now the old place was a fine sight. But would Elizabeth think so?

The dirt road wound into the foothills surrounding the town, and he turned his full attention to guiding Midas. The horse shied at every strange noise or movement and slowed to check out clumps of grass along the way.

They'd head through Saddleback Pass to reach the Carters' valley on the other side. He wondered if Miss Hamilton appreciated the mountain scenery. Snow still capped the tops of the mountains, but spring had arrived in the valley. Buffalo grass covered ranges that, until a few weeks ago, had been mud. Peeking up through the thick grass, the first of April's wildflowers unfurled their buds.

He knew Miz Carter was eager to have Elizabeth stay on. Maybe if she came to appreciate this land, she'd remain. He looked forward to showing her his favorite places: the swimming hole, his thinking rock, the land he planned to buy. Maybe she was too fine for him, but there wasn't any harm in being kind to her. After what she'd endured in Boston, she deserved some happy times.

He straightened in the saddle. Life had certainly taken an interesting turn, and he wondered what might happen next. He certainly hoped she'd take to the ranch. The sight of a lady like Miss Elizabeth Hamilton would sure brighten a man's day.

* * *

Richard's brown eyes filled with love. He reached out to her. "Beth." The tenderness of the softly spoken word made it an endearment.

"Richard," she cried, filled with joy. She stretched out her hand to him and felt her fingers warmly clasped.

"Miss Hamilton?"

The question jerked her awake. She realized she was inside Pamela's carriage, holding the hand of a man who leaned in the doorway. Nick Sanders, not her dear Richard. She almost cried out at the loss. She snatched back her hand.

"Are you all right, Miss Hamilton?"

"Yes," she whispered, but she wasn't. She'd never be. Richard had taken her heart with him to his grave.

Still disoriented, she asked, "Have we arrived?"

"No, ma'am," Nick replied. "I had Jed stop so you could see a view of the ranch before we start down into the valley."

"We're not there yet, and you woke me up," she choked out, groggy with sleep and disappointment. "This horrible journey has been endless, and I was finally getting some rest."

He pulled back. "I'm sorry, ma'am."

"And please don't call me 'ma'am.'" *It makes me feel old.*

He looked down at his feet, the color rising in his face making slight freckles stand out through his tan. "I didn't mean to upset you, Miss Hamilton." His gaze shifted back to her. "It's a beautiful sight, and I thought you'd like to see it."

By this time, Elizabeth was fully awake and ashamed of her rudeness. "I'm sorry. I'm just exhausted." She attempted a weak smile. "It might do me good to get out for a few minutes to see this view of yours."

A relieved smile brightened Nick's face. He held out his hand.

Elizabeth couldn't help smiling in return. She placed her fingers in his palm and allowed him to help her out of the carriage. At his touch, she shivered in unexpected pleasure. Then, uncomfortable with her reaction, she pulled her hand away. Taking a few deliberate steps away from him, she gasped in delight at the vista before her.

Distant purple mountains framed lush green meadows speckled with brown dots of cattle. A silver river threaded through clumps of trees. In the middle of the valley, ranch buildings clustered around a large white house.

Elizabeth inhaled crisp air into her lungs, as deeply as her corset allowed; all the staleness of the journey faded away. In an instant her tiredness and irritability dissolved, replaced by fresh excitement. *Montana. I'm so glad I'm here.* In absorbing the grandeur spread below her, she forgot Laurence, Genia, and her life in Boston.

She turned to Nick, who watched her closely, his look one of tenderness. Absurd thought. He barely knew her, and she'd been rude to him.

"I'm so glad you stopped," she said. "This is the most beautiful view I've ever seen."

Nick flushed with pleasure at her words and seemed to once again lose his ability to speak. Finally, he cleared his throat and gestured to the carriage. "It'll still be some time before we reach the house. I reckon we'd best be goin'."

Although impatient to end her journey, Elizabeth wouldn't have minded lingering with Nick for a few more minutes. But she remained silent, allowing him to help her back inside.

No longer sleepy, Elizabeth stared out the window. Ahead, the muddy road still held puddles where the moisture hadn't soaked into the rich brown soil.

Unfamiliar trees and bushes caught her interest. She'd never been much of a horticulture student and was only familiar with the types of flowers growing in her garden or given to her by an admirer. Curiosity arose within her. She wanted to know the name of the little brown bird that flitted away, startled by the passing of the carriage, and what kind of overgrown evergreen it took refuge in. Surely Pamela would know.

She certainly had a lot of questions for Pamela. Beginning with the man she'd seen getting on the train. She hoped as soon as possible, they'd have some privacy to talk. Luckily, the new surroundings continued to capture Elizabeth's interest, distracting her from her thoughts of that man; otherwise she'd be climbing out of her skin with impatience.

Finally they reached the bottom of the mountain road, and it straightened like an arrow pointing toward the ranch. They drove past a herd of reddish-brown cattle, the nearest ones veering away from the carriage.

Several men on horses attended the cattle. Like Nick, the horsemen wore faded indigo or tan denim pants, striped shirts, and colorful handkerchiefs tied around their necks. Wide-brimmed hats shielded much of their faces from Elizabeth's view. As the carriage passed, each man tipped his hat to her.

In the distance, she heard faint shouts. Leaning out the window, she saw two young boys galloping their ponies toward the carriage.

"Aunt Elizabeth!" called the taller one. He swept off his hat and waved at her. As they neared, Jed slowed the carriage to allow them to pull up and ride beside Elizabeth's window.

The older boy's sorrel pony danced closer to the carriage.

"You must be Mark," Elizabeth said to him.

His blue eyes sparkled with excitement, and he flashed her a contagious grin. "Yes, ma'am," he said. Elizabeth couldn't help but return his smile.

"And I'm Sara," piped up the younger child, whose grin showed tiny white nubs growing into gaps left by missing baby teeth. "We've watched for you all day!"

"Sara!" exclaimed Elizabeth, shocked that the boy was really Pamela's daughter. "I never would have guessed. You look so…big."

"Mama says I'm tall for my age."

"Indeed."

Elizabeth could perceive the children's resemblance to Pamela. How odd to see their father's blue eyes looking at her from small replicas of Pamela's plump, well-loved face. Elizabeth felt immediately drawn to them.

"Come on, you two," Nick called. "Your folks are waiting for Miss Hamilton. Ride ahead and tell them she's here."

They both flashed impudent grins at him, but obediently reined their ponies away from the carriage and galloped off toward the house. Jed snapped the reins, and the horses and carriage followed the children.

Elizabeth leaned back against the seat cushions and watched the children on their ponies. They rode like little centaurs. Although both children dressed like the ranch hands she'd seen earlier, the indigo of their denim pants wasn't as faded, and the blue handkerchiefs hugging their necks looked new.

She shook her head in disbelief. Sara not only wore what looked to be her brother's outgrown clothing, she also rode astride. What was Pamela thinking to allow such a thing! Her friend had written how her daughter enjoyed the outdoors, and had even mentioned Sara was a tomboy. But it shocked Elizabeth to see how Pamela allowed Sara to run wild rather than teaching her to be a little lady.

Elizabeth's stomach tightened in apprehension. She reached up and clutched her locket. *Maybe Pamela has changed more than I'll be comfortable with. Have I been too impetuous in coming to Montana? Dear God, please tell me I didn't jump from the frying pan into the fire!*

CHAPTER SIX

Two black-and-white dogs barked ferociously at the arriving carriage. "Whoa, you two. Stop making such a racket," Nick commanded. The barking tapered off to a few friendly yaps. With tails wagging, the dogs kept pace with the carriage until it pulled to a stop.

The large, freshly painted white clapboard house drew Elizabeth's attention. A broad porch ran the width of the first story, and several dormer windows graced the second story. While the architectural style differed from that of the residences in Boston, it was still an impressive home, worthy of Pamela.

Yellow daffodils decorated the planters in front of the house, and the beginnings of a big flower garden poked through the earth at the west side. Later in the summer, the yard would be beautiful. Early in Pamela's marriage, she had written Elizabeth a letter complaining of Montana's lack of flowering bulbs. Elizabeth had sent her several packages of tulip and daffodil bulbs, but had never expected to see the blossoming flowers herself.

Her earlier doubts vanished. Happiness bubbled in her stomach and rose until the joy reached her face, causing her to smile in delight. She had to restrain herself from bouncing in her seat like a child.

Pamela, John, and the children spilled out the door to greet her. John barely had time to open the carriage door and assist her to the ground before she and Pamela ran into each other's arms.

As Elizabeth hugged Pamela, tears glistened in her friend's eyes. The breeze tugged at tendrils of Pamela's hair—the same wisps that in Boston refused to stay properly pinned—and blew them across her forehead.

At the familiar sight, Elizabeth could only laugh through her own tears. As always, she reached up and tucked the hair back in place, following the gesture with a kiss on her friend's plump cheek.

The eagerness of the rest of the family to meet her broke the two apart. John stepped forward to take her hand between both of his. "Welcome, Elizabeth." A broad smile lit up his craggy face. "Pamela has been like a cat on hot coals waiting for you the last two days."

"John, thank you so much for having me."

He shook his head and ran a hand through his thinning sandy hair. "I hear you've met two of our rascals," he said, dropping his hand on Sara's head and ruffling her brown bangs.

"Yes, they've given me quite a welcome, but I haven't met this one." She stooped to address the little girl in a pink flower-sprigged dress, who peeked out from behind Pamela's blue calico skirt. "You must be Lizzy."

The child gave a slight nod before ducking behind her mother. Then, seemingly unable to resist the lure of a new visitor, she peered back out.

Elizabeth looked closer at the little girl and raised a hand to her mouth to suppress a gasp of astonishment. Lizzy was the image of Pamela's beloved little sister. Mary had died of diphtheria before her fourth birthday, devastating both Elizabeth and Pamela. A shiver went up her spine. Did Pamela see the resemblance? She'd never written of it. She glanced up at her friend, but Pamela's gaze slid away from hers.

She tried to set her fears for Lizzy's health aside. After all, the child looked healthy.

Dark brown hair curled around a delicate face. Long brown lashes lowered shyly over big blue eyes, and a few freckles sprinkled across her tiny nose. Unlike the two older children, with their sturdy bodies, Lizzy was small-boned.

Elizabeth found herself tumbling into love with the beautiful little girl. She longed to pick her up, but judged it best to wait until the little girl felt more comfortable with her.

"Hello, Lizzy, I'm your Aunt Elizabeth," she said. "When I was your age, everyone called me Beth. Sometimes your Mama still calls me Beth."

Lizzy gave her a brief smile before once again ducking out of sight behind her mother. Elizabeth straightened up and smiled at Pamela. "I guess it'll take a while for her to get used to me."

"Just give her some time." Pamela wrapped her arm around Elizabeth's waist and led her to the house. "You must be exhausted," she said with sympathy. "Which would you like first—a rest, a bath, or food?"

"A bath would be heaven. I've wanted to crawl out of my skin for the last two days! After that I'd like to sleep."

"I thought you'd feel that way," Pamela replied with a laugh. "I remember how it was for me. The tub is already in your room. I just need to send up hot water."

"Pamela, you're an angel." Elizabeth put her hand over Pamela's. "I can't wait to see your home, get acquainted with your children, and talk with you, but first I simply must scrub myself clean."

Out of the corner of her eye, she caught a suppressed smile from Nick. Heat seeped into her cheeks. How could she have so forgotten herself? She couldn't believe she'd just spoken in such a personal way about her body. And in the presence of men! Avoiding Nick's eyes, she turned toward Pamela and said with forced gaiety, "Lead the way."

The two women entered the house. Elizabeth's possessions followed in a grand procession. John and Nick each carried one end of a trunk, and all of the children insisted on helping. Even Lizzy hugged a hatbox to her chest.

Elizabeth scarcely had time to notice any details in the broad entryway before the chattering group swept her up the stairs. They trooped along a wide hall. Through canted doors, she glimpsed simple pine beds covered in colorful quilts.

"The children's rooms," Pamela said with a gesture toward the open doors. "I'll show you around later."

"I look forward to the tour."

"And this will be your room." She opened a door and ushered Elizabeth inside. The procession followed them into the spacious room and deposited her belongings on the polished plank floor.

"I'll go get that last trunk," Nick said, and left.

John pushed the trunk into the corner next to an armoire, then stacked her carpetbag, satchel, and hatboxes on top.

In a few minutes Nick reappeared carrying the trunk. He made it look so easy, but Elizabeth knew its weight.

"Look out, children." She herded them out of the way. "How about that wall, Nick?" she asked, pointing to the only available space. He lowered the trunk.

John cleared his throat. "I'll take the children and leave you in my wife's capable hands, Elizabeth. We'll see you at dinner if you're up to joining us."

Elizabeth smiled in acknowledgment, and he ushered the children out of the room. Before leaving, Nick sent her his shy smile and touched his hat. Something about his smile elicited an answering one from her. For a few seconds, she forgot the clamor around her. "Thank you for your help, Nick," she said. "You provided a lovely introduction to Montana."

Behind Nick's retreating back, Pamela cocked a questioning eyebrow.

Once again, Elizabeth's cheeks warmed. She rushed into an explanation. "He stopped to show me the view of the ranch from the top of the valley. I must confess, at first I was a little rude to him." She hoped Pamela would attribute Elizabeth's pink cheeks to her confession of discourteous behavior and not anything else. *Not, of course, that there's anything else to it.*

"Stopping like that sounds a little unusual for Nick," Pamela said. "He's usually reserved around strangers, especially women."

Elizabeth was eager to turn the subject away from Nick. Finally she could ask the questions she'd bottled up for the last hour. "Pamela, there's something I must ask you. In town, I caught a glimpse of a man who looked strikingly like Richard."

The look on Pamela's face changed from curiosity to concern. Her gaze dropped to Elizabeth's gold locket, then flitted back to her face. "You must have seen our banker, Caleb Livingston."

"I almost fainted from shock! Nick actually had to support me." Elizabeth shook her head at the memory. "Poor man. I don't know what he must have thought."

Pamela's eyes filled with sadness, and she reached for Elizabeth's hand. "I wish I'd been with you. I know how affected I felt when I first saw him, and I wanted to spare you that. It never occurred to me that you'd see him in town." One tear dripped down her plump cheek.

Matching moisture welled up in Elizabeth's eyes, and she leaned forward to kiss her friend's cheek. Still holding Pamela's hand, she led her over to the bed, and they both sat down.

"I understand why you kept it a secret. Perhaps it's just as well." Elizabeth gave a shaky laugh and pulled out a lace-edged handkerchief from her sleeve. With gentle fingers she dabbed the tears from Pamela's eyes before brushing her own away. "It gave me an interesting welcome to Montana." She made her voice sound light.

Pamela managed a smile.

Elizabeth leaned in. I'm pleased to know there's at least one cultured gentleman in Sweetwater Springs. I was afraid you'd taken the only eligible one for yourself!"

Pamela gave her a playful look. "There's more than one. I've arranged a dinner party so you can meet some of our friends. Of course, Mr. Livingston will be in attendance."

"At least this time I won't faint. I'm so glad he didn't see my reaction. And how horrid I looked. I'd hardly have made a good impression."

"Your bath!" Pamela stood up. "I'll send Annie up with hot water. She hugged Elizabeth. "I'm so glad you're here. Now I'll stop talking and get your water. Oh, and I'll send up a tray with some food."

Once she was alone, fatigue overwhelmed Elizabeth. She sank down on the bed. The cozy featherbed on the four-poster invited her to sleep. Although tempted to lie down and relax, she knew she wouldn't remain awake. Instead, she studied her surroundings.

The large room had two windows curtained in white lace looking out to the mountains. Elizabeth couldn't work up the energy to go over and examine the view.

The walls, covered with white wallpaper dotted with purple violets, matched the embroidered violets on the white linen bedcover. Pamela's handiwork. She'd always embroidered so beautifully. Violets were Pamela's favorite flower; similar paper had hung in her childhood bedroom. Elizabeth liked the feeling of familiarity the wallpaper gave her.

A knock on the door interrupted her thoughts.

"Come in," she called.

The door opened. A stout Chinese woman, lugging two buckets of hot water, walked and bowed to Elizabeth before pouring the water into the tub. A taller girl with similar black hair, but whose round brown eyes and dark skin proclaimed her Indian heritage, followed her into the room. The Indian girl also carried two pails of steaming water, which she added to the tub.

"You must be Annie," Elizabeth said to the first woman.

"Yes, Missy."

Pamela appeared behind them. "Dawn helps as my personal maid," she said, laying her hand on the tall girl's shoulder. She also takes care of the children. Her Indian name means beautiful dawn, so Dawn is what we call her."

She smiled at Dawn. "I'd like you to help Miss Elizabeth with her bath and settling in."

Pamela motioned Annie out the door and followed her. Dawn silently helped Elizabeth undress. Once in the water, Elizabeth gave herself over to the girl's ministrations. Lavender-scented soap, the same kind she'd used in Boston, cleansed the last of the travel aches from her mind and body. Never in her life had she been so grateful to soak in a warm bath!

"Dawn," Elizabeth said, "Will you please unpack some of my clothes and iron one of my dresses? I'd like to relax for a while until you return and can help me wash my hair."

The girl nodded and crossed the room to the nearest trunk. Piece by piece she removed the clothing, hanging them in the large mahogany armoire. Almost as large as the one Elizabeth had in her room in Boston, this one would easily house the reduced wardrobe she'd brought with her.

"That one will do," Elizabeth said indicating the lawn nightgown Dawn pulled out of the trunk. "Please get rid of the clothes I've been wearing. I don't care what you do with them. I don't ever want to see them again."

Dawn bundled up the discarded clothes and left the room. Elizabeth lay back and closed her eyes. Despite her fatigue, her body tingled with elation at her welcome, especially at being reunited with Pamela. So different from her recent experiences in Boston.

If she wasn't exhausted and soaking in a bath, she might have danced around her room in pure childish delight. Instead, she allowed herself to bask in the soothing hot water. She couldn't remember feeling this happy for a long, long time. Not since Richard…

"Oh, my darling," she whispered. "If only you were here, everything would be perfect. If you're watching from heaven, please wish me well."

❋ ❋ ❋

Birds chirping outside Elizabeth's window dragged her out of a dreamy sleep. She opened her eyes, gazing blankly at the violets on the wallpaper and struggling with a moment of disorientation. As her memory returned, she snuggled deeper into her pillow in drowsy contentment.

The night before, Pamela had urged her to sleep as late as she wanted. So Elizabeth allowed herself to enjoy the first peaceful, rested morning since receiving the telegram announcing Laurence's marriage.

After a period of pleasant dozing, Elizabeth recalled their reunion dinner last evening. The children had been so excited about the presents she'd brought. All during dinner, she'd basked in the glow of the loving Carter family. She couldn't wait to experience more.

That thought propelled her out of bed. She chose a Swiss embroidered muslin shirtwaist and a brown calico skirt that she could easily don without a maid's assistance.

She managed to brush her hair into the style she'd worn the evening before. She missed Josie's help and decided to tie her corset as best she could. Thankful for her small waist, Elizabeth knew she couldn't handle the tight lacings by herself. She supposed in the future, Dawn would wake her and help her dress.

When she finished, she studied her image in the looking glass over the dressing table and decided she could be taken for a pioneer woman. She smiled and then whirled around to inspect her back. *Genia would faint if she saw me wearing calico. I must mention it in my first letter home.*

On her way downstairs, she noted the white painted walls and bare wooden steps. She stopped to examine a framed watercolor of a seascape and realized she'd painted it. Pamela had requested several of Elizabeth's paintings before she left and had chosen views of the sea to remind her of Boston.

Elizabeth smiled at the memory of clambering over the jagged rocks to reach this particular view. She'd almost been cut off by the tide before finishing the picture. How lovely to see her work again. It had been a long time since she'd scrambled around to find the perfect scene. *How young and energetic I was then.*

For the first time in a long while, her fingers longed to paint. Good thing she'd brought her art supplies, both watercolor and oil. Attempting these majestic mountains should be quite a challenge.

Elizabeth proceeded down the steps and strolled along the hall. She stopped and peered through the first open door into Pamela's parlor.

Brown-and-green floral paper covered the walls. The brown velvet sofa sported plump, embroidered pillows. Several tan-and-green damask wing chairs invited comfortable lounging. One of her oil paintings hung above the sofa. Pamela had displayed a portrait of her and Elizabeth over the fireplace. How young they looked…and how happy…

Pamela glanced up from her embroidery. "Good morning," she greeted her, with a warm smile.

"Morning." Elizabeth crossed the room, sat down on the sofa, and picked up a green pillow embroidered with pink roses to study the pattern. "You still do beautiful work."

"Not as much as I used to," Pamela said. "The children keep me too busy, but there's more time for handwork in the winter." She folded her embroidery and put it aside in a woven basket on the round oak table next to her. "Did you sleep well?"

"Very. The best rest I've had for weeks."

"Good. I'm afraid you've missed breakfast," Pamela said with a playful smile. "Luncheon will be served in about half an hour. At least you didn't sleep through dinner." They both laughed. "Are you hungry or can you wait?"

Elizabeth smiled ruefully. "I'm sure I can manage to wait. Where are the children?"

"They're in the barn. One of the mares foaled last night, and they were eager to see the filly."

"Oh, I'd like to see her too."

Pamela's forehead scrunched up in a question.

Elizabeth laughed. "I've never seen a newborn foal…or any foal, for that matter."

"The children would love to give you a tour of the outdoors after we eat. Since we have some time now, do you want to see the rest of the house?"

"Of course. In a way I feel as if it's already familiar because you've written so much about it."

"I've enjoyed furnishing and decorating the house." Pamela ran her hand over the smooth finish of the table next to her. "The decor is much more informal than what I was used to in Boston, but it suits us."

"It's different, but I like it." Elizabeth hesitated a moment then added, "How do you keep it up? I haven't seen many servants around."

An uncomfortable look crossed Pamela's face. "I have to warn you, I do some of the housework myself."

"Really?" Elizabeth tried to control her shocked reaction to such a statement. In Boston, upper-class women did *not* do their own housework. That's what servants were for. Yet Pamela didn't look unhappy…

"It isn't the same," Pamela said as if she'd read her thoughts. "In Boston, women in domestic service are plentiful. Out here, men outnumber women, and an available woman marries quickly. Even if I hire someone from the East, she doesn't stay for long. So I just have Dawn. The ranch foreman's wife comes in twice a week to clean or do laundry. With Dawn's help, I keep things neat the rest of the time."

"What about Annie?"

"Annie has her hands full with the cooking. In addition to the family, she cooks for most of the men." There was another pause. "Sometimes I help her."

"You help her cook?" Elizabeth said in an amazed tone of voice. This was a facet of her friend's life she hadn't anticipated. "Did she teach you?"

"No, the woman I had before her taught me a few things. I mostly do some baking and preserving, but sometimes Annie needs to have time off, so I've learned to cook a simple meal."

"I'm shocked you have to work so hard."

"Beth, I wish you could understand. I like to do these things. In Boston, all we did was socialize and shop. I don't think we even knew how unimportant our daily lives were."

Elizabeth wasn't sure she understood. Pamela's domestic duties sounded very unappealing. She hoped she wouldn't be expected to cook and clean. She wouldn't have the faintest idea what to do.

She glanced down at her smooth, white hands with their perfect nails. She'd always been proud of her beautiful hands. Pamela's looked brown and rather work-worn, so different from the way they'd been back home.

She rose and hugged her friend to soothe away her distress. "I'm amazed at your zeal for life, that's all. Now, please give me the grand tour. I want to see the rest of your house."

I might make my home here.

❋ ❋ ❋

Pamela led Elizabeth upstairs, showing her the children's rooms and the other guest bedroom. Then she brought her to the room she shared with John. A carved four-poster bed, with its crisp white linen cover, dominated the room where Pamela and John spent so much of their intimate lives.

As if reading her mind, Pamela said, "The children were all born in this bed." She sat down on it, smoothing an imaginary wrinkle on the cover, then patted the bed in an invitation for Elizabeth to join her. "After each birth, when I finally held my baby in my arms, I was so incredibly happy."

"I remember how I waited for days wondering about your delivery and whether you'd had a boy or girl. Thank goodness for John's telegrams."

Pamela reached over and clasped Elizabeth's hand. "There was always something lacking because my parents and brothers, and you, my dearest friend, weren't here to share my joy." She smiled mistily at Elizabeth. "It means so much to have you here."

"I envy you," Elizabeth said, with a frankness of emotion she rarely exhibited. "Since Richard's death, I've made myself stop thinking of having babies. Meeting your children makes me realize how much I want some of my own."

"Beth, I'm sure having children will happen for you." Pamela squeezed her hand in reassurance.

Elizabeth leaned over and kissed Pamela's cheek. "It's so nice to talk to someone who knew Richard and how much I adored him."

"We all loved him," Pamela murmured. "But the love you two shared was special." She reached out and, with one finger, lightly touched Elizabeth's locket. "I see you still wear this."

"Yes, always. Since Laurence's marriage, I've thought about Richard a great deal. Before their wedding, I kept myself so occupied that on many days I managed not to think of him. Now it seems the pain is always with me."

Pamela's hand tightened over hers.

Elizabeth remained silent for a moment. "I haven't wanted to settle for less than what we had," she said with a sigh. "Perhaps that was a mistake. But I want a marriage like yours with John. A husband who adores me. Someone I can love and respect."

Pamela's brown eyes sparkled with mischief. "Maybe Mr. Livingston will fit your description. You'll have a chance to find out at tomorrow night's party."

The thought of meeting Mr. Livingston made her nervous. "I'm sure it will be a pleasant evening." She refused to give in to her friend's teasing; having Pamela and John watching her reactions wouldn't help matters. "Who else is invited?"

"You'll like Dr. and Mrs. Cameron. They're good friends. Why if it wasn't for him, we wouldn't have our Lizzy."

"What!"

"I had a long, difficult labor." Pamela shuddered. "She wasn't breathing properly when she was born."

Elizabeth pressed her hand in sympathy. "You never wrote me that. I wish I'd been with you."

"It was a frightening time. We'll always be grateful to Dr. Cameron. We still require his services more than I'd like. Lizzy's so frail, and she seems to catch any passing illness."

"I'm pleased you have him to help you," Elizabeth murmured. But within her chest, an insidious fear about Lizzy's frailty wrapped around her heart and squeezed.

CHAPTER SEVEN

Pamela stood up from the bed, pulling Elizabeth with her. "Come on. It's almost time to eat."

"Good."

"I'll show you the downstairs. Did you know I've a music room?"

"You wrote about John surprising you with the piano on your first anniversary, so I brought some of my favorite music. I wasn't sure if you had some of the newer pieces."

"Oh, how wonderful. I'm sure I'll enjoy playing them. When I first came here John worried that I might miss my music," Pamela said as they walked downstairs. "I actually don't play much anymore, at least not every day like I used to. More in the winter. The winters here do tend to be fierce, and we spend a lot of time cooped up in the house. This winter, I'm going to start teaching Sara to play."

Pamela guided Elizabeth through the door and into the music room. The large room had simple wooden chairs scattered around a cherrywood piano. In addition to Pamela's piano, a violin rested in an open case on one of the chairs, next to a stand.

"Who plays the violin?"

"Nick does, although out here we call it a fiddle. Last winter he started teaching Mark." Pamela smiled and rolled her eyes. "You can imagine the screeching. We try to stay out of earshot."

Elizabeth gave her a mischievous smile. "I'll have to ask Mark to play for me."

"Believe me, you'll only ask once. However, you'll hear Nick and me play. We have musical evenings for the family and sometimes invite everyone else from the ranch."

"You invite everyone?" Elizabeth echoed. "You mean the ranch hands?"

"Yes," Pamela replied. "It started when we had Sunday prayer services. Much of the winter we can't make it into town to attend church, but we feel that it's important for everyone to observe the Lord's day. We have to set an example, you know."

"I suppose you're right."

"So Sunday mornings during the winter everyone gathers here. John reads the service out of the prayer book. I play the piano, and we sing hymns."

"I'd like to see John's attempt at being a minister."

Pamela laughed. "Actually, he does a good job. It's not too difficult when you don't have to preach a sermon."

The whole concept sounded strange to Elizabeth. However, she could see the importance of John and Pamela upholding civilized values in this wild place.

❋ ❋ ❋

"We'll stop by the kitchen. I want to tell Annie you'll be joining us," Pamela said as the two walked downstairs and along the hall. "It's in here." She motioned to a partially opened door and stepped back to allow Elizabeth to precede her into the room.

A large table covered with a red-checked cloth and set with blue tin spatterware dominated the center of Pamela's big kitchen. Annie leaned over a monster black stove, stirring something in a huge pot. The smell of baking bread wafted from a brick oven set into one of the outside walls. A long-handled indoor pump meant Annie didn't have to carry water from the well outside.

Sunshine streamed through white-curtained windows and played across several colorful, braided rag rugs. A gray cat, curled up on a cushioned rocking chair, lifted his head, regarding Elizabeth with an unblinking yellow gaze.

"Meet Smoky, the terror of the kitchen," Pamela said. "He doesn't look like it right now, but he's a great mouser."

"Hello, Smoky." Elizabeth greeted the cat with a scratch behind his ear.

He yawned in reply, then gave his side a perfunctory lick. Seeming to change his mind abruptly, the cat stood and arched his back in a stretch, then jumped off the chair.

Elizabeth cocked her head at the thud of approaching footsteps.

"Unless you want to be knocked over by the stampede, we'd better go into the dining room," Pamela commented with a wry face. "Or you can wait and meet the men?"

Elizabeth inwardly shuddered. "I definitely have no desire to be run over," she informed Pamela.

Nick bounded up the steps and through the partially open door.

"Too late," Pamela said. "Here's the first of the horde."

At the sight of the women, Nick smiled and swept off his hat. "Miz Carter, Miss Hamilton."

Pamela greeted Nick, but Elizabeth only nodded and gave him a polite smile that belied the warmth in her stomach at the sight of him. She smoothed imaginary wrinkles from the front of her calico skirt to avoid further eye contact. *Why does this young cowboy make me feel so unsettled?*

"This room's going to be very crowded in another minute," Pamela said, jerking Elizabeth from her musing. "Let's move into the dining room. Annie," she said to the cook, "do you need us to carry anything?"

"You could set out the biscuits." The cook picked up a towel and wrapped it around each end of a tin tray holding several dozen golden round biscuits. "Be careful; they hot," she said, thrusting the tray into Elizabeth's hands.

Startled at the unexpectedness of the hot tray in her possession, Elizabeth took a step backward and tripped over Smoky. Juggling to keep the tray from tipping, she started to fall.

Nick leaped to grab her, catching her arm, one hand accidentally brushing her breast, while his other arm steadied her back. The tray banged into his side, knocking most of the biscuits to the floor.

Hot with mortification, Elizabeth murmured apologies. Trying to ignore Nick, she stooped to scoop up the biscuits. Nick leaned over to help her, and they bumped heads.

Elizabeth let go of one end of the tray to rub her head, causing the rest of the biscuits to slide toward the floor. In a vain attempt to save the remaining biscuits she grasped the tray, searing her palm.

Near tears from pain and embarrassment, she threw Pamela a mute glance of appeal.

"Beth, you're hurt!" Pamela rushed to her side.

Elizabeth turned her hand over to show her friend the red welts beginning to mar her skin.

Pamela pulled her over to the sink, thrusting Elizabeth's hand under the pump and pushing the handle up and down. "We must cool your hand."

As the soothing water gushed out, behind her she could hear the sounds of Nick picking up the biscuits and setting them on the tray.

It all happened so fast," Pamela said with distress. "I feel horrible. Your first day here, and you're hurt."

Nick strode over to a shelf by the stove, grabbed a small brown crock, pulled off the top, and held it out to them. Pamela dabbed Elizabeth's palm dry, then dipped the cloth in the crock.

Elizabeth tried not to shiver from the touch of the cloth against her raw skin. Pamela gently slathered some salve over the burn. "Let me go get one of my clean old gloves to put over this."

Left alone with Nick and Annie, Elizabeth sat down on a chair and stared at the floor, trying to breathe away the pain. Remembering the accidental intimacy when Nick had touched her made her warm cheeks glow even hotter. Elizabeth glanced up at him from beneath lowered lashes, but could see only concern on his face.

Outside she could hear the sound of male voices. *Oh, no. The ranch hands.* Just what she needed to worsen the situation.

As if reading her thoughts, Nick spoke up. "I'll keep the men outside for another few minutes. Right now, you don't need a bunch of cowboys crowding the kitchen." He reached over and lightly touched her shoulder. "I'm real sorry about this, Miss Hamilton. I shouldn't have gotten in your way."

She looked up in astonishment. "Nick, this wasn't your fault. If you hadn't caught me, I'd have landed on the floor, probably broken something, and still been burned. I haven't thanked you because I've been too mortified to speak."

Her words brought a flush to his face. He bent to pick up his hat from the floor. "I'm just sorry you're hurt." He headed toward the door. "I'll go head off those men."

Pamela hurried back into the kitchen, waving a glove. "Here's an old one. It's stretched out, as I've used it as a bandage before. Cooking does tend to cause cuts and burns."

Elizabeth had had enough of cooking for today. "Pamela, if you don't mind, in the future I'll stay away from your kitchen."

Her friend gave her an understanding smile. "I don't blame you. Let's go into the dining room so the men can eat."

* * *

After the meal, the children asked Elizabeth to accompany them to the barn. With Lizzy holding her unburned hand, and Mark and Sara leading the way, Elizabeth headed outside. As soon as the children stepped through the door, the two black-and-white dogs ran over.

"This is Shep." Mark patted the head of the larger one. "The other is Sally."

"Shep and Sally, I'm so-o-o glad to meet you," Elizabeth teased with mock formality as she stooped to pat the dogs. "I regret I was rather preoccupied last night with greeting people, so we were not properly introduced. I hope you don't think me rude."

The dogs didn't seem to mind her breach of etiquette, and with wagging tails and lolling tongues, they trailed after the group.

"You'll have to explain what each of these buildings is." She pointed at a small whitewashed hut set on stilts. "What's that little one over there?"

"That's the henhouse," Mark said.

"Every day I collect the eggs from the chickens," Sara told her, a proud lilt in her voice. "Lizzy helps me. She knows how to be real careful."

Lizzy nodded in agreement.

"My favorite hen is Mrs. Hooch," Sara continued. "She sits on my lap and lets me pet her." She cast a triumphant glance at her brother. "She pecks at Mark."

"Who cares about an old hen," Mark grumbled. "I'd rather be with the horses."

"That's the men's bunkhouse." Sara pointed to a long, narrow building. "And over there's where the foreman, Carl, lives with his wife, Daisy. They have a little baby boy named Johnny."

Set back several hundred yards from the barn, a small house sat, dwarfed by its large porch. Two rocking chairs invited hardworking folk to sit and relax. Porches and rocking chairs seemed an inevitable part of homes in Montana. *Rather charming.*

By this time they'd reached the enormous whitewashed barn. The children led her past the entrance.

"Where are we going?" Elizabeth asked.

"To the corral," Sara said. "Nick's there working with Outlaw. He's wild."

"Outlaw?"

"His horse," Mark said. "He works with him every afternoon. Nick is probably having a hard time with him today. That stallion has been two weeks without exercise. No one else dared."

With a sideways skip, Sara scooted in front of Elizabeth. "He's a real outlaw."

"He is?"

"Bucked off anyone who tried to ride him. His bad owner whipped Outlaw." Sara's words tumbled out in a rush. She took backward bouncing steps to stay in front of Elizabeth. "Nick saw the whipping and got real mad. Know what he did?"

"What?"

Sara's gap-toothed grin flashed, and her eyes lit with pride. "He grabbed the whip and said he'd hit the man with it. Then he made the bad man sell him the horse."

"Good for Nick." Warmth and admiration filled her. Nick had seemed so quiet and shy. Evidently, there was more to him…

"It took Nick months of work before Outlaw trusted him," Mark said.

"You be careful, though, Aunt Elizabeth," Sara warned. "Outlaw's still dangerous."

"We aren't supposed to go close to him unless Nick is with us," Mark added. "Nick's the only one he trusts."

Mark reached the edge of the barn first. He peeked around the corner, then waved his hand and motioned for the others to come forward.

Elizabeth stepped behind him, leaned over his head to peer around the corner, and caught her breath at the sight.

Nick stood in the center of a small corral, holding a long rope attached to the halter of a magnificent charcoal-gray stallion. The horse cantered in a circle around him, its long black mane and tail flowing behind. As they watched, Nick flicked the rope and uttered clicking sounds. With each one, Outlaw changed paces, the horse's movements so smooth there seemed to be no transition.

"Ow! Get off my foot." Sara elbowed her brother, causing Mark to stumble away from the shelter of the barn. He dance-stepped to get his footing. A tin pail clanged to the ground.

Outlaw reared up, his powerful muscles bunching. The rope pulled taut, yanking Nick forward. The horse backed away. Tossing its head, the stallion snorted and banged against the wooden rails of the corral.

CHAPTER EIGHT

Elizabeth's heart thumped, and a jolt of fear jagged through her body. She gasped as Outlaw reared again, and she pulled the girls close.

Nick braced himself. He spoke in a soothing voice, his gloved hands on the rope. Elizabeth couldn't hear his words, but the horse seemed to respond. Tossing his head again, a wild look in his eyes, Outlaw allowed Nick to take a step forward. Nick held out his hand, murmuring until Outlaw moved against him, permitting Nick to caress his nose.

The tension seemed to drain from the horse. His mouth opened and closed several times.

"That means he's all right," Sara whispered.

"What does?" Elizabeth whispered back. As Outlaw quieted, Elizabeth's own rapid heartbeat slowed, and she relaxed her grip on the girls.

"When he steps toward Nick and moves his mouth like that, he wants to know that he's safe."

Nick has such a calming touch—

"Nick'll be working for a few more minutes," Mark interrupted. "Wanna see the other horses?"

A strange reluctance to leave the sight of Nick and Outlaw almost rooted her to the ground. The bond between man and horse drew her. She took a breath. Who was she trying to fool? Nick drew her—his quiet masculinity, his thoughtfulness…

Lizzy tugged on her hand. "Foal," she said.

Elizabeth smiled down. "All right, darling. Let's go see the foal."

"A few horses and the milk cows are in the barn." Mark led the way toward the large double doorway. "Unless it's winter, the rest of the horses are out in the pasture."

They entered the barn. After the brightness outside, Elizabeth's eyes took a few seconds to adjust to the dim interior.

She grimaced at the redolent smell of horse, leather, dirt, and hay, but the odor wasn't too overwhelming. Curious horses gazed out of stalls along each side of the barn, some nickering as the group walked past. Overhead, a loft held loose hay. A few wisps had floated down on the otherwise cleanly swept dirt floor.

The children led her past each stall until they reached the one holding Mark's chestnut-colored pony.

"This is Billy." Mark stroked the pony's head, allowing it to puff his palm.

Little Lizzy, who up to this time had stayed silent, tugged on Elizabeth's hand and pointed to the brown pony in the next stall. "Susie."

"Is that your pony, dear?"

Lizzy nodded.

"She's beautiful. I'd like to see you ride her. Maybe we can do that later."

Lizzy nodded again, but this time a smile lit her solemn little face.

Mark gestured toward a chestnut mare. "Come meet Mama's mare. Her name is Belle. Mama doesn't ride her very much. She's usually too busy."

Elizabeth stroked the sleek nose, and the horse blew soft breaths on her hand.

"She's looking for a carrot. Mama always brings her one," Mark said.

Sara impatiently pulled on Elizabeth's skirt. "Father's horse is black. He's named Midnight. You can see him later when Father brings him back to the barn."

Elizabeth looked down the row. "Where's Midas?"

"Out in the pasture," Mark said. "After the train ride, Nick wants him to enjoy some freedom. He'll probably work him later."

"He will?"

"Nick doesn't always ride with Father and the other men," Mark told her. "He's in charge of the horses. He spends a lot of his time schooling them. Everyone else works with the cattle."

"He also plays with us," Sara added. "He's our best friend."

"What do you mean, he plays with you?" Elizabeth asked, thinking Nick a strange type of playmate.

"He taught us to ride," Sara said with a proud tilt of her chin. "He teaches us about the plants and animals. He lets us help him with the horses."

Lizzy tugged at Elizabeth's hand.

Sara patted her sister on the head. "Lizzy loves to ride on his shoulders. I used to, but I'm too big now."

"I should think so," Elizabeth murmured.

The children passed by the stalls of mares in foal without introducing them. They were anxious to see the filly. They'd just reached the newborn's stall when footsteps behind them warned of Nick's approach.

"You children think you can be quiet around the foal?" Nick asked with a quirked eyebrow.

Mark and Sara exchanged guilty looks. "Sorry about spooking Outlaw," Mark said, hanging his head.

Nick looked amused and ruffled Mark's hair. "No harm done."

Elizabeth glanced at Nick from under lowered lashes. His worn tan shirt clung to his muscled body, a few dirt streaks marring the fabric. He leaned against the stall in a casual pose that provoked a fluttering response in the vicinity of her stomach.

Uncomfortable, she dropped her gaze to study the newborn filly. The little chestnut foal, tugging busily at her mother's teat, ignored her admirers.

"She has a white star on her forehead," Sara pointed. "So, I've named her Star."

"She's a darling," Elizabeth said. "Can I touch her?"

"Yes, Miss Hamilton," Nick told her, opening the door to the stall. "But first come and meet her mama." He held up his hand to stop the children. "You three stay back and let Miss Hamilton do this alone."

He beckoned to Elizabeth. "Approach her slowly, stroke her nose, and let her smell you. Talk to her gently."

Elizabeth complied. "Hello, mama." She rubbed the mare's nose. "I've come to admire your baby. She's very beautiful, and I'm sure you must be very proud." She glanced at the nursing foal. "Your baby has a good appetite. I'm sure she'll grow up to be strong and as fast as the wind."

"That's good," Nick said in encouragement. "Now she'll let you near her foal. The baby's stopped nursin', so approach her the same way you did her mama."

Elizabeth advanced slowly. She held out her hand until the filly wobbled to her with cautious steps.

"Hello, Star."

Star let Elizabeth stroke her head and body. Elizabeth sank to her knees in the straw, disregarding the possible damage to her skirt.

"Oh, you're so beautiful," she crooned to the baby. "You do have a star on your forehead."

Star nudged Elizabeth's face, and she kissed the filly's soft nose. Her own reactions amazed her. Who'd have ever thought that proper Elizabeth Hamilton would be on her knees in a barn kissing a horse!

Happiness arose in her, as if this foal brought an awareness of the possibilities of Elizabeth's new life. For a moment, her heart opened, taking in the horses, the children, and even Nick.

* * *

That strange feeling came back to Nick's stomach, although this time it traveled upward to the vicinity of his heart. His hands stroked and soothed the mare, but all his attention centered on the woman kneeling in the straw.

The haughty attitude Elizabeth sometimes displayed had vanished. Happiness lit up her face, and her eyes shone with love.

Look at me that way, he silently pleaded. He knew Star didn't appreciate her loving attention the same way he would.

As if hearing his thoughts, Elizabeth glanced up. As their gazes met, it took all his willpower to continue stroking the mare.

He wanted to go to her, take her hand, kneel down in the straw, and tell her how he felt. Only he didn't know how he felt. And even if he did know, he didn't know what words to say, and even if he did know the words, she wouldn't…

Sara's voice, begging to pet Star, brought him back to the moment. Nick looked away from Elizabeth, and she scrambled to her feet.

"Of course, Sara," she said. "I didn't mean to be selfish. It's just that I've never fallen in love with a horse before." She shook the straw out of her skirt. "It's had quite an effect on me. I forgot you were waiting."

What about me? Nick thought. *Could you bring yourself to let some of that love spill over to me?* He mentally shook his head at his fantasy and made an effort to sound normal. "One of you at a time. Let Lizzy go first."

When Elizabeth turned to leave, he stopped her with a light touch on her shoulder. "You can stay with Lizzy, Miss Hamilton. I just didn't want all the children in here at once."

After each child had time with Star, Nick shooed them off. "I think the baby's had enough company for today," he said over their protests. "You can see her again tomorrow."

"Aunt Elizabeth wants to see Lizzy ride her pony," Mark said. "Can we show her?"

"If it's all right with your mama," Nick told Mark. "Just let me finish up here."

"Come on, Aunt Elizabeth." Mark grabbed Elizabeth's hand. "You gotta see the rest of the animals."

Elizabeth obediently followed.

The only animals in the barn left for Elizabeth to meet were the milk cows. Elizabeth learned more than she ever wanted to know about milking, churning butter, and making cheese.

She'd never given a thought to where dairy products came from. They had just magically appeared on the table, and she took them for granted. Elizabeth almost wished she'd remained ignorant. She didn't like to think about where her food originated.

During the warmer months, the Carters kept the pigs in back of the barn. While Elizabeth was not unfamiliar with the smell of horse droppings, pig stench was another matter. Elizabeth held her hand over her nose while they introduced her to the pigs, including a huge sow nursing her piglets.

The sow rose to its feet, tumbling the piglets off. It gave Elizabeth a baleful look, then shook its ungainly body, sending mud droplets all over the place.

Elizabeth didn't step back soon enough and ended up with smelly mud flecked across her face and clothes.

"Uggggh," Mark said. His sisters burst into giggles.

Dismayed, Elizabeth took out her lace-edged handkerchief and scrubbed at her face, knowing she might have left smudges. Then she tried to wipe her shirtwaist, to no avail. She sighed. *Welcome to the West, Elizabeth.*

Sara sobered. "Mama can lend you a clean one, Aunt Elizabeth."

Elizabeth regarded the soiled piece of cloth, no longer recognizable as fine linen, and shuddered. "Don't worry, sweetheart. I have more." She tossed the handkerchief in the pigpen, where the sow proceeded to collapse on it.

Beyond learning that they slaughtered the pigs in the fall, and the children liked playing with the cleaned and blown-up bladders, Elizabeth was thankful to avoid a long discussion of living pork and ham. They didn't linger in the vicinity of the pigpens, but left the livestock and headed to the front of the house.

Now Elizabeth had more time to examine the ranch house. Pamela's yellow daffodils had faded around their edges, but the tulips displayed all their scarlet glory. The lilacs near the side of the house showed purple buds that in a few weeks would burst into fragrant flowers. Several tall trees shaded a rough-cut lawn of new grass. One of the trees had a white bench circling the trunk. The limb of another tree held a swing.

"That's our swing," Sara told Elizabeth. "Nick made it for us. It's strong enough to hold Mama, although she doesn't ever play on it. She tested it to make sure it could hold us."

"Your father would be a better test," Elizabeth joked. "Couldn't Nick persuade him?"

"No," Sara answered seriously. "Father offered, but Nick wouldn't let him. He said he'd not only break the swing, but he'd probably break the tree."

"Why don't we go back so Lizzy can show me how well she rides," Elizabeth suggested. "Mark, run ahead and ask your mama if Lizzy can ride her pony."

Mark raced off. Elizabeth and the two girls followed. By the time they arrived at the house, Pamela had joined Mark on the porch.

"Just a quick ride before supper," she told her youngest daughter. "You children run and tell Nick to get Susie saddled up." She turned to Elizabeth, surveying her face. "I was about to ask if they've been taking good care of you."

"An encounter with one of your pigs."

"They've gotten me a time or two. You learn to watch and dodge."

"I'll just stay away," Elizabeth said, her tone ironic. She changed her tone. "Your children are darlings. Although Lizzy didn't say more than two words to me."

"She doesn't talk as much as the others did at her age. It's not that she doesn't know the words, it's just that she doesn't use them."

The two women headed toward the corral.

"She worries me," Pamela confided. "She's so fragile. She has the appetite of a sparrow."

"She's small-boned and tiny like a bird. I can see why you'd worry. Perhaps it's just a stage she'll grow out of."

"I hope so. But it's the way she's always been. I keep hoping that when she gets older, she'll be stronger."

"Too bad you don't have the recipe for your nanny's tonic," Elizabeth said in an attempt to lighten Pamela's mind. "She always told you it would help you grow big and strong."

"Ugh," said Pamela with a shudder. "That horrible drink. I had to hold my nose in order to swallow it. I used to envy you because your nanny didn't make you down a nasty tonic."

"Well, it worked." Elizabeth laughed. "You and your brothers all grew up strong and healthy."

Pamela wrinkled her nose. "I think we survived in spite of the tonic, not because of it. I could never inflict something like that on my children." A shadow crossed her face. "And it didn't work for Mary."

The same clutch of fear she'd experienced yesterday tightened Elizabeth's heart. So Pamela did see Lizzy's resemblance to her frail sister. And it was clear she worried about her daughter. Elizabeth didn't know what to say to comfort her friend, so she reached out and touched her shoulder.

By this time, the two women had rounded the barn and stood in front of the corral. With her dress hitched to her knees, Lizzy rode astride her brown pony.

As Nick led the pony at a sedate walk, Lizzy's face glowed with delight. "Look at me, Aunt Elizabeth!" The child waved so strongly, she almost lost her balance. A quick hand from Nick righted her.

Hearing Lizzy actually direct a sentence toward her caused Elizabeth to exchange an astonished look with Pamela. "I see you, dear," she called and waved back.

Nick touched Lizzy's leg and reminded her to grip the pony tighter with her knees. He continued to lead the pony around the edge of the corral, instructing the child in a quiet tone.

Elizabeth watched how patient Nick was with the little girl—his love for Lizzy was apparent in the tone of his voice and every careful move. His teaching techniques contrasted with the few lessons she'd received as a child. To her instructor, she'd just been another pupil, and he'd been rather abrupt with her. She'd been frightened by the whole experience.

No wonder the children rode so well. They'd had the best instruction possible. She thought about the gentle way Nick guided the pony and the touch of his strong hands. Becoming uncomfortable with such physical thoughts, and to distract herself, she focused instead on her disapproval of Lizzy riding without a sidesaddle. "Pamela, why are your girls riding astride? Is that common out here?"

Pamela let out a sigh. "With a few women, though most use a sidesaddle. But it's something John feels strongly about. Riding astride is safer and gives the rider more control of the horse."

"It just seems so unladylike."

"It's not like riding in the park in the city or on someone's country estate, Elizabeth." Pamela's tone sharpened. "Living on a ranch means living near cattle. Sometimes they stampede."

"I had no idea." Elizabeth suppressed a flash of apprehension. "You're poking a hole in the idyllic picture I had of the peaceful bovine," she said in a wry tone of voice.

"Under the conditions here, the girls need to be able to react quickly, and they can do that better if they're astride."

"Oh."

"The alternative is to keep them in the house all day." Pamela gestured to the children watching Lizzy's lesson. "As you can see, that's not an option they'd be happy with. When they're older, I'll insist the girls at least learn to ride sidesaddle, so if they need to make a ladylike impression, they can."

Elizabeth could see the sense of Pamela and John's decision.

"I suppose you're also wondering why Sara is wearing boys' clothes?"

"Yes, I was. Do other girls out here wear trousers?"

"Not many," said Pamela with another sigh. "And she doesn't wear them to school. John had a little sister he adored. Sara's named after her. When his sister was six, there was a terrible accident. The children were playing near an open fire. Her dress flared out over the flames and caught on fire. Terrified, she ran. John tried to catch her. But it was too late. She died of her burns."

"Merciful God!" Elizabeth stiffened and covered her mouth with her hand. It had been heartbreaking enough for the two girls when Pamela's sister, Mary, died. But she'd died of an illness, and the family had had a few days to prepare themselves. How much more tragic to lose a beloved younger sister in such a horrible way!

"He still blames himself. So that's why the girls wear trousers—although Lizzy doesn't usually…"

The flames of the long-ago tragedy burned Elizabeth's critical feelings to ashes, leaving her shaken. If wearing boys' clothes would keep Sara and Lizzy safe, she'd wholeheartedly support John and Pamela's decision.

Life was fragile enough, especially for children. Parents had to do everything in their power to protect them. Even then, it often wasn't enough…

Pamela seemed to sense Elizabeth's feelings. "John would be fine if I wore trousers," she said in an apparent attempt to lighten the conversation. "Could you imagine me in men's clothing?"

Elizabeth made an effort to shake her melancholy thoughts. "I don't even want to think about it," she said with mock firmness.

Pamela laughed, then called out to the children. "Time to wash up before dinner. Remember, you're taking a bath tonight so you'll be clean for our guests tomorrow."

"Oh, Mama," Mark groaned. "Does that mean we have to stay in the house all day?"

"Yes. That's the only way you'll stay clean. Besides, you have to do your lessons for school. You've missed two days of studying."

Mark let out another groan, but along with his sister, obediently headed to the house.

Nick opened the gate of the corral and led Lizzy's pony toward the two women.

"Lizzy, you ride so well," Elizabeth told the child. She directed a warm smile to Nick. "And you're lucky to have such a good teacher."

Nick raised an eyebrow and tipped his hat to her.

"Do you think I could ride your pony?" she teased Lizzy. "Or do you think I'd be too big?"

Lizzy shook her head. "Too big."

Elizabeth laughed, delighted to get a second sentence from the child.

"It's time to wash up, Lizzy," Pamela said to her daughter.

Lizzy dropped the reins and held out both arms to Elizabeth.

Elizabeth's heart warmed with love at the little girl's trusting gesture. She gave a quick look to Pamela for permission, and at her friend's nod, lifted Lizzy off the pony.

Lizzy wrapped her arms around Elizabeth's neck and squeezed her thin legs around her waist. Surprised, Elizabeth directed an astonished look at Nick and Pamela. They laughed in response.

"Lizzy's just being a monkey, Miss Hamilton," Nick said. "Would you like me to take her?"

Elizabeth nestled the child to her, inhaling her little girl scent. She shook her head. Now that Lizzy had finally reached out to her, she wasn't going to give her up.

Nick seemed to understand her reaction. "Does something to you, doesn't it, when she puts those skinny little arms around you and hangs on that way?"

She nodded in wholehearted agreement.

"Come on, you two." Pamela turned to walk to the house.

Elizabeth smiled good-bye at Nick, but his words disturbed her.

The child in her arms felt too much like Mary. Light in weight. Limbs stick-thin. Her fingers could feel every rib. She dropped a soft kiss on Lizzy's forehead.

Lizzy laid her head on Elizabeth's shoulder and snuggled closer.

Touched to tears by the feeling of the child in her arms, she could only hug her tighter and say a prayer. *Please, please, let her grow up strong and healthy.*

CHAPTER NINE

The next morning Elizabeth awoke eager for her first horseback ride. As she headed for the barn, she lifted the wide skirt of her hussar-blue velvet riding habit, careful to keep the hem off the ground. She didn't even want to think of the velvet absorbing the smelly muck around the horses.

Dressed in a blue shirt and indigo denim trousers, Nick was waiting for her. Up close, she noticed his clothes made his green eyes look almost blue.

When he saw her, his blue-green gaze lit with appreciation. "Morning, ma'am."

Elizabeth made a face at him.

"Sorry." His eyes lit with laughter. "Let me try again. Morning, *Miss Hamilton*."

She grinned back at him. "Good morning, Nick."

"How's the hand?"

She held her hand, clad in a blue leather riding glove, and gave it an experimental flex. "Much better."

"Let me know if it bothers you. Perhaps we'd better just go for a short ride."

"That would probably be best."

"How much have you ridden?" he asked.

"Only a little in the summers when I stayed at a friend's country estate. I had some lessons as a child," Elizabeth admitted. "It's been quite a while. I only rode once last summer."

"Belle should be fine for you." He gave her a knee up onto Pamela's sidesaddle, adjusted the stirrup, then smiled reassuringly. "She has spirit, but she's also very gentle. Besides, we'll stay at a walk."

A brown horse with white speckles on his hips and back waited, already saddled. Nick went over to him and stroked his neck. "Freckles, this is Miss Elizabeth Hamilton." Freckles nuzzled Nick's face, making soft blowing noises. Nick untied the horse and mounted him in a smooth, practiced motion.

Nick rode next to Elizabeth. She could tell he watched her closely, his body alert to any possible assistance she might need.

"You can relax, Nick."

"I'm responsible for your safety, Miss Hamilton."

"I'm sure Belle won't run away with me."

He didn't change his watchfulness. "Just want to be sure."

It had been a long time since she'd experienced a man's protectiveness. She liked the feeling of security his care gave her. Her mind flashed to Caleb Livingston. He, too, would be quite the gentleman. She imagined him placing his arm around her—

"We'll ride along the river," Nick said, interrupting her fantasy. "It's a mighty pretty sight."

A mighty pretty sight indeed. Puffy white clouds floated across the azure-blue sky. Pine-covered mountains, crowned by snowcaps, folded down into foothills that ringed the valley. Beneath the clouds, the play of sun and shadow cast hazy blue-green patches on the mountainsides. A distant large-winged bird rode an air current before diving into a clump of trees.

Side by side, the two horses meandered along a path, heading toward a strand of trees. The bubbling sound of water flowing over rocks reached her before she saw the river. Budding trees threw shadows over the swiftly moving translucent green water. Brown mossy rocks jutted up throughout the river, causing small rippling waves. Here and there, quieter pools looked calm.

The sounds and sights of the water relaxed muscles Elizabeth hadn't known she'd tensed. She loved to be near water and had been afraid she'd miss the ocean. That concern eased from her mind.

Elizabeth knew she'd be spending a lot of time on this riverbank. She'd bring a book to read, or her paints. Soon there'd be river scenes to add to Pamela's seascapes.

"How deep is the river?"

"'Bout three foot in the middle, but it's deeper now from snowmelt."

Nick pointed out what looked like a slatted wooden box placed under a small waterfall. "That's my fish trap," he told her. "The trout swim in, and, unless they're real small, can't get out."

How clever, she thought, looking at him in admiration. "Do you eat fish often?"

"On Fridays. Miz Carter says it's a Boston custom. But it's sure been a change for a beef-lovin' man."

"I can imagine." She laughed. "Although we usually have codfish, and they're caught in the ocean." She glanced around. "What kind of trees are these?"

"They're aspen. Wait until you see them in the fall. The leaves turn yellow, and it looks like the sky hereabouts is filled with gold."

"Sounds lovely."

"This is the children's favorite place." Nick reined in Freckles next to a large pool formed by a crescent-shaped dam of rocks, reaching halfway across the twenty-foot-wide river. The still pool contrasted with the swiftly flowing water around it, inviting Elizabeth to hitch up her skirts and wade.

"John swam in this pool when he was a boy, but Miz Carter didn't think it was safe enough for the children, so we added more rocks between the pool and the fast water."

"They must turn blue with cold."

"It's better in the summertime when it's hot outside. Swimming is refreshing then. Sometimes even Miz Carter takes her shoes off and puts her feet in the water."

So Pamela gave in to temptation. Elizabeth grinned at the thought. "Do the girls swim too?"

"Yes, Miz Carter lets them swim in their shifts."

Elizabeth raised an eyebrow at that. "What do you men wear?"

Laughter glinted in his green eyes, and he slanted her a mischievous grin. "Since Miz Carter came here to live, we swim in old pants cut off at the knees."

Warmth crept up her cheeks. Bad enough thinking about a bare-chested Nick swimming in the pool without thinking of him naked!

She nudged Belle with her heels, urging her ahead. Freckles caught up to her, but Elizabeth ignored Nick.

As she became absorbed in the scenery, she forgot her embarrassing feelings. The overwhelming grandeur of the surroundings through which they rode entranced Elizabeth. Montana's beauty filled her until she could barely think; she could only be part of it with every breath she inhaled.

She could understand how different the beauty of the countryside could be from the city, but the sky...How could the same sky over Boston look so much bluer in Montana? In Boston, she'd never even looked up except for the occasional glance to see if rain threatened.

Almost involuntarily, she murmured, "The sky is the most glorious blue I've ever seen."

He must have heard the quiet words. "I used to think there couldn't be a more beautiful blue in all the world."

The sound of his voice pulled Elizabeth into the awareness of his presence. She sent him a curious glance. "What changed your mind?"

He flushed, although his green gaze remained steady on her. "I saw your eyes."

His cheeks reddened further, and he glanced down at the neck of his horse.

Elizabeth's dreamy state vanished. One part of her mind skittered away from his attraction to her, but another part felt moved by the appreciative look he'd given her and the lovely simplicity of his compliment.

And she couldn't help thinking how beautiful his eyes were. She even liked how his freckles stood out on his skin when he flushed. But before these thoughts could go any further, the first part of her mind won out. His words had broken Montana's spell, and she had to resist the urge to gallop away.

"I'm ready to return." She didn't look to see his reaction. Would there be a closed-off look in the green eyes that just a moment ago had been so vulnerable?

She kicked Belle into a trot. A bird flew out of a nearby bush, startling the horse.

Belle shied away.

Elizabeth sawed at the reins.

Nick wheeled Freckles around, leaned over, and caught Belle's bridle. "Whoa, girl. That's just a little ole bird. It's not goin' to hurt you."

The horse slowed to a walk.

"You all right, Miss Hamilton?"

"I'm fine, thank you," she said, embarrassed that he had to rescue her. "I have her under control. You can let go."

He dropped the bridle, but petted Belle, soothing her. Reining in Freckles, Nick allowed Elizabeth to precede him back to the ranch.

With his compliment, Nick had destroyed the peace of her ride and aroused uncomfortable sensations within her. She'd really have to watch these absurd reactions she had toward him. Shaking her head, she kneed Belle forward, careful not to glance back in Nick's direction.

When they reached the barn, Nick dismounted and reached to help her down. His strong hands circled her waist, and a shiver of pleasure coursed through her body. Suddenly, she had trouble ignoring him.

"Thank you," she murmured before turning toward the house.

* * *

Nick watched her retreat, chiding himself for being a fool. He'd enjoyed being in Elizabeth's presence, watching her face as she fell under the spell of Montana's beauty. While he'd basked in the pleasure of her reaction, he'd lowered his guard. He hadn't meant to say anything, but it had slipped out. Now upset with his familiarity toward her, she might never trust herself alone with him again.

His stomach had knotted the entire ride home. He hadn't known what to do or say to make the situation right, so he'd said nothing. He cursed his inexperience with women. Being good with horses just wasn't the same as expertise with ladies. Besides, any knowledge he had about western women probably wouldn't apply to a high-society beauty like Elizabeth.

Nick let out a sigh. *Hell. I shouldn't be mooning over her anyway.* He took hold of the horses' reins and led them toward the barn. And even though he told himself not to think of her, as his hands busied with unsaddling and grooming the horses, his thoughts returned to the look on her face as she rode beside him under the deep-blue Montana sky.

❋ ❋ ❋

Once inside the house, Elizabeth searched for Pamela. She found her in the kitchen discussing the party menu with Annie.

Pamela glanced up when she came through the door. "There you are. Did you enjoy yourself?"

"Yes, but I'm feeling a little stiff. It's been a long time since I've ridden. I'll probably be sore later."

Pamela's smile commiserated. "I feel that way when I haven't ridden enough. Taking a bath helps. Yours is ready in your room. I'll send Dawn up with hot water. After you bathe, you'd better rest before the party. When it's time to dress, I'll send Dawn to wake you."

"But won't you need her help with dressing?"

Pamela blushed, then laughed. "Actually John's become quite an expert lady's maid. He sure can pull my corset strings tight."

Elizabeth read between the lines of what her friend was saying. "But your hair," she teased. "Don't tell me John is as good at putting hairpins in as he is at taking them out."

Pamela hugged Elizabeth and whispered in her ear, "Beth, you wretch. Only you'd dare have a conversation like this with me. It's a good thing Annie doesn't speak English very well."

Elizabeth laughed and left the kitchen. As soon as she reached the solitude of her room she wanted to think about the ride she'd taken. But Dawn walked in right behind her with the hot water, so she concentrated instead on the enjoyment of soaking her stiff muscles. After she'd bathed and lain down to rest, she expected to stay awake and think, but ended up falling asleep.

A soft knock woke Elizabeth. Dawn entered, carrying a tray with a cup of tea. She moved across the room and handed the tray to Elizabeth.

"Thank you." Elizabeth sipped the tea, directing Dawn to lay out her undergarments. "Would you please bring me my jewel case?"

Dawn took the case out of the bottom of the wardrobe and handed it to her. Elizabeth turned the key in the lock, opened the top, and lifted each piece of jewelry out, spreading them on the blanket in front of her. She'd brought all her jewelry with her, even the coral bead necklace and gold locket from her childhood.

She debated whether to wear her pearls or her diamonds. Her mother's delicate diamond necklace had matching tear-shaped diamond earrings. They were Elizabeth's favorite pieces, and she wore them far more often than she'd worn the more ornate Hamilton diamonds, now in Genia's possession.

As Elizabeth hesitated between the two sets, her throat tightened with sadness. She rubbed the pearl necklace between her fingers, savoring the memories evoked from the silken beads. She knew if she stayed in Montana she'd rarely wear such elaborate jewelry.

Tonight, however, she was the guest of honor, so she dropped the pearls into their silk pouch and picked up the diamond necklace. The waning light from the windows sparkled across the stones. *I'll wear this.*

That decision made, Elizabeth scooped up the rest of her jewelry and replaced them in the jewel box. She pulled Richard's locket over her head, carefully set the necklace in the corner of the box, then closed the lid.

Elizabeth slid out of bed and placed the diamonds on the dressing table. She gestured for Dawn to begin helping her dress.

Dawn carried over Elizabeth's best silk chemise and drawers, both decorated with punchwork embroidery and edged with lace, and helped her into them.

Elizabeth chose her favorite A La Spirite corset and had Dawn pull the laces as tightly as possible. The familiar pressing sensation against her ribs gave her some reminiscing thoughts to how loosely she'd been tying her stays in the last few days. Maybe she wouldn't be able to wear her diamonds very often in this primitive place, but wearing a loose corset meant she'd at least be able to breathe!

She stepped into several silk taffeta petticoats that fitted her figure at the hips and finished at the bottom with layered ruffles. The petticoats boasted row after row of hand embroidery added by Josie's clever fingers. Elizabeth loved the rustling sound taffeta made when she walked. It always made her feel more elegant than when she wore plain silk or linen petticoats.

Lastly, she donned the horsehair bustle, designed to add fullness to the back of her dress. She'd not worn one for the last few days. At least this bustle wasn't as big as the ones she'd worn a few years ago. She'd never liked the cagelike bustle with steel springs. Thank goodness the fashion had changed to smaller ones.

Dawn helped her into the two-piece peacock-blue silk dress. Then she buttoned her up.

Elizabeth slid her hands over the skirt, which fitted snugly over her hips, falling into a slight train banded with peacock-blue velvet. The bottom of the polonaise fitted over the top of her skirt in a velvet-edged V. The long sleeves, slightly puffed at the shoulders, ended at her wrists in velvet points. She twitched the Belgian lace of the low-cut neck, showing an expanse of bosom, which, while proper in Boston, might shock Pamela's friends.

Elizabeth giggled at the thought, earning a look of surprise from Dawn, and seated herself in the chair in front of the dressing table.

Dawn fastened the diamond necklace while Elizabeth screwed the earrings to her ears. The girl gathered most of Elizabeth's hair in an intricately braided knot.

A knock sounded. Pamela pushed open the door and entered the room.

Wearing a claret-colored velvet dress that wasn't cut as low as Elizabeth's, her friend sparkled with the garnet necklace, earrings, and bracelet, which Elizabeth remembered as once belonging to Pamela's mother.

"You look beautiful," Elizabeth told her.

Pamela smiled. "You know I was never a beauty. You're the one who truly looks lovely. You'll cast the rest of us in the shade."

Elizabeth sent her a reassuring smile. "Pamela, you glow with love, and that's beautiful."

Pamela blushed.

"What's more," Elizabeth added in a playful tone, "I'll bet John's already told you so."

Pamela smiled and changed the subject. "We're both wearing our mothers' necklaces. Remember when we were children, and we'd spy on our parents when they held a party?"

"I used to sit on top of the steps to catch glimpses of them until Nanny sent me to bed."

"Me too. How beautiful my mama looked. I couldn't wait until I was old enough to dress up and go to parties." Pamela sighed. "Now it's we who are grown-up and wearing their jewelry. Don't you wish they could be here tonight?"

Elizabeth echoed her sigh. "Wouldn't that be wonderful? And our fathers too...At least your father is still alive and can visit you."

"Yes, though he's only done so once. Maybe in the next few years he'll come again."

Dawn used the curling iron to position loose curls around Elizabeth's face and from underneath a knot of hair pinned high on the back of her head. With satisfaction, Elizabeth watched her reflection in the looking glass. Josie couldn't have done it better.

"I just wanted to check up on you," Pamela said. "I'm going downstairs. Our guests should be arriving soon." She frowned. "We'll be one short. Sweetwater Springs has another eligible bachelor that I wanted you to meet, Wyatt Thompson. He owns a ranch on the other side of town. He sent word that his daughter's ill, and he won't be able to make it."

Elizabeth pretended to pout. "I'll just have to make do with Mr. Livingston."

"I'm sure you'll do very well with him." With one finger, Pamela tapped Elizabeth's shoulder. "I'll see you downstairs."

"I'll join you in a few minutes."

As Dawn put the finishing touches to Elizabeth's hair, Elizabeth dusted her face with rice powder so she'd have the desired pale complexion.

The girl draped a white lace shawl around Elizabeth's shoulders. "Pretty," she said, with her first smile for Elizabeth.

The compliment touched her. "Thank you, Dawn. You did a wonderful job."

The girl nodded, then glided from the room.

Elizabeth sat a little longer to collect her thoughts. Aside from Genia's disastrous party, it had been a long time since she'd experienced anxiousness before a social occasion. She explored the feeling for a moment, rolling the idea around in her mind as though tasting a new wine.

An excited nervousness, actually…She rather liked it, although it also saddened her.

When did I lose my eager anticipation for life?

Those feelings must have died with Richard, and in the greater losses of the time she'd never noticed the lack.

"Now you're becoming melancholy," she scolded herself. "It's a party; you're supposed to be happy." She stood, arranged her skirts, and glanced one more time in the looking glass. Then she walked resolutely out the door and down the stairs.

CHAPTER TEN

From the doorway to the parlor, Elizabeth could see John and Pamela seated on the sofa. John, clad in a brown broadcloth jacket and trousers with a tan vest and lighter tan shirt, looked the way she remembered him in Boston. How quickly she'd gotten used to seeing him in his working clothes.

John rose to his feet when Elizabeth entered the room, an appreciative smile on his face. "Elizabeth, I'm going to have every available man for miles haunting my doorstep, hoping to catch a glimpse of you," he teased. "It's a good thing my men won't see you—I'd never get a lick of work out of them. But I can't answer for Nick's reaction. Perhaps we should keep him away."

"Nick?" Elizabeth echoed, disconcerted by the idea of the handsome cowboy attending the party. "Will he be here?"

"Of course," John told her, looking at his wife for confirmation. "Didn't Pamela tell you?"

"I guess I never thought to mention it. I only told her about the invited guests."

Nick walked in at that moment, and Elizabeth caught her breath. She'd seen him wearing a suit in Boston, but even though he wore the same suit tonight, he looked different somehow. Maybe he fit the surroundings better, or maybe her awareness of him had changed. She slid her thoughts away from that disturbing idea.

Nick greeted Pamela and John, then turned to Elizabeth. "You look lovely, Miss Hamilton." Their eyes met, and again

Elizabeth experienced that tingling down her spine that always happened in his presence.

"See, Elizabeth, I told you how it would be." John laughed. "I'll be stumbling over all your admirers."

"I saw some of the others arriving," Nick told Pamela in an apparent attempt to change the subject. "They should be here any minute."

Elizabeth's discomfort about Nick's unexpected presence vanished with his appearance, replaced by an odd excitement. His compliment had been so polished, without a trace of his usual shyness. With amusement, she wondered if he'd practiced it beforehand.

The appearance of the Carters' nearest neighbors, the Addisons, interrupted her thoughts. The schoolteacher, Harriet Stanton, and the mercantile owners, Frank and Hortense Cobb, arrived together. The Cobbs stopped to talk to John, while Miss Stanton approached Pamela.

"Miss Stanton, how nice of you to come," Pamela greeted her.

"I'm so happy you invited me."

"This is my friend from Boston, Miss Elizabeth Hamilton. Elizabeth, this is the children's teacher, Miss Harriet Stanton."

The two women smiled and nodded to each other. Petite and pretty Miss Stanton's gray eyes and light brown hair showed to advantage in her green calico gown patterned with gray feathers. Fastened at her neck, a round gold pin shone in the candlelight. Elizabeth immediately thought of her as a modest young lady.

"I'm delighted to meet you, Miss Stanton. You're quite a favorite with Mark and Sara."

"They're such dear children. But as for me being a favorite...When they talk to me at school, it's Nick who holds that position." She looked around the room. "There he is now." Her eyes lit up, and her body quivered with eagerness. "Excuse me. There's something I must ask him." She lifted her hand to wave at him. "Oh, Nick." Apparently without a further thought for Pamela and Elizabeth, Miss Stanton made a beeline for him.

The joyful note she'd heard in the woman's voice caused Elizabeth to revise her opinion of the teacher. Not so demure after all. She glanced at Pamela to see her reaction to Miss Stanton's impolite behavior.

Pamela gazed at Miss Stanton and Nick, a speculative gleam in her eyes.

Elizabeth had an uneasy tightening in her stomach. She hadn't seen that expression on her friend's face for many years, but she knew what it signified. *Pamela's just switched into her matchmaking mode.* Before Elizabeth could figure out why the idea of a match between those two bothered her, John strolled over with the Cobbs and introduced them.

The Cobbs reminded Elizabeth of the Jack Sprat rhyme: he, tall and lean; she, short and stout. A fringe of gray-and-brown hair circled Mr. Cobb's bald head, and his red, bulbous nose made her wonder if he spent too much time imbibing spirits.

Wearing a black silk dress, ornamented with a froth of lace pinned on her bodice with a cameo, Mrs. Cobb looked Elizabeth up and down. Her small brown eyes seemed to shrewdly assess the value of each article of Elizabeth's apparel.

Elizabeth tried to show interest in being introduced to the Cobbs, while at the same time keeping an eye on Miss Stanton and Nick. Across the room, the teacher chattered away, her hand intimately placed on the wrangler's arm, her gaze locked on to his face. Elizabeth couldn't overhear their words, but judging by

Nick's rigid stance and the tug he'd just given his collar, he wasn't comfortable.

Reverend Norton, clad in a rusty black suit, ministerial dignity radiating from his thin, white-bearded face, entered the parlor, his wife in tow.

"Miss Hamilton, welcome to Montana." Reverend Norton's voice boomed over Elizabeth. "I understand you're from Boston."

"Yes, I am."

"We originally hail from Cambridge."

"I know several families there."

"Elizabeth." Pamela waved her over to meet the late arriving Dr. and Mrs. Cameron.

The couple exuded vitality, and the other guests greeted them with warmth. Traces of a Scottish accent laced their apologies for tardiness. As she talked, Mrs. Cameron's mop of sandy curls almost sprang from the confining hairpins. Freckles danced across her nose, in tune to the cadence of her speech.

Her husband, although wearing the traditional side-whiskers and Prince Albert coat of a successful doctor, had straight auburn hair that looked as if he'd run his fingers through it. His coat pockets sagged and bulged.

He reached into one and pulled out a sweet for Lizzy, chucking her under her small chin and eliciting one of her shy smiles. *What a kind man. He must be a good doctor.*

When would Mr. Livingston arrive? She held her neck locked to avoid glancing toward the doorway every few seconds, instead politely focusing on her conversation with Mrs. Cameron. But the lively doctor's wife pulled her into an interesting exchange of ideas about adjusting to Montana.

Intent on their discussion, she missed his entrance. But Pamela guided him straight toward her.

Elizabeth's breath caught, and her heart beat with a slow, painful rhythm. The tall, handsome man moving toward her looked the very image of her beloved Richard. The same wide-set brown eyes, the same straight nose. Richard, yet not Richard. She reached up to touch her locket, remembered she wasn't wearing it, and dropped her hand to her side.

Beside him, Pamela gestured. "Mr. Livingston, I'd like you to meet my dear friend from Boston, Miss Elizabeth Hamilton." She turned. "Elizabeth, meet Mr. Caleb Cabot Livingston, our town banker."

"Mr. Livingston." Elizabeth greeted him with an extended hand, while at the same time struggling not to show her reaction at his resemblance to her dear, departed Richard.

The man bowed, lifted her hand to his lips, and kissed it. "Mrs. Carter didn't tell me what a beautiful friend she had." His voice was lighter than Richard's, more tenor compared to her beloved's baritone, but warm, just as she remembered. He held her hand a few seconds longer, then turned it over and lightly ran his thumb over the center of her palm.

Shock reverberated through Elizabeth; tears sprang to her eyes. She lowered her lashes in what she hoped would be taken as an appearance of modesty. He'd given her Richard's secret signal—the extra touch of the thumb on her palm after the more conventional kiss on the hand. It had been her beloved's way of saying, "I love you," whenever he greeted her in public.

"I'm delighted to meet you, Miss Hamilton. I sincerely hope you enjoy your visit to Montana."

Please, please don't let him notice my reaction, she prayed. How could she possibly explain tears? Caught between painful memory and exciting reality, Elizabeth blinked the moisture away, summoning her composure.

From the corner of her eye, she caught Nick staring at their joined hands, a stormy frown on his face. Miss Stanton tapped him on the arm, and he looked at her.

Elizabeth turned her attention back toward Mr. Livingston. "Thank you, Mr. Livingston," she said a trifle breathlessly. "Montana is..." She caught her breath. "...more than I'd ever hoped."

She steadied herself with her other hand on the back of a nearby chair and cast a covert glance at Pamela. The mischievous look on her friend's face banished her strange feeling of faintness. Apparently Pamela didn't comprehend the intensity of her reaction.

As Elizabeth moved to withdraw her hand from Mr. Livingston's, he again stroked her palm with his thumb. Shivers of warmth raced up her arm, setting fire to her rapidly beating heart. She wanted to sink into his embrace, but before she could speak, Mrs. Cameron claimed his attention.

As he talked with the doctor's wife, Elizabeth studied him. Richard's hair had been darker, and he'd had a cleft in his chin. Mr. Livingston stood taller, and his shoulders weren't as broad as Elizabeth remembered Richard's being. The Patrician nose matched Richard's, although perhaps Mr. Livingston's was slightly longer.

She kept the banker in her awareness even as she interacted with the other guests. She barely knew what she said, but she wasn't receiving any strange looks, so her behavior couldn't be too odd.

To distract herself, Elizabeth watched the children greet the adults. They looked quite different from the urchins of the past few days: scrubbed, dressed in their good clothes, and warned to be on their best behavior.

Tomboy Sara had transformed into a little lady. Her hair, held back with a navy velvet ribbon, dangled in corkscrew curls halfway down her back. The child kept smoothing her matching blue velvet dress, as though pleased with the material.

Mr. Livingston didn't seem to be a favorite with the children, which gave Elizabeth an unexpected pang. They greeted him with politeness. He acknowledged their presence, said a few short words, then moved away from them to join the Addisons. Belatedly, Elizabeth realized that they didn't know Mr. Livingston well. They'd hardly spend time with the town banker.

Across the room, the children swarmed around Miss Stanton and Nick. Mark and Sara competed to tell their teacher something, while Lizzy slipped her hand into Nick's and leaned into his leg, a trusting expression on her face. Elizabeth couldn't make out what they said, but she recognized the argumentative postures Mark and Sara used with each other.

Judging by the pout on Sara's face, Mark won the competition. As if in consolation, Miss Stanton seated herself on the sofa and drew Sara toward her, while Mark continued talking. Miss Stanton looked up at Nick, said something, and patted the place next to her. He shook his head, but she persisted until he complied.

Elizabeth struggled with envious feelings about the familial tableau before her. Why did it matter to her if Miss Stanton held Nick's and the children's attention? Her gaze strayed to Mr. Livingston. In watching his profile, so like Richard's, her attraction to him strengthened, and the feelings of envy subsided.

Annie entered the room and nodded to Pamela. Pamela signaled Dawn to lead the children upstairs, while the guests followed the Carters toward the dining room.

To Elizabeth's great pleasure, Mr. Livingston approached her. "May I escort you to dinner, Miss Hamilton?" He extended his arm.

She flashed him a brilliant smile. "I'd be delighted, Mr. Livingston." She slipped her hand through the crook of his arm. She rested her fingers on his sleeve, her cheeks flushed, smile wide like a giddy girl's. *Our first walk to dinner. How well we fit together. Does he feel the significance of this moment?*

She glanced upward to see his reaction. His smile, so like Richard's, set her heart pounding. Her body felt so light she could practically walk on tiptoe. She floated through the few steps to the dining room, where their brief contact concluded far too quickly; she could have walked beside him for hours.

"In this room, one might feel he was back in Boston," Mr. Livingston commented, looking around at the mahogany table set with the rose Pompadour service. Maroon flowered wallpaper and matching heavy velvet curtains complemented the rose pattern on the plates. Elizabeth recognized some of the silver pieces as belonging to Pamela's mother. She hadn't seen them here before; Pamela clearly only brought them out for special occasions.

"Yes, it does," Elizabeth agreed. "Pamela and I picked out the pattern of the dishes before her marriage. She decorated the room to match."

John strode to the head of the table and sat down. Mr. Livingston seated Elizabeth on John's left, then pulled out the chair to her right. It pleased Elizabeth to see Mrs. Cameron take a seat across from her, with Nick by her side, although her pleasure dimmed when Miss Stanton seated herself on Nick's other side. Nor did she like how Mrs. Cobb settled next to Mr. Livingston and immediately claimed his attention.

Elizabeth made eye contact with Pamela, who was taking her place at the foot of the table. The two women exchanged warm smiles before her friend turned to her left to answer a question from Dr. Cameron.

Over dinner, talk ranged from a discussion of ranch matters, to community problems, to politics. Elizabeth let the conversation flow around her. In a blur of joy, only vaguely aware of what was being said, she joined in very little of the discussion. However, she managed to focus her attention on the conversation when Mr. Livingston made a comment. His responses sounded intelligent and conservative.

She tried not to be obvious in her sideways glances at him. Even in profile, he had Richard's high cheekbones. She couldn't get over her reaction to his appearance. His presence felt so familiar, she found it difficult to refrain from touching him. With Richard there had always been an exchange of discreet light touches on the arm or brushes of the leg whenever they sat next to each other.

Once she looked across the table at Nick and noticed him watching her with a shadowed expression in his green eyes. For a moment, her happiness dimmed. Could he sense her attraction to Mr. Livingston? Their glances held, then he turned away to reply to a remark addressed to him by Miss Stanton.

Seated next to Miss Stanton, Mr. Addison, who'd been quietly attacking his food, spoke up when the conversation lulled. "My mare cast a shoe. Second time this month."

John chuckled. "Never was much of a blacksmith, Addison. Better ask Nick, here, if he'll reshoe her."

"I'm not much of a smith either," Nick said. "Sure will be glad when Red Charlie gets his blacksmith shop up and running." He glanced across the table at Mr. Livingston. "Know how much longer it'll take?"

Mr. Addison gave the banker a curious look. "He going to buy it from Reinhart's widow?"

"That's what he wanted," the banker said, "but I had to refuse him the loan."

Across the table Nick's knife clattered against his plate. "Why on earth did you do that?" he asked.

Mr. Livingston lifted his eyebrows. "Loan money to an Indian without collateral? I hardly think so."

The warm glow in Elizabeth's heart faltered.

Nick scowled back. "Red Charlie's a good man and a hard worker. It shouldn't matter that he's an Indian."

"You mistake me, Sanders." Mr. Livingston sent a quelling look across the table. "I'm not making a judgment on his ability to work hard, nor on him being an Indian. It's his lack of collateral I object to. Banks have gone under by overextending themselves in that way. I'm not going to allow that to happen in Sweetwater Springs. Too many people have entrusted me with their savings."

Nick's eyes glittered like emeralds. "Red Charlie knows more about horses than anyone around these parts."

Miss Stanton touched him on the arm. "Not more than you, Nick. After the way you tamed Outlaw—"

"I didn't tame him. I just worked with him in a way he could trust." Nick's words sounded calm, but one hand crumpled the linen napkin in his fist. "Much of what I did with Outlaw, I learned from Red Charlie."

Mr. Cobb waved his fork in a big circle. "Shouldn't have one of those redskins running a business anyway. Looks bad for the whole town. As my pa always said, the only good Indian's a dead Indian." He stabbed the fork into the table.

Elizabeth winced at the harsh words and lack of respect. At the foot of the table, Pamela echoed her movement. Even John frowned at the man. Cobb shoved a forkful of potatoes into his mouth and smiled vacantly at the minister.

Clearing his throat, Reverend Norton reproved in his best pulpit tone. "Now, Mr. Cobb, that's hardly a Christian attitude. Remember, it's our duty to bring the word of the Lord to the heathen."

Mrs. Cobb's plump bosom quivered with indignation. "They're always hanging around outside the store, the lazy, drunken thieves," she said, with a shrillness that caused Elizabeth to wince again. "I don't let them inside until I see their money in hand."

A wave of dislike for the Cobbs and their attitude swept over Elizabeth. In Boston, she'd never given any thought to Indians. Dawn was the first Indian she'd met. Elizabeth liked her. Thank goodness the girl wasn't around to hear the Cobbs's horrible words.

Nick spoke with controlled emphasis. "There's good Indians and bad, just as there's good and bad white men." He shot a dagger-glance at the merchant. "Red Charlie's a good one."

At the head of the table, John shifted in his seat. "Actually, Livingston, I'd appreciate it if you'd reconsider." The tone sounded quiet, but the words, uttered by the foremost rancher in the county, hung heavily in the air. "Being fairly new to Sweetwater Springs, you might not be aware of his reputation. I agree with Nick. Red Charlie's a good man and a fine blacksmith."

"You'd save me a great deal of trouble," Dr. Cameron added. "I've had to patch up several men who tried to do their own smithing. We could use an expert."

"How 'bout if I stand pledge for him?" Nick asked.

Mr. Livingston raised a questioning eyebrow. "With what?"

"My string of horses."

"How many?"

"Eleven. Eight in foal."

"Good offer," Mr. Addison spoke up. "Best horses in the county."

The banker looked unconvinced. "Horses are speculative. Especially since you haven't established yourself with your own ranching operation, Sanders."

"I'll stand pledge, Livingston." John spoke with firmness. "I think I'm established enough for you. You'd hardly turn me down."

"If you're willing to do that for him, Carter, then I believe we can work out a deal."

Murmurs buzzed around the table.

Elizabeth relaxed.

"I'll ride into town next week, and we can draw up the papers." John reached for his wineglass and saluted the banker.

Annie entered the room carrying a towering seven-layer chocolate cake. As if to dispel the tension in the room, everyone focused their attention on dessert. Between bites of Annie's delicious cake, Pamela turned the conversation to a safer subject.

"Elizabeth has brought the latest music with her," she announced. "Unlike me, she's kept up regular practice."

"I hope you'll play for us, Miss Hamilton," Mr. Livingston said.

"I'm sure Elizabeth will oblige," Pamela said.

"Only if you all remember that I haven't touched an instrument for a week. Perhaps," she said with a teasing smile directed first toward Pamela and then Mr. Livingston, "my fingers won't play as well in Montana."

"I'm sure we'll take that into consideration," Mr. Livingston responded, with a grave look on his face.

Taken aback by his serious response, Elizabeth's cheeks heated in embarrassment. Obviously, he hadn't been able to tell she was joking. Well, she couldn't wait to demonstrate her skill.

"In addition to hearing Miss Hamilton play, I'd love to hear that lovely composition of Nick's," Miss Stanton said with a flirtatious smile in Nick's direction. "Mark has mentioned to me how much he likes it."

"I'm afraid Mark's musical taste isn't very well developed," Nick said.

Pamela set down her fork. "Nick, don't be so modest," she chided. "It's a beautiful piece, and I'd love you to play for us."

"Oh, yes, please, Nick." Miss Stanton tugged on his arm.

He ignored her, glancing in Elizabeth's direction.

She smiled encouragement.

Seeming to make up his mind, he nodded at Pamela.

"Wonderful," Pamela said.

"Oh, Nick, I'm so delighted," Miss Stanton gushed, sending him another flirtatious smile.

The schoolteacher's fawning over Nick irritated Elizabeth. Did she have to be so obvious in her preference for the cowboy?

"Perhaps if everyone is finished eating," Pamela said, looking around the table, "we could proceed to the music room. I'll have Annie bring the tea tray there."

Mr. Livingston stood up, pulled Elizabeth's chair back, and assisted her to her feet. Across the table she saw Nick do the same for Miss Stanton. The proprietary way the teacher put her hand through Nick's arm bothered Elizabeth. *The woman's too forward.* She immediately chided herself for her uncharitable thoughts. Why should it matter to her how Miss Stanton behaved with Nick?

But it did, and for a moment confusion unsettled her.

CHAPTER ELEVEN

Pamela and John led the way to the music room. Everyone stood to follow.

Elizabeth caught up with them and hooked her arm through Pamela's. "Thanks for warning me," she said with mild sarcasm.

"About what?" Pamela asked with a puzzled look.

"Playing tonight."

Pamela tilted her head. "I'm sorry. I just took it for granted. In Boston you always played for company."

"I could have done with a little practice."

"I haven't practiced either. Besides, on your worst day you still play better than I do."

"Why don't you play first?"

"I'll end the evening playing some songs we can sing. That way it won't matter if I make mistakes. Why don't you start with that piece by Mr. Liszt?"

Inside the music room, Elizabeth went over to the cabinet where she'd placed her music, selecting several new pieces and a few of her old favorites. Although she was accustomed to playing in company, butterflies of nervousness fluttered in her stomach. Tonight she had a special audience.

She set the sheets on the stand, seated herself at the piano, arranged her skirt, and then started to play. After a few measures, she fell under the spell of the music, and her tension floated away. Her heightened awareness flowed through her fingertips, producing music more beautiful than she'd ever played. The feeling stayed with her even when she stopped to announce the next piece.

When she finished, she could feel exhilaration bringing a glow to her eyes, yet she almost couldn't bring herself to glance at Mr. Livingston. What might she see on his face? What did he think of her playing? But when she turned toward him, the warm light in his brown eyes and his appreciative smile sped up her pulse and caused her hands to shake. So like Richard after he'd heard her play...She balled her fingers in an effort to hide the telltale quivers.

Annie entered carrying the tea tray. While Pamela poured for everyone, Elizabeth received compliments on her playing. Impatient for Mr. Livingston's approach, she barely paid attention to her admirers.

She wasn't kept waiting for long.

Mr. Livingston carried two cups of tea and handed one to Elizabeth. "Miss Hamilton, I haven't heard such playing since I was last in Boston."

"Thank you, Mr. Livingston." She relaxed at his praise and took a sip of her tea.

"And even there I've heard few performances to rival yours. I don't think I've ever enjoyed one more, not even a professional one."

"You flatter me, Mr. Livingston," Elizabeth said, immensely pleased. "Although I must admit, I enjoyed playing for such an appreciative audience."

"It's not often we have a chance to hear such fine music. I hope I have more opportunities in the future."

She took a deep breath of satisfaction. She'd been treated so coldly over the last few months. She hadn't realized how much

Genia's attitude had wounded her. The warmth of Mr. Livingston's admiration soothed her bruised heart.

John called to everyone to resume their seats.

Mr. Livingston seated himself in the first row next to Elizabeth. Conscious of his presence by her side, she tried to distract herself by observing Nick.

He lifted his violin out of the case and, cradling the instrument between a broad shoulder and his neck, tuned the strings. Glancing around the room, he smiled at Pamela and then at Elizabeth. "This is called 'Lizzy's Theme.'"

Elizabeth stiffened. Surely he didn't mean her? He'd been looking at her, but he must mean little Lizzy. She relaxed back into her seat, and sipped her tea.

The first lilting notes reassured her. The music called to mind a tiny bird, flitting from tree to tree. She smiled in delight. Nick had musically caught the character of Lizzy. As Elizabeth watched Nick play, she forgot the man next to her.

For the first time, she studied Nick's face. Lowered eyelids hid his beautiful green eyes, making his long lashes stand out against his cheeks. He had the kind of fair skin that freckled and then tanned only after repeated days in the sun. His jaw rested on the violin. Without his hat, she noted his prominent cheekbones. The bump on his nose gave his face character, and she wondered how he'd broken it.

As she studied Nick, a new appreciation arose in her. He had a depth she'd never suspected. As if sensing her thoughts, Nick looked up. As he met her eyes, the violin's vibrations shivered through her body.

Playful and delicate, the music joyfully followed the little bird through her day, then became more serious, although no less lovely, and ended with a tune like a lullaby. In her mind,

Elizabeth saw the bird growing tired of playing and settling into her nest to rest for the night.

When he was finished, Elizabeth clapped with the others.

Nick bowed in acknowledgment. Again, he met her eyes. His shy smile elicited an answering one from her. His music had formed a bridge over the differences between them, building a harmony with him she'd never thought she'd experience.

Then Mr. Livingston leaned forward to say something to her. In looking into his dark eyes, so like Richard's, she lost her connection to Nick.

"That was well done," he commented. "The boy shows talent."

Pamela stood up and moved forward to the center of the room. "Thank you, Nick. That was beautiful." She smiled and glanced around. "Although perhaps I shouldn't say so, since it is a composition about my daughter. However, I still think it's wonderful."

"Nonsense, Mrs. Carter!" Dr. Cameron called out. "No false modesty allowed."

Laughter flowed around the room.

"Now if you'd play for us, we could have a song." The doctor allowed his voice to thicken into a burr. "How about something for a homesick Scot." He leaned back, and winked at his wife. "Let's sing 'Highland Mary.'"

Pamela passed out booklets, which she'd made by copying notes and words of songs onto sheets of paper. She'd then sewn the papers together along one side. In turning the pages, Elizabeth saw many songs she knew, but also some that weren't familiar.

Pamela started playing. Contrary to her friend's earlier disclaimer, the notes flowed smoothly.

One by one, each person picked a song. It had been a long time since Elizabeth had participated in a pleasurable evening of singing. Mr. Livingston's presence made the experience even more special. She listened to the pleasant tenor beside her, pleased at how well their voices blended.

Pamela chose the final rendition. "This last song expresses our feelings for our home and our friends," she said with a loving glance at her husband.

Elizabeth had never heard the song before. As she sang, she pondered the words.

We journey along quite contented in life
And try to live peaceful with all.
We keep ourselves free from all trouble and strife
And we're glad when our friends on us call.
Our home, it is happy and cheerful and bright.
We're content, and we ask nothing more.
And the reason we prosper, I'll tell to you now:
There's a horseshoe hung over the door.

Elizabeth remembered the horseshoe hanging over the door of the kitchen. She'd wondered why the Carters displayed such a rustic decoration, but hadn't asked. Now she understood. Maybe if she had a house out here, she too would display a horseshoe over the kitchen door. At the thought, "Lizzy's Theme" played sweetly in her mind.

With the singing ended, everyone stood up and prepared to leave. Mr. Livingston glanced down at Elizabeth. "If you're attending church with Mr. and Mrs. Carter on Sunday, I'd like to invite the three of you to my home for luncheon after the service."

Elizabeth tried not to show her elation. "Thank you, Mr. Livingston. I'd be delighted. I'm sure it'll be fine with the Carters. Although I believe the children attend church too."

"They do. Of course they're invited also. My housekeeper can look after them."

"Then I'll look forward to Sunday."

With a brief bow, he turned and left the room. Elizabeth's gaze followed him. A movement to her left caused her to glance at Nick. Had he overheard their conversation?

He nodded at her. "Good night, Miss Hamilton." He turned to leave.

"Nick, wait." He stopped, facing her.

She stepped forward, extending her hand to him. "I loved your composition."

He took her hand and bowed. "Thank you."

It amazed her how this callused hand touching hers, so different from the smooth feel of Mr. Livingston's, could play the most delicate music. "I could actually picture Lizzy as you played. You're very talented."

Mrs. Cobb bustled over.

Nick hastily dropped her hand.

"Oh, Miss Hamilton. Before we left I wanted to tell you how much we enjoyed your playing."

"Thank you, Mrs. Cobb."

Behind Mrs. Cobb's back, Nick gave Elizabeth a slight bow and left the room.

Elizabeth forced herself to politely say good night to Mrs. Cobb instead of making a face at her for spoiling the moment with Nick. They'd only started talking, and she still had so much to say to him about his music. Oh, well, perhaps they could continue their conversation another time. Surely in the next few days they'd find some private moments that no Mrs. Cobb could spoil.

❋ ❋ ❋

John left the house to see the departing guests to their carriages. As soon as they were alone, Elizabeth turned to Pamela. "What a wonderful evening," she said, with a sigh of pleasure.

Pamela hugged her friend. "Do tell."

"Do you remember the secret signal Richard gave me whenever we met in public?"

Pamela's eyebrows scrunched together in thought. "The thumb-press on your palm?"

"Yes." Elizabeth leaned forward and touched her forehead to her friend's. "Pamela, Mr. Livingston gave me that same signal!"

Pamela's eyes widened. "*No-o-o.*"

"I almost melted."

"I can imagine."

Elizabeth straightened up and grimaced. "Actually it brought tears to my eyes."

Pamela touched her cheek. "Oh, my dear."

"I didn't think you'd noticed. You sent me a mischievous look."

"I didn't notice. I'm so sorry."

"Don't be." Elizabeth smiled ruefully. "It helped me regain my composure. If you'd have looked sympathetic, I'd have dissolved into tears."

"I'm glad I could help," her friend said with an ironic lift of her eyebrow.

With a sigh of pleasure, Elizabeth raised her shoulders and flung out her hands, spreading her fingers wide. "Pamela, I'm so pleased about meeting Mr. Livingston."

"Then you liked him?"

"Yes, very much. He's quite the gentleman."

"And so handsome," Pamela teased.

"He's invited us to his house for dinner on Sunday after church. I thought it would be fine if I accepted for all of us."

Pamela tilted her head and tapped her finger on the side of her chin, pretended to think about it. "I don't know, Elizabeth, we have so many other invitations for that afternoon. I really think we'll have to check our social calendar and reschedule for a few weeks from now."

"Silly," Elizabeth said, hugging her friend. "I'm so happy. Thank you, thank you, for inviting me here. Now I'm off to bed."

"To dream of Mr. Livingston, no doubt," Pamela called to her.

Elizabeth didn't dignify that remark with a reply, but there was a bounce to her step when she left the room. Too bad she had almost a whole week to wait. In spite of her prior reservations about Reverend Norton's sermons, Elizabeth eagerly anticipated Sunday morning. She didn't care if the minister was boring. She might not even listen to the sermon!

* * *

Nick and John walked the Camerons to their buggy. Although the light of the full moon illuminated their surroundings, John held the lantern so the Camerons, unfamiliar with the ground, would be able to see their way.

"I loved your composition, Nick." Mrs. Cameron reached over and gave his arm a squeeze. "I could listen to your playing for hours."

"I agree, Nick," Dr. Cameron added. "You're really quite talented. Have you ever thought of seriously pursuing a musical career?"

"When he was younger we tried to get him to go back east to music school, but he wouldn't," John said.

"As much as I love music, I love horses more."

"At times you can be stubborn as a mule."

"I take after my godfather." Nick elbowed John in the arm, causing the lantern to sway, sending shadows dancing in their path.

They all chuckled.

"It's not too late, lad." Dr. Cameron continued in a more serious vein. "Those music schools in the East and in Europe accept adults."

"I don't regret my decision."

"Don't try too hard to convince him, Doc," John said. "I don't know what we'd do without him. And my children would miss him. I'd have to tell them it was your fault he left."

"Oh, no, you don't." Dr. Cameron's Scottish accent broadened. "We can't be upsettin' the bonnie lad and lassies. Sorry, my laddie, you'll just have to be a-stayin' home and not a-traipsin' off to foreign parts."

They laughed again. John held the lantern higher so the couple could see to climb into their buggy.

Mrs. Cameron settled her skirts. "Thank you so much for a lovely evening."

"It was nice to enjoy a party without being called away on an emergency," her husband added, untying the horses. He climbed into the seat, picked up the reins, and flicked his hands.

As the horses started forward, Mrs. Cameron leaned out the side, her curls disheveled, and waved. "Good night."

"Night." The two men waved good-bye.

John turned to Nick. "That's the last of them. Did you enjoy yourself?"

Before Nick could answer, John continued, "The little schoolmarm seems mighty taken with you."

Grateful the darkness hid any telltale sign of his embarrassment, Nick remained silent.

"I'll bet Pamela's thrilled. She loves playing matchmaker."

Remembering some of Pamela's previous attempts on his behalf, Nick winced. Just what he needed: Miz Carter takin' up the idea of matchin' him with Miss Stanton.

"Livingston seemed impressed with Elizabeth," John continued.

So John had noticed too. Regret choked Nick's throat. He had to force his next words out. "Miss Hamilton looked happy to meet him."

"I'm glad he changed his mind about the loan to Red Charlie."

"He didn't." Nick growled. "You offered your pledge. That's what got Red Charlie the loan."

"He should've taken you up on your offer of the horses."

"He couldn't believe a cowboy'd actually own something." The words came out with more heat than Nick intended.

"Remember, Livingston's only been here since '91. He just doesn't know you or Red Charlie."

"He's the banker. It's his business to know."

"Give him a little more time, Nick. He'll learn. Especially if he comes a-courtin' Elizabeth."

"Maybe." Nick knew it was probably futile to hope the man wouldn't come around. How could Livingston resist Elizabeth? *I certainly can't.*

"My wife told me Livingston is the living image of the fiancé Elizabeth almost married. Apparently he died only months before the wedding, and Elizabeth hasn't been interested in any man since."

Nick's stomach knotted. Bad enough competing with Livingston the man—but Livingston as the ghost of a beloved fiancé…

"Having two matches to work on will make my wife mighty happy."

After seeing the attraction between Elizabeth and Caleb Livingston, Nick hadn't thought he could feel any worse. But now he knew the truth of the saying about how your heart could drop, because his heart had just landed somewhere in the vicinity of his boots. If he wasn't careful he'd step on it.

Nick didn't want to cut John off, but he was anxious to end the conversation and be alone with his thoughts. "It was a nice party."

"It was." John paused as if to say more, then stopped himself. "Good night, Nick. I'll see you in the morning."

"Night, John."

Nick strolled toward the bunkhouse. But when he knew he was out of John's sight, he changed direction away from the ranch buildings. He headed toward his favorite thinking spot—a large boulder in the middle of one of the pastures.

The moon's light made the evening bright enough for him to avoid any obstacles. Calm and chill, the night held only the sounds of nickering horses and the distant hoot of an owl. He climbed over the fence and made clicking noises with his tongue to reassure the nearby horses, but didn't stop until he touched the rough surface of the rock.

Over six feet tall, the rock had a depression about halfway up that made a semi-comfortable chair. In his "chair" he could slightly recline and look at the sky, while his legs dangled over the side. Ever since he'd come to live at the ranch, he'd climbed up on the rock whenever he had feelings or problems he needed to think through.

He'd spent a lot of time perched on this rock when he'd first come here to live. He'd been fourteen that year, grieving the death of his parents and little sister Marcy from a wagon accident, struggling to live his new life when most of his heart had died.

While John, his godfather, had been kind, it had taken Nick a long time to adjust. Working with the horses—the silent communication between them and trust they'd placed in him—had helped. But the arrival of Miz Carter, and later, the children, had made all the difference. It was almost like having family again, and for the most part, he'd been content.

But now, with the appearance of one Boston lady, that contentment had vanished. The Carter family was no longer enough. Tonight he realized he wanted a family of his own. But that would mean opening up the withered places of his heart to Elizabeth.

He'd risk being hurt all over again, especially if she became Livingston's wife. Could one's heart perish twice? Could he bear it a second time? He massaged his chest, feeling the ache as the warmth of his love for Elizabeth flowed into places long numb—like blood rushing into fingers and toes after they'd been frozen.

In the distance, only a few lights showed through the windows of the ranch house. The candles in Elizabeth's room cast a soft glow, beckoning his thoughts to drift through the window to her. He could almost see her sitting in one of those fancy robes women wore over their nightgowns, seated at her vanity table. She'd pull out each hairpin until she could shake her hair free. Shining golden in the candlelight, her mane would cascade past her waist, a glorious sight to be seen only by a husband…

In his vision, she picked up a silver-backed brush and stroked the long fall of hair. He imagined himself taking the brush from her hand. As their eyes met in the mirror, he'd sensuously stroke every tress. He could see himself picking up a lavender-scented lock, kissing it, and then kissing her shoulder, her forehead, her lips.

The light in the window vanished. "Good night, Elizabeth," he said softly. "Sleep well."

He tilted his head back until it rested on the rock and studied the sky above him. He seldom went to his rock at night. Usually he did his thinking while looking at an azure sky, perhaps with puffy white clouds. Sometimes just the vastness of that overarching blueness would put his thoughts in perspective. Tonight he had velvety blackness broken by the glowing light of the moon and the pinprick white of the stars.

The big dipper gleamed down at him, the first constellation he'd learned. He'd been a youngster when his pa had traced the lines in the sky for him. Later, Pa had taught him the others. And he, in turn, had taught Mark and Sara. For a minute the memories distracted him from his feelings. The night, although cold, shimmered with beauty. He wished he could share the experience with Elizabeth.

He imagined her on the rock beside him, his arm slipping around her while they looked at the stars together. Did she know the constellations? If not, he'd teach her. And after the lesson, he'd kiss her and hold her sweet body close. New lessons. Lessons in love. Together they'd share in the learning.

He sighed. *Stick to reality, cowboy.*

Elizabeth would probably never choose a ranch hand. But at least he knew she'd be around. And he thought he'd have time. Time to quietly woo her…to show his love through his deeds. It was too hard to get words around the crippling shyness he felt. Or, like what happened on their horseback ride, they seemed to be the wrong words.

The chill night air pricked at his skin. Livingston had words, plenty of them. And an attitude to match. How dare that highfalutin easterner deny Red Charlie a loan. Remembering the dinner conversation angered him all over again, and the heat of his feelings protected him from the cold.

It'd taken everything he had not to make a spectacle of himself by hauling off and punching the man. Wouldn't that have wrecked Miz Carter's fancy party? Probably wouldn't have been too good for his chances with Elizabeth either. Not that he had much of a chance with her anyway. He tried to swallow down his anger but couldn't. The thought of her as the wife of that dull stick Livingston stuck in his craw.

His mind drifted to Harriet Stanton. She'd embarrassed him, suggesting he was better with horses than Red Charlie. Did she have to make her feelings so obvious? He'd never asked for them and certainly didn't return them. And it didn't have anything to do with Elizabeth; he just wasn't attracted to Miss Stanton.

He'd been waiting for someone to come along who'd make him feel the way Elizabeth did. He laced his fingers behind his head, cushioning it from the rock, and grinned at the stars. A woman worth waiting for. *Worth fighting for.*

He'd handle the problem of Miss Stanton by avoiding her. He could easily skip church for the next several weeks with the excuse of the mares in foal needing him. Maybe Miss Stanton would turn her interests to someone else.

He continued gazing at the stars and tried to formulate a prayer, but he couldn't put his desires into words. Instead a melody came to him, drawn from the beauty of the stars, his longing for Elizabeth, and his connection with God. He spun the notes out in his mind until he'd composed the entire piece and knew he wouldn't forget the music in the morning.

Maybe he'd play it for Elizabeth and let the music speak to her in ways he couldn't. Somehow, he knew she'd love his composition. They'd shared that minute, right after he'd finished "Lizzy's Theme," when they experienced a musical bond—until Livingston broke it between them.

The boy shows talent. The overheard words still rankled. Boy! At twenty-four! He'd like to see that banker do a man's work around a ranch. He'd have blisters on those smooth hands inside of two hours. Not to mention how he'd feel after a long day in the saddle.

Elizabeth wouldn't be happy with Livingston. He knew it. True, the man had money, a large house, and a purebred pedigree—all the things she probably wanted in a man. But it wouldn't be enough.

He had instincts about her in the same way he knew horses—what they needed, how to touch them. In the last week, there'd been times when she'd thawed and shown her feelings. He'd bet anything a special woman lurked beneath her proper Boston exterior. With Livingston, that woman would never emerge.

He straightened and ground a fist into his palm. He couldn't step back and let Livingston waltz away with her. It wouldn't be right. He'd have to change. Force himself past his shyness. Force himself to open up.

Nick wasn't sure how he'd do it. Aside from what he'd learned from Miz Carter, he'd not had any training in proper society manners. Now, he'd seen for himself how different things were in the East. But something in Elizabeth had touched him, something that went beyond social barriers, and he knew she'd sensed it too. He might not have much wealth to offer, but there were other things he could do to make her happy, and he'd love her with all his heart.

She might still choose Livingston, but I'll put up a damn good fight for her first.

CHAPTER TWELVE

Sunday morning, Elizabeth dressed with care in royal-blue silk with a black lace overdress. Black velvet trimmed the sleeves, waist, and hem. A black velvet bow circled the high neck. Her pearl brooch, pinned to the bow, added the final elegant touch. She smiled at herself in the mirror, imagining Mr. Livingston's reaction, how his brown eyes would light up at the sight of her… just like Richard's…

No, not today. I won't think of Richard.

Swinging her hat by its matching blue ribbons, with her skirt held higher than considered proper, Elizabeth skipped down the stairs. She peeked into the empty parlor, then continued down the hall, searching for Pamela.

The tantalizing smell of frying bacon and the sound of voices lured her to the kitchen. Inside, Annie deftly turned strips of bacon, sizzling in a huge cast-iron pan.

Pamela, holding a white porcelain pitcher of milk, spoke with Nick. "So you don't mind if we leave the children with Dawn?" Her tone sounded uncertain. "I'm sure they'll be out pestering you and the foal."

"I don't mind. There's another foal on the way." He waved his hat in the direction of the barn. "The children will probably want to watch." He caught sight of Elizabeth, and his eyes widened in obvious approval. "Morning, Miss Hamilton."

"Good morning."

"You look mighty nice. The reverend will have a hard time keeping his mind on his preachin'."

"Thank you." Whatever had gotten into Nick this morning? Elizabeth hoped Pamela wouldn't notice the pink creeping into her cheeks. For distraction, she pounced on what she'd just overheard. "You can't mean the children will watch the foal being born?"

Nick lifted an eyebrow at Pamela, deflecting the question to her.

"On a ranch you can't keep children ignorant of the birthing process," Pamela said, a placating note in her voice. "The children have already seen all kinds of animals being born."

Elizabeth shook off her prudish reaction. Of course birth would be a familiar part of their lives. "I'm sorry," she apologized to both of them. "I didn't think before I spoke." She looked at Nick. "You won't be attending church with us?"

"Not today. I make it a rule to be around when a mare's foaling. She might need my help."

Elizabeth abruptly changed her mind. "I know this might sound a little unusual based on what I just said, but sometime I'd love to watch the birth of a foal. It would be an interesting experience." She shot a mischievous glance at Pamela. "Imagine what Genia would say if she knew."

Pamela smiled and raised one shoulder.

"You'll probably miss this one," Nick said. "But there'll be plenty more. They're often born when no one's around. Although if I think there are going to be difficulties, I'll bed down in a nearby stall."

He laughed at the uncertain look that must have shown on her face. "It's all right, Miss Hamilton. I promise not to wake you in the middle of the night. I'm sure there'll be another daytime arrival."

Annie rang the triangle for breakfast, and Elizabeth turned away to hide her second blush of the morning. She couldn't imagine why the thought of Nick awakening her caused her to have such a reaction. She walked from the room with outward composure, resisting the need to put her hands up to cover her warm cheeks like a silly schoolgirl. She hadn't blushed so much in years.

What's the matter with me?

* * *

The morning sun shone with enough warmth for John to drive the buggy instead of the closed carriage. The three of them together on the seat made a snug, but not uncomfortable, fit. Preoccupied with thoughts of Caleb Livingston, Elizabeth absentmindedly answered John and Pamela's comments about the surrounding countryside.

"Elizabeth," Pamela chided her, "I think you're still half asleep. Or is your mind occupied with other things—a handsome banker, perhaps?"

Elizabeth resisted the impulse to give Pamela an unladylike elbow to the ribs. She didn't want to be teased about Caleb Livingston in front of John. John loved to joke with his family and friends. Her feelings for Mr. Livingston felt almost sacred, not in the least bit humorous, and she protectively guarded them.

"Forgive me for being inattentive. I didn't sleep well, and I'm still tired."

As Elizabeth knew she would, Pamela changed from teasing to solicitous. "I hope nothing's wrong."

A little guilty for being evasive, Elizabeth reminded herself that she *had* stayed awake late into the night. She'd been thinking about certain Montana men…And she would have felt tired this morning, if she didn't have anticipation, like champagne bubbles, coursing through her body. However, she'd keep such thoughts to herself!

"No, nothing's wrong," she said. "I was just musing about my new life. We've been so busy since I arrived, I simply haven't had much thinking time."

The conversation lapsed, and they drove the rest of the way in a companionable silence.

A few scattered frame houses, complete with porch and rocking chairs, marked the outskirts of Sweetwater Springs. Elizabeth barely remembered the town from her exhausted arrival, and she looked around with interest. Most of the wooden false-fronted buildings also had porches. The only brick buildings in sight were the bank and Cobb's mercantile store. She noticed several buildings with "Saloon" written on the outside window.

Seeing her glance at them, Pamela remarked, "It's a shame that we have three saloons in Sweetwater Springs." She glanced playfully at her husband. "At least John doesn't spend much time in them."

"Much time!" John said with mock indignation. "How about rare time. You keep me too busy." He leaned forward and winked at Elizabeth. "That's the problem around here: not enough men have wives to keep them on the straight and narrow."

Pamela elbowed him in the ribs, and they all laughed.

Soon they arrived at the white frame church. Unadorned except for a bell tower with a cross on the top, the windows held plain, instead of stained, glass. Although very different from the imposing edifice where Elizabeth worshiped in Boston, it showed a simple charm that appealed to her.

Pamela had told her the banker had a large brick house, but Elizabeth didn't see one anywhere nearby, and she didn't want to ask. She'd see Caleb's house soon enough.

John reined in the horses and applied the brake. Elizabeth scanned the small crowd outside the church, but didn't see Caleb Livingston. Her champagne feelings flattened with disappointment. For the last few days, she'd been imagining how happy she'd feel as he clasped her hand with that special signal and guided her down from the buggy.

Perhaps he's already inside.

She greeted her new acquaintances, suppressing her impatience. She acknowledged an introduction to an older couple, trying to hide her haste to get into the church.

Finally Pamela and John, with Elizabeth following, strolled inside. She discreetly glanced around, under the guise of examining the church, but didn't see the banker.

"That's where we usually sit," Pamela whispered, nodding to a pew near the front.

Elizabeth followed her up the aisle, looking around with interest. A simply carved cross affixed to the wall over the white linen–draped altar was the only religious symbol in the room. Red tulips set in a green glass vase made a bright splash of color. A plain wooden pulpit stood to the right of the altar, and to the left, an organ, positioned to face the congregation.

Elizabeth smiled at the Cobbs, seated across from the Carters. The stuffed finch decorating the crown of Mrs. Cobb's straw hat bobbed forward when she nodded in return. Again, she seemed to scrutinize Elizabeth's apparel.

Elizabeth seated herself next to Pamela near the center aisle, leaving just enough room in case a certain eligible bachelor decided to join her.

Out of the corner of her eye, she noticed Mr. Livingston arrive and take a seat behind the Cobbs.

Disappointment stabbed her at his choice. She turned to smile at him.

He gave her a slight bow and smiled.

She nodded back and then quickly looked straight ahead, pretending to study the church. She didn't want to make her interest too obvious.

I wish he'd have chosen a different seat. Then I'd be able to study him during the service. So much for the entertainment I'd expected during the sermon.

The Nortons entered the church together. Mrs. Norton, wearing the same black dress she'd worn to the party, seated herself at the organ, while Mr. Norton strode to the pulpit. "'Amazing Grace' will be our first hymn," the minister announced.

Elizabeth loved to use her well-trained voice to "make a joyful noise." Singing hymns made her feel connected to God, and being in church gave Elizabeth an opportunity to sing strongly instead of modulating herself as she did in social situations. Her unladylike loudness usually blended into the many other voices raised in song.

Today, with a smaller congregation, her voice sounded more obvious. She thought about modifying the volume, but decided to hold her course. Singing in this way was special to her, and she didn't care how anyone might judge her.

In spite of her reservations, Elizabeth enjoyed the service. To her surprise she found Mr. Norton's sermon contained no hint of fire and brimstone. He tied biblical examples to current-day situations, making the old precepts seem relevant. Elizabeth found the sermon simple yet wise, and her estimation of Mr. Norton rose considerably.

At the conclusion of the sermon, with a feeling of virtue, she noted that, for the most part, she'd put Mr. Livingston to the back of her mind. She followed the Carters down the aisle and out of the building, and a sense of peace wrapped around her like a shawl.

Once outside, the Carters and Elizabeth kept busy greeting people. Several minutes passed before Mr. Livingston approached them.

"A most interesting sermon," he said to all of them. Then, turning to Elizabeth, he took her hand. "I know that church services in Montana are different than in Boston. I hope you don't judge us negatively." His finger brushed across her palm, releasing those champagne bubbles inside her.

"On the contrary, Mr. Livingston." Elizabeth reluctantly eased her hand from his and strove for a tone of normalcy. "The buildings may differ, and the congregation is smaller, but the hymns are the same, and the Lord is still present. I agree that the sermon was interesting. I enjoyed it very much." She smiled at him with just a hint of flirtatiousness. "I will look forward to Sundays."

He returned the smile. "I usually walk to church when the weather's pleasant. Today, however, I drove. Would you like to accompany me to the house? It's only a short distance."

Elizabeth glanced at Pamela and John to check if the invitation was all right with them. At Pamela's nod of acquiescence, Elizabeth smiled at Mr. Livingston. "I'd love to."

He extended his elbow to escort her to the waiting vehicle. She tucked her hand into the crook of his arm. How long since Richard had offered this familiar gesture, sending a thrill through her? For so many years, a man's arm had just been a guiding prop to lean on. Except at that horrible dinner party in Boston. Nick's arm had offered her support then. She shoved that memory out of her mind.

She caught a reproving look from Mrs. Cobb and smiled graciously at her in return. *Grumpy woman. Does she disapprove of everyone?*

At the sight of Caleb's buggy, Elizabeth lifted her chin in approval. The shiny black equipage, drawn by two matching brown horses, appeared newer than the Carters'.

Mr. Livingston caught Elizabeth's admiring glance. "I bought the horses from John Carter," he told her with a proud smile. "Carter's horses are quite admired in these parts." He helped her into the vehicle, then walked around to the other side and climbed in beside her.

"They're beautiful." She gave him a sideways glance. "I'm learning more about horses than I ever dreamed I would."

"Horses are important in the West."

The smile he directed at her caused a lump to rise in her throat. She couldn't get over how like Richard he appeared—and how he moved her. Richard's smile had been equally charming. Although when her fiancé had flashed her his gamin grin, his eyes full of mischief, she knew a prank or joke was sure to follow. Richard had always been so full of life. She suppressed a sigh. Would he have matured into a more serious man like Mr. Livingston?

Would I have wanted him to?

She swallowed to clear the constriction in her throat. "I never paid attention to our horses at home unless I was riding. And that wasn't very often."

"There aren't many opportunities to ride in Boston. I usually rode on one of the estates of my Cabot cousins," he said.

"A foal was just born a few days ago at the ranch. I quite fell in love with it." She almost told him about the hug and kiss she'd given the foal, but changed her mind. The idea sounded too strange. And after all, this man wasn't really her Richard, in whom she had always confided all her thoughts.

Caleb drew the buggy to a stop before an imposing three-story brick mansion. A brick and iron fence surrounded a large front yard blanketed by thick grass. Against each side of the steps to the house, yellow daffodils bloomed in white planter boxes.

"Your home is beautiful." The perfect residence for a successful banker.

"I'm glad you like it. I wanted something that reminded me of the East."

"Then you didn't grow up here?"

"We lived in several parts of Montana. However, I also spent a great deal of time with my grandparents in Boston. I'm a relative newcomer to Sweetwater Springs."

A bushy-bearded man wearing faded blue overalls appeared from the stable positioned toward the back of the house. Mr. Livingston climbed down from the buggy and handed the reins to him.

John and Pamela stood waiting by the fence. Under their watchful eyes, Mr. Livingston helped Elizabeth from the vehicle, tucking her hand in the crook of his arm.

He led them up the brick path and several steps to a large wooden door surrounded with Tiffany stained-glass windows. A thin woman, her gray hair pulled into a tight knob on top of her head, opened the door.

"Ah, Mrs. Graves, I see you returned before us," he said, ushering everyone into the house.

"I didn't linger after church," the woman said, smoothing the immaculate white apron she wore over a gray dress without a bustle. "I had too much to do."

"Very good." He turned to Elizabeth. "Miss Hamilton, this is my housekeeper, Mrs. Graves."

The housekeeper gave Elizabeth an unsmiling nod, the sagging flesh under her chin folding into accordion pleats. Without a change of her expressionless face, she conveyed disapproval of Elizabeth.

"You already know the Carters."

Another solemn nod.

"Perhaps you can escort the ladies upstairs to freshen up."

Elizabeth discretely glanced around the entrance hall with a tiled black-and-white floor like in her home in Boston, a sweeping carved stairway, and lacy plasterwork ceiling. An immediate sense of familiarity relaxed her shoulders. *This is the kind of house I'd expect back east, not in Montana. I could be very happy as its mistress.*

As the two women followed somber Mrs. Graves up the stairs, Elizabeth noted the mahogany furniture and rose-patterned wallpaper. The house was very different from Pamela's more casual home, but similar to many Elizabeth had known in Boston. Everything was meticulously neat. Elizabeth frowned. Caleb's home somehow lacked a lived-in feeling.

"This house needs the touch of a loving woman," Pamela whispered to her.

Elizabeth nodded, but didn't dare reply in case Mrs. Graves overheard. No use making an enemy of Caleb's housekeeper. Although it might be too late. Already the woman seemed to dislike her.

❋ ❋ ❋

Mrs. Graves led them back down the stairway and stopped at an open carved oak door. "Mr. Livingston and Mr. Carter will be in there." She waved a work-worn hand at the doorway. "I must see to the meal."

"Thank you," Pamela murmured to Mrs. Graves's stiff retreating back.

That woman would be hard to live with, Elizabeth thought in apprehension, anticipating future problems. *I wonder how attached Mr. Livingston is to her.*

Elizabeth followed Pamela into the drawing room. Her thoughts about the housekeeper vanished. She looked around, inhaling and releasing a contented breath.

From the pair of tufted chenille ottomans in the corners and the blue velvet settee in front of the fireplace, to the Chinese oxblood vases on the mahogany display shelves over the mantel, everything pleased her. She could picture herself entertaining guests in this room.

Mr. Livingston approached the two women. "Mrs. Carter, Miss Hamilton, I trust Mrs. Graves made you comfortable?"

Both women nodded.

Elizabeth rushed into speech. "Mr. Livingston, I must tell you how comfortable I feel in your home. This room especially.

I love blue and have decorated my parlor in Boston in similar shades to what you've done here."

"I'm glad, Miss Hamilton." He looked around. "The colors suit me." *And you suit me,* his brown eyes seemed to tell her.

Elizabeth's knees quivered, and she had to look away.

Pamela glanced with amusement at her husband. "I'm amazed you even care about the decor, Mr. Livingston. I could change the colors in our parlor, and John wouldn't even notice."

They all laughed.

John's face wrinkled in a grin. "Maybe so." He held up an admonishing finger. "However, I would notice if you changed something in my study."

Pamela continued her teasing. "Especially if I removed that horrid bear's head." She turned to Mr. Livingston. "John has the head of a bear, teeth and all, hanging on the wall in his study." She gave a theatrical shudder. "I don't know how he can stand it."

Elizabeth nodded in agreement. "I haven't seen it yet, but it sounds horrible."

Mr. Livingston exchanged commiserating glances with John. "Trophies are important to a man." He turned to the women. "But, I can assure you, there are no animal heads hanging anywhere in this house."

The warm glow inside Elizabeth intensified. She would have been disappointed to find his home furnished in a way that lacked good taste, but to feel so compatible...She waved to a draped piano in the corner. "May I look at your instrument?"

"By all means, Miss Hamilton." He crossed the room and lifted the long fringe of a beige scarf, revealing the black piano underneath. "Perhaps another time you would honor me with playing."

"I'd be delighted." Before she could do more than glimpse the piano, Mrs. Graves entered the room.

"Luncheon is served, Mr. Livingston."

"Splendid."

Without another word the woman left the room, and the four of them followed.

Elizabeth and Pamela exchanged a meaningful glance. In Boston, she'd never keep the dour woman as her housekeeper. However, looking around the immaculate room, she had to remind herself that good servants were scarce in Montana. As long as the woman did a good job…

When they entered the dining room, Elizabeth's pleasure in the decor increased. The blue flowered French wallpaper lined a room that could accommodate a dinner party of twenty. The table, loaded with silver, and blue-and-white china in a pattern Elizabeth didn't recognize, looked every bit as formal as any she could have set in Boston.

Mr. Livingston drew out the chair to his right for Elizabeth. "If you don't mind, I'd like us to all sit at one end of the table." He waved Pamela and John to sit across from Elizabeth. "That way we won't have to shout to be heard." As if asking for Elizabeth's approval, he smiled and lifted an eyebrow.

"That seems very sensible," she agreed.

She scanned the room. A painting of a young couple, the woman wearing a green-belled dress of an earlier era, caught her attention.

Mr. Livingston noticed her interest. "My Cabot grandparents."

"Are they the ones you'd stay with when you were younger?"

"Yes." He sent a warm glance in the direction of the portrait. "I loved my time with them. Their home was always filled with my cousins. We got into plenty of mischief."

"That sounds familiar." Pamela's smile to Elizabeth acknowledged their shared memories.

Mr. Livingston, his brows raised in inquiry, invited further explanation.

"Elizabeth has an older brother, and I have three. They were the best of friends and enjoyed playing tricks on their poor little sisters," Pamela said.

Elizabeth rolled her eyes in agreement. "I hope you were kinder to your female cousins than our brothers were to us, although knowing boys..."

His brown eyes filled with laughter, and he actually grinned at her. "I can't say that we were."

At the sight of his grin, so like Richard's, Elizabeth caught her breath and had to restrain herself from putting a hand to her mouth. Across the table she saw from Pamela's rounded eyes that her friend had seen the same resemblance.

A wave of sadness mixed with excitement washed over her. Like in a fairy tale, she'd received a second chance at happiness, and she didn't know whether to laugh or cry.

Mrs. Graves's entrance with a large platter interrupted the moment. As if her presence cast a pall over them, the conversation ceased while she moved in and out of the room with the serving dishes. Elizabeth had to give her credit. Only one woman, serving a formal meal, yet Mrs. Graves did it with ordered efficiency.

While the men talked of ranch matters, Elizabeth concentrated on assessing Mrs. Graves's cooking ability. Although not as elaborate as a Sunday afternoon meal for company in Boston, it was similar to the food served at Pamela's—a fish course of fresh trout, a tender filet mignon, accompanied by several types of vegetables and light-as-air rolls. The sweet new carrots must be the first of the season, Elizabeth thought, accepting a second helping.

Caleb turned his attention to Elizabeth. "Miss Hamilton, are you by any chance related to the family who owns the Hamilton shipping business?"

"Yes. My great-grandfather started the company. My brother runs it now."

"I believe I've met your brother on a number of occasions… three or four years ago, however."

She could almost see his estimation of her rise.

They spent the next few minutes comparing acquaintances. They had several in common.

"I wonder why we haven't met before," Elizabeth mused.

"It does seem strange. However, I haven't been back east in two years. It's not the same since my grandparents passed away."

"I know what you mean. I've lost too many beloved family members." Their glances locked in mutual sympathy.

Mr. Livingston cleared his throat. "The worst was losing my cousin, Richard. Second cousin, actually. We were very close as boys, although we didn't see each other much when we grew older. I'm in the West. He was in the East. Didn't even write. I regret that now…Richard died from influenza in his early twenties." He briefly looked away.

Elizabeth's breath caught, and dizziness rushed to her head. *Richard? My Richard!* She couldn't even muster the strength to ask.

With a concerned glance at Elizabeth, Pamela came to her rescue. "Do you by any chance mean Richard Harrison?"

Mr. Livingston looked surprised. "Why, yes."

Briefly Elizabeth closed her eyes, as if to hold back the wave of old pain. Then she found her voice. "Richard and I were engaged to be married. He…" The words jammed, and she had to take a deep breath before she could go on. "He died in my arms."

She saw a familiar sorrow linger in his eyes—one she'd seen many times in her own mirror. He too had suffered over the loss of Richard.

The attraction Elizabeth felt for Caleb Livingston strengthened into a bond.

Richard, my love. Have you sent this man to me? A man you loved and trusted. Is he supposed to take your place? Be my husband?

Mr. Livingston interrupted her internal conversation. "Richard wrote of you. I remember his happiness. I remember how much I envied him. I'm so sorry you lost him—we lost him." Mr. Livingston moved his hand as if to place it over hers.

Mrs. Graves entered carrying a cloth-shrouded pie, and placed it on the table between them, dispelling the heavy emotion in the air.

The woman has the worst timing. Elizabeth so needed the sympathetic touch of Caleb Livingston's hand. Couldn't Mrs. Graves have delayed her appearance by a few minutes?

"Dried apple pie," Mrs. Graves announced. She unbent enough to give her employer a faint smile. "Your favorite."

"Mrs. Graves makes the best pies." He beamed at his housekeeper.

At the taste of her first bite, Elizabeth had to agree with him. Despite her sour personality, the woman certainly could bake.

The last few minutes of the meal flew by. Elizabeth savored every moment in Caleb's presence, impressing each nuance into her memory. She probably wouldn't see him again until church next Sunday. How did a man go about courting a woman in the West? The distance to the Carter ranch would preclude the normal social calls gentlemen made to show interest and get to know a lady. She'd have to ask Pamela.

"Mr. Livingston." Pamela gave Elizabeth a barely discernible wink. "Perhaps you'd like to join us after church next Sunday?"

"I'd like that very much."

His gaze connected with Elizabeth's. The smile of pleasure in his brown eyes sent warm waves of happiness through her.

"Miss Hamilton, would you care to drive with me after church?"

Yes. Yes. Yes. So this was how it was done in the West. Not so different from Boston after all.

Somehow Elizabeth managed to tone down her joy enough to give him a polite social smile. "I'd be delighted, Mr. Livingston."

CHAPTER THIRTEEN

Elizabeth picked up the letter resting on the dining room table, recognized Genia's handwriting, and wrinkled her nose. Somewhat to her surprise, her sister-in-law had proven to be a regular correspondent, writing several times a week.

Unfortunately, her news didn't bring Elizabeth much pleasure. All social gossip, something Elizabeth hadn't been interested in even when she lived in Boston. She preferred the letters from her friend Sylvia. Sylvia wrote about her children, other friends they had in common, and Elizabeth's special charities. They were much more meaningful, and she looked forward to receiving them.

She shrugged her shoulders, sat down, and started to read. At the sight of the first sentence she gasped and dropped Genia's letter on the table.

I know you will be overjoyed, my dear sister, to learn we are expecting a welcome addition to the family just in time for Christmas.

The sadness and regret that swept over Elizabeth didn't feel in the least joyful. Shame followed when she realized she wasn't rejoicing over her brother's good fortune. Clutching her locket, Elizabeth tried to separate her confused feelings.

During her engagement to Richard, in a favorite fantasy she'd imagined their children. She'd wanted four, two boys and two girls. In her mind's eye, they all had Richard's laughing brown eyes, although the girls had her long golden curls. She'd even pictured her children and Laurence's playing together. She'd loved the anticipation of being a beloved mother and aunt and could hardly wait to experience the reality.

Elizabeth released a pent-up sigh. When Richard died, she had stopped seeing herself as a wife and mother. The idea of children who would never exist had been far too painful. Even now the feeling stabbed through her heart, and she pressed the hand holding the locket against her breast as if to stop the ache.

In the following years, when Laurence hadn't looked like he'd ever marry, she'd given up on the idea of nieces and nephews, resigning herself to a life without children. Now she didn't know what to feel about a baby of Genia's. What kind of mother would her sister-in-law make? Would the child be horribly spoiled?

A picture of the spiteful women at the last dinner party in Boston flashed through her mind. At least Elizabeth wouldn't be there to overhear any more comments about her being a maiden aunt. But at the same time, she'd miss the opportunity to know and love her niece or nephew. She smoothed her thumb over the cover of her locket, torn between regret and relief.

The old daydream of her firstborn drifted across her thoughts. A boy with mischievous eyes and a lock of brown hair that, like his father's, constantly fell across his forehead. A miniature version of Richard...

With a shock of awareness, Elizabeth straightened, the sadness banished by a feeling of excitement. A son of Caleb's would look the same way as a child of Richard's—although perhaps without the errant strand of hair...

A smile played about her mouth. Her old dream could still come true. Still holding her locket, she stood, walked into the parlor, sank into a comfortable chair, and lost herself in her rosy vision of the future.

For the first time in ten years, Elizabeth allowed herself to dream of her own children. She wiggled with childish happiness. It shouldn't be too long before Caleb proposed, maybe only a few weeks. There was no reason to wait to get married. Hopefully he wouldn't want a large Boston wedding. She certainly didn't.

Perhaps by this time next year, she'd have a baby of her own!

❋ ❋ ❋

Several days later, on her way to the barn to track down the children, Elizabeth paused by the wood-and-wire chicken pen. She wrinkled her nose at the distinct ammonia smell of the coop and almost moved on. But one petite rusty brown hen scratching in the dirt by itself caught her eye. The bird bobbed its head, moving away from the flock in a search for bugs and seeds.

A shuffling sound made Elizabeth turn to see Annie waddling toward her, wiping her hands on her blue calico apron. The sun glinted off the cook's shiny black hair. She shuffled to a stop next to Elizabeth. "Missy Erizabeth, what you doing?"

Elizabeth pointed to the little hen. "Is that Sara's Mrs. Hooch?"

Annie shook her head, squinting to examine the flock. "Mrs. Hooch, she be a skinny biddy. Too tough."

"Oh."

Annie waved toward the little hen. "You rike?"

Puzzled, Elizabeth tried to make sense out of Annie's words. "I like what?"

"You rike chicken. You want?"

Still not sure of the cook's meaning, Elizabeth nodded. "She seems like a sweet little bird."

"She be sweet. Not rike Mrs. Hooch. I get for you."

"Wait, that's not necessary." Elizabeth raised a hand to stop her.

Annie ignored her, flinging open the gate, and stepping inside.

The chickens scattered, squawking and flapping their wings.

With determined steps, Annie waded through the flock, cornering the petite chicken against the henhouse. Leaning over, she grabbed it by the throat, and swung it around over her head.

Elizabeth stood frozen, repulsed by the snapping sound of the bird's neck.

The body separated from the head and flew against the fence, dropping to the ground where it flopped back and forth.

Elizabeth gagged.

Annie, the chicken head still clutched in her hand, picked up the carcass, and marched out of the pen, slamming the gate behind her. She strode a few yards away to a square block of wood, and tossed the body of the fowl onto the top, where it continued to twitch as if still alive. Removing a knife from her pocket, she deftly sliced open the breast.

Sickened, Elizabeth didn't wait to see more. She clapped a hand over her mouth, grabbed up her skirt with her other hand, and fled to the outhouse. When she reached the tiny building, she jerked open the rickety door. Inside the stench only added to her nausea, and she became violently ill. She emptied the contents of her stomach, vowing to never eat chicken again.

When she finished, she exited the outhouse, tottered to the trough near the barn, and pumped some water. Wetting her handkerchief, she wiped it over her face, then rinsed out her mouth. She straightened, glancing around to see if anyone had witnessed her weakness, but the barnyard area remained empty, except for a brown horse tied to a hitching post.

Shaken, needing to escape from the sight and smell of animals, she wandered past the garden to the wooden seat circling the oak tree and collapsed onto it.

Her mind, blank from horror of what she'd just witnessed, slowly came back to life.

I can't do this. I can't live this way.

Elizabeth closed her eyes and laid her head back against the tree, resisting the urge to run into the house, pack her trunk, and catch the next train to Boston. Surely, residing with Laurence and Genia couldn't be as bad as living on a ranch. At least in Boston, she wasn't subjected to the daily cruelties of sustaining life—would never witness a sweet little chicken slaughtered in front of her.

The vision of the hen's carcass jumped back into her thoughts, and she grimaced, feeling nausea once more rise. Even in Boston, she wouldn't be able to escape the vision. Every time someone served the fowl, no matter how elegant the setting, she'd remember today's scene, and feel repulsed by the artistic creation displayed on the fine china in front of her. Just the thought took away the potential glamour of future dinner parties.

And if Genia found out about Elizabeth's new aversion to chicken, the meat would probably be served in every main course for the rest of Elizabeth's life.

No, when she weighed the options of chicken with Genia or chicken in Montana, she knew she wanted to stay in Sweetwater Springs. But, oh, through her blithe decision to move to the West she had acquired a gruesome reality.

* * *

Several days later, with a swish of her leaf-patterned brown skirt, Pamela entered the dining room. Elizabeth looked up from the overdue letter she'd been writing to Laurence and Genia to congratulate them about the news of Genia's pregnancy.

"Elizabeth, I'm going to practice shooting this morning. Would you like to join me?"

"Practice shooting," Elizabeth echoed. "You mean with guns?"

"Yes, of course with guns, silly." Pamela's eyes crinkled with laughter. "I have my own Winchester rifle and Colt 45. John gave them to me the first year we were married."

"But why would you want to shoot a gun? What would you need it for, and however did you learn?"

"John taught me. In fact, he insisted I learn."

"How very odd." She raised her eyebrows.

"Not at all, my dear. I was reluctant at first, but I wanted to please him, so I let him teach me. Now I practice with Nick when John's not around."

Elizabeth's shock must have shown on her face, for Pamela laughed again.

Elizabeth remembered the slaughtered chicken. She'd never be able to kill an animal. "But, Pamela, have you ever actually used your gun to shoot and kill something?"

"No, but I like knowing I could if I had to," Pamela replied, her tone practical. "We usually have enough men around here to take care of any danger, but some wives have to protect their gardens from marauding deer and their chickens from wolves. And you'll have to get John to tell you the story of how his mother shot a grizzly bear."

Elizabeth shuddered.

"Elizabeth, I've told you about the dangers of living around cattle, but there's more. Even though we have a civilized ranch, this is still the wilds of Montana. Some of the Indians around here aren't very friendly. We even have an occasional outlaw."

"I hadn't really thought of that."

"You've only seen the town and our ranch." Pamela made a sweeping movement with her arm. "We have a large, nice house, with staff and ranch hands, but that isn't true for many of the homesteads here. My life is easier and safer than that of most of my neighbors."

Although a little shaken by the idea that Montana wasn't as secure as she'd assumed, Elizabeth still had reservations about handling a gun.

"Out here, even the children learn to shoot," Pamela continued. "John taught Mark. He's quite good for his age, and he sometimes joins me when I practice."

"What about the girls?"

"Next year John's going to start teaching Sara, but the little imp's trying to persuade him to start sooner."

Elizabeth wavered. "I'll come along and watch you. Maybe I'll bring my sketchbook and draw a picture of you shooting a gun. I'll send it to Genia!"

"Don't you dare! Imagine the gossip that would fly around the city."

"Just think of her reaction. Do tell me, Pamela, dearest," Elizabeth mimicked her sister-in-law in a falsetto voice. "What does one wear when shooting guns?"

Pamela laughed. "I'm just glad Genia isn't here. You might accidentally shoot her!"

Elizabeth joined in her laughter, then she said more soberly, "No, I wouldn't. I don't hate Genia. I just don't like her. Besides, if Laurence hadn't married her, I wouldn't be here."

"That is true. However, Beth, I do want you to learn to shoot."

"I'll learn because you insist. But I'm *not* killing anything."

Pamela walked over, linked arms with Elizabeth, and pulled her out of her chair. "Come along, dearest Elizabeth," she teased. "I find your pink calico dress perfectly appropriate for a morning of shooting."

Elizabeth laughed and left her half-written letter behind. Arm-in-arm with Pamela, she walked out of the room and down the hall to John's study.

Pamela opened the door. "This is the only room in the house that John asked me to leave alone," she said as they entered his domain. "It's been this way for the last ten years and probably will stay the same for at least the next ten."

"The sacrosanct male bastion. Laurence feels the same about his library. Although I don't think my poor brother will stand a chance against Genia's changes."

"You're probably right."

Elizabeth glanced around at the big, cluttered oak desk, shabby leather chairs, and the guns mounted on the wall. She pointed at the mounted head of a huge bear, hung over the fireplace, its mouth frozen in a fierce growl. "That's the bear you told Caleb about. Ugh, Pamela, how can he stand to have something like that on his wall?"

"John shot that grizzly bear when he was fourteen and is still very proud of it."

"Looking at that thing would give me nightmares."

Pamela shrugged. "I try not to notice it."

Elizabeth reached up to the mantel and took down one of several tan baskets woven with geometric black designs. "What are these?"

"Indian baskets. They used to trade them to John's father for supplies."

She rotated the basket from side to side, admiring the workmanship. "Do they still make them?"

"Yes."

"I'd like to get one to send to Laurence."

"Ask Dawn. She'll know where you can buy some."

Pamela went to the wall and lifted off a rifle. "This one's mine." Walking over to the desk, she pulled open a drawer. "Here's where I keep my Colt revolver."

Elizabeth wrinkled her nose.

Pamela shook her head and rolled her eyes. "It won't bite you, Beth." She reached into the drawer again. "We keep the ammunition in this." She handed a wooden box to Elizabeth. "You can carry it."

Elizabeth tucked the box against her side.

Pamela pulled out two pieces of cloth. "The rifle has quite a recoil. The first time I used it, I had bruises for weeks."

Elizabeth winced.

"I made these to cushion my shoulder." Pamela held up what looked like a gray dishcloth with padding on one end. "I wear it like this," she said, draping the cloth over her shoulder with the padded side in front. "The stock of the rifle rests here." She patted the cushioned part, then handed the other one over to Elizabeth. "This one's Mark's. He doesn't use it much anymore because he likes to think he's tough."

"I don't know about this, Pamela. I'm liking this idea less and less."

"It's not so bad. Let's go find Nick."

"Nick?"

"John is out with the men, so Nick will teach you."

Reluctantly, Elizabeth followed Pamela out of the house and to the barn. They found Nick in one of the stalls inspecting a very pregnant bay mare.

"A few more days, girl, before you're ready to foal," he said, with a light slap on the horse's rump.

"Nick, we'd like to have some shooting practice," said Pamela. She glanced playfully at her friend. "Elizabeth is eager to learn."

Elizabeth scrunched a face back at her, but didn't reply.

Nick laughed. "It won't be that bad, Miss Hamilton. You might even like it."

Nick's grin was so infectious that, in spite of her apprehension, Elizabeth couldn't help but acquiesce. "I'll give it a try, but I won't promise to like it."

❋ ❋ ❋

John had designated a small meadow near a part of the river Elizabeth hadn't yet explored for the shooting range. As they approached through the trees, Elizabeth saw faded canvas stretched over stacks of hay bales, riddled with bullet holes. On each one was a rough sketch. She could identify the side view of a deer, and one of a steer, but it was the outline of an erect bear, extended paw showing wicked claws, that made her shudder.

"You can see my lack of artistic talent," Pamela said with a wave of her hand toward the targets. "I have to make new ones every few months, and these are about due to be changed. Maybe I can get you to help me, Elizabeth. Then they'd look more realistic."

"I'd rather paint animals than shoot at them," Elizabeth said, trying not to think about the possibility of killing any living thing. "Why is the bear standing up?"

Nick gave her a serious look. "A bear has a skull like iron. It's best to hit it though the heart."

Elizabeth's gaze slid away from the target. "It's best to stay away from one entirely," she echoed.

Pamela tapped Elizabeth on the shoulder. "I'll go practice on the bear. I'll use the Colt." She pointed to the side view of the deer. "You and Nick can use the Winchester."

Nick and Elizabeth walked over to stand about twenty yards in front of the deer. He held up the rifle. "Ever seen one of these fired before?"

"No, for some reason, I've never had that opportunity," Elizabeth answered in a wry tone.

"You do now." He took the box from her hand, placing it on the ground. "First we need to load it." He pulled a cartridge from the box. "You shove the nose of the cartridge into the loading gate." With a push of his fingers, the cartridge disappeared. "Just like this, see? Hear it snap into place?"

Elizabeth nodded.

"Load as many as it will hold." He bent over to pick up another cartridge. "Here, you try." He placed the cartridge in her palm. "I'll hold the gun while you load this one."

Feeling fumble-fingered, Elizabeth leaned forward and forced the cartridge through the loading gate. At the sound of the snap, she straightened, smiling in accomplishment. "That wasn't too hard."

"Naw." Nick grinned at her. "That's the easy part. Now go on, load the rest."

She scooped up a few more cartridges and one by one loaded the rifle.

"That's enough," Nick said. "Now it's time for the fun part. Place the stock against your shoulder like this." Nick demonstrated. "Sight along the top toward the deer. Aim for the heart—right behind the front shoulder." He glanced over at her, his green gaze penetrating.

She nodded her understanding.

He lowered the rifle and pointed to the sights along the top. "Frame your target through these." He raised the rifle again, aimed it at the side of the deer. "Then press this lever down and forward." He motioned with his finger. "That chambers the cartridge and cocks the hammer." His voice took on a cautionary note. "Once that's done, all it takes is a squeeze of the trigger. Watch."

Crack!

Elizabeth flinched.

A new hole appeared in the area of the deer's heart.

Nick lowered the rifle, turned and smiled at Elizabeth. "See. Not hard at all."

She'd regained her outward composure before Nick turned to her. But inside, her stomach churned. This shooting business didn't look quite so easy to her.

"Are you ready?" Nick's encouraging smile lessened some of her nervousness. "Or do you want me to take another turn?"

She took a deep breath and tucked her locket inside her shirtwaist. "I'm as ready as I'll ever be."

A shot rang out from Pamela's Colt.

Elizabeth winced and tried to ignore the sounds of her friend's target practice.

Nick handed the rifle over.

Elizabeth awkwardly tried to set the stock of the Winchester against the pad on her shoulder.

"Here, let me help." Nick stepped behind her, reached around her body, and placed his hands over hers, steadying the rifle against her shoulder. At his touch, unusual tingling sensations coursed through her.

"Look down the sights to the target," he murmured in her ear. His finger pressed over hers, guiding her movement.

Her whole body warmed at his closeness. Too aware of him, she couldn't concentrate. She just closed her eyes and squeezed the trigger. The noise of the shot reverberated in her ears. The recoil of the gun sent her staggering back into Nick.

His arms tightened around her.

She lowered the rifle.

"You missed," Nick's voice teased in her ear.

Elizabeth's heart raced. She relaxed against his chest, loving the feel of his strong arms around her.

The sound of Pamela's pistol firing brought her back to an awareness of her surroundings. She allowed herself the luxury of another few seconds of leaning against Nick before she reluctantly wiggled away.

"I closed my eyes when I fired," Elizabeth admitted with a sheepish look, turning to face him.

He laughed and made as if to hug her, but instead pulled back. "How'd you expect to hit what you're aimin' at with your eyes closed?"

"I don't know. I don't like the whole idea." Her voice quavered. "I'm not sure I want to try it again."

She couldn't tell him the problem wasn't the rifle, but her reaction to being in his arms. She wasn't supposed to feel that way about Nick. But perhaps she'd have those feelings if any attractive man put his arms around her in that manner. She tried to imagine herself in a similar situation with Caleb, but couldn't muster up a vision of it.

"Why don't we trade Miz Carter for the Colt? You might be more comfortable with it."

Although aching with a vague sense of disappointment, she knew she should be relieved to avoid further intimate contact with Nick. Surely he wouldn't have to put his arms around her when she shot a pistol. Pamela managed by herself without any problem.

Her shoulders relaxed, and she flashed him a smile of agreement. "Yes, that would be better."

Without waiting for Nick to respond, Elizabeth walked over to Pamela. "If you don't mind, I'd like to switch guns with you." She shuddered. "I don't think I'm ready for a rifle yet."

"It's still difficult for me too." Pamela handed over the Colt and took the rifle from Nick. "That recoil can be painful. The first time knocked me clean off my feet."

Elizabeth sent her an exasperated look. "Why didn't you warn me?"

A sly smile tugged at Pamela's mouth; her plump cheeks crinkled in mischief. "I trusted Nick to catch you."

Elizabeth shook her head at Pamela and walked back to stand in front of the deer target. "Show me what to do with this." She handed Nick the gun.

"You aim it with one hand like this." He shifted his body slightly back and to the side, and straightened his right arm. "However, when you're just startin', it might be easier for you to use two hands to hold it like this." Facing forward, he pulled back his hand enough to place his other hand around it, then extended and locked his arms. "This way'll be more steady. Why don't we start with you holdin' the gun with both hands?"

Her brow wrinkling in concentration, Elizabeth nodded agreement.

"Thumb the hammer back after each shot. When you pull the trigger, the hammer falls, and the gun shoots the bullet."

With a flourish, he presented the Colt to Elizabeth, handle first. "Think you can keep your eyes open this time?" The corner of his mouth twitched as he tried to suppress a grin.

"Yes," she retorted, "but that doesn't mean I'll hit the target."

"Keeping your eyes open will be a good first step, Elizabeth—uh, Miss Hamilton." As Nick slipped up and called her by her first name, his instructive mode vanished, and he stepped away from her.

In spite of her feeling of connection with Nick, Elizabeth tried to ignore his familiarity. But it wasn't easy, given how her body reacted to his touch.

She raised the gun with both hands and pointed it toward the deer, surprised by how heavy it seemed.

Nick reached over from the side and cupped her hands, his touch warm and steadying.

"Are you lookin'?" he asked.

"Yes."

He dropped his hands, stepping behind her. "Then shoot."

Elizabeth pulled the trigger. With a loud report, the pistol jerked into the air, startling her backward into Nick's waiting arms. To her disappointment, no new bullet hole appeared in the target. She lowered the gun until it pointed to the ground, twisted out of his hold, and looked up at him with a question in her eyes.

He lightly tapped her forehead between her eyebrows, leaving a warm spot from his touch. "Did you keep your eyes open?"

"Yes. But I still missed."

"You're just learnin'," he reassured her. "It's more important for you to first get the feel of the gun. Eventually, you'll hit what you're aimin' for."

"And why'd I lose my balance like that?"

"The Colt has a strong recoil that yanks your arms up. After each shot, you're going to have to lower the gun and re-aim."

Elizabeth shook her head and rolled her eyes.

"You'll get used to it," he reassured her. "Ready to try again?"

She nodded and turned to face the target. Much to her surprise, on her next attempt she hit the edge.

"There, you're gettin' closer. In no time at all we'll be callin' you Dead Eye Hamilton."

Elizabeth glowed at Nick's teasing. "But I didn't hit what I aimed for."

"You came close. You've got the hang of it now. You just need more practice."

She fired one more shot.

Then Nick stopped her. "We need to reload."

"How do you know?"

"Because I saw Miz Carter reload and fire two shots before turning the gun over to you. You fired three more. This gun's called a six-shooter because it holds six bullets. However, only five chambers are loaded."

Elizabeth tilted her head in puzzlement.

"The hammer should always be sitting on an empty chamber to prevent an accident." He held out his hand. "Let me show you how to reload."

Elizabeth placed the Colt in his palm.

Slowly Nick pulled the hammer back until she heard a *click*. "Now it's half-cocked. Swing this loading gate out, reach under the barrel, and press this rod to eject the empty cartridge, then rotate the cylinder. Eject all of them first." He demonstrated and glanced over at her.

She nodded in understanding.

"Then slide in a fresh cartridge and once again rotate the cylinder." He loaded four more cartridges and handed the Colt back to her.

Elizabeth fired five more times, exhilaration building within her at each shot. She managed to hit the target at least half the time. But by the end, exhaustion dropped over her, which was strange considering how little physical energy she'd expended.

"Why don't you take a turn now," she suggested. "I want to see an expert in action."

A flush climbed his cheeks, but he took the Colt from her, reloaded, and stepped over to the steer. With an effortless lift of his arm, he rapidly shot five rounds dead center into the heart area. He lowered the gun, turned, and, lifting an eyebrow, waited for her reaction.

Impressed by his quiet confidence, Elizabeth mirrored his raised eyebrow. "You make it look so easy."

Nick laughed. "Been shootin' since I was Mark's age."

She teased back. "That's not so long ago."

"A man grows up fast in these parts. When you need to survive," he spun the words into a drawl, "you learn to hit what ya aim for."

Nick's right. He has grown up fast. In spite of his age, he doesn't seem younger than me. Elizabeth shook her head, unable to explain her connection with this man. As she continued to stand there, gazing into his eyes, the feeling deepened. This close, she could see a gray ring circling the green irises. *So that's why his eyes sometimes look blue.*

"Elizabeth." She barely heard Pamela. "Elizabeth!" Pamela called again.

Reluctantly, she broke eye contact.

"Are you finished?" Pamela said. "I'm ready to go back to the house."

"I'm ready too." She tossed the words at Pamela before smiling at Nick. "Thank you for the lesson. It was quite an experience."

He touched his hat. "My pleasure. But first we need to reload the gun. Remember how?" He handed the Colt to her.

This time as she loaded the gun, her fingers moved with more sureness, although nowhere near as smoothly as Nick's.

He grinned and nodded.

A flush of happiness warmed her cheeks, then rolled all the way down to her toes. With a final smile at him, she turned and strolled over to Pamela, resisting the urge to dance on tiptoe like a little girl.

"Well, how'd it go?" Pamela asked.

Her body still tingling, Elizabeth touched a finger to the corner of her mouth. "It was interesting…I might even be willing to try again."

Pamela, you don't know how interesting.

CHAPTER FOURTEEN

The last note of the hymn trailed away, and Reverend Norton intoned the final blessing that concluded the church service. Through lowered eyelashes, Elizabeth glanced sideways at Mr. Livingston, who was sitting in the same pew as last Sunday.

She'd been disappointed when, in spite of his invitation to drive her to the ranch, Mr. Livingston had not taken a seat next to her. Then she'd realized changing his place might be considered making a declaration of his intentions. She wasn't sure either of them felt ready for that kind of public scrutiny. Perhaps in a few weeks...

This Sunday, Elizabeth was more relaxed. Once outside the church, she greeted and exchanged a few words with the people she knew. Anticipation over Mr. Livingston still bubbled within her, but she'd gotten over the shock of his appearance and felt more secure about his courtship of her.

A tug on her pink silk dress caused her to look down to see Sara and Lizzy, in identical blue flower-sprigged calico dresses, vying for her attention. Lizzy clutched a fold of Elizabeth's skirt in her hand.

"Aunt Elizabeth, will you sit between us on the way home?" Sara asked, giving Elizabeth the gap-toothed grin that tugged at her heart.

Elizabeth dropped a kiss on Sara's forehead and stooped to give Lizzy a hug. "Oh, my dears, I'd love to. However, Mr. Livingston is coming to dinner. I'm riding home with him."

Both girls stuck out their lower lips in disappointment. "I can tell you're sisters," she said, touching Lizzy's mouth. "You even pout the same." She reached over to pull gently on Sara's braid. Elizabeth's necklace swung out, almost hitting Sara in the nose. The child's gaze fastened on the locket.

"Here." Impulsively, Elizabeth raised the necklace over her head and dropped the chain around Sara's neck. "You can wear this home. That way, it's almost like I'm with you."

Sara's eyes widened. She reverently cupped the locket in her palm.

As if she'd never seen the necklace before, Lizzy stood on tiptoe to examine it.

"Let your sister wear it halfway home."

"Yes, Aunt Elizabeth."

Elizabeth patted Lizzy's head. "After we eat, we'll have some music. I'll let you choose the first two songs. One for each of you."

Their faces brightened.

Sara grinned. "I'm going to pick a not-Sunday song."

"Little imp." Elizabeth gave Sara's braid another tug. "Good thing Reverend Norton won't be there." She smoothed brown wispy bangs back from Lizzy's delicate face. "What about you, little bird? Do you have a song you want me to play?"

The child nodded.

A male voice behind her said, "I hope I get to pick a song too."

At the sound of Mr. Livingston's voice, Elizabeth straightened, feeling a flush rising in her cheeks. "Of course, Mr. Livingston," she said. "However, I've promised the girls the first two choices, so you'll have to go third."

"I'd be happy to allow two such lovely little ladies to precede me." He gave them a playful bow.

Sara giggled and clapped a hand over her mouth. Pulling Lizzy like a caboose behind her, she skipped over toward her parents.

"Well, Mr. Livingston, I can see you're quickly going to become a favorite with those two," Elizabeth said.

He reached over to pull her hand gently through the crook of his arm, placing it on the sleeve of his brown wool jacket. "It's their Aunt Elizabeth with whom I intend to become a favorite," he said, smiling down at her while he led her in the direction of his buggy.

Warmth swelled within her heart and expanded throughout her body. Surely the glow radiated from her face, apparent for him to see.

His smile intensified. Stopping before the buggy, he studied her face, his brown eyes warm. He brought her hand to his lips.

Elizabeth thought she might faint from joy.

He helped her onto the seat of the buggy, then walked around and climbed up beside her. Reaching into his pocket, he pulled out a pair of brown leather driving gloves, then tugged them on. He released the brake and flicked the reins. For the first few minutes, they remained silent while he drove through the town.

Elizabeth admired his handling of the reins. Her artist's eye was always quick to catch the shape of a person's hands, and she wished he hadn't put gloves on so she could study his. She longed to compare them with her memory of Richard's. Underneath the leather, it seemed he had narrow hands with long fingers. With an inner shiver, she wondered what they'd feel like on her skin.

"Miss Hamilton." His quiet voice interrupted her thoughts.

She blushed, glad that his concentration had to remain on his driving. "Yes, Mr. Livingston."

"I'd very much appreciate it if you'd call me Caleb."

Yes, things were progressing quite nicely. "I'd like that, Caleb."

He gave her a quick smile. "May I call you Elizabeth?"

"Certainly, Caleb."

He relaxed back against the black leather seat. "Do you think you'll make a long visit with the Carters?"

"They've extended an invitation for me to make my home with them. So far everything's been wonderful, but I'm not sure yet just what I'll do."

"I've been wondering what brought such a refined lady out to the wild, uncivilized West."

"It's a rather long story."

He smiled down at her and slowed the pace of the horses. "We have plenty of time."

She related the details of her brother's unexpected marriage. The serious expression in his eyes during his quick, sideways glances at her told her how attentively he listened. She tried to keep a light tone of voice, but some of her feelings must have seeped through.

"You've had a difficult time. Your brother's behavior sounds very selfish."

"I don't think he meant to be. He thought it would be good for me to have a sister-in-law."

Caleb transferred the reins to one hand and with the other reached out to clasp hers. "Your brother's a cad." He squeezed her hand before taking back the reins into both of his.

"Thank you, Caleb." Tears rose in her eyes, and she blinked them back. She felt protected and cherished, just like when Richard used to stand up to Laurence on her behalf. She wished her brother could hear Caleb's words. Not that anything would change.

Companionable silence prevailed while Caleb guided the horses through the pass.

"It's a beautiful sight, isn't it?" Elizabeth asked, looking down at the ranch spread out below them.

"It's a prosperous ranch, the best in these parts, but perhaps not the best setting for a lady like you."

His words made her a little uncomfortable. After all, Pamela was a lady, and this was her home. And so far Elizabeth had enjoyed her stay at the ranch. Still, good thing Caleb didn't know about the shooting practice she'd had this week. He might not approve. "I've been happier here the last few weeks than I've been since Laurence married."

"I'm sorry you've had to suffer through the difficult circumstances that caused you to come to Montana; however, I'm pleased you're here, Elizabeth. You deserve to be happy." Again, he shifted the reins back into one hand and, reaching for hers, he lifted it to his lips. He brushed her palm with his finger, sending her into a blissful daze.

* * *

Nick strolled out of the barn just as John and Pamela pulled up in the buggy. *Where's Elizabeth?* He automatically went to stand by the nearest horse, then held the harness and stroked its neck while John dismounted.

"The mare foaled yet?" John asked.

"Not yet. Probably be a few more hours till she's ready."

John grunted and walked around to help Pamela down.

Pamela smoothed her green silk skirt and smiled at Nick. "I'm glad most of the foals are born. You've been missing too much church."

"Only two more to go. And it'll be several weeks before that gray mare foals."

"You'll join us for Sunday dinner?"

Before he could nod an affirmative, Pamela added, "Mr. Livingston's driving out with Elizabeth."

Nick shuddered at the thought of another meal with the banker. And with him courting Elizabeth…He shook his head. "I should stay with the mare."

Pamela's brown eyes held understanding. "Soon you'll not have those mares for an excuse," she said in a voice only Nick could hear.

In the distance, Nick saw Livingston's buggy and nodded in that direction. "Company's comin'."

"Goodness, I'd better warn Annie they're here." Pamela lifted her skirt a few inches off the ground and sailed toward the house.

John had climbed back into the buggy. Nick stepped out of the way then followed, intending to help unharness the horse.

Thoughts whirled around in Nick's head, and his stomach knotted. He'd promised himself he'd fight for Elizabeth, yet at the first chance he'd gone and backed down.

Chicken. He was worse than the rooster that kept running away from Sara's hen, Mrs. Hooch.

Nick Sanders, he sternly told himself in a mental voice that sounded like his mother's. *You march right into that house and tell Miz Carter you're coming to dinner. Then you hightail it to the bunkhouse to wash up and change into something decent!*

The decision made, he relaxed. Turning, he glanced into the birthing stall. The mare lay on her side in the straw, panting, the whites of her eyes straining. All thoughts of courtship fled. He unlatched the door and slid inside. Kneeling down, he ran his hands over her sweating side. "What's wrong, girl?" he murmured. Underneath his probing fingers, he could feel her strain.

John stopped at the stall. "How's she doing?"

Nick rolled up his right shirtsleeve, held the mare's tail aside, and continued his manual examination. "Foal's breech," he said without looking up.

"You'll need help."

"You've got company. Get one of the men."

"All right, but send him to the house if you need me."

Nick heard John's quick footsteps recede, and he became lost in the battle to save the mare and foal.

❋ ❋ ❋

Nick walked slowly from the barn feeling exhausted but content. It had been a struggle, but both mare and foal were doing fine. His peacefulness fled at the sight of Caleb Livingston's buggy. *Oh, no.* He'd completely forgotten about dinner. Glancing down at his blue denim work shirt and pants covered in muck and blood, he shook his head in disgust.

Piano music floated on the air. *Elizabeth's music.* He recognized the piece by Liszt. If he'd been in the room, he'd have had another chance to play for her. He hadn't forgotten the connection they'd experienced the night of the party when he'd performed "Lizzy's Theme."

He'd finished the piece he'd composed for Elizabeth, but hadn't made the opportunity to play for her. Nor did he want to debut that music in front of Livingston. That music belonged to Elizabeth alone.

Glancing around to make sure no one saw him, he headed in the direction of the house. Outside the music room, he leaned back against the house where he could hear every delicate note.

A sigh squeezed up from his midsection. He slid down the wall until he sat on the ground, his hands on his knees. He closed his eyes and pictured Elizabeth bent over the keys, blue eyes intent on her music, blonde tendrils curling around her face.

Then he imagined Livingston hovering over her.

Nick clenched his fist. The man would probably listen attentively, thinking what an asset Elizabeth would be as his wife. Livingston could be entertained by her fine playing whenever he wanted. Then when he had guests, they'd admire the banker even more because of his lovely, talented wife.

He brushed a straw off his pants, inhaled a deep breath, and vowed silently: *I'm out here now, Livingston, because I had a job to do. But I promise you, I won't always be the mucked-up cowboy on the outside of her life.*

❋ ❋ ❋

I'm pleased you're here, Elizabeth.

As she blissfully drifted through the rest of Caleb's visit, his words echoed in her mind. The flow of the day washed over her and carried her along. Cocooned in joy, she floated through the meal and the music afterward. Even bidding Caleb good night didn't settle her down to earth, for she was lost in the rosy glow of their future together.

Later that night, Elizabeth sat in dreamy contentment in front of her dressing table, brushing out her hair and humming "Lizzy's Theme." A shaft of moonlight peeking through the gap in her curtains made her stand and move to the window. She leaned against the wall and slowly stroked the brush through her hair, gazing out into the night.

A movement below caught her attention, and she leaned forward to make it out. A shadowy male outline walked toward one of the horse pastures, the one with the large, oddly shaped rock in the middle.

Nick. She recognized his walk.

As she realized she'd missed him, her humming ceased. Only then did she realize she'd been humming Nick's music. The lack of his presence had been the only prick in her happiness. Where had he been? How strange that he'd stayed out of sight. Even stranger was how much it mattered to her.

CHAPTER FIFTEEN

Sara burst into the parlor, Mark following on her heels. "Mama, Mama, the saskatoons are ripe! May we go pick them?"

"The birds are already at them," Mark added. "We'd better hurry if we want any."

"That berry patch is so big, there'll still be plenty for us," Pamela said.

"What are saskatoons?" Elizabeth asked.

"Similar to blueberries, except smaller and redder." Pamela smiled at Elizabeth. "A delicious purple berry. Picking berries is always an occasion. We take a picnic lunch and enough pails and baskets to ensure we have plenty of fruit for jam and pie."

"I love saskatoons," Sara said, rubbing her stomach in anticipation.

"And I love saskatoon pie!" Mark said.

"You'll come, won't you, Aunt Elizabeth?" Sara begged. "Please, please."

Elizabeth hadn't even thought about offering to help pick berries, but capitulated at the pleading look on Sara's face and the eager way Mark rocked forward on his toes while he awaited her answer. "Of course I will."

Pamela's brown eyes twinkled with mischief. "Then you'd better put on your oldest dress and your straw hat. Unless you want to borrow one of my sunbonnets."

Elizabeth knew her friend was teasing, but pretended to be shocked. "Pamela, don't tell me that you actually have a sunbonnet?"

"No, of course not. That's one unfashionable item I haven't yet succumbed to wearing." She ruffled her daughter's bangs. "But Sara has one she never wears."

Sara crinkled her nose and shook her head.

Her mother shrugged. "As you've noticed, she prefers her Stetson."

Sara nodded vigorously, her braids bouncing on her shoulders.

"Lizzy has several sunbonnets because she can't take the sun. And they're more practical than the straw hats, although she has those, as well as a Stetson." She turned her attention to her son. "You'll need your hat too, Mark. And run and tell Annie to pack a lunch for us." She looked at her daughter. "Go find Dawn. She'll have to keep an eye on Lizzy. It'll be too hot for her to go with us."

The children ran out of the room.

"We'd better go change," Pamela told Elizabeth. "Those two will be back in a minute and raring to go."

* * *

The uneasy feeling refused to go away. It settled between his shoulder blades like an itch he couldn't scratch. Nick tried to shrug it off his shoulders and out of his mind, but the sensation persisted. No matter how he busied himself with the horses and foals, the ominous feeling stayed and distracted him. Even the horses sensed his preoccupation. After the third normally placid mare shied away, he gave up.

Collapsing on the nearest hay bale, he tried to figure out what was bothering him. When he thought about John, the cowboys, and the cattle, his apprehension didn't intensify. But when he turned his thoughts to the women and children picking berries, his gut tightened with an almost physical cramp.

Elizabeth! Is something wrong with Elizabeth?

His uneasiness increased.

Thinking himself a fool for rushing off on a possible wild-goose chase didn't stop him from quickly saddling Outlaw and leading the horse outside. He tossed the reins around a hitching post, ran into the bunkhouse, pulled his gun belt off a peg, and strapped it on. The Winchester rested on the gun rack. He grabbed it and ran outside, shoving the rifle into the scabbard on his saddle. He flung himself on the horse and, urging Outlaw to a canter, headed for the berry patch.

❋ ❋ ❋

The heat of the afternoon sun burned through Elizabeth's blue calico shirtwaist, sticking the material to her shoulders. Damp tendrils of hair curled around her face. She'd long since given up brushing them out of the way for fear of leaving purple berry smudges across her cheeks.

For the first few hours, she'd enjoyed picking saskatoons. The acre-long thicket, situated close to where the river ran down from the mountains, provided multitudes of warm, ripe berries. In the beginning, they'd all picked near each other, and, with talk and laughter, the morning had passed quickly. The children ate almost as many as they put in the baskets, and the women weren't much better. Elizabeth loved the tart sweetness of the fruit.

Even with all the saskatoons they'd eaten, they had plenty of room left for a picnic in the cool shade of the cottonwood and aspen trees near the river. Watching the bubbling green water play over mossy rocks had been so peaceful that Elizabeth had promised herself she'd return another day to paint. After lunch they once again settled in to serious picking. Elizabeth had worked her way around to the right of the patch, out of sight and earshot of Pamela and the children.

She set her basket down and untied the strings of her straw hat. Yanking it off, she vigorously fanned herself. She debated about walking over to splash some cool water on her face. Rustling in the bushes about thirty feet in front of her caught her attention.

That's odd. I thought the others were picking berries in the opposite direction. "Mark, Sara, is that you?"

With a growling grunt, a huge bear poked his snout through the bushes. Small brown eyes glared at her. Elizabeth jumped back. *Oh, no.* Her heartbeat quickened.

The beast pushed out of the brambles, and opened its mouth about a foot, displaying huge yellow fangs.

Terror jolted through Elizabeth. Her knees shook and threatened to buckle under her. She didn't know whether to turn and run, or back away. "Shoo!" Steeling herself, she waved her hat. "Shoo! Go away!"

In horror, she watched the bear rear up, a grizzled monster with long, wicked claws. Lowering itself back down on all fours, it rumbled toward Elizabeth faster than she'd believed possible.

She screamed. Her hat slipped from her limp fingers, and she took a few faltering steps back. *Please, God, please.*

The crack of gunshots from behind her startled Elizabeth, and she screamed again. The bear staggered, then collapsed less than five feet away from her.

Elizabeth almost joined the animal in a heap on the ground. Her heart pounded so hard it seemed to pull the blood from her head, leaving her dizzy. She looked behind her and saw Nick mounted on Outlaw, his Winchester still aimed at the grizzly.

"Nick," she whispered. Never in her life had she seen such a wonderful sight.

Nick leaped off the horse. Still pointing the rifle at the bear, he nudged the carcass with his foot, then lowered the rifle and turned to Elizabeth.

She threw herself against him. His arm tightened around her. Setting the rifle on the ground, he pulled her close.

Elizabeth clung to him, still too shaken to even burst into tears. Nick had saved her. She glanced back at the carcass, still hardly believing what had just happened, then shuddered and buried her face in his shoulder.

"Elizabeth, are you all right?"

She nodded, but didn't lift her face. Her body trembled. A few relieved tears squeezed through her tightly shut eyelids.

Nick reached up and stroked her hair, placing several comforting kisses on her head.

"I was so frightened," she murmured into his shoulder. "Thank goodness you came."

He pressed another kiss to her head.

Elizabeth sighed in relief, her body shaky. Everything had happened so fast. But she was safe in Nick's embrace, and she didn't want to leave anytime soon.

Nick scooped Elizabeth into his arms.

She gasped, flung her arms around his neck, and clung to him.

"Nick, I'm too heavy," she protested.

"Lighter than those hay bales," he teased. "You make a better fit too."

Elizabeth blushed and hid her face against his shoulder. She'd never literally been swept off her feet before, and she loved the protective feeling of being held against his body while he carried her toward the river.

All too soon they reached the water. He lowered her down by the edge, then knelt beside her. Still keeping one arm around her, he reached up and pulled off his blue bandana. Dipping the cloth into the water, he bathed Elizabeth's face.

"That feels good." Nick's tenderness touched her all the way to her toes. She tenuously smiled at him. "I'm feeling better."

"Beth!" Pamela sounded anxious as she hurried toward them, Sara and Mark running behind. "What happened? I heard shots. Are you all right?"

Nick kept his arm around Elizabeth and jerked his head in the direction of the bear.

"Oh, my!" gasped Pamela. "Beth, did it harm you?"

"No, Nick shot it in time. But, Pamela, I feel so weak. I've never been so frightened before."

Pamela knelt down and took Elizabeth's hand. "What happened?"

Elizabeth relayed everything. She finished, a shiver running down her spine.

Nick's arm tightened around her.

"The monster reared up on its hind legs, and it was so big!" she said. "It had the longest teeth and claws. I didn't know what to do." She managed a wry smile for her friend. "I didn't think a ladylike faint was my best option."

Pamela squeezed Elizabeth's hand. "I never would have forgiven myself if something had happened to you."

Elizabeth gave Nick a sideways glance. "I never even knew you were behind me."

Pamela looked at Nick. "Why did you come out here? It's a miracle you were there."

"Perhaps that's the reason. I think the good Lord was trying to tell me something." He looked down at Elizabeth, still cradled against him. "The children told me you all were going berry pickin', and for some reason the idea just didn't sit right." He shook his head. "I tried to put it out of my mind, but it kept on worryin' at me. I finished up with the horses and decided to head out and check on things."

"The Lord was watching over us," agreed Pamela with a sage nod. "We have much to be thankful for."

"I'm just glad you listened to Him," Elizabeth told Nick with a slight return of her playfulness.

Sara cuddled against her mother. She'd lost her hat, and the freckles stood out on her pale skin. "I don't want to pick saskatoons ever again," she said in a small, fearful voice.

"Now, honey, don't you worry none," Nick told her in an exaggerated drawl. "You've been picking berries here for years and never saw any ole bears until today." He winked at her. "Besides, I don't think that grizzly was after Miss Elizabeth. I think it was more interested in her basket of berries."

"Then why'd you kill it?" Sara asked, looking a little less fearful.

"I saw that there grizzly, and I thought to myself, bear steaks! I sure do love bear steaks. And since your pa don't let me keep any bears in the barn, I rarely get to eat any."

Sara laughed, and color returned to her cheeks. "Silly Nick. You can't keep bears in the barn!"

"Well, maybe not. But I couldn't let an ole bear frighten a pretty little lady like Miss Elizabeth, now could I?"

Elizabeth's heart lightened at the compliment, but she pretended not to hear. As Nick reassured the child, she could feel the strain inside her ease.

"We'll get that bear's head stuffed and mounted," Nick continued. "Then Miss Elizabeth can hang it in her bedroom."

"Don't you dare," Elizabeth exclaimed in mock horror. "I'd never be able to sleep!"

Sara giggled.

"Maybe the next time we pick berries, Nick will accompany us," Elizabeth suggested to Sara. "That way, we'll feel safe."

Sara pulled away from her mother and leaned toward Nick. "Yes, Nick, will you?"

He gently tugged one of Sara's braids. "I won't let you out of my sight."

Pamela reached over and brushed some stray tendrils from Elizabeth's forehead. "You sound like you're feeling better, Beth. Would you like to head back to the house?"

"I could put you up on Outlaw," Nick offered. "If I lead him, he'll carry you without a fuss."

Elizabeth had a ridiculous vision of herself riding Outlaw. She'd make an outlandish sight straddled on a man's saddle. Why, her dress would be hitched up to her knees!

"Thank you for the kind offer, but if it's all the same to you, I'd rather walk. However, my knees still feel a little shaky, so perhaps you could walk beside me and allow me to hold your arm."

Mark tilted his shoulder in her direction. "I'll help you too, Aunt Elizabeth. You could put your other hand on my shoulder."

"That would be a big help, dear," she told him.

Their concern and support sparked a feeling of love and warmth inside her that melted the last of her tension. She'd not experienced anything like this since before her parents and Richard had died.

Nick released her. "Elizabeth, you sit right here with Pamela," he ordered, rising to his feet. "I'll take the children and gather up the berry baskets."

He held out his hand to Sara and motioned Mark to follow.

The two women watched until they'd walked out of sight. "He's a good man," Pamela said. "He's been such a comfort to me ever since I came to Montana." She looked at Elizabeth. "He's John's godson, you know. His parents died when he was thirteen, and he's been with John ever since. He lived in the house for a few years, then insisted on moving into the bunkhouse. He's quite an independent young man."

"That's why you invited him to your party!" Elizabeth exclaimed. "I couldn't understand it at the time, and I was going to ask you, but then I met Caleb, and everything else went out of my mind."

"He used to dine with us more often, but since you've been here, he eats with the men. I haven't said anything to him because I thought he might be uncomfortable. He's always been shy around women. But now I'm going to insist that he start having meals with us again." She reached over and squeezed Elizabeth's hand. "You don't mind, do you?"

"Of course not. He saved my life. Right now I couldn't deny him anything. I thought Nick was just a hired hand. I didn't know he was John's godson. Why didn't you ever tell me?"

"I thought I did when I first moved out here and wrote to you."

"You probably did." Elizabeth's smile was rueful. "That was a long time ago."

The two women relaxed in silence for a few minutes. Elizabeth offered up a prayer of gratitude that came from her whole being.

Nick and the children rounded the bushes. Sara and Mark had regained their hats and baskets. Nick took each of the baskets of berries and tied them to Outlaw's saddle. At first, Outlaw objected to having the strange objects against his sides, stamping a leg and shying away. Nick petted and soothed him, and soon the horse settled down.

He was the same man she'd seen every day for the last six weeks, but suddenly Elizabeth saw him through new eyes. She watched how his muscled body moved with a graceful economy of motion and the gentle way he touched the gray stallion and the children. She'd gotten used to his longer hair, but now it reminded her of the swashbuckling heroes from the adventure tales she'd read about in her childhood. He'd saved her today, just like in the storybooks. And he'd swept her off her feet too.

Wait until Laurence and Genia heard about her adventure. Well, maybe she wouldn't write them about it. They hadn't expressed a very high opinion of Nick. She smiled to herself. They couldn't understand him, and he'd never fit into their Boston ways. He was a western man and belonged in this milieu. Yet she was still an eastern woman. Wasn't she?

❋ ❋ ❋

He'd been in tight situations before, but Nick had never been as scared as when he'd seen that grizzly charging for Elizabeth. He glanced down at her, reassuring himself she was all right. Her straw hat blocked him from seeing her face, and she clung to his arm. He'd have liked to place his other hand over hers, but he didn't trust Outlaw to obediently follow if the horse wasn't led.

Nick had underplayed the danger Elizabeth had been in. He hadn't wanted to further frighten the women and children, but his knees had shaken for several minutes afterwards. What if he'd ignored his feeling and not ridden to check things out? He'd never have forgiven himself if something had happened to her. His heartbeat quickened as he imagined what could have happened.

As if sensing his thoughts, Elizabeth looked up. Her pale face still showed signs of strain. He winked at her to see if he could bring out the dimple in the left corner of her smile.

It worked. Her skin pinked up, and the dimple briefly appeared. That seldom-seen dimple really did something to his heart. The tiny indentation changed her from the proper Miss Hamilton to his Elizabeth. He had to restrain himself from leaning down to brush his lips across it. *Maybe someday.* Right now his heart overflowed with enough gratitude because they walked together, safe. If she hadn't just had such a dreadful experience, he imagined they could stroll for hours.

❋ ❋ ❋

Bear steaks and saskatoons smothered in cream made for interesting supper conversation. Elizabeth joined the others for the meal, having recovered enough from her traumatic afternoon, even though she'd been reluctant to eat the meat. She felt certain that if she took a bite, she'd picture the sight of that grizzly and feel nauseous.

However, Nick's presence made the idea palatable. When he'd arrived in the dining room, the good-natured teasing had started. Bear innuendoes and jokes had been tossed around the dinner table. Even the children joined in, and the meal passed in merriness. To Elizabeth's surprise, she even liked the slightly sweet taste of the steak.

At the conclusion of dessert, Nick leaned back in his chair, satisfaction apparent on his face. "I sure do love berries and cream."

"Me too," Sara piped up.

"'Bout the only thing better is a taste of one of your ma's saskatoon pies."

A chorus of agreement echoed around the table.

Elizabeth cocked an eyebrow at Pamela. "*Your* saskatoon pies?"

John answered for his wife. "Best around these parts."

Pamela's plump cheeks flushed at the praise. "Our last cook taught me," she explained to Elizabeth. "Her secret recipe. I've never shared it with anyone."

"Sounds like an experience to look forward to. When will I have the honor of trying this famous pie?" Elizabeth teased.

"How about tomorrow?"

The three children emphatically nodded, eager looks in their eyes.

"Oh, yes, Mama," Mark said.

His mother smiled back. "Perhaps I should ask your Aunt Elizabeth to help me." She slanted a mischievous glance toward Elizabeth. "I'll teach you the recipe."

"Oh, no, you don't, Pamela." Elizabeth shook her head. "You know I've never baked anything in my life."

John joined in the teasing. "Now, Elizabeth, knowing how to make Pamela's saskatoon pie would surely be seen around these parts as an increase to your dowry."

As he tried to suppress a laugh, Nick choked, then raised his napkin to his mouth. But his eyes danced with emerald glee, and Elizabeth knew the napkin hid a grin.

Elizabeth stiffened, then with exaggerated haughtiness lifted her nose in the air. "My dowry is quite sufficient as it is, thank you, John." She said each word with snooty emphasis that ended with a smile and relaxation of her body.

John gave a mournful shake of his head. “I don’t know about that, Elizabeth. Good cooking is a sure way to a man’s heart.”

Elizabeth shook her finger. “John Carter, I happen to know that when you fell in love with Pamela, she’d never even been near a kitchen except to give orders to the staff.”

With a rueful shrug, John grinned at his wife. “She’s got me there, my dear. I’d love you even if you’d never cooked a day in your life.”

Pamela rolled her eyes.

Elizabeth sat back, enjoying the banter. Somewhere in the conversation she had decided to learn to bake. Excitement thrummed in her stomach at the idea. She’d tell Pamela later. An Elizabeth Hamilton pie would be a nice surprise for Nick—a small token of her appreciation for saving her life.

CHAPTER SIXTEEN

Elizabeth gingerly pulled the saskatoon pie from the oven. As she saw the golden crust, she exhaled with relief, then inhaled the fragrant aroma that filled the kitchen.

Pamela glanced over her shoulder from the dishes she was washing. "It looks wonderful."

Elizabeth glanced around to make sure Smoky wasn't in sight. The gray cat had made his presence known earlier, following the proceedings with his golden eyes, rubbing around the two women's legs, and getting tangled in their skirts. After all her hard work, Elizabeth wasn't about to trip over the cat and drop her precious creation.

She took four cautious steps from the stove to the oilcloth-covered table, then set the pie on the rack next to Pamela's. She pushed away the towel she'd used to carry it so she'd have an unobstructed view. After a moment of anxious scrutiny, she straightened in satisfaction.

Just like Pamela's.

As she caught her friend's proud smile, Elizabeth felt her face crinkle in a lighthearted grin. Rubbing the back of her wrist across her forehead, she realized she'd just added a white streak to her already flour-smudged face. She shrugged and grimaced ruefully at her friend.

"Shall we sit down and have a cup of tea?" Pamela asked.

"Yes, let's." Elizabeth smoothed the berry-and-dough-stained apron she wore over her pink calico dress. "I'm exhausted. You didn't tell me baking was such hard work."

Pamela lifted the copper teakettle from the stove. Elizabeth took down two teacups and saucers from the cabinet and set them on the table.

"It'll get easier with practice," Pamela said in a practical tone of voice.

"Practice!"

"Yes, practice. You can't fool me, Elizabeth. I know you enjoyed making that pie."

Elizabeth laughed. "You're right, I did. I never realized the satisfaction one could achieve from baking something. It reminds me of...packing mission boxes for charity. Except that was for strangers, not someone...people I care about." Warmth crept into her cheeks. *Care for Nick? Well, of course. He saved my life. I'll be forever grateful.*

Pamela didn't seem to notice Elizabeth's slip. "There's nothing like using your efforts for something you know will bring others pleasure."

Elizabeth hurried away from her feelings for Nick. "I enjoyed the experience. You're a good teacher, Pamela." She twisted her right hand to examine the pink burn on her smooth skin. "In spite of everything that went wrong." She shook her head, then collapsed onto the chair at the end of the table. "Baking's a hazardous occupation."

"Life's a hazardous occupation." Pamela poured the tea, set the teakettle back on the stove, and sat down at Elizabeth's right.

Elizabeth pushed several straggling wisps of hair away from her eyes. "You made everything look so effortless, while I was all thumbs."

"You'll have plenty more opportunities while the saskatoons are in season."

Elizabeth sipped her tea and then smiled at her friend. "You win. I admit I'm pleased with myself. Although there were some moments when I was about to give up." She gestured toward the flour-dusted sideboard.

Pamela nodded. "I could tell."

"Eggshells in the bowl. Nearly adding salt instead of sugar. Good thing you stopped me." She pushed her hair back again. "In Boston they'd never believe what I've experienced in the last few days. She shook her head. "I don't dare write them either."

They both laughed.

"You never wrote me what your life in Montana was really like."

"It's not always like this, Beth. But I didn't think you'd understand."

Elizabeth started to protest, then stopped. Pamela was right. "I wouldn't have. I'd just have worried." She reached across the table and clasped her friend's hand. "But now we can share everything." She thought of her confused feelings for Nick. *Well, perhaps not everything.*

Quick footsteps sounded on the steps. "Annie," Nick called, before peering around the partly opened outer door. "Oh. Hello, ladies." He pulled off his hat and stepped into the room. "Is that saskatoon pie I smell?"

"Yes, it is," Pamela said.

Elizabeth couldn't help it—she beamed at him.

Nick's gaze lingered on her disheveled appearance.

Heat rushed into her cheeks. Anticipation started a drumroll in her heart.

He cocked an inquiring eyebrow. A pleased smile started in one corner of his mouth and spread across his face. "It appears, Miss Hamilton," he drawled, "that you've been bakin'."

His twinkling green eyes sent a happy flush to her face.

"I made it for you, Nick. For rescuing me yesterday."

It was his turn to flush. "You baked a pie for me?"

She proudly lifted her chin. "I did."

"I'm much obliged, Elizabeth."

His slip-up of her name went unremarked by both of them.

Pamela stood up. "Why don't you join us for tea, Nick." She walked over to the cupboard to get him a cup and saucer.

"Actually, I came to see if Annie had the liniment bottle; it's missing from the barn." He glanced around the kitchen. "I don't see it around here."

Pamela frowned. "Maybe it's in John's study. I'll go look." She left the room.

"Please stay to tea, Nick," Elizabeth coaxed. "I'll slice you a piece. Pamela's pie is cool enough to eat."

Nick rocked back on his heels. "I'll take yours even if it's too hot. He walked around the table to pull out the chair opposite Elizabeth. "Can't rightly pass up an offer like that."

Elizabeth jumped up to make him a cup of tea, then served him a slice of pie.

Nick's appreciative smile sent quivers down to her toes. With great ceremony, he scooped up a forkful, blew to cool it, then took his first bite. He chewed for several long moments, his face deadpan. Then his grin burst forth. "Best pie I've ever tasted."

Elizabeth's heart swelled with pride. Footsteps tapped in the hall behind her. "He likes it, Pamela," she called without turning around.

Caleb Livingston's voice sounded behind her. "I'm afraid I'm not Mrs. Carter."

Elizabeth froze in dismay.

A thundercloud crossed Nick's face.

She whirled around. "Caleb!"

He was immaculately dressed in a tan suit, a sharp contrast to her own appearance, and carrying a bouquet of lilacs.

Embarrassment flooded her. Dropping the knife on the table, she futilely tried to smooth back her hair, then untied her apron, balled the material up, and tossed it onto her chair. "I didn't expect you."

His eyebrows rose as he surveyed the scene before him. "I thought I'd surprise you. I knocked, and Sara answered. She said I'd find you in the kitchen." His tone sounded carefully neutral. "You have flour on your face."

Elizabeth wanted to run to her room. *Composure, show composure,* she told herself. She walked to the sink, picked up the dishtowel, wet an end, and rubbed her face. Using a dry section of the towel, she blotted her face. "Better?"

Caleb nodded; he handed her the bouquet.

"Thank you, Caleb. They're beautiful." She took a fragrant sniff, then placed the flowers into a vase, filled it with water from the pump, and set it on the table.

Caleb glanced from Nick to her, with puzzlement in his eyes. "Elizabeth, what are you doing in the kitchen?"

He sounds like he caught me playing in the pigsty, Elizabeth thought resentfully. Then she reminded herself that a few weeks ago, except to give orders to the cook, she'd rarely been in a kitchen.

"Pamela taught me how to bake." She pointed to her pie. "That one's mine. We'd just finished and were having a cup of tea."

Nick stood up. "Mrs. Carter makes the best saskatoon pies around. Miss Hamilton's is just as good, if not better. If you taste it, I'm sure you'll be proud of her."

Caleb ignored Nick, directing a pointed look at Elizabeth. "Menial labor will ruin your hands."

She looked down at her hands, then curled her fingers to avoid exposing the purple berry stains around her nails, but that only made her burn evident. She twisted her hand to hide it.

Too late.

Caleb stepped forward, gently clasping her hand. His thumb brushed around her burn, careful not to touch the tender skin. "You've injured yourself. From now on you must avoid the kitchen. Leave the cooking to others."

Nick's voice was edged with steel. "You're making a mistake, Livingston. Taste that pie, man, and you'll change your mind."

"Miss Hamilton has no need to bake."

"Caleb," Elizabeth said, verbally stepping between them. "I can assure you that I'll never bake you a pie."

His face relaxed.

Pamela walked into the room holding out the bottle of liniment in front of her. "Here you go, Nick. It took me forever to find." She became aware of the banker's presence. "Why, Mr. Livingston, I didn't know you were here."

"I thought I'd surprise Miss Hamilton with a midweek visit."

Pamela's rueful gaze swept the room. "I'm afraid you haven't caught us at our best."

He lifted an eyebrow. "I'm aware of that. Perhaps I'd better leave."

Elizabeth gave him a coaxing smile. "Caleb, don't be silly. I'm delighted you've come to visit me." *I just wish I'd known in advance.* "Why don't you wait in the parlor while I freshen up."

Nick held out his hand to Pamela for the liniment bottle. "I'd better head back to the barn." His tone sounded clipped. He replaced his hat. "Thank you for the pie, Miss Hamilton." His green gaze met hers in support and understanding. "It was delicious. I'd like another piece—later."

"Thank you, Nick." Elizabeth gave him a strained smile before turning to Pamela. "Could you send Dawn up to help me change?" She touched Caleb's arm. "I'll be down in a few minutes."

His face softened. He took her hand, his finger brushing her palm. As always, she melted at his special signal. He lifted it to brush his lips next to the burn. "I hate to see this beautiful skin marred in any way."

Still embarrassed by his scrutiny of her hand, she slipped her fingers out of his grasp. "The burn will heal in a few days. Now, if you'll excuse me, I'll go tidy up." She paused to pick up the vase of lilacs. "I'll take these to my room." She hurried from the kitchen.

Lifting her skirts, she rushed upstairs to her room. Her stomach churned, and her mind raced with the changes she needed to make. She set the vase on her dressing table, and yanked hairpins from her hair, wincing when she pulled some strands in the process.

Dawn opened the door and came to her rescue, pressing Elizabeth into the chair before the dressing table and efficiently extracting the rest of the hairpins. With a few swift strokes, the shining blonde tresses lay smooth on Elizabeth's shoulders.

The Indian girl's calm penetrated through to Elizabeth, and she took some deep breaths. *Relax*, she told herself. It shouldn't matter that Caleb had found her at a disadvantage. After all, he'd still given her their special signal. That must mean everything's all right.

Actually, there'd been times with Richard when she'd been in an equally bedraggled state. Once they were caught in a sudden rainstorm without an umbrella. Her new red hat had drooped, leaking dye in rosy streaks across her face. Trying to wipe them away had resulted in red marks on her gloves. Richard had just laughed and kissed her. For days afterward, he'd called her his rosy-cheeked maiden.

Then there were all those times when he'd found her painting at the shore, wearing an old dress liberally dabbed with various colors and her hair tossed by the breeze. Richard always loved those moments. They certainly provided him with fodder with which to tease her.

But Caleb didn't seem to have Richard's sense of humor. Or maybe he needed to be better acquainted with her before he'd relax and allow that facet of himself to show.

Would Richard have cared if she'd baked a pie? He would have laughed and joked about it, but he probably wouldn't have approved her continuing to spend time in the kitchen. After all, that's what cooks were for. At least for the wealthy in Boston.

She reached out to touch a lavender petal. Richard had often brought her lilacs in the springtime. Their sweet scent always made her happy.

Elizabeth smiled at her memories and let go of the last of her worries. Surely Caleb would be the same. Perhaps not today, but sometime soon, they'd laugh about the day he paid her an unexpected visit and found her with a flour-smudged face and berry-stained hands.

* * *

Like a locomotive at full speed, Nick barreled straight for his rock. Angry thoughts roiled in his head. His heart beat to the pounding of his stride, and he could almost feel steam blasting out his ears. Dropping the liniment bottle on the nearest clump of grass lest he throw it at the rock, Nick envisioned shattering it over Livingston's head. Better yet, a punch in the nose to wipe that haughty look off the banker's face. A broken nose could only improve the man's countenance.

Vaulting the pasture fence, he didn't even acknowledge the horses that shied away from his agitated movement. He scrambled up the rock, then sat panting, trying to rein in his outrage. How dare the man treat Elizabeth that way! Nick didn't care what Livingston said to *him*. He was riled up that the man would imply to Elizabeth, who was a lady no matter what menial tasks she did, that baking was beneath her. Good thing Livingston didn't know about her shooting, her berry picking, or the bear attack.

If Livingston won her, he'd keep Elizabeth in a cage like a gilded bird and never let her blossom into the vibrant person she really was. Nick shook his head in disbelief. How could that man want to clip her wings? Elizabeth had glowed with pride at her achievement. Her blue eyes had sparkled with pleasure. Beneath the dusting of flour, her cheeks had been pink. For the first time she'd been totally relaxed with him. Despite her disheveled appearance, Nick had never seen her look happier, nor more beautiful.

Then, with Livingston's arrival, her body had stiffened, the glow fading from her eyes. A few words of praise from that man would have brought the light back to her face. Instead he'd squelched her spirit. And even worse, Elizabeth had accepted his criticisms.

Nick's anger drained away, only to have frustration take its place. He leaned his head back against the rock. The brilliant blue sky arched overhead, a few small puffy clouds floating into different shapes. He tried to slow his breathing to match the languid movement of the clouds, a calming trick he'd learned when he was younger.

Underneath the frustration, helplessness churned. Even when he'd been enraged with the men who'd abused Outlaw, he'd been able to do something. But Elizabeth was a person, not a horse. She controlled her own destiny, and he was powerless to stop her, even if he knew she teetered on the edge of making a mistake.

Breathe with the cloud, he reminded himself. Charging around like an angry bull would only make things worse. There had to be something he could do; he needed to think things through. He wished Miz Carter heard what Livingston had said to Elizabeth. Knowing Miz Carter, she'd have given the man what for.

With a sigh of relief, Nick realized the time would come when Livingston would again reveal his feelings about inappropriate female behavior. Then Nick would put his foot down about Livingston's attitude. Hopefully Elizabeth would listen to him. Even better, Nick hoped the man would reveal himself in front of the Carters. *That* would set off fireworks.

Nick grinned. He could imagine how John would react to Livingston's implications about his beloved wife. He grinned at the thought. Regardless of future financial consequences, the banker would be ordered off the ranch at gunpoint. And Nick would be right at John's side, Colt in hand.

Meanwhile, the next time he saw Elizabeth he'd renew his praise and admiration, and not just for her baking, but for every other new thing she tried.

Before she chose to step into Livingston's gilded cage, he wanted her first to experience flying free.

CHAPTER SEVENTEEN

A tap at the door woke Elizabeth. She rose on an elbow to glance out the window. Early morning sun streamed through the curtains, deliberately left open to give her an awareness of the weather. She relaxed back against the pillows in relief. A beautiful day. "Come in," she called.

Dawn entered, carrying a silver tray with tea and toast. The normally solemn-faced girl's eyes sparkled, and pink brightened her tanned cheeks.

"Mornin', Miss Hamilton."

Elizabeth raised her eyebrows in surprise. Usually Dawn went about her duties without a word. This was the first time she'd ever given Elizabeth a morning salutation.

Elizabeth sat up. "Good morning, Dawn. Is Miss Lizzy up?"

"Hoppin' around like a grasshopper." Dawn handed Elizabeth the tray.

Elizabeth smiled and took a sip of the tea. Little grasshopper, indeed. Well, every girl had a right to be excited on her birthday.

"Just set out my blue calico dress and my straw hat. I've too much work to do. Later I'll wear the rose silk. It'll need pressing."

She took a bite of her toast and chewed, reviewing her list of tasks for the day. Pamela planned on overseeing the food and setup for the party, while Elizabeth needed to arrange the flower decorations and make sure the children looked their best. "You'll have your hands full keeping those children clean and neat."

Dawn rolled her eyes and nodded.

"I don't know how well Sara's hair will stay curled. You'd better keep her curl papers in until just before the party." She took another sip. "Thank goodness Lizzy's hair curls naturally."

Elizabeth slid out of bed and set the tray on her dressing table. She slipped her nightgown over her head and motioned for Dawn to help her dress. In between donning her undergarments and her dress, she finished her toast.

With a few strokes, Dawn drew the brush through her hair and twisted it into a simple bun. Elizabeth dropped a faded blue gardening apron of Pamela's over her dress, tying it behind her back. She grabbed her hat off the bed, hurried down the stairs, and found Pamela and the children in the dining room.

"You must take a few bites of toast, Lizzy," Pamela said with exasperation.

Elizabeth grinned. She could remember Pamela's mother using that exact tone of voice.

"Good morning." The words came out in a warble. "How's the birthday girl?"

Lizzy's beatific smile answered her.

"Morning, Aunt Elizabeth," chorused the children.

She set her hat on an empty chair and walked over to place a hand on each of Lizzy's cheeks. She briefly studied the delicate little face. Blue eyes bright, translucent skin tinged peach with pleasure. "Happy birthday, my dearest goddaughter." She dropped a kiss on the child's forehead, then flashed a triumphant glance at Pamela. "Four years old!"

Her friend's eyes echoed Elizabeth's emotion, but her words sounded tart. "A four-year-old who won't eat her breakfast."

"I remember another little girl who couldn't eat when she became too excited."

"Beth," Pamela warned.

"I think your daughter comes by it naturally."

Mark grinned. "Was Mama really like that, Aunt Elizabeth?"

The corners of Pamela's lips twitched with a smile, and she shook her head.

Elizabeth tilted her head and tapped her finger alongside her mouth. "Let's just say that your mama sounds an awful lot like her mama this morning." She leaned over and hugged her friend, and they both laughed.

Lifting her hat from the chair, she placed it securely on her head and tied the blue ribbons under her chin. "I'm off to gather flowers."

❋ ❋ ❋

In the garden, Elizabeth snipped the long stems of larkspur and laid each stalk in the basket, carried in the crook of her arm. Pamela always grew a large selection of larkspurs in colors varying from pale lavender to blue to purple, just for Lizzy's birthday.

How lucky Lizzy was to have such beautiful blooms for her July birthday. Elizabeth's January birthday flower was the snowdrop. It had always been difficult to gather enough of the tiny white blossoms to make the wreaths and decorations so important to a child's celebration.

Pamela and Elizabeth had spent days preparing, determined to celebrate this special birthday with all the hoopla a child's celebration in Boston received. Even the children had helped. Mark and Sara had addressed the birthday invitations given to all the children in town and at nearby ranches and homesteads.

Nick would soon take the carriage to gather some of the children. The Camerons would bring more, and the rest would ride over.

She stooped to smell one of her favorite pink roses and inhaled its spicy-sweet scent. A smile played at her mouth. Last Sunday, Caleb had brought her a bouquet of these pink beauties. One of those roses still hung upside down in her room, a flower she'd plucked from the bouquet and dried to preserve as a special memory.

They'd invited Caleb to the party. He'd ordered a special doll from Boston for Lizzy, with brown curls and blue eyes. Elizabeth had commissioned a larkspur-blue silk dress from her dressmaker for her goddaughter and also had the woman make a doll's dress in the same material. Caleb's doll, dressed in birthday blue, lay swathed in tissue paper and ruby ribbons on the bottom of Elizabeth's armoire.

She gave the rose another dreamy sniff. The doll was an extravagant gift for a non-family member to give a child—rather a message to Elizabeth that sometime soon he expected to become one of the family. Her body tingled at the thought. She hummed a dance tune, swaying as she strolled among the flower beds.

Carefully stuffing the last of the larkspur stalks into her overflowing basket, Elizabeth paused by the edge of the kitchen garden. In her first weeks at the ranch, she'd assisted Pamela and the children in planting the vegetables. Now she felt a proprietary interest in their progress. She'd enjoyed watching the tiny shoots push through the rich earth and ripen into plants. The produce she'd grown herself surpassed anything she'd eaten from the greengrocers in Boston.

The plants in the section of the garden assigned to little Lizzy straggled in uneven, crooked rows. The child loved her garden. Elizabeth often watched her happily playing in the dirt and pulling up shoots to discover what was happening "underearth." It amazed Elizabeth that given Lizzy's ministrations, anything still managed to grow.

She stooped to straighten a green stem listing to the right, tucking the dirt firmly around the plant's roots. She brushed her fingers against her apron, uncaring of the earthen stain they left behind.

Straightening, she lifted her face to the sun. Like the plants, Elizabeth knew she had blossomed this spring, bursting forth like a flower from the hard, brown bulb she'd grown around herself. Day by day, her soul rooted into the Montana soil. From hothouse flower to western wildflower...Well, she didn't think she'd actually ever become a wildflower. She touched a pink rose petal. Perhaps a western rose.

Glancing at the sun, Elizabeth retraced her steps. She still had the flowers to arrange and wreaths to make. She wanted to have plenty of time left to bathe and dress. After all, even though it was Lizzy's birthday, Caleb would be here, and Elizabeth wanted to look her best.

* * *

Pamela set the cardboard crown covered with blossoms plucked from the larkspur stalks on Lizzy's dark curls. The children circling around them on the porch burst out clapping.

Pamela stepped back, proudly eyed her youngest daughter, then glanced around at the other guests. Each wore a paper cap and a larkspur boutonniere. "Now," Pamela said, "everyone line up in rows of four and follow Lizzy down to the river." She motioned to Mark. "You and Sara go in the first row."

Elizabeth helped Pamela shepherd the children into the proper order. Then, while Nick played a merry march on his violin, Lizzy started out, hand-in-hand with her mother and father, to lead her birthday procession down to the river. As the children passed, the adults fell in line behind them.

Elizabeth, escorted by Caleb, a folded fan dangling from her wrist, held up the hem of her rose-colored silk dress so it wouldn't trail in the dirt.

Caleb smiled down at her. "I remember having parties like this with my cousins, but we didn't march in such orderly rows. There usually was quite a bit of scuffling and a jabbed elbow or two."

Elizabeth shook her head in mock disapproval. "Boys! Pamela's brothers and Laurence did the same thing at parties." She smiled at the flower-crowned little figure, clad in her new blue silk dress, marching at the head of her parade. "Something about Lizzy makes everyone more gentle around her." She pointed with her chin. "Look, even the boys are behaving."

"You're right." His eyebrows lifted. "She's a special child." He glanced down and laid his other hand over hers. "I have become quite attached to her."

"Yes, I know. She's going to love the doll you bought." Elizabeth exhaled a blissful breath. She'd never felt happier. The pinpricks of worry over Lizzy's health had vanished, and she enjoyed the attention of handsome Caleb Livingston.

And, like her Richard, who'd adored children, Caleb loved her goddaughter. He'd make a good father. She restrained herself from taking waltz steps. A few months ago she'd been miserable. How things had changed. Life in Montana was wonderful!

"I do believe Lizzy's Aunt Elizabeth loves that doll too." Caleb, his brown eyes warm with laughter, smiled down at her.

She gave an extravagant sigh. "Yes, I wish I'd known you when I was a little girl. I'd have adored a doll like that."

"Actually, you probably wouldn't have liked me. I'd have teased you just as much as your brother did. And I certainly wouldn't have given you a doll. Or if I did, I'd probably have chopped its head off first."

Stopping midstep, she looked up at him, half in laughter, half in exasperation. "You boys! Once, when I was younger than Lizzy, Laurence pulled all the arms and legs off my favorite doll, Gretchen." She resumed their walk.

Brandishing his arm like a sword, Caleb said, "I'll make sure to zealously guard Lizzy's doll from all masculine marauders—at least for today."

She squeezed his arm. "Then she's sure to be safe."

By this time they'd arrived at the river. There, on the rug taken from the dining room, stood a long trestle table covered with a white cloth and decorated with larkspurs. Wooden benches flanked each side. White linen sheets pinned with blue ribbons hung from the trees, and blue draperies covered the shrubs encircling the area, creating an enchanted outdoor bower.

After breakfast, John and Nick had sweated over moving the heavy dining room table and chairs in order to slide out the rug. They'd grumbled and teased the two women about "Boston" notions of a child's birthday party. But both Elizabeth and Pamela had been adamant—even though the party took place by the water, where it would be cooler, the area still needed to look like a "room."

On the table, the white-frosted birthday cake, with Lizzy's name in blue icing and four white candles in the middle, held the place of honor. A few minutes earlier, Annie had carried down dainty sandwiches cut in triangles, tiny biscuits, individual molds of jelly, and small spice cakes with the name of each guest written on them in icing. Bonbons arranged in tiny wicker baskets nestled at each place.

Even though Pamela had fretted that a party without ice cream would be like breakfast without bread, they'd had to give up on the notion of a fancy molded ice cream bombe; it would have melted long before the dessert reached the table. But John had assured her that with all the other goodies, the children would never know the difference.

With much oohing and ahing, the young guests found their places. The adults sat clustered together at one end of the table, Caleb next to Elizabeth and the Camerons on the other side of the Carters. Nick stood, playing tunes on his violin.

Amid the children's giggles, everyone quickly consumed the food. Pamela brought out Lizzy's cake, complete with lit candles. The child hesitated, puffed her cheeks with air, then blew out all four. Everyone clapped.

John reached over and hugged his wife, his face beaming with pride. Elizabeth exchanged glances with Pamela, and saw the same relief in her friend's eyes. They could stop worrying. Unlike Mary, Lizzy had survived to her fourth birthday.

After the meal, Lizzy unwrapped her presents, inspecting each with bright-eyed, silent wonder. It was Pamela who, on Lizzy's behalf, thanked each guest for the gift they'd given. When she opened Caleb's gift, Lizzy's eyes grew big. She clasped the doll to her chest, rocking her new baby back and forth. The adults laughed.

"See," Elizabeth murmured to Caleb. "I told you."

John clapped Caleb on the shoulder. "That doll takes first prize, Livingston. Her mother and I are sure obliged to you."

Pamela nodded in agreement. "We appreciate such a generous gift, Mr. Livingston. And since that doll's dress matches Lizzy's birthday dress, you and Elizabeth must have been in cahoots."

Caleb sent Elizabeth a conspirator's smile.

Elizabeth laughed. "Perhaps."

Only one wrapped parcel remained, but Lizzy, involved with her doll, ignored the other children's urging her to open it. The restless children got up from the table to play, and the adults wandered after them. The men gathered to talk business, while Mrs. Cameron oversaw the children in a game.

Seeing Caleb engrossed in conversation, Elizabeth drifted over to Nick, who'd continued playing throughout the party. When he concluded the song she said, "It's so nice of you to play for us, Nick."

Over the violin, his green eyes met hers. "It's a special day. I'm not sure who's enjoying herself more, Lizzy or her mama."

They exchanged a smile of understanding. Elizabeth's heartbeat quickened, and heat stole into her cheeks. Sliding her fan into her hand, she snapped it open and waved it back and forth.

"Look at Lizzy," Nick said. "She's finally ready to open my gift." He set his violin on the bench.

Lizzy laid her doll down on the table and picked up the last present. Unwrapping the paper, she pulled out a carved wooden horse.

"My pony!" She held it out to her mother. "Look, Mama."

Pamela looked at Nick. "I'll bet Nick carved that for you."

Lizzy looked in inquiry at Nick, who nodded back at her. She jumped up, ran over, and hugged his legs. "Thank you, Nick."

She looked up at him with a sunny smile. "My pony is my bestest present."

Nick laughed, swung Lizzy up in his arms, and gave her a squeeze. She squealed and clung to him. He whirled around, eliciting a gleeful giggle.

Elizabeth watched their interaction with pleasure, and her heart turned over. How she'd loved it when her father had picked her up in that same way when she was a child.

Out of the corner of her eye she saw Mark's friend, George, sneak up to the table and snatch the doll. "Oh, no. Nick." She pointed. "George has taken Lizzy's doll."

Flourishing his prize overhead, George ran over to the group of boys tossing stones in the river.

Her mouth rounded with distress, Lizzy stretched out her hand. Nick handed the child over to Elizabeth. "Don't worry, little bird. I'll save your baby."

As George dangled the doll over the water, Lizzy wailed and clung tightly to Elizabeth.

"Everything will be just fine," Elizabeth assured Lizzy. "Nick won't let your baby go for a swim."

Nick grabbed George by the shoulder, then forced his arm away from the water. Much to Elizabeth's surprise, he didn't immediately take possession of the doll. Instead, he stood in front of George, holding both the boy's shoulders, and quietly spoke with him.

George hung his head and scuffed a booted foot in the grass, then looked up and answered.

Nick smiled and, dropping a casual arm around George's shoulder, guided him over to Elizabeth and Lizzy. The boy held out the doll.

Lizzy reached both hands out, embraced her baby, then protectively cuddled it between her body and Elizabeth's.

Nick gave George a prompting push forward. "I'm sorry, Lizzy," the boy apologized. "I didn't mean to scare you."

With a small smile and slight nod, Lizzy indicated her forgiveness.

Turning George around, Nick indicated the other boys. "Go play," he ordered. "And stay out of trouble." George ran and joined the other children. "See, darlin'," Nick said to Lizzy, "everything's fine with your baby."

Lizzy held an arm out to Nick, and Elizabeth transferred her over. Nick stroked the child's hair, and she laid her head on his shoulder.

What a tender picture they make. With a feeling of wistfulness, she glanced over at Caleb, and some of the bliss seeped from her day. Engrossed in his conversation with John and Dr. Cameron, he'd never even noticed the doll had been in peril.

So much for the defender against masculine marauders!

CHAPTER EIGHTEEN

For the second straight week, the August sun's rays scorched the valley. Not a single cloud drifted across the intense turquoise sky.

John engaged Nick in worried conversations about grazing and fodder for the winter. In the early morning, Pamela, Elizabeth, and the children carried pails of water to the garden to nourish the wilting plants.

During the midday heat, the women and children languished on the porch. Even Mark and Sara played quietly in the shade, while Lizzy drooped like a withered violet.

Elizabeth tossed the shirt she'd been mending into a wicker basket overflowing with clothes. "That's the last one, thank goodness." She leaned back in her rocking chair, picked up her fan, and made a futile effort to cool herself.

Pamela looked up from her embroidery. "Thank you, Elizabeth. It's the first time since the winter that we're caught up with all the mending."

"Glad to help." She wafted the fan harder.

Pamela set another careful stitch into a purple pansy. "Knowing your dislike of sewing, I'd have thought mending might bore you."

"It does. I don't know how you can calmly sit there and embroider for hours."

Her friend gave her a serene smile. "Why don't you try it?"

"Pamela, you know I'm not good at embroidery."

"Of course I know that. Remember who secretly finished your sampler for you?"

Elizabeth scrunched a face at her.

"Then there was that other piece of embroidery, which you'd take out and pretend to work on whenever you were supposed to be showing off your ladylike accomplishments."

"That horrible thing. I hated it."

"Did you ever finish it after I left?"

"I finally threw it away." She gave a rueful laugh. "That's the nice thing about being an adult. No one makes me embroider."

"Just don't tell Sara," Pamela said with a slight toss of her head toward the end of the porch, where Mark and Sara played a game of checkers. "It's difficult enough to get her to work on her sampler."

Elizabeth glanced at Sara, the rag doll cuddled on her lap. "Have her make a new dress for Catherine."

"Maybe that will work," Pamela said. "Clinging to that doll is about the only feminine behavior she exhibits."

"Well, I'm sure Lizzy will take after her mama."

Both women looked over at the child asleep on a cushion. Sweat-dampened tendrils curled around a face flushed with heat. Even in slumber she clutched her wooden pony.

"I'm going to start teaching her next winter."

"Winter. It's hard to believe we'll be surrounded by snow."

"Believe it," Pamela said with a tired sigh. "We'll be so cold that we'll reminisce about this unusual heat wave. I wish you had a better introduction to our regular summer weather." She scanned the brilliant sky, looking for any sign of a cloud. "I hope it breaks soon. John's afraid we'll have a drought."

"Here comes your husband now."

As John approached, dust puffed up with each step he took, powdering his tan pants a darker brown. Reaching the shelter of the porch, he paused to pull a blue bandana from his pocket, and wiped his face. "We've finally gotten all the cattle into the north pasture. With the increased shade and water there, they should be all right."

Lizzy had awakened at the sound of his voice. "Papa," she murmured, stretching a hand to him.

John sat down in the chair next to Lizzy, leaned over and brushed the damp hair off her face. "Would my little bird like to turn into a little fish?"

Lizzy gave him a puzzled look. He glanced over at his wife. "How about taking a picnic down to the swimming hole?"

"What a marvelous idea." Pamela straightened in her chair. "I've been wanting to, but I knew you and Nick were too busy."

"I've sent Nick to get his bathing things." He lifted an eyebrow. "What do you think, Elizabeth?"

"Just putting my feet in the water sounds heavenly."

John raised his voice. "Mark, Sara, shall we go for a swim?"

Both children scrambled up and hurried over.

"Now? Can we go now?" Mark asked, his expression pleading.

John laughed and ruffled his hair. "Soon as you're ready."

Both children charged off into the house.

Pamela folded her embroidery, placed it in the sewing basket, then stood up. "I'll go tell Annie to pack a picnic basket. Elizabeth, why don't you help me gather up some towels and blankets to sit on?" She stepped over and placed a loving hand on her husband's cheek. "We'll be ready in a few minutes."

* * *

At the sight of the swift green water bubbling over mossy rocks, Elizabeth sighed with relief. During the long, hot walk, she had to force her tired feet to keep to the pace of the others. She shifted the bundle of blankets she held in her arms and tried to restrain her eagerness. The days since she'd come to Montana had flown by, and she'd not been back to the water as she'd promised herself the day she and Nick had ridden by the river.

Elizabeth glanced over at Nick, striding along with Lizzy on his shoulders. Once in the shade, the child had perked up enough to giggle as she bounced along on her moving perch.

Nick caught Elizabeth's glance and winked.

She blushed and looked ahead at John and Pamela strolling arm in arm. John carried a hefty wicker picnic basket. Pamela had several folded towels tucked under her other arm.

Sara and Mark ran ahead, each eager to be the first to reach the pool.

Pamela shook her head at them. "Such energy in this heat." She raised her voice. "Just don't go in the water until we get there."

The children were out of sight when the adults reached the pool, but giggles coming from two separate clumps of bushes betrayed their whereabouts.

Nick waved his hand at the nearest bushes. "Behold the ladies' dressing room."

Elizabeth raised an eyebrow toward the other cluster. "Then that must be the gentlemen's dressing room."

"Precisely, my dear lady," Nick uttered in dramatic tones, his green eyes teasing her. "Or perhaps I should say the gentlemen's *un*dressing room."

"Nick!" Elizabeth tried to sound disapproving, but ended up laughing.

He threw her another wink, then lifted Lizzy off his shoulders and patted her in the direction of the ladies' dressing room. "Get your sister to help you."

He took the blankets from Elizabeth, then dropped the gray Indian-striped one in a heap on the grass. "Come help me with this." He jiggled the navy-blue bundle.

She took an end, and together they spread out the blanket. John set down the basket on the corner. "Ready, Nick?"

"Just let me lay this one on the ladies' log." He picked up the Indian blanket, folded it, and smoothed it over a fallen tree trunk that had been moved next to the pool. "There, ladies, you'll be able to cool your feet in comfort." He touched his hat, and vanished into the male "dressing room."

Elizabeth placed her hands on her cheeks. "Pamela, I can't believe we're doing this."

Her friend laughed sat down on the blanket, and patted the spot next to her. "Come on."

Still holding her cheeks, Elizabeth walked over and sat down.

"Off with your shoes and stockings, Elizabeth." Pamela started to undo her shoes. "Just think how cool that water will be."

As she complied with Pamela's edict, Elizabeth wrinkled her brow in thought. She couldn't remember ever going barefoot outdoors. "Pamela, before you lived in Montana, did you ever go outside with bare feet?"

"Of course not." She stood up, reached out a hand for Elizabeth, and pulled her to her feet. "Just wait until you try it. The grass tickles, but watch for any sharp stones or sticks."

Bunching her skirts above her ankles, Elizabeth gingerly extended the toes of her right foot and stepped onto the grass. It felt cool and springy. She could feel individual blades tickling her sole. She took another bouncing step and looked up to see Nick grinning at her.

Gasping, Elizabeth released her skirts to decently cover her ankles, but there was nothing decent about Nick. At a glimpse of his naked chest, pink crept into her cheeks, and her body flushed warmer than the air around her. She glanced down at her toes, but then couldn't resist another look. The sight of the curly brown hair covering his well-muscled chest sent a shiver through her as if she were feverish. *I never knew males had chests like that.*

John emerged from the dressing room, followed by Mark. John had reddish hair covering his chest, which matched the sandy hair on his head. Pamela should have warned her. No wonder men were often compared to animals. *I don't want to even think about where else they might have hair.*

As Nick had told her on that long-ago ride, they all wore trousers with the legs cut off, giving her a view of Nick's muscular calves.

Mark stepped from behind his father and raced toward the pool, his pale arms flailing. "Last one in is a rotten egg." He splashed into the water until he was waist deep. "Come on!" He waved at his father, then dunked under and came up sputtering. Shaking the water out of his face, he grinned at them. "The water's great."

Nick's eyes danced emerald with mischief. "You can't stand there all day, Miss Hamilton. You're going to have to display those lovely ankles sooner or later." He held out a hand to her. "Shall I escort you to the water?"

Pamela had already settled herself on the log and was dangling her feet in the pool. Elizabeth's blush deepened as she tried and failed to think of a rejoinder and instead placed her hand in his. Sliding her gaze away from his bare chest, she focused her eyes on the water.

She didn't notice the ground underneath her feet until she stepped on a sharp stone. Wincing, she picked up her foot and balanced on the other.

"Shall I carry you?" Nick's words were serious, but a grin played about his mouth.

She flashed him a flirtatious look. "It's just a few more paces. I'm sure I can manage." She'd walk, even if her feet were on fire. Being carried against that chest would cause more than her feet to burn.

Elizabeth sat down next to Pamela and carefully gathered her blue calico skirt to expose as little skin as possible. She pointed a toe into the water. Cold, but refreshing. She allowed both feet down. Her cheeks remained hot, and, if she'd been alone, she'd have knelt down and splashed water on her face.

The girls, wearing their white cotton shifts, joined them. Sara plunged into the pool and paddled over to the men, clambering onto her father's back. Lizzy hovered near her mother, dabbling her toes in the water.

Elizabeth pulled her handkerchief from her sleeve. "Lizzy, dear, will you dunk this in the water for me?" She held out the handkerchief to the child.

Lizzy stooped and spread the material over the surface of the water. Watching the handkerchief float, she poked it under. In playing with the handkerchief, she relaxed, taking a few steps into deeper water. When the material seemed to be wet enough for her, she scooped it into a ball and handed it to Elizabeth.

"Thank you, dear." Elizabeth wiped her face and neck. The cool water soothed her parched skin, but failed to dampen the blushes caused by Nick's half-naked body.

John stood in the center of the pool, the water to his chest, talking to Nick. In shallower water, Mark and Sara splashed one another. Elizabeth's gaze strayed to Nick, who'd slipped behind Lizzy. Grasping the child under her arms, he swung her back and forth. Lizzy's toes skimmed the water, and her giggles punctuated the air.

In fascination, Elizabeth watched his muscles flex as he played with Lizzy. The warmth in her cheeks heated, and she took refuge behind her handkerchief. Watching Nick warmed her inside far more than the Montana sunshine. With difficulty she glanced away from him.

"This is marvelous, Pamela. Why didn't we do it days ago?"

"I never think to do it without the men. They're the ones who go into the water with the children."

"We could still bring the children ourselves. Mark and Sara swim well, and if something happened, the water's not so deep that we couldn't go in ourselves if we had to rescue them."

"We'll have to try it."

"Then we wouldn't mind the heat." Elizabeth became more animated. "I could paint, and you could embroider while the children played in the water."

"It certainly would be cooler," Pamela agreed.

It would be cooler without a certain almost-naked male body frolicking in the water. Although she wasn't sure she'd ever visit this pool and not remember Nick.

* * *

The next day, Elizabeth stood at the table in the quiet kitchen arranging the flowers she'd just picked in a crystal vase. She chose a rosebud, inhaled the sweet fragrance, then tucked the stem into the edge of the vibrant grouping.

The sound of footsteps caused her to look up and see Nick walk through the outer door. He doffed his hat.

"Mighty beautiful, Elizabeth."

Warmth crept into Elizabeth's cheeks. "Thank you, Nick. I'm trying to enjoy the garden before the heat kills off all the flowers."

"Just let me know if you need help watering. I know that's a tiring task for you and Miz Carter."

"The children are a big help. Even Lizzy carts her tiny pail to splash drops on her plants."

He smiled at the thought, then held out a letter. "Something from Boston."

Elizabeth glanced at the address and saw her brother's scrawled handwriting. *How odd.* He hadn't written her since she'd arrived here, instead sending messages through Genia. She tore the envelope open and began to read.

Dear Elizabeth,

Eugenia has been having difficulties with carrying the baby. In the morning, she feels quite ill and is also suffering strain to her delicate nerves. Doctor Sherman was here today and ordered complete bed rest for her until the baby is born.

I cannot withhold from you, my dear sister, my uneasiness of mind about her health. I don't know what I'd do if I lost my beloved wife. I implore you, please return home to be with us during this perilous time. With you by Genia's side to comfort and succor her, I know she will safely weather these next few months until she can deliver our child.

Laurence

P.S. Don't mention any of this to Genia. I'd like your return to be a pleasant surprise for her.

Go back to Boston? Oh, no. Thinking furiously, Elizabeth pulled out a chair and sat down.

Nick's voice penetrated her thoughts. "Bad news?"

"You know Genia's expecting?"

He nodded.

"She's having trouble with…The doctor's ordered her to remain in bed. My brother writes"—she briefly glanced down at the paper—"in a florid style quite unlike him…begging me to return home to take care of her. He seems to think my being there would help."

Nick looked stricken. "You'd leave?"

Blindly she reached out and straightened one of the roses in the vase. "I'm sure it's my sisterly duty. It's only until Christmas."

"But is it what you want?"

No, no, no.

"It's not about what I want. There's the responsibility I have to the baby." She tried to smile. "I do want my niece or nephew to arrive safely in the world. If I wasn't there and something happened, I'd never forgive myself."

"I know about living with that kind of guilt."

Elizabeth looked closer at him and saw old sorrow in his eyes. She opened her mouth to ask.

Seeming to anticipate her, he rushed on, "You don't have to stay away. You can return here after the baby's born. 'Course, that's midwinter. You might want to wait till spring."

She rolled the stem of a rose between her fingers, trying to sort through her reluctance.

"I don't know what to do, Nick. I'll have to spend the next few days thinking about it."

Because I can't bear to leave.

❋ ❋ ❋

As he left the kitchen, Nick swallowed down the dryness in his throat. He hurried into the music room, grabbed up his violin, and left the house. Although he'd planned to work with Outlaw, the horse could wait.

Outside, he climbed the pasture fence, careful not to knock his violin on the wooden rail. He headed toward his thinking rock; the dry grass crunched under his feet. The horses clustered in the shade of the trees, so nothing impeded his straight line to the rock.

He needed to do a quick rehearsal before he could let Elizabeth know of his feelings. Yet lately he'd been too busy to actually play much. The lack of practice might cost him dearly. When he played his composition for her, he would need the best performance of his life.

Nick settled on his rock, tucking the violin under his chin. While he tuned the instrument, he took the time to go through the music in his mind. Then he sat and played, stopping and starting, running through sections over and over, dissatisfied with the results.

Finally, he gave up in frustration. It was too hot to remain on the rock, so he slid off, then strayed over to the horse trough under the trees. Once in the shade, he set the violin on the grass and pumped out clean water. Cupping his hands, he scooped some up, wet his face, and took a long drink.

Cooler, he lay on his back, trying to figure out what was wrong—besides Elizabeth's probable departure. He took a deep breath, inhaling the scent of grass and horses, to ease the tightness in his chest. His thoughts wormed into the knot in his stomach, attempting to untangle the heavy mass. But it took another series of breaths before he recognized the fear and pain constricting his innards.

He'd lived with these emotions for a long time after his family had died. Later he had dared to care for the Carters, but it wasn't the same as his feelings for Elizabeth.

He'd chosen to open his heart to her, knowing he had only a slight chance of her coming to see him as husband material. But recently he'd been gaining ground on Livingston. He'd become hopeful that with time…But now he wouldn't have that time.

What if she leaves and never returns?

Then he'd always be alone, because he could never love another woman like he did Elizabeth.

CHAPTER NINETEEN

With a sigh of irritation, Elizabeth kicked the sheet off her warm body. She raised herself up on an elbow and turned her pillow over, hoping to find a cooler spot, but it was no use. The moonlight streaming through the open window could just as easily have been the bright rays of the sun. With little fanning motions, she pulled her cotton nightgown away from her chest.

Having to make a decision to return to Boston wasn't helping her repose. Her thoughts had tumbled around in her head, and her body had tossed and turned for hours.

Think of snow. Snowflakes drifting down to trace lacy patterns on her hand. Pristine snowdrifts, perfect for lying back and making angels. Icy wind reddening her face and numbing her hands and toes. What she wouldn't give to hold a snowball and run it over her cheeks, down her neck, and between her breasts, feeling the ice melt into dribbles tickling as they ran down her stomach and sides.

Her feverish body refused to respond to her cool coaxing. She'd been hot for days. Would this heat wave ever break? Elizabeth thought back to the afternoon spent at the pool—how she'd longed to cast aside ladylike behavior and join the men and children in the water. But instead she'd had to content herself with wetting her feet.

If only I could be there now. With a dreamy smile, Elizabeth imagined herself at the pool, wading into the water, her nightgown floating around her. Perhaps Nick…

She sat up abruptly. She wouldn't let herself think improper thoughts about Nick! Although she had to admit, the recollection of his bare chest made that resolution difficult. She waved her hand in front of her face. Such memories made her even hotter. Shaking her head, she slid out of bed and stepped to the window in hopes of a breeze.

Below her the moon's glow bleached the familiar view into silvery shadows. Elizabeth strained for the slightest flow of air, but felt none. With another sigh of frustration, she plopped down on her bed, her thoughts straying back to the river. How refreshing to dangle her toes in the water. As if wading into an imaginary stream, she pointed her foot at the floor.

Well, why not?

Elizabeth stood. She could go to the pool and take the dogs for protection. It was certainly light enough for her to see the way. She wouldn't even have to get dressed. Everyone else was asleep.

Before she could change her mind about her impulsive decision, Elizabeth pulled her necklace over her head, set the locket on the dressing table, slid her feet into slippers, and crept out of the room. Moving through the still house, she let herself out the kitchen door.

Shep and Sally rose to their feet. As they rushed to greet her, their nails clicked on the wooden porch. Moist noses pressed into her hands, followed by soft licks. As the dogs became excited at having a late-night playmate, they pressed forward, their tails thumping against her legs.

"Shush, Shush," Elizabeth whispered, in case their exuberance led them to bark. She stepped off the porch, then turned and patted her leg. With a few short bounds the dogs joined her.

As she strode into the gray darkness, the familiar surroundings took on an eerie air. She shivered, almost deciding to return to bed. But the sticky skin beneath her nightgown goaded her toward the river.

In the solitude of her walk, the voices of the night took on a greater meaning—the snap of a twig underfoot or the rustling of the dogs' passing through the long, brittle grass sounded more noticeable. Above her, an owl hooted. She didn't recognize the call of another bird that flitted through the trees. She stepped into a puddle of moon glow and realized just how seldom she'd been alone since she'd arrived in Montana.

Flashing a smile at the bright orb overhead, Elizabeth threw out her arms and spun around. During those last lonely months in Boston, she'd felt so hurt and angry. The warmth, love, and attention she'd found at the ranch had been healing. Yet now she enjoyed the peacefulness of the quiet evening.

Shep parked himself in front of her.

"I know, I know. I look crazy."

The dog's tail made a thumping sound in the dirt, as if to say, "What are we waiting for? Let's go."

She reached down and patted him. "You're right. The water's waiting for us."

The dogs trotted on ahead. With a spring in her step, Elizabeth followed. The burbling of the water cascading over rocks reached her ears before the scent of dampness wafted to her nose. She inhaled, enjoying the change from the dusty smells of the dry earth.

Reaching the river first, the dogs lapped some water, then ranged upstream.

Elizabeth crouched and scooped water into her palms. Splashing it onto her hot cheeks, she then ran a wet hand around her neck. She repeated the process several times, ignoring the water dripping on her nightgown, plastering the material to her skin. How delightful. But not enough. She continued downstream toward the pool.

Rounding the bushes of the ladies' dressing room, Elizabeth saw a movement in the pool and realized she wasn't alone. With a gasp, she shrank into the bushes, hoping not to be seen.

Eventually curiosity overcame her fear. From her hidden vantage point, she peeked out at the swimmer. Definitely male. The moon's light played over a broad shoulder and muscled arm, lifted in a stroking motion. The strokes stopped, and the man stood up in water to his hips, shaking long hair out of his face.

Nick. Even at night she recognized that chest—she'd been trying not to think of it all day.

Butterflies floated in her stomach, and their tickling spread throughout her body, lingering in the vicinity of her heart, which thudded so hard she thought he'd hear. She knew she should leave before he discovered her, but her stubborn feet remained rooted to the spot.

The dogs returned from their explorations. Elizabeth made a futile grab for the nearest one. With a bark, the dogs rushed forward to the pool. Then, as if asking her to join in the fun, with an eager whine, one trotted back to her.

"Who's there?" Nick called.

Conflicting thoughts flashed through her mind. How mortifying to be caught spying on Nick as he swam. She couldn't hide; the dogs would give her away. And she couldn't run. What if Nick, not knowing who she was, chased her?

Blood rushed from her head, and she almost swooned with embarrassment. She took a deep breath to steady herself.

"It's Elizabeth." She kept her body screened by the bushes, but leaned her head out so he'd see her face.

Nick stepped back into deeper water. "Elizabeth! What are you doing here?"

"I was hot, and I couldn't sleep." She ducked her head back into the bushes. "I thought I'd cool off with a swim. I never dreamed anyone…"

Time drew out. A bird called.

"The last foal was born tonight," Nick said. "A filly. Afterward, I…" his voice trailed off.

"Oh, I missed the last of the births."

"There'll be plenty…next year."

This time the silence lengthened.

Elizabeth knew she should excuse herself and return to the house, but a reckless feeling of abandonment seized her. "Nick, I'm still so hot. Do you think I could—that is, I'd like to cool off."

Laughter edged his voice. "Then come on in. The water's just fine." He made a splashing motion with his hand. "If you'll turn your back, I'll hustle into my clothes."

Elizabeth's heart sped up again. A swim. At night. With a man present. A naked man! What was she thinking?

Banishing her prim thoughts, she took a cautious step into the open, then another. Surely he'd notice that all she had on was her nightgown. What would he say?

"Close your eyes," he ordered.

She complied. Senses heightened, she listened to the sounds of his movements in the water. When she heard him step onto solid ground she couldn't resist the urge to peek. Just a brief lift of her eyelids showed the curve of his back and buttocks as he bent to pick up his pants, and the long line of legs, hardened from hours in the saddle. She admired the way the silvery moon's glow gleamed over his well-muscled body, like the marble statues she'd seen during a long-ago trip to Italy.

Elizabeth shivered in delight. Fire raced through her veins. She flexed her hands. She'd never painted portraits of the human figure, but she wanted to paint Nick. No, model him in clay, a medium she hadn't ever been interested in before. She imagined running her hands down his leg, molding the pliable clay under her fingers; she could almost feel the strength in the—

"You can open your eyes now." Nick's voice interrupted her reverie.

She gave a guilty start, hoping he hadn't noticed her peeking.

"I'll trade places with you," he continued. "You swim, and I'll keep watch."

"Swim?" she echoed. "In front of you?" *What a scandalously wonderful thought.*

"No," he teased. "Behind me. I'll sit on the tree trunk with my back to you."

"You could just leave." *But please don't.*

"No." His voice was firm. "I'll stay to guard you." His tone turned teasing. "Don't you want me to protect you from any wolves or bears who might be interested in a beautiful mermaid?"

Well, when he put it that way..."Just don't look."

"My word of honor, ma'am."

"And don't call me *ma'am*."

"Yes, Elizabeth."

He turned away, a resolute stiffness in his bare back. She admired the curve of his spine before quickly pulling off her nightgown and stepping into the water. She sighed with pleasure as the blessed relief from the heat enveloped her parched skin. But even the coolness of the water didn't quench the fire raging inside her.

* * *

Nick heard the soft slither of fabric as it slid from Elizabeth's body to the ground, then the gentle splash as she paddled in the water. He'd faced bears, wolves, stampeding cattle, buckin' horses, and maraudin' outlaws, but in retrospect, that had been nothin' compared to the fortitude it took to keep his back to the pool while the vision of a nude Elizabeth threatened to buckle his knees.

He groped behind him for the tree trunk. When he touched the rough bark, he backed up until he could drop down and sit. Another splash and glide sounded as though she was swimming on her back. He could envision her hair floating around her and the splendor of her beautiful body shining in the moonlight. With a groan, which he bit off before it could become audible, he sank his head to his knees and hung on with both hands.

"You lasso those thoughts, cowboy," he muttered. As if to keep himself firmly planted, he dug his heels into the ground and began to pray for the strength to resist temptation.

"The water's marvelously refreshing." Her voice sounded as bubbly as the water over rocks. "I'm so glad to be cold again." He heard the sound of her hand running over her satin-cool skin. "I have goose bumps."

He almost groaned again. Hopefully Elizabeth wouldn't swim for very long, because when she was through, he'd need to be jumpin' back in that water to cool down.

"I should have brought a towel," she continued, as he heard her emerge and move up the bank. "My nightgown will be soaking wet."

You're making this very difficult for me, Elizabeth. "Just stand there for a few minutes, and you'll dry off."

"My hair won't." She laughed. "It'll keep me cool."

He must be dreaming. This couldn't possibly be happening. Miss Elizabeth Hamilton stood behind him with nothing but wet hair to hide her nakedness. And laughing about it. She made it damn hard for him to remain a gentleman.

Cloth rustled, and he knew she'd stepped out of the water and put her nightgown back on.

"You can turn around now."

Ever so slowly he stood, then shifted to face her. He restrained himself from gasping at the sight of her beauty. In the moonlight she glowed like a silver angel.

Almost without his volition, his hands reached toward her.

With a mischievous smile, she stepped onto the tree trunk. Perched above him, she took his hands. "I can't believe I'm doing this. Tomorrow I'll feel so embarrassed, but tonight everything is perfect," she said in a soft voice.

The distant howl of a wolf startled her. She glanced behind and lost her balance.

Before she could fall, Nick caught her and slowly lowered her to the ground.

Elizabeth looked up at him, lips slightly parted. In a trance, he bent his head and slowly brushed her lips with his.

Elizabeth raised her arms and clasped his shoulders with her hands. Taking that for an invitation, he feathered kisses across her cheeks until he reached her waiting mouth. Beneath his hands, he felt her quiver in response.

He paused, looking into her eyes with all the love he could give her, and tenderly brushed her cheek with his finger. Then, sliding his hand behind her neck, he kissed her again. This time he deepened his kiss, sliding his tongue into her mouth, teasing her tongue into a response.

Her arms tightened around his neck, and she pressed her breasts against his chest. Through the damp material he could feel their lush fullness. He dropped his hands to span her waist, and spread his fingers across her back, his thumbs just touching her navel. A shudder sped through him, and it took every ounce of discipline he had to not run his hands up her body.

With reluctance he disengaged his mouth from hers.

"Elizabeth." He stroked a damp tendril off her forehead, then kissed her brow. "We'd better go back to the house. I can't answer for my behavior if we keep this up."

Her lips parted in a sigh of protest. He gave them a quick kiss, then, with great effort, resolutely stepped back.

"Come on." Nick could hear the thickness in his voice. He leaned over to pick up his soiled shirt. Tossing it over his shoulder, he took a few steps away from her. "I don't want to leave you, but perhaps it's best if you and the dogs go back first. I doubt anyone's up, but we can't risk being seen together like this."

"You're right," Elizabeth whispered. "We'd scandalize everyone."

"Of course, I'd fight any of the men who said anything bad about you." He laughed and shook his head. "But I sure couldn't do that with the women."

"Pamela would be shocked, but she'd believe me if I said nothing happened."

"Hardly nothing, Elizabeth." He moved closer, took her hand, brought it to his lips, then cupped her palm to his cheek. "I love you."

She stepped back, but didn't release his hand. Even in the dim light he could see the uncertainty leap into her eyes. Her mouth opened in shock. "But—"

He placed a finger on her lips. "Don't say anything. I know you don't feel the same."

The uncertain look eased to relief.

"Good night, Nick." Elizabeth dropped his hand, stepped past him, and started toward the house.

"Good night, Elizabeth."

The dogs looked from her retreating back to his still form. He shooed them to follow her.

Nick watched until the darkness swallowed her white figure, then turned back for that cold swim he'd promised himself. The chill water would douse his body's passion, but now that he'd held Elizabeth in his arms, tasted her sweet lips, and felt her respond to his touch, nothing could wash the aching emptiness from his heart.

* * *

Elizabeth hurried to the house, her mind and emotions torn by what had just happened. Somewhere inside, she knew she should be feeling ashamed, but she wasn't. Excited, confused, shaken—but not ashamed. As she pondered her emotions, her steps slowed.

She'd never experienced anything like Nick's kisses. Not even Richard had stirred her to such depths. And Caleb had never given her the opportunity. She wondered if Caleb's kisses would move her the same way Nick's had? Surely they would. She'd better make certain before she made an irrevocable decision.

Fingering a strand of hair tickling her neck, she relived the thrill of Nick's embrace. If he hadn't stopped, would she have wantonly abandoned herself to the tide of feelings that had swept over her? What about Caleb? A spurt of guilt darted across her mind. If he knew…

Confused, Elizabeth tossed her wet hair over her shoulder. She should feel grateful Nick was a gentleman, but the tight tingling in her breasts and the lingering memory of his lips on hers almost made her wish they'd continued and made love under the wild Montana sky.

CHAPTER TWENTY

The next morning as Elizabeth, lost in her reverie of last night's encounter with Nick, walked down the hall, she casually glanced up, only to stop short at the sight of her goddaughter, curled like a napping kitten, halfway up the staircase. She smiled and shook her head at the child's choice of resting place. "Lizzy, dearest, what are you doing?"

The child turned her head slightly from where it lay on her arm, but didn't answer.

"Little bird, you've chosen a strange place to make a nest," Elizabeth teased, climbing the stairs to sit beside Lizzy. "Why don't you go lie on your comfortable bed?" She stroked the child's long brown curls away from her face.

"Hot," Lizzy murmured.

"I know, darling." Elizabeth gathered the child onto her lap.

Lizzy sprawled in her arms like a rag doll. Her little body felt warm—too warm. Faint stirrings of alarm crept into Elizabeth's mind. "Lizzy, dearest, tell Aunt Elizabeth what's wrong." She rocked the child back and forth.

Lizzy lifted heavy eyelids. "Hot," she repeated.

Elizabeth studied the child's face. Lizzy's normally pale skin was translucent, with dark circles under her eyes. A bright flush of unhealthy color dotted each cheek.

Oh, no. Elizabeth bit her lip to stop its quiver.

Mark clattered through the front door, sliding to a stop when he caught sight of the two of them on the stairs. "Whatcha doing, Aunt Elizabeth?"

"Run and get your mother," Elizabeth said, trying not to sound as worried as she felt. "I'm putting Lizzy to bed."

Gingerly, she straightened, careful to balance her precious burden. Moving slowly enough so as not to trip on the hem of her skirt, she took one step at a time. When she reached the landing, she quickened her pace into Lizzy's room. She turned back a quilt sprigged with pink flowers, laid Lizzy down, and sat next to her.

The child didn't even reach for the well-worn brown bunny with which she slept.

Elizabeth's concern increased. Lizzy always grabbed that stuffed animal when she climbed in bed. She slept with it cuddled next to her, and only with the greatest reluctance did she relinquish her beloved bunny in the morning.

Elizabeth reached for the animal. "Here's your bunny, dearest." She placed it on Lizzy's chest and gently pulled the child's arm around it.

Still carrying the pansy embroidery she'd been working on, Pamela hurried through the door. "Elizabeth, Mark said you wanted me?"

Elizabeth rose. "Something's wrong with Lizzy. I think she's feverish."

"Oh, dear Lord." Pamela tossed the embroidery onto a wooden chest, rushed to her daughter's side, and placed a hand on her forehead. She looked over at Elizabeth, fear in her eyes. "You're right." Sitting on the bed, she tenderly lifted Lizzy to a sitting position. "Here, sweetie. Let Mama help you into something more comfortable." Propping the limp child against her side, Pamela untied the bow on the back of Lizzy's white pinafore.

Elizabeth twisted her hands into the material of her skirt. "What can I do to help?"

"John's with the men at the south pasture. Nick will have to go to town for Dr. Cameron." Pamela slipped off the pinafore.

"I'll go tell him." Elizabeth placed a hand on her friend's shoulder and squeezed. "And I'll send Mark to get John."

Pamela looked up at Elizabeth, anxiousness pulling the skin around her eyes. "I'm so glad you're here with me, Beth."

Elizabeth swallowed the lump in her throat and leaned over to tuck Pamela's usual straying strands of hair back into place, then kissed her cheek. "I am too." She turned to leave. "I'll be back in a few minutes."

Please, please, dear Lord. Let her be all right. The words tumbled through her mind in rhythm to her quick steps.

Out in the sun, the heat blazed down on her. The dust kicked up in the hot air, drying her lungs and making it difficult to breathe. Maybe, she wished, just maybe, Lizzy was only affected by the heat. But even as Elizabeth tried to console herself, in her heart, she knew differently.

As she rounded the barn, to her relief she saw Nick and Mark exactly where she'd expected them to be—working with Outlaw. Nick, the back of his blue shirt soaked with sweat, was lunging the horse on a long lead. Mark, perched on the top rail on the opposite side of the corral, waved at her.

"Nick," she called and waved, forgetting to be careful in front of Outlaw.

At the unexpected sound, the horse shied, then reared on his hind legs, eyes showing white.

"Whoa, boy." Nick gathered the rope in, crooning soft words of comfort. Outlaw took reluctant steps toward him. Nick rubbed the horse's nose, then turned toward Elizabeth.

The smile that brightened his eyes darkened when he saw the expression on her face. He flipped the lunge rope several times around a rail of the fence. "What's wrong?"

"It's Lizzy!" Elizabeth gasped for a breath. "She's...She's feverish. Pamela wants you to ride for Dr. Cameron."

Without a word, he strode to the saddle and blanket resting on the top rail of the fence, and threw them on Outlaw's back. He motioned to Mark. The boy jumped down and ran across the corral to him, making a wide berth around Outlaw.

"Lizzy's sick. Your ma wants me to get the doctor."

Mark looked from Elizabeth to Nick, tension draining his face of color, making his freckles stand out against his pale skin. "Is she going to be all right?"

Nick gripped Mark's shoulder with a comforting squeeze. "I'm sure she'll be fine, son. You know what a good doc Dr. Cameron is."

"Yes, sir," he said, but fear still tightened the muscles in his jaw.

Nick gave him a gentle shake. "I want you to saddle up and ride for your pa."

Mark nodded.

"Good. Now get movin'."

With one hand holding the hat on his head, Mark took off running toward the barn, dust puffing with every step.

Nick finished saddling the horse, exchanged Outlaw's halter for a bridle, opened the gate to the corral, and led the horse through. In one fluid motion, he gathered the reins and vaulted into the saddle.

Outlaw danced sideways.

Nick brought him back. Looking down at Elizabeth, he leaned over and touched a tender hand to her cheek. "I promise Dr. Cameron will be here soon." He kicked the horse into a lope.

Elizabeth placed one hand on her chest while the other cupped her cheek. Somehow Nick's gentle touch warmed the cold fear in her heart. She whirled and hurried toward the house.

❋ ❋ ❋

A few hours later, Lizzy's small room overflowed with people. At the foot of the bed, John, still clad in his dusty work clothes, rested a supportive arm around his wife. Elizabeth stood in the doorway watching Dr. Cameron's examination of Lizzy. The man's gentle yet professional manner reassured her. So different from that of the brisk, stern man who'd been the family doctor when she and Pamela were growing up. She'd always been afraid of him.

In the hallway, Nick paced back and forth, while Mark and Sara, clutching each other's hands, sat on the top step of the stairway.

Dr. Cameron bent over the bed, his fingers moving gently over Lizzy's body, his brogue broadening as he tried to coax responses out of the child. When Lizzy rewarded him with a slight smile, Elizabeth relaxed a little. The child was in good hands. Surely Dr. Cameron would have her feeling better in no time.

Elizabeth looked behind her, trying to meet Nick's eyes. He stopped pacing, but his green eyes, made bluer by the color of his shirt, still looked serious. Inside her, the dread grew colder. She clutched her locket for comfort and glanced toward the bed. *Please, God...*

Dr. Cameron straightened. With a wave of his hand, he beckoned everyone out of the room. They all stepped onto the landing. The doctor's concerned gray gaze first met Pamela's eyes, then John's. He cleared his throat. "She has influenza."

Pamela gasped. John pulled his wife close, lowering his chin to the top of her head.

Elizabeth's knees grew weak. A fleeting longing for the shelter of Nick's arms went through her. She pressed a shaking hand to her mouth. An influenza epidemic had taken the lives of Elizabeth's parents. And Richard.

"I hate to have to tell you this." Dr. Cameron briefly looked down at the floor before his eyes came back to their worried faces. "There are several other cases in town, and the Meager baby died of it yesterday."

CHAPTER TWENTY-ONE

A few days later, Pamela took her hand off Lizzy's forehead and straightened. "She's still feverish," she said to Elizabeth, "but at least she's finally asleep."

Both women gazed at the sleeping child. Lizzy had suffered a restless night, tossing fretfully and whimpering for her mother whenever Pamela left the room. But now the fan of her long eyelashes hid the dark circles under her eyes and, deep in slumber, the child looked peaceful.

Pamela put both hands in the small of her back and stretched. "Beth, I don't know what I'd do without you here. But what about Genia?"

"I'm not going anywhere until Lizzy's well."

"Is it selfish to say I'm grateful?" Pamela reached for Elizabeth's hand and patted it.

"I'm the selfish one. I'd fret myself to cinders, worrying about Lizzy…about you. Being away…not being able to do anything but pray."

"Do you realize it's Sunday?"

"Is it really?" Elizabeth asked with a weary shake of her head. "The days have all run together. Well, we know the Nortons won't be driving out today."

"They have been kind, haven't they? There's so much sickness, and they're not sparing themselves any more than the doctor is."

"I'm ashamed of my first opinion of them." Elizabeth kept her voice low. "I thought him rigid and controlling, and she a downtrodden wife. I was wrong to judge. They're truly good people."

"I'd give anything to be in church with my whole family sitting beside me in the pew." Pamela swept her hand across an imaginary pew.

"Maybe by next Sunday." Yet, even as she spoke, Elizabeth knew Lizzy wouldn't be well enough to attend church next Sunday, or maybe not even for a month of Sundays.

"Caleb's coming today." Pamela flashed Elizabeth a tired smile, the first Elizabeth had seen on her friend's drawn face during the three-day vigil. "You'd better freshen up and put on a nice dress."

Elizabeth smoothed the rumpled apron, one of Pamela's, covering her blue calico dress. Hardly the appearance she wanted to present to a gentleman caller. Surely Caleb would understand. He must know she'd been nursing Lizzy, and the child was special to him.

"Caleb will just have to take me as I am."

Pamela shook her head. "It will be good for you to go for a drive, Beth. You've been cooped up here too long."

"What about you? You've barely slept all night."

"I couldn't have slept anyway. But now that Lizzy's finally peaceful, Dawn can sit with her so I can get some rest."

"All right." With a last glance at her sleeping goddaughter, Elizabeth withdrew and walked down the hall to her room.

Opening the armoire door, she looked over her wardrobe and shrugged. Except for that disastrous baking day, Caleb had never seen her wearing anything but her good clothes, with her hair carefully coiffed. Now, because Dawn sat with Lizzy and couldn't help her dress, Caleb would just have to see her in something simple. A clean shirtwaist and skirt would have to do.

Elizabeth undid the buttons of her dress, slipped it down over her hips, stepped out of it, then unbuttoned her shirtwaist. The room felt so close and hot, she wished she could take off her corset and put on something cooler. Maybe one of those loose-fitting Mother Hubbard dresses Annie and Dawn wore. She shook her head, amazed at her own thoughts. She'd been scandalized by the very idea of those dresses—yet here she was, actually considering wearing one.

Elizabeth poured tepid water from the pitcher into the ewer, dipped a cloth. She ran it over her face, neck, and arms, wishing for reviving cold water.

Her thoughts slid back to the night at the river with Nick. How long ago it seemed. At times during the last tense three days, the memories would creep into her mind, sending warm tingles through her body, temporarily easing her fear for Lizzy, and lifting the tedium of the long, silent watches at the child's bedside.

What a good man Nick was—so patient with the children. Although he'd kept Mark and Sara occupied around the ranch or played games with them, he'd also been in and out of Lizzy's room almost as much as the child's father.

Guilt pricked her. She shouldn't be thinking about Nick. Caleb would be arriving any minute. It seemed like forever since she'd seen him. Maybe today she'd get the chance to test the power of Caleb's kisses. She slowed the motion of the washcloth and smiled mischievously at her reflection in the mirror. She'd just have to be forward and make it happen. Too bad she couldn't arrange a midnight swim in the pool...but perhaps after they were married...

When the crisis with Lizzy was over, she'd have to talk to Nick, although she didn't know what she'd say. It would be so much simpler if he didn't love her.

She pulled on a fine white cotton shirtwaist. The light material and lowered neckline made it the coolest one she owned. And the lace edging on the bodice and sleeves fancied the plainness up a little. She stepped into a robin's-egg-blue gingham skirt with little red flowers patterning the cloth.

She plucked out hairpins, then shook her hair loose. She briefly massaged her scalp, then brushed the long fall back into a bun. Stabbing the hairpins back in, she anchored the heavy mass in place and was done.

As she walked down the stairs, from outside the half-opened front door she heard the sound of a buggy. Caleb's here! Her heart lightened, and her feet responded, increasing her pace the last few steps and out the door. After the past difficult days, she could hardly wait to see him.

On the porch she blinked to adjust her eyes to the bright sunlight. Dr. Cameron looked up from the reins he'd wrapped around the porch rail and smiled.

"Oh, I thought you were Mr. Livingston." The words escaped before Elizabeth realized it.

An uncomfortable look crossed the doctor's face. He picked up his black leather satchel with one hand, while the other tugged at the collar of his shirt.

"Hot day, isn't it, Miss Hamilton?"

"Like every other day has been." *Whatever is wrong? Why does he look like that?* She raised an eyebrow in inquiry, hoping he'd answer her unspoken question.

He tried to ignore it—stepping up onto the porch and setting his satchel on one of the wicker chairs. Taking off his hat, he fanned his face, then ran his fingers through sweat-dampened auburn hair.

"Dr. Cameron, is anything the matter?"

"Well, lass," Dr. Cameron added in a Scottish brogue. "Mr. Livingston was askin' me a lot of questions about Lizzy's illness."

Elizabeth smiled. "Lizzy's a favorite of his. He must be very worried about her."

"I'm sure he is, lass." He swallowed, then his gaze finally met hers.

At the concern in his tired eyes, she took a small step back.

"I didna get the impression he'd be payin' the Carter ranch a visit ana time soon."

Elizabeth straightened her shoulders and gave him a polite social smile. "I'm sure you must be mistaken."

Dr. Cameron heaved a huge sigh. "I hope I am, lass. I hope I am." He set his hat back on his head and picked up his satchel. "Now, perhaps I could wash up before I see my patient."

"Of course." Elizabeth led the way into the house and down the hall to the kitchen. "Lizzy had a very restless night, but she's finally sleeping."

"That's to be expected."

"Pamela just laid down to steal some rest, and John's in the south pasture. Do you want me to wake her?"

"No, no." He shook his head. "Let the puir woman get some sleep. I know my way around."

Elizabeth walked back out to the porch. She sat down in a rocker and picked up the fan she'd left outside several days before. She felt more disturbed by Dr. Cameron's information than she'd wanted him to know. She shook her head and vigorously wafted her fan. No. Not Caleb. The doctor must have misunderstood.

He'll come. I only have to wait. He'll be here soon.

❋ ❋ ❋

The sound of rapid hoofbeats woke her.

Caleb.

Elizabeth bolted upright in the rocker, then slumped back at the sight of the rider. Nick, not Caleb. Confusion flooded through her. She didn't know whether to feel glad or disappointed. She should be wishing for Caleb, but her heartbeat raced out of control at the sight of Nick's broad shoulders. Raising a quick hand to pat her hair, she checked to make sure no tendrils had strayed from the bun.

Nick reined Freckles in next to the doctor's horse. Dust covered the Appaloosa and powdered Nick's tan shirt and pants. Pulling down the blue bandana from over his mouth, he grinned at her and held up a bulging gunnysack.

She cocked her head. "What?"

"I had them sent from California." Anticipation glinted in his green eyes, lightening his tired, dusty face.

"What?" Elizabeth repeated, getting up and moving to the edge of the porch.

"Lemons."

"Oh, Nick." Elizabeth's voice choked, and tears welled in her eyes. "How wonderful. Oh, Pamela will be so pleased."

Getting any nourishment into Lizzy had proved almost impossible. Neither coaxing nor ordering had any effect. Yet Dr. Cameron had been so firm about the necessity of Lizzy having plenty to drink that Pamela continued to struggle to get water or milk into her feverish daughter.

"How did you know I'd been wanting lemons for Lizzy?"

He slid out of the saddle and looped the Appaloosa's reins around the porch rail. Striding up the stairs and onto the porch, he placed the rough sack into her hands. He leaned forward until the brim of his hat almost touched her head. "Must have read your mind."

"Thank you," she whispered, wondering if she should give into the urge to drop the bag and throw her arms around Nick. She didn't care if her clothes became covered with dust. Nor did she care if it was broad daylight. She couldn't help herself; she wanted him to kiss her.

From the tenderness in his eyes, he wanted the same thing. The pause between them stretched out. Then Nick moved back several steps, glanced down, and tried to brush himself off. He gave her a rueful twist of his lips. "I reckon I'd better get cleaned up," he drawled, looking at her. He seemed to note the lace-edged shirtwaist, and a curious look flashed across his face.

Elizabeth answered his unspoken question. "I was waiting for Mr. Livingston, and I must have dozed off."

Nick's mouth tightened. He looked toward the horizon, squinting in the glare of the late afternoon sun. "He's late." He cocked an eyebrow.

"I know." She exhaled a slow breath. "Dr. Cameron doesn't seem to believe he's coming." Distress tinged her tone.

"Why?" Seeming to restrain a kick, Nick scuffed his boot across the wooden floor.

"Because of Lizzy's illness."

"That lowdown—" Nick caught himself, turned, and paced a few quick steps before coming back to face Elizabeth.

To say any words might bring on tears. Instead, hefting the laden sack between them, Elizabeth tried to smile. "I'll just take these to Annie. Why don't you go wash up so you can see Lizzy drink your lemonade?"

Footsteps sounded behind them. The doctor appeared in the doorway, carrying his hat in one hand and his bag in the other. At the sight of their anxious faces, he shook his head. "She didna wake up when I examined her." He placed his hat on his head. "I have ta tell ye, I didna like the look of the wee lass. She's fadin' away."

Elizabeth's racing heart thudded to a stop, and she had to catch her breath before she could speak. "Nick's brought some lemons to make lemonade for her." Her eyes pleaded with him. "Do you think it will help?"

"Aye, lass, I'm sure it will." Dr. Cameron tried to infuse some hope into his voice. "Now, I'd best be goin'. I've more patients yet to see. I'll be back tomorrow."

"Thank you, Dr. Cameron, for driving out every day to check on her," Elizabeth said, struggling to get the words out. "We're blessed to have a doctor like you."

For an instant, the doctor's weary face eased, then his expression settled back into careworn creases. He took her hand and squeezed it. "I can only do so much, lass. Sometimes it's not enough."

* * *

Elizabeth deposited the lemons with Annie and drifted outside to wait for Caleb. Unwilling to sit still, she paced back and forth, fanning herself to bring a hint of coolness to her face and neck. Her spirits, which had risen at Nick's gift, drooped.

Heavyhearted, with a knot growing ever tighter in her stomach, she forced herself to walk, hoping the exercise would banish her feelings of gloom.

After what had been a horribly gray time in her life, she'd emerged into the happy, blue skies of Montana. A new life and a new love...Now, however, the intensity of the heat melted her resilience, and she had to fight giving way to tears. She loved Lizzy so much and couldn't bear the pain and fear she felt and saw on the faces of her dear friends.

Now there arose a new fear inside her. Richard's death had charred her heart to cinders. But with meeting Caleb, a new love had blossomed from the ashes, only to be threatened with doubt. She wrapped her arms around herself. *Where is Caleb? Why isn't he here when I need him the most?*

Annie called from the doorway, "Missy Erizabet."

Elizabeth turned.

The cook carried a wicker tray holding a pitcher of lemonade and several tall glasses. A slight smile crossed Annie's broad face, and she hefted the tray higher.

"Marvelous, Annie." Elizabeth crossed the porch, and lifted the pitcher off the tray. "I'm sure Lizzy will drink this." She relished the feel of the coldly beaded glass and lifted the decanter to touch her warm cheek. "It feels so good." She closed her eyes, sighed, then opened them.

A worried look crossed Annie's face. "Ice almost gone."

Elizabeth pulled the pitcher away from her cheek. "All the ice in the icehouse is used up?"

"Too hot."

Another problem. Elizabeth shook her head to still the tears that wanted to spring forth, then squared her shoulders. *Just be thankful for what we do have,* she told herself. Today Lizzy has cold lemonade. "We'll worry about that later, Annie." She placed the pitcher back on the tray. "I'll take this upstairs and see if Lizzy's awake." She took the tray from Annie.

Stepping through the doorway, she paused for her eyes to adjust to the interior. The sound of rapid steps made her peer down the hall and smile when she recognized Nick.

With his hair slicked back and dangling in wet curls to his shoulders, he reminded her of their night together by the pool. Warmth crept into her cheeks. She hoped he wouldn't notice. At least he was wearing clothes. She lifted an eyebrow at his clean blue shirt. "That was fast."

"Dunked myself in the horse trough." He ran his fingers through his hair. "Didn't want to miss Lizzy drinkin' her lemonade."

"Horse trough!" Elizabeth wrinkled her nose.

He grinned at her. "Don't worry. I pumped in clean water."

"Here." Elizabeth handed him the tray. "You do the honors."

"Yes, ma'am." The words came out in a drawl and from the teasing light in his eyes, he expected a response.

Elizabeth held up a finger to stop him. "If you're going to *ma'am* me, I'm going to start calling you *sir*." She shook her finger. "Now, how would you like that?"

"No, ma'am." He shook his head, spinning out the words. "I sure wouldn't like that, ma'am."

Elizabeth rolled her eyes and started up the stairs. Entering Lizzy's room, she smiled at Pamela sitting in a chair next to the bedside. "You're awake."

Lizzy briefly opened her eyes, then closed them again. "We have a treat for you, dearest." Elizabeth waved her hand at Nick. "Look."

This time Lizzy kept her eyes open. A curious look flitted across her face—the first animation Elizabeth had seen Lizzy show for the last several days.

Pamela stood up and took a few steps away from the bed so they could approach the child.

Under Lizzy's solemn gaze, Nick placed the tray on a table next to her bed, pushing aside an unlit lamp, an empty glass, and a bowl.

"Nick sent all the way to California for lemons so you could have lemonade to drink. What do you think of that?"

Lizzy didn't reply, only continued to watch Nick.

Nick poured some lemonade into a glass and held it up so Lizzy could see.

Elizabeth leaned over Lizzy. "Here, dearest. Let me prop you up." She slid her arm under the child's skinny shoulders and pushed her to a sitting position, then deftly slipped some extra pillows behind her. "There, now." She walked to the chair at the foot of the bed and sat down.

Nick knelt down by the side of the bed. "Here, little bird. Take a drink and tell me if you like it." He placed the glass to her lips and tipped it.

Lizzy took a small sip, and Nick held the glass away a few inches. "Like it?"

She nodded.

"More?"

Another nod.

Elizabeth and Nick exchanged pleased glances.

Nick helped Lizzy take another, longer swallow, before she shook her head.

"No more?" Nick made a comical face of dismay. "Did it turn sour? Let me taste it." He pretended to take a sip. "Tastes plenty sweet to me. Why don't you try again?" He placed the glass against her mouth, and she took another drink. "Good girl."

Elizabeth watched as Nick, alternating between teasing and coaxing, persuaded Lizzy to drink the entire glass of lemonade. He's so good with her—with all the children. Someday, he'll make a wonderful father. That unexpected warmth crept into her cheeks again.

As if Nick read her mind, his eyes met hers.

Elizabeth blushed. Surely he wasn't having similar thoughts about her?

CHAPTER TWENTY-TWO

Nick's boots felt as if they had rocks in them instead of feet, making it difficult to drag them up the stairs to Lizzy's room. The heat had pressed down on him all day, until he felt his muscles had shriveled to strips of bacon. When he'd glanced in the looking glass after washing up, he could see new lines etched around his eyes, making him look ten years older. The other men, and Mark and Sara, who'd stayed with him all day, had a similar parched appearance. Heat and fear had taken a toll on all of them.

Entering the room, he saw Pamela and Elizabeth sitting quietly, the air thick with their exhaustion. He nodded at them and received quiet nods back, although Elizabeth managed a slight smile. Pamela's cheeks had lost their plumpness, and she had dark circles under her eyes, while Elizabeth looked pale and drawn. He ached to be able to hold her and make everything all right.

"Nick," Lizzy murmured. She opened heavy-lidded eyes and moved her fingers in a pathetically weak gesture toward him, which wrung his heart.

"Little bird." He folded her tiny, bony hand into one of his while soothing back the hair from her face. A couple of tendrils caught in his knuckles. Even the texture of Lizzy's hair was different, its usual springy softness brittle against his skin. He twisted his work-roughened fingers until the delicate strands untangled.

Her eyes closed, then opened again. "Music." He barely heard the plea from the pale, dry lips.

"Do you want me to play for you?" He glanced at Miz Carter for permission.

Pamela nodded. It seemed to him that the idea of soothing music for her daughter relaxed the tight muscles around her eyes.

He flicked a quick glance at Elizabeth, who smiled in approval. His heartbeat quickened, and he grinned back. He hadn't seen a smile cross Elizabeth's drawn face for the last three days—not since the day Lizzy had first drunk some lemonade.

"I'll be right back." On his way to the music room, he pondered his eager mood. Nothing had changed. Lizzy was still in danger. Only now he could do something. To know the child he adored hovered near death, and to see the pain and suffering of the Carters and Elizabeth had near driven him crazy. His helplessness during the entire week of Lizzy's illness had burdened his heart. Only when he'd gotten the lemons, or taken Mark and Sara with him on his jobs around the ranch, had he felt like a contributor.

The violin lay on the chair where Nick had left it. Shaking his head, he picked up the instrument and bow. The party seemed like it had taken place years ago instead of just weeks. So much had happened since.

He tucked the end of the violin under his chin and tuned the strings. Something lively first. Playing the catchy strains of "Pop Goes the Weasel," he started out of the room, down the hall, and up the stairs, the sounds of music announcing him.

He entered the room just in time for Lizzy's favorite part. Making sure he had eye contact with her, he pantomimed a monkey face, and made the popping sound with his finger on the strings.

Lizzy's wan face brightened, and a small laugh escaped her. Nick's heart lightened in response, and he could see from the joy on Elizabeth's face that she felt the same way.

Pamela's face and shoulders relaxed, and she sent him a look of gratitude.

With a flourish, he finished the rest of the song. "What next, little bird?"

"'Lou, Lou.'"

"'Lou, Lou' it is." Nick winked at Elizabeth and watched the pink rise in her cheeks. Tapping his foot, he began to play "Skip To My Lou."

When he'd finished, he slid right into another song, playing every tune he knew. Then he started in with hymns. Lizzy's eyelids drooped, but he could see her fighting to stay awake.

Nick's fingers started to ache, and the pads of his fingertips were tender, but he wasn't going to stop until Lizzy fell asleep.

Running out of hymns, he began the strains of "Lizzy's Theme" and watched the child's eyes grow heavy. Soon she lost her battle with Morpheus. Her dark lashes fluttered, then her eyelids stilled.

A sob from Pamela shifted his attention. For the first time since her daughter's illness, Pamela's rigid control broke. She pulled a handkerchief from her sleeve and mopped away the tears running down her cheeks.

Nick almost stopped the music, but didn't want to break the sleeping spell he'd cast over Lizzy. "Ah, Pamela," he said softly.

"Pam." Elizabeth rose from her chair, reaching out her hand to her friend.

Pamela shook her head, motioned for Elizabeth to stay in her seat, and fled the room.

❋ ❋ ❋

Elizabeth's extended hand folded over her heart. She had to resist moaning and bending forward to hide her face in her lap. *Oh, dear God, I wish there was something...anything I could do to console Pamela.*

She glanced at her sleeping goddaughter, so pale and weak. *Please, dearest Lizzy, please get well.* For the thousandth time, she silently pleaded the words. Would the nightmare of this illness ever have a happy ending, or would a silent grave and an ever-present emptiness take Lizzy's place in all their hearts?

Nick shifted his weight and brought "Lizzy's Theme" to an end.

Elizabeth looked up at him and saw her feelings—sorrow and fear—mirrored in his eyes.

Nick began playing another piece—a beautiful one she'd never heard. The feelings in his eyes changed until they held love and compassion. "This is for you," he whispered.

Mesmerized, she became lost in the emerald enchantment cast over her by his gaze and the seductive music. Although not releasing her from her cares, the music soothed away the harsh edges so they didn't cut so deep into her soul, giving her the strength to continue to bear them.

The heavy sound of boots pounding up the stairs interrupted her reverie. John slowed to a stop when he reached the landing, attempting to enter the room quietly.

Usually the men cleaned up before coming into the house, but dust covered John's clothes, and his hat remained on his head. He beckoned them from the room.

Nick brought the music to a gentle close, and they followed John out the door.

Although she was disappointed not to hear the rest of the music and continue exploring her feelings for Nick, Elizabeth's stomach clenched at the sight of John's face. *My God, what's next?*

"Where's Pamela?" he asked.

"Probably in her room." Elizabeth waved her hand at the closed bedroom door. "She broke down in tears when she heard Nick play Lizzy's music, and she wanted to be alone."

The creases around John's eyes and mouth deepened. "I'll go to her in a minute." Seeming to belatedly become aware of his hat, he lifted it off his head. Underneath, his thin, rust-colored hair lay plastered to his skull. "Jed shot and wounded a grizzly near the north pasture."

"The north pasture?" Nick sounded surprised.

"The fence was down. Some cows and calves had gotten out. Jed went after them. The grizzly caught him by surprise. His horse reared, and he barely got a shot off."

"Is he all right?"

"Yeah. He decided to round up the cattle instead of trackin' the grizzly."

Nick's forehead wrinkled. "That bear's too close by."

John nodded. "At first light, I want you to go after it. Just what we don't need around here: a wounded grizzly."

"Done."

"Elizabeth." John turned toward her. "I want everyone to stay close to the house. Keep the children inside."

Elizabeth caught her breath. "Would a bear come this close to the house?"

"Probably not, but there's no tellin' what a wounded grizzly will do," Nick said.

"'Bout twenty years back, one killed the youngest O'Brian child." John glanced toward Lizzy's room. "Best not to take chances."

* * *

Elizabeth couldn't stand another minute of being cooped up in Lizzy's room. The long, hot day drew to a close. Lizzy slept peacefully, so Pamela wouldn't need Elizabeth for a while. She stood up and shook out her rumpled blue calico skirt. "I'm going for a walk."

Pamela looked up from her embroidery. "Stay close."

"I'll walk in circles around the house."

Pamela gave her a faint smile. "You'd better take a hat. It's still hot out there."

"I will."

Elizabeth made a quick trip to her room, where she scooped up the straw hat hanging on the bedpost. Plopping it on her head, she hurried out the door, anxious to get out of the house. If she didn't get some exercise, she'd burst. Elizabeth suppressed a smile. What an unladylike image. Being in Montana had even changed the way she talked to herself.

Once outside, she blinked in the early evening sunshine. While still hot, the air had lost the dryness that made her feel as if every drop of moisture had leached from her body.

Where to go? She looked around carefully, making sure no grizzly was in sight. Surely it wouldn't come this close to the house. And besides, Nick must have shot the bear by now. Still, she wouldn't venture too far.

Despite the heat, Elizabeth stepped briskly, hoping to banish the anxious feelings inside her. She felt a little light-headed.

Between the oppressive heat and the knot of fear in her stomach, she'd barely eaten anything in two weeks. With the loss of weight, she didn't even need to wear a corset.

She took deep breaths, relishing the freedom from her tight stays. Maybe she'd remain at this weight and never wear corsets again. She shrugged her shoulders. Maybe she'd regain her weight and still never wear corsets again.

As she walked, her thoughts turned to Laurence and Genia. Although she'd written to them briefly about the crisis with Lizzy, she hadn't mentioned anything to her brother about returning home. Nor had she given the baby much thought. But Lizzy's illness reminded her of the preciousness of children and the frailty of those little lives. If she could do anything to aid the safe delivery of her nephew or niece…

When Lizzy's well, I'll go home.

And if she doesn't make it?

No. Don't even think that.

Reaching the whitewashed fence of the horse pasture, she opened the gate, let herself in, and closed it behind her. Several of the horses seemed to be milling around a large boulder in the middle of the field. Wondering why, she squinted for a closer look and spotted a solitary figure perched on the rock.

Nick.

Her heart raced. She debated retreating, but decided to stay her course. Humming "Lizzy's Theme," she walked along the fence until she reached a gate. Unfastening the latch, she pushed the gate open, then closed it behind her.

Taking a deep breath, Elizabeth tried to quiet her rapid heartbeat and still her shaking hands, but couldn't. She approached the boulder.

Nick, clad in a dusty brown work shirt and blue denim pants, appeared lost in studying the sky. It wasn't until the horses shied away that he noticed her.

"Elizabeth!" He jumped off the rock. "What are you doing out here?" A look of alarm crossed his face. "Lizzy?"

She shook her head and waved her hand in negation. "I just needed to get out and walk."

His mouth tightened. "Elizabeth, John told you to stay in the house." His voice sounded firm.

Nick's tone halted her. He'd never spoken to her that way before. "I looked around, and it seemed to be safe. I didn't plan on going far."

"It's too dangerous for you to be outside."

"You're outside."

With his boot he nudged the rifle on the ground next to the rock. Then he turned and picked up the gun belt from behind him.

"Oh."

"Promise me you won't go wandering off again."

"I promise."

His shoulders relaxed.

"But now that I'm here, can I stay? I can't bear to be in the house another minute."

He touched his hat. "I'll keep guard."

Elizabeth motioned to the rock. "May I join you?"

He bowed slightly and set the gun belt on the ground. "Allow me."

Placing his hands around her waist, he gave her a little lift onto the rock. "How's that?"

"Fine," she managed to stammer. He'd touched her uncorseted waist! Could he tell? The blood raced through her veins, and her heart beat so loud, she thought he'd hear. Settling back against the rock, she willed her pulse to still.

From her vantage point, she concentrated on the view. The dusky orange of the setting sun coated the undulating grassy hillocks amber and gold. The black, brown, gray, and chestnut mares grazed peacefully, their foals beside them. Her heartbeat slowed in response. She finally looked down at him. "I take it you didn't find the grizzly."

Nick shook his head. "That ole bear's a smart one. I tracked it to the water and lost it."

Elizabeth tilted her head in puzzlement.

"It must have stayed in the river. I went upstream and down on both sides and couldn't see any tracks where it came out." He rubbed his face with his hand. "I don't even know which way it went. It might even have been badly wounded, drowned, and washed away."

"What are you going to do now?"

"Keep after it. It was getting late, so I came here to my thinkin' rock"—he gave the stone an affectionate pat—"to see if I could figure out where to find that darn bear."

"Thinking rock?" She lifted an eyebrow.

"Yep. After my parents died and I came to live with John, I spent a lot of time on this rock just looking at the sky." He glanced up and, as if to frame a view, lifted his hand in the air.

Elizabeth watched the golden rays of the setting sun play across his face, turning his green eyes to hazel.

"I would look at that vast expanse of blue and imagine my parents being up there, watching from heaven." He dropped his hand and looked at her. "Somehow it comforted me."

"Pamela told me you were only thirteen when your parents died. What happened?"

"They were killed in a wagon accident."

"How awful for you."

"Yes. My little sister too."

"Oh, no!"

"Marcy was Sara's age. Always carried around a rag doll just like Sara does. I found it after..." He lowered his head and kicked at a clump of grass. When he looked back at her, she saw the shadow of old sorrow shading his eyes. "I was angry they died and left me alone. Part of me died with them."

A lump rose in Elizabeth's throat, and her heart ached for him. She understood only too well what Nick had gone through, even though she'd been older.

"John was always good to me, but it really got better when Miz Carter came out here, and the children were born. Almost like having a family again." He paused. "But not quite. A part of me always felt on the outside."

Nick had made the Carter family a solace from the pain of losing his own...and so had she. Now the specter of Lizzy's illness hung in the air between them, threatening to tear apart the contented surrogate family they'd made.

Elizabeth's deepest fear welled up into whispered words. "I'm afraid she's dying."

Nick remained silent, but his face tightened, and the shadow in his eyes deepened to sea green.

"You're afraid too. I can see it in your eyes."

He swallowed and nodded.

"She grows more transparent every day. And I feel so helpless." Her voice choked on a sob.

Nick reached up, lifted her off the rock, and gently set her down. He slipped off her hat, cradling her to him. "Elizabeth," he whispered into her hair.

Elizabeth ignored her hat drifting to the ground. Being held in the security of Nick's arms loosened the tears she'd been suppressing since Lizzy's illness began. She tucked her face into his shoulder and cried. Her chest heaved with gasping sobs, and she clung to him.

Nick feathered a kiss across her brow, then rested his cheek on the top of her head while lightly rubbing her back with his hand.

Elizabeth couldn't stop the flood of tears and made no attempt to try. The relief of releasing her sorrow and fear felt necessary. It had been so long…not since Richard and her parents had died…At the memory of those earlier losses, she cried more, the tears welling up from a deep pool of grief. She seemed to cry forever, for years and years.

Finally all the feelings squeezed out of her, like a dishrag wrung dry. She allowed herself to remain limp in his arms. How wonderful to be held like this.

She sniffed. Poor Nick. She'd drenched the front of his shirt. Not wanting him to see her red, tearstained face, she turned within his hold, pulling a handkerchief from her sleeve. Keeping her face averted, she delicately blew her nose several times, then laid her head back on his shoulder.

"I hate death," she said. "The worst time of my life was when my parents died. And my fiancé, Richard was only nineteen. An influenza epidemic just like this one. Pamela's little sister, Mary—Lizzy looks just like her—died of diptheria too. And my fiancé, Richard." Her voice choked.

Nick kissed the top of her head.

She twisted slightly within his arms in order to cup her locket, snapping the case open. "Here's his photograph." She held it up to him. "He gave me this locket on my eighteenth birthday. I've worn it ever since."

Nick kept his arms around her while he studied the photograph. "He was a handsome man."

Could Nick see Richard's resemblance to Caleb?

Nick's voice softened. "I can see why you always wear this necklace." He lifted his gaze to her, his eyes so full of understanding that once again her tears welled up.

He hugged her to him. "I'm so sorry you lost him…lost them all," Nick murmured into her hair.

Elizabeth lifted her eyes to his. "Richard was a strong man. If *he* died, how can our frail little Lizzy survive?"

With a tender finger, he brushed a tear out from under her eye. "Elizabeth, we must trust and pray."

She turned away from him. "Sometimes that's not enough." She scooped up her hat and took a few steps toward the house. "I'd better get back. Pamela might need me."

"Wait." Nick grabbed his gun belt and buckled it around his waist. He picked up the rifle and caught up to her.

Elizabeth stopped and looked up, watching angry red and orange streak across the dusky sky. "It felt like a miracle to be here in Montana. When I met Caleb Livingston, and he appeared so like my Richard, I thought I had a second chance at love. I felt so happy…so alive." She lowered her gaze. "But then Lizzy came down with influenza, and Caleb stopped visiting…" Her voice trailed away.

They walked in silence; their connection lingered between them. When they reached the house, Elizabeth stepped on the first stair of the porch.

"Wait." Nick grabbed her arm. "Elizabeth, you mustn't give up hope."

"I don't know what I feel, Nick. I'm numb." She tried to smile, then reached out and touched his face. "Thank you for letting me cry. It's what I needed."

"I know." His fingers tightened on her arm. "Promise me you won't give up hope."

Elizabeth hesitated.

"Promise."

Unable to resist the love and intensity in his eyes, her heart warmed to him. "I promise."

* * *

Nick strode away from Elizabeth, vowing the promise he'd coaxed from her would not be in vain. His stomach churned with a maelstrom of emotions: the constant fear for Lizzy, his old grief about the death of his parents and sister, Elizabeth's sadness about her losses, anger with Caleb Livingston, and his pain over her feelings for the banker.

Flexing his hands, he thought about holding Elizabeth—how right she'd felt in his arms. He'd never have guessed that beneath her refined exterior she'd kept so many tears bottled up. While she'd sobbed against his shoulder, his heart had ached for her. Stroking her back, he'd imagined his hand sending his love into the lonely hurt places inside her.

But after she'd finished crying, the hopeless expression on her face punched him like a bronco's kick. He'd do anything—he clenched his fists—*anything* to wipe away her feelings of despair and light her face with happiness.

Nick turned the corner of the house, stopped, and leaned against the building. *A second chance at love.* His stomach twisted further at the memory of her words, and he rubbed his hand across his face. Now he knew Elizabeth loved Caleb Livingston. The hope that she'd come to love him withered in his heart like the fresh green grass beneath the scorching Montana sun.

He ground a clump of dry grass under the heel of his boot. The love he'd give anything to possess, Livingston had so carelessly tossed aside—something the banker would return to when the threat of Lizzy's illness disappeared. He wished he could shoot Livingston for hurting Elizabeth—for not being here when she needed him.

Nick fixed on the one stable rock in the tide of hopelessness washing over him. Although he couldn't do anything to cure Lizzy, there was something he could do for Elizabeth. He shifted his gun belt. First thing tomorrow, he'd head into town and hunt down Livingston.

❋ ❋ ❋

I promise...not to give up hope. The words echoed in Elizabeth's mind. She took weary steps across the porch, dropped her hat on a table, sank into a rocker, and wrapped her arms around herself. Across the gray horizon, the last remnants of orange and red faded away. Within the inner darkness and fear of her soul, hope did indeed flicker—a trickle of warmth, warding against despair.

Nick's hope. Nick's love for her.

Taking a deep breath, she leaned her head back against the rocker, her nostrils quivering at the scent of dry grass and dust. Never before had a man held her while she cried. Not even her beloved Richard. The years with Richard had been happy. She'd never had a need for tears. His death, rapidly followed by the deaths of her parents, had caused the pain she'd lived with ever since.

At the time, no one else could comfort her, although Pamela and Sylvia tried. Laurence had shut himself off, suffering his own grief over the loss of his parents and best friend.

Elizabeth's tears had either been shed in the lonely silence of her room or locked away deep inside her. As painful as it had been to cry them out with Nick, she'd also experienced a sense of relief, as if chest muscles that had clamped down years of sorrow had finally relaxed.

Nick had been the key. Elizabeth knew she hadn't shed her entire load of buried feelings—more grief and pain existed within her—but now she knew if she needed him, Nick would be there to hold her. And not just now. If in the future, she needed the release of tears…Her mind shied away from thoughts of Lizzy.

Pulling the damp, crumpled handkerchief from her sleeve, Elizabeth patted away any lingering wetness from her face. She shifted her head to avoid a hairpin pricking into her scalp, then closed her eyes.

Think only of Nick, Elizabeth told herself. She relived the sensation of his arms around her, relishing the reminder of how her body trembled when his featherlight kisses brushed across her brow. The trembling began again, somewhere deep within her. Tingling warmth flooded her body.

Elizabeth couldn't stop her thoughts from drifting. Memories of the hot moonlit night at the river, when he had held her against his almost-naked body, floated across her mind. Her lips tingled at the thought of his remembered kisses.

The tip of Elizabeth's tongue touched her lower lip. She slipped her hands to the center of her chest, just above the cleft between her breasts, and pressed against her heart in an effort to still its rapid beating. Instead, the rising shivers of need warmed her body; wantonness flamed through her veins.

Dropping her hands to the arms of the rocker, she clasped her fingers around the smooth wood and rocked. If she didn't anchor herself to this chair, her feet might follow the pounding of her heart, sending her breathlessly racing after Nick.

At her vision of throwing her arms around him and the surprised look he'd have, a mischievous smile danced across her face. She imagined Nick laughing with joy. He'd pick her up and swing her around. Then he'd kiss her and say, "I love you, Elizabeth." And she'd say, "I lo…

Elizabeth straightened in the chair, shocked at the fantasy words she'd almost uttered. *Love Nick? Do I really love Nick?*

Her mind whirled, fragments of pictures of him flashing in and out so fast she could barely settle on any one: the day he'd brought her from the railway station and stopped so she could see the view…the horseback ride beside the river when he'd said her eyes were the most beautiful blue he'd ever seen…teaching her to shoot…saving her from the grizzly bear…eating the saskatoon pie she'd baked…coaxing Lizzy to drink her lemonade… the magical night at the pool…his long-lashed green eyes glowing with love for her…

The blinding scales of Caleb fell from her eyes, and the truth blazed in fiery letters across her heart—spelling out: NICK!

Elizabeth suppressed a gasp. *Nick! It's true. I love Nick, not Caleb—never Caleb.* Rocking back and forth so hard the runners of the chair thumped against the side of the house, she shook her head in disbelief. Her heart raced. She'd been so busy searching for a re-creation of Richard and trying to control her heart, she hadn't recognized her growing love for Nick.

Lost in her thoughts, Elizabeth slowed her rocker to just a slight, soothing push with her toes. Tears filled her eyes, and she reached up and carefully pulled her necklace over her head.

Cupping the locket in her left hand, she snapped open the cover and, for the last time, kissed Richard's beloved face. "Good-bye, my dear," she whispered.

Balling her fist around the locket, she dropped her hand into her lap. Later, she'd tuck the necklace away in her jewelry box.

Resolutely, Elizabeth blinked back the tears, and her rocking grew more forceful. Now what? Should she tell Nick about her feelings for him? Of course. But would that be too forward? Elizabeth straightened her shoulders.

I don't care.

I'm through with being a proper Boston lady. From now on, she'd be a western woman who could shoot at targets, bake pies, and tell her man that she loved him.

CHAPTER TWENTY-THREE

Nick reined in before the whitewashed brick bank. He dismounted, led Freckles over to a nearby trough, and let the horse have a brief drink before he looped the reins over the rail. Freckles stretched his neck toward the drooping daisies blooming in a planter on the small porch, then seemed to decide they weren't worth eating.

On the ride to town, Nick had rehearsed about ten different versions of the talk he meant to have with Livingston. In his favorite, he walked in, pointed his gun at the banker, and ordered Livingston to ride with him to the ranch. Once Livingston caught sight of beautiful Elizabeth, everything else should just happen naturally.

Nick's stomach clenched in pain. He ignored the feeling and, instead, kept his mind on how happy Elizabeth would be when the banker resumed his courtin'.

He stepped up on the porch, sending a sleeping brindle-colored cat running for cover. Unfortunately, waving a gun around in a bank and kidnapping the banker would send the sheriff and a posse out after him. He didn't fancy that would sit too well with Elizabeth and the Carters.

Nick shrugged. He had better, although less satisfying, ways. He shouldn't have too hard a time reasoning with Livingston. He'd make his talk short and to the point so he could get back to the ranch and track down that grizzly.

Pausing before the door, lettered with "Livingston's Boston Bank" in black paint, Nick turned the handle and entered.

In the dimmer interior light, Nick made out an elderly clerk perched on a high stool behind the wooden counter. "Horace," Nick greeted him.

The door to Livingston's office remained closed.

Nick hung his hat on the rack near the entrance.

"Morning, Nick." The clerk's ink-stained fingers suspended a pen over the inkwell. "How are things at the ranch?"

"Not good. Little Lizzy's mighty sick, and we're a-chasin' after a wounded grizzly."

Horace shook his head. The sunlight from the barred window next to the door played in stripes across his balding pate.

"Heard about the child. Preacher's been praying for her every Sunday. Wife and I have too."

"Thank you." Nick hoped he hid his surprise. Usually the clerk never uttered more than a greeting and stuck strictly to business.

Horace glanced away, then looked back at Nick. A shadow of old sorrow lingered in the fading blue depths of his eyes. "Wife and I lost our baby boy to influenza."

Nick swallowed. He'd always thought the couple childless. "I'm sorry. I never knew."

"Near thirty years ago." The clerk's voice quavered. "This here influenza epidemic brings it all back. And with the Meager baby dying—"

The door to the inner office opened. "Horace, where are those"—Livingston nodded at Nick—"reports about the Mason property?"

"I have them right here, sir." The clerk scuttled around the counter and handed over a sheaf of papers.

"Sanders." The banker, clad, despite the heat, in a three-piece brown suit, made no move to advance into the room. "May I help you with something?"

"Yes, as a matter of fact. I'd like to speak to you." Nick jerked his chin toward the office. "Privately."

"Certainly." Livingston led the way into his spacious office, and after Nick had entered, shut the door. A large mahogany desk, placed near the bar-covered window on the far wall to catch the light, dominated the room. The few chairs and the small table holding a silver tea service seemed lost in the space.

In the corner, a gilded cage held three finches perched on swings. After one glance, Nick kept his gaze away from the birds. His heart constricted from the thought he might be helping Elizabeth step into a similar cage. But she wanted this man, and he'd sworn to give her hope.

Livingston walked around the paper-spread desk, straightened a seascape on the wall, and motioned for Nick to sit in the high-backed wooden chair in front of him.

"I've been concerned for my little Lizzy," Livingston said. "How is she?"

Nick almost choked. What a hypocrite. How dare Livingston say he was concerned for *his* Lizzy. They all had certainly seen enough evidence of his *concern*.

If my errand weren't so important...Nick balled his hands into fists so he wouldn't reach over the desk and strangle the man. "Not well at all, I'm afraid."

Livingston ran a hand across his eyes, momentarily veiling his expression. "I'm sorry to hear that." He dropped his hand onto the desk and shuffled one stack of papers. "You must be anxious to get back to the ranch. If you've come about Red Charlie and his blacksmith shop—"

"No. I've come about something else. Something personal."

An uncomfortable look flashed in the banker's brown eyes. "Indeed?"

"It's about Miss Hamilton."

"Miss Hamilton?" Livingston frowned, then straightened in his chair. "Is she all right? Don't tell me she's ill as well?"

His anger subsiding somewhat, Nick unclenched his hands and settled back in his chair in satisfaction. The man actually sounded as if he cared. "No, no. She's fine. Just worn out from the strain of nursin' Lizzy."

Livingston relaxed. "She must be a great help to the Carters."

"She's an angel."

Livingston lifted his eyebrows.

"But she's frettin' over you."

"Me?" Livingston frowned again and fingered a pen on the desk.

"You. You've stopped your courtin' ever since Lizzy took sick."

"You'd hardly expect me to go to the ranch when there's illness. The last thing the Carters need is a visitor."

"Not ordinary visitors." Nick's anger rose again, and he fought to keep his tone level.

"Do you presume to tell me my business, Mr. Sanders?"

"A man who's courtin' a woman shouldn't disappear at the first sign of a little trouble."

Livingston set down his pen and straightened. "An influenza epidemic is not a little trouble," he snapped. "The Meager baby died of it."

"Elizabeth needs your support. This is a terrible time for her—for all of them."

"I have a duty to the town. What would happen to the bank if I became ill?"

"Horace would manage just fine."

"He's only a clerk."

"A damn fine one."

A condescending frown crossed Livingston's face. Looking Nick up and down, he said, "What would a cowboy like you know about the responsibilities of a man like me?"

Nick couldn't take any more of the man's excuses. "A *man* puts his duty to his loved ones first," he growled. Standing up, he placed both hands on the desk and leaned forward. "I expect you to leave this office in Horace's capable hands." He emphasized each clipped word. "Get in your buggy, head out to the ranch, and see Elizabeth."

"Impossible." Livingston rose to his feet and stepped from behind the desk. "I have work to do. Please give Miss Hamilton my regards, and tell her I'll drive out to visit when this crisis is over." He took another step toward the door. "And not a minute before."

"You coward." Nick slammed his hands on the desk. "Hidin' behind your duty."

The insult pulled Livingston up short. His face reddened, and he inhaled a sharp hiss that puffed out his cheeks almost as if he were about to spit air. Raising one stiff arm, he pointed to the door. "Get out!"

Nick's fingers itched to slide toward his gun; he resisted the temptation by clenching them into fists again. Instead, he took two deliberate strides, his boot heels clicking on the polished wooden floor, to stand face-to-face with Livingston. "She's better off without you."

Livingston narrowed his eyes. "I see which way the land lies. If I didn't trust Miss Hamilton's superior values and morals—"

Nick's fist snaked out, aiming for the banker's nose. Livingston barely had time to turn his head before Nick's knuckles connected with the man's cheek, sending him stumbling back against the wall. The seascape crashed to the ground. With shock and disbelief in his eyes, Livingston slid to the floor, cradling the rapidly forming red mark on his face.

Nick shook his head in disgust. Pity he hadn't broken the man's nose. But perhaps he'd taught him some manners. Nick yanked open the door and stalked out.

With a look of horror on his face, Horace hovered in front of the counter, wringing his hands.

Nick nodded to him, picked his hat up off the hat stand, and placed it on his head. "Settled my account with your boss."

The clerk tried to speak, but only a gurgle issued forth.

"I'll pass along your respects to the Carters," Nick murmured as he turned and strode out the door.

Out in the sunshine, the straight set of Nick's shoulders belied his feelings. He'd failed in the promise he'd made in his heart to Elizabeth—and not only failed, but he'd probably made things worse.

* * *

"Dawn," Elizabeth called down the stairway. "Dawn." Hearing no response, she started down the stairs. "Dawn?" She walked into the kitchen. "Annie," she said to the cook kneading dough at the kitchen table, "have you seen Dawn?"

"Dawn, no here." Annie waved a plump, flour-covered hand at the door. "She say she go git herb woman."

"Herb woman?"

"For Missy Rizzy."

Elizabeth crinkled her forehead, hoping Dawn had anticipated Lizzy's need. "Dr. Cameron?"

"No tink so. Tink Injin herb woman."

"Oh, dear." Elizabeth whirled, rushed out of the room and hurried down the hall. She knew Mark and Sara were playing on the front porch. She could send one of them to find Nick. Or maybe Mark could ride to town for Dr. Cameron.

Outside the sun blazed in the brilliant blue sky, and the heat pressed against her. In the shade of the porch, the children bent over a checkerboard, engrossed in their game.

"Children, have you seen Nick?"

"No," Mark said without glancing up.

"We looked in the barn and the bunkhouse, but couldn't find him," Sara said. "He's probably hunting that grizzly."

Elizabeth had forgotten about the grizzly. Now she couldn't send Mark for the doctor either.

"I'm so sick of playing in the house," Sara complained. "I hope Nick kills that ole bear."

"I'm sure you are." Elizabeth brushed damp wisps of hair off Sara's forehead. "If Nick returns, send him upstairs, will you, dear?"

Dear Lord, what are we going to do now? With a heaviness to her step, Elizabeth entered the house and trod up the steps to the sickroom.

At the bedside, Pamela looked up from bathing Lizzy's forehead, a question in her puffy, red eyes.

"Nick's not here. He and John must both be out hunting that wounded grizzly."

Lizzy's breath rattled in her throat. Even in sleep, the dark circles under her eyes turned her gaunt face into a death mask.

"What are we going to do?" Pamela whispered. "Her fever's higher, and we're out of ice."

Elizabeth sat down in the chair next to Pamela, reached for her friend's hand and squeezed it.

Pamela leaned toward her. "Beth, I'm afraid Lizzy's dying," she whispered. "My baby doesn't have much time left." Her voice broke.

At the sight of the pain on her friend's face, Elizabeth felt her heart tear into little pieces. "No," Elizabeth said fiercely. "We won't let her. Pamela, we have to break her fever."

"How? There's no ice."

"The river. We'll take her to the pool."

"Moving her might kill her."

"Not reducing the fever will kill her, Pamela. It's our only hope."

Pamela squeezed her eyes shut for a few seconds. When she opened them again, Elizabeth saw a new resolve replace her previous look of despair. "We'll take the horses." Pamela said. "Go ask Mark to saddle them. I'll bring Lizzy down."

Elizabeth gave Pamela's hand a final squeeze before rising from her chair and racing out the door. As she ran, she bundled up her blue calico skirt. Once outside, she skidded to a stop. "Mark, run to the barn and saddle horses for me and your mother."

Both children jumped up at the tone in her voice.

"We're taking Lizzy to the pool to cool her fever."

"But Aunt Elizabeth," Mark protested. "Only Outlaw and Belle are in the barn. The others are in the pasture. And we've only one ladies' saddle."

Elizabeth knew if she stopped to think about what she was going to do, she'd be too afraid to act. "Put the ladies' saddle on Belle for your mama and Lizzy. We'll let them start ahead to the river. Then saddle Outlaw for me. Do you think you can handle Outlaw?"

"I've been helping Nick with him."

"Good. Get him. And don't tell your mama. She'd waste time arguing with me, and we don't have it to waste."

"Nick's going to kill you, if Outlaw doesn't." Mark took off running, Sara at his heels.

That's the least of my worries. Elizabeth hurried back inside.

Pamela, with a blanket-wrapped Lizzy in her arms, carefully descended the stairs.

Elizabeth rushed to help her. "Mark's saddling up Belle for you and Lizzy." She slid one arm around Pamela's waist while the other supported the child. "I'll grab some more blankets and anything else we might need and follow you."

"Mama, Mama." They heard Sara's piping voice through the open door and hurried out to the porch. Sara perched atop Belle, one blue denim–clad pant leg draped over the horn of the ladies' saddle. "Here's Belle." Sara unlocked her leg from around the horn and slid from the saddle. "Mark's bringing Aunt Elizabeth's horse."

"Very good, darling." Pamela tenderly handed Lizzy over to Elizabeth.

The child felt too light in her arms. She'd withered away to nothing. Elizabeth remembered the first time she'd carried Lizzy—how, like a monkey, the child had wrapped her arms and legs tightly around her. Now, as she looked down at Lizzy's limp body, she prayed. *This has to work. Please, God, let the river cool her fever.*

Pamela led Belle over to the mounting block, hoisted herself into the saddle, and gathered the reins. Elizabeth dropped a quick kiss on Lizzy's pale cheek, then handed her goddaughter up to her mother's waiting arms.

Pamela cuddled Lizzy close. "You and Mark remain here," she ordered Sara. "Stay in the house."

"Yes, Mama."

"Get going," Elizabeth said. "I'll be right behind you. I'm just going to get a gun."

Pamela nodded and urged Belle to a walk.

Elizabeth waited until Pamela rode out of earshot. "Tell Mark to get Outlaw," she told Sara. She turned back to the house. Once inside, she ran down the hall to John's study. She hadn't been inside it since that day she and Pamela had had target practice.

Her gaze roamed the rack of rifles before she crossed over to the desk and slid open the drawer that held Pamela's Colt. As she picked up the gun, her fingers trembled. She opened the loading gate, pulled the hammer to the half-cocked position, and rotated the cylinder. Five cartridges nestled inside—just as Nick had left it. She lowered the hammer on the empty cylinder and closed the loading gate.

Looking around, Elizabeth spotted a worn leather gun belt and empty holster hanging on a peg by the door. She slipped the Colt into the holster, lifted it off, and buckled the belt around her waist. It slithered down past her hips, and she made a hasty grab before the gun landed on the floor.

With an exhalation of annoyance, she unbuckled the belt and wrapped it twice around her waist. There. She slid the Colt into the holster and grabbed a faded red Indian blanket tossed across one of the leather chairs. Now to face Outlaw.

Outside by the porch, Mark held Outlaw's reins, apprehension etched across the boy's freckled face. His eyes widened when he saw the gun belt draped around her waist. "That pistol won't stop a grizzly, Aunt Elizabeth. You'd better take a rifle."

"I can't even hit the target with the rifle."

Mark shook his head. "Probably won't see that ole bear anyway. It's Nick you'd better worry about. When he sees you've taken Outlaw, he's going to be mighty angry."

Elizabeth shifted her blanket to one arm and with her other hand tilted Mark's chin. "I have to do this, Mark," she said, trying to project an assurance she didn't feel. "We have to get Lizzy to the river, and I can't let your mother go alone, not with the threat of the grizzly."

Mark nodded, his eyes still unhappy. "Outlaw's never been ridden by anyone but Nick. You'll have to ride him astride. And your skirt might spook him more."

Elizabeth bit her bottom lip, but resolutely stepped forward and caressed the horse's gray nose. "Outlaw," she murmured. "Please, I need to ride you. Please." Her voice caught on the last word.

Outlaw snorted and shook his head.

Elizabeth clamped down on her fear. "Here." She handed the blanket to Sara, who'd been standing silently. Gathering up the middle of her blue skirt, she tucked it into her waistband, wishing she'd worn the trousers she'd disdained when she'd first arrived.

Without stopping to think, she reached for the saddle horn. Outlaw shied away before her fingers could clasp it, and her fingers slithered across the leather. Stepping closer, she grabbed for the horn again. This time her fingers securely grasped it, and she placed her foot in the stirrup. It was a long reach, and she wondered if she should use the porch steps as a mounting block.

Outlaw took two dancing steps sideways, forcing Elizabeth to hop to keep up with him. Feeling foolish and angry, Elizabeth wondered if she'd even manage to get in the saddle, much less ride the darn beast. She pulled her foot. "Please, Outlaw, we don't have time for this."

Mark pulled on the horse's reins with one hand, and with the other, pushed Outlaw's side in an effort to stop him.

Taking advantage of the momentary pause, Elizabeth hoisted herself into the saddle.

The horse rose on his hind legs, pulling Mark off balance. Elizabeth clenched her legs around his girth and clung to the saddle horn, praying Mark could hold him.

With a snort and a toss of his head, Outlaw settled to the boy's soft talk and pressure on the reins. Holding tightly to the saddle horn, Elizabeth reached down and tucked her skirt securely around her legs.

Mark adjusted the stirrups, looped the reins over the horse's head, and handed them to her. She reached out to Sara for the blanket and set it on her lap, tucking a folded corner into her waistband.

For a tense moment, Elizabeth waited for the explosion she was sure would come. When nothing happened, she flashed a nervous grin at Mark and spared one for Sara. Then, she kicked Outlaw and took off after Pamela.

At first, Elizabeth held herself stiffly against the movement of the horse, trying to anticipate whatever tricks Outlaw might play on her, but after a few moments, she settled into his rhythm. She enjoyed the unusual sensation of riding astride and feeling the powerful muscles of the horse move beneath her legs. She'd never experienced anything like it. If she hadn't been so fraught with fear over Lizzy, Elizabeth would have lost herself in the experience. Maybe someday…

She caught up with Pamela and Lizzy when they'd almost reached the river.

Pamela glanced over at her, and her eyes widened. "Elizabeth Hamilton! What are you doing riding that horse? Nick's going to be so angry with you!"

"Nick's not around," Elizabeth said tartly.

"Well, you'd better not break your neck. We've enough problems as it is."

"I won't."

Pamela glanced down at her frail daughter—a feeble bundle in her arms. "Will this help her, Beth?"

"It will, Pam." *It has to.*

At the pool, Elizabeth reined in. Uttering another prayer, she slid her foot from the stirrup, awkwardly swung her leg over the horse, and dismounted. She tied the reins to a nearby bush and gave a quick stroke to the horse's neck. "Thank you, Outlaw."

Elizabeth reached up for Lizzy, and Pamela handed her down. Holding the child close, Elizabeth placed a kiss on the hot, dry skin of her forehead. Lizzy barely opened her eyes before her eyelids drooped shut.

Pamela tied Belle to the bush and, sitting on the log by the water, removed her shoes. Kilting her dress up, she reached out for her daughter. With one more kiss, Elizabeth handed her over. Helping Pamela unwind the blanket, she then pulled off the child's shift. With Lizzy in her arms, Pamela waded out into the pool, and slowly lowered her into the water.

Lizzy stirred enough to utter a mewing protest.

"It'll help you, darling," Pamela crooned, submerging her daughter until, except for her face, water covered her entire body. "It feels good, doesn't it?"

Elizabeth sat on the log, undid her shoes, and pulled off her stockings. She unstrapped the gun belt and folded it into the blanket to protect the gun from errant splashes.

Stepping into the water, she relished the coolness against her feet and legs. The pool looked shallower, and the water didn't seem as chill as it had been several weeks earlier.

With the dangerous ride on Outlaw safely over, the peaceful silence of the quietly flowing river gave Elizabeth a sense of relaxation. Surely this beautiful pool would help Lizzy.

Wading over to Pamela, she slipped a hand under Lizzy's shoulder and waist, helping to support the little girl. Buoyed by the water, Lizzy's slight weight felt even lighter. Her skin gleamed pale against the green water, dark hair fanning around her head. Elizabeth moved her hand from under Lizzy's bony shoulder, trying to cool the child's face by brushing her palm across the little girl's forehead and cheeks. "Her skin's still too warm."

"But she does seem a bit cooler, doesn't she?" Pamela's eyes begged.

Elizabeth dribbled more water over Lizzy's face, careful not to trickle any in the child's eyes, then she cupped her forehead. "I do believe you're right. She does feel cooler."

Minutes passed quietly, with the two women hardly daring to hope.

A snap of broken branches cut the stillness, a rustling of the bushes downstream across the river. With a flash of frightened intuition, Elizabeth knew.

The grizzly.

* * *

A breeze caressed Nick's cheek, a touch of coolness in the oppressive heat. The breath of humidity differed from the scent of the river where he and John searched for bear signs. He lifted his head in surprise at the hint of moisture in the dry air. He hadn't felt any breeze in weeks. Scanning the sky, he saw gray clouds building in the distance. A storm. He whooped with excitement.

Across the water and upriver about twenty feet, John Carter knelt, examining the embankment. At Nick's whoop, he scrambled to his feet, reaching for his rifle.

"Look," Nick called, pointing at the corner of graying sky. "Storm clouds."

A grin split John's weary face. He clasped his hands together and waved them over his head, almost knocking his hat off. "We'd better head back," he called.

Nick untied Freckles's reins from the bushes, pulled them over the horse's head, and mounted. Downstream about fifty feet, the river flowed over a sandy bed, free of the boulders that made most of the river too dangerous to cross.

He urged Freckles into the water. The horse balked at the current swirling around his knees, but a firm nudge with a boot heel sent Freckles plunging into the cold green depths. In the last weeks, the drought had tamed the river—the water didn't even reach Freckles's belly.

The horse had almost crossed the river when an ominous feeling clenched Nick's gut. He yanked out his Colt and kicked Freckles up the bank, through the trees, and out into the open. *Nothing.*

Angling Freckles around in a circle, he studied each bush and tree. Nick's nostrils flared. Searching for any clue of danger, he listened with all his might. *Still nothing.*

The area seemed peaceful, but his unease only deepened. The focus appeared to be located quite a ways downstream. He sheathed the Colt and rubbed his neck. The familiarity of the feeling itched at his memory. Mentally he scrolled back over the past weeks, searching to remember. Then it came to him—he'd felt this way the day the women and children had picked berries!

"John," he shouted. "John!"

John galloped into sight from around the tree-shaded bend in the river and reined his black stallion in next to Nick. "What?"

"I don't know exactly. Something with the women and children."

John was familiar with Nick's instincts, and his face paled under his ruddy tan. "Where?"

"Downstream."

"Downstream? Why the hell would they be at the river?"

"No idea." Nick pulled at the reins, turning Freckles. "Let's go." He kneed Freckles into a gallop. *Please, God, let us get there in time.*

CHAPTER TWENTY-FOUR

More bushes crackled. Elizabeth's heart pounded at the sound. "Get Lizzy to the horses," she whispered, moving in front of Pamela and pushing her toward the shore.

Pamela looked confused. "Elizabeth, what are you doing?"

"The grizzly, Pam. The one the men are hunting. It's here."

The recognition came too late. The bear broke through the brush opposite them, thirty feet from the bank of the river.

For Elizabeth, time slowed. She'd faced a grizzly before. But this time she grew even more afraid. She had more at stake and no Nick to rescue them.

Her stomach clenched. Her knees shook, but her brain remained clear. Elizabeth's eyesight sharpened on details: how the bear's face and body were a silver-tipped brown, with only a brown bib surrounding its neck…how the shoulder wound oozed glistening blood, darkening the brown fur to black…how, as the grizzly started toward the water, she could see what must be four-inch claws extending from its paws.

The bear planted its forelegs wide and lumbered side to side, luffing its jowls.

A scream gurgled up from Pamela. Clutching Lizzy to her breast, she splashed toward the bank.

Elizabeth angled toward the shore where she'd left the blanket. *Why, oh, why didn't I keep the Colt nearby?* She scrambled over the log and grabbed the blanket, yanking its folds loose. The gun belt and holster bounced to the ground. She scooped the holster up, pulling out the Colt.

Pamela cried out again. Lizzy whimpered and struggled in her mother's arms. Hampered by the child, Pamela slipped, and they both fell under the water.

Elizabeth hopped back over the log and dragged Pamela up with one hand, trying to ignore Lizzy's weak wails. The other shaking hand pointed the gun toward the grizzly, which plodded toward them, seeming to favor its right side.

As the animal approached the water, Elizabeth thrust Pamela behind her. Willing herself to calmness, she steadied the gun with both hands. *Keep your eyes open*—she heard Nick's voice in her head. The warmth of the memory strengthened her arms, but didn't slow her rapidly beating heart.

Elizabeth took a deep breath, thumbed the hammer back, and squeezed the trigger.

Crack.

The monster jerked, but continued its hulking shamble to the water.

She shot again. *Missed.*

Steady, Elizabeth. Nick's voice again.

Taking another breath, she fired. Another jerk from the bear, but it continued into the water. The animal reared to its hind legs. Its mouth opened, showing long yellow fangs. The sight of the huge monster towering a few yards away from her threatened to make Elizabeth faint, but she forced the waves of dizziness away from her.

Nick, where are you? She bit her lip.

Aim for the heart. Nick's words focused her aim.

In rapid succession, she fired off the last two rounds.

The grizzly froze, then leaned forward.

"Oh, no," Elizabeth moaned. *Why, oh, why didn't I bring more bullets?*

Then the bear slowly toppled sideways, landing with a splash in the water.

❋ ❋ ❋

At the sound of a scream, Nick thought his heart would stop with fear. Bending low over the horse's neck, he kicked Freckles to a faster gallop, wishing he'd ridden his wind-racer, Outlaw. He pulled his Colt from the holster. From the corner of his eye, he saw John do the same.

The *cracks* of gunshots scared him right down to his boots. *What's happening? God, please keep her safe.*

Rounding the bushes, Nick and John burst into the clearing by the pool, almost running down Belle and Outlaw, who skittered out of the way. Their horses skidded to a stop. *Why the hell is Outlaw here?* But his concentration focused on Elizabeth, standing in front of Pamela and Lizzy—facing down the wounded grizzly with only a pistol.

Nick jammed his Colt back in the holster and yanked out the Winchester. Sighting down the barrel, he watched the animal collapse before he could pull the trigger.

His shoulders relaxed. Relief burst through his body, setting his hands to shaking. Keeping a wary eye on the bear, he lowered the rifle.

John holstered his Colt, leaped off his horse, and ran toward his wife and daughter. Nick slid off Freckles. Still holding the Winchester aimed at the grizzly, he raced around John and splashed over to Elizabeth.

Pulling Elizabeth sideways with his free arm, he kept his body between her and the bear. He spared time for a quick kiss, two kisses, relishing the feeling of having her safe, then released her. "I'll be right back. Need to check out that bear."

Without waiting for a response, he waded out of the water, then climbed back in below the rocks that dammed the pool. Keeping the rifle aimed at the animal, he forded the river, clambering over slimed green rocks.

Gingerly he approached the carcass, ready to shoot should it rise to life. Studying the animal, he prodded it with his foot. Dead, all right. He picked up one claw-tipped paw, his gut clenching at the thought of how close those claws came to rending his beloved.

He examined the grizzly. The old shoulder wound, with its caked, seeping blood, must have been driving the bear crazy with pain. One of Elizabeth's bullets had caught the animal in the heart. A very lucky shot. "You're going to make Elizabeth one warm rug," he told the dead carcass. He dropped the paw. "I'll deal with you later."

Turning, he waded back across the river. Elizabeth stood where he'd left her, a forlorn figure in a sodden blue gown, still clasping the pistol with both hands. His heart swelled with pride at her courage, but he also wanted to shake her for scaring ten years off his life.

* * *

Elizabeth didn't know whether to let out the yell of triumph that had knotted in her throat or succumb to her dizziness and tumble headfirst into the pool. The sensation of Nick's kisses lingered on her lips, adding to her feeling of unreality. She watched him prod the bear, flinched as Nick lifted its paw, and shut her eyes.

Collapsing into the water will not do, she sternly told herself, trying to instill strength into her trembling knees. Nor did she intend to let her nerveless fingers drop Pamela's gun into the river.

Behind her, she could hear John and Pamela babbling to each other in relief. She knew she should go to them, but her feet felt glued to the sandy bottom of the pool. She peeked from underneath her lowered eyelids to see if Nick had finished his gruesome examination of the beast.

Across the river, he met her gaze. Emotions blazing in his eyes turned them to emerald fire. Beneath his tan, his skin was still pale, and lines bracketed each side of his mouth. Her stomach tightened at the thought.

Nick plunged into the water. Mesmerized, Elizabeth watched his hips move against the current. As she stared at the wet shirt plastered to his slim waist and muscled chest, her heartbeat, which had started to calm, quickened.

She rotated her body with his progress across the river like the shadow of a sundial following the sun. When Nick reached the bank of the river, he set the rifle on the ground, climbed around the rocks of the dam, and waded purposefully toward her.

The tension between them increased with each stride. Vaguely, out of the corner of her eye, Elizabeth saw John wrapping Pamela and Lizzy in blankets. As her pulse raced in anticipation, she realized she didn't care if John and Pamela witnessed Nick kissing her. She wanted to declare her love to the world.

Nick took the pistol from her, turned, and tossed it onto the grass. Placing his hands on her arms, he pulled her to him, the pressure of his fingers biting into the softness of her flesh.

"I don't know whether to shake you"—Nick emphasized his words with a joggle of her arms—"or kiss you." His tone sounded playful, but seriousness glimmered in his gaze.

A dry laugh escaped her lips. She leaned toward him. "Kiss me, please, Nick." She put every ounce of her love and longing in the words.

He searched her face. "Are you sure?"

"Yes, oh, yes."

Ever so slowly, he tilted her chin with one callused finger, bent down, and brushed her lips with his. Elizabeth's body quivered in response, and his kiss deepened. He slid his hands around her shoulders, pulling her closer while his tongue explored her mouth.

Elizabeth melted into his embrace. Her arms crept around his waist. The wet shirt clung to his body, reminding her of the hot night at the pool and how her palms had felt against his bare skin. Her body shivered with pleasure at the memory.

In response, Nick's arms tightened around her. On that night, she'd been shocked and tentative about her feelings for Nick. But now everything was different. She ran her fingers over the hard muscles in his back. Rocked with passion, filled with his love, for one glorious moment, all her cares and concerns disappeared.

A pitiful cry from Lizzy pulled Elizabeth and Nick apart. Elizabeth's joy fled, and she saw her fear mirrored in Nick's eyes. As one, they turned and splashed to the log where the Carters sat.

"Hush, dearest," Pamela crooned to the child cradled in her arms. "The water will make you feel better."

John had his arm around Pamela's waist, while the other held his daughter's limp hand. Pamela looked up at Elizabeth, hope in her eyes. "I think the immersion helped. Her skin feels cooler."

Elizabeth placed her palm on Lizzy's forehead. "You're right. She does seem cooler."

The sound of hoofbeats startled them. Both men's hands dropped to their guns. John swiveled around on the log and stood up. Nick stepped in front of Elizabeth.

Elizabeth's nerves jangled. She resisted the temptation to clutch Nick. What other disaster could possibly happen today?

Dawn, mounted astride a gray Appaloosa, appeared around the bushes. She'd exchanged her proper clothes for a dress of soft, tan leather, patterned in tiny colored beads. Hitched to her knees, the dress exposed shapely brown legs. She wore moccasins of beaded leather.

Both Nick and John's postures relaxed, and their hands ceased to hover near their guns.

"That grizzly's made me as jumpy as all git out," muttered John, a sheepish look on his ruddy face.

Elizabeth barely had time to wonder why Dawn was wearing such strange clothing, when an elderly Indian woman, riding a brown Appaloosa with a white spotted rear that looked almost like Freckles's, followed Dawn around the bushes. She nodded in greeting.

Elizabeth gasped in surprise. Like Dawn, the old woman was dressed in beaded leather, but a brightly patterned blanket was draped across her shoulders. Blue feathers were tucked into white hair braided back from a dark face, which was wrinkled like a walnut. Her wise brown eyes surveyed everyone before dropping to Lizzy.

"Herbal woman," said Dawn. Then she repeated a long, unpronounceable Indian name. "She make Lizzy better."

"It's Good Earth Woman," Nick said. "Red Charlie's great-aunt. She's a renowned healer among the Indians."

"I've heard of her," John said. "Helped Joe Green when nothing else seemed to work." He turned to look at his wife, whose face had brightened with hope. An unspoken message passed between them. John ran his fingers through his sandy hair. He gave the Indian a slight bow and waved toward Lizzy. "Please."

The medicine woman dismounted, approached Pamela and Lizzy, knelt down in front of them, and spoke in her language to the child.

Lizzy shrank against her mother. Then the gentle tone of the old woman's voice and the power in her ancient eyes seemed to reassure her. She relaxed, and a spark of life glimmered in the blue eyes, which had been lifeless for so many days.

The medicine woman gestured for Pamela to lay Lizzy on the grass. Silently, she examined her, her gnarled brown hands moving in a slow but competent way over the wasted little body.

When she finished, she rocked back on her heels and spoke to Pamela. Dawn translated.

"It is good you brought her to water to quiet her inner fire." She pulled her medicine bag into her lap and opened it. Bringing out a leather-wrapped packet, she exposed crumpled brown leaves that gave out an aromatic scent. "Make into tea. Drink several times a day. Make her strong."

Pamela nodded, her gaze never leaving the old woman's face.

The Indian leaned down and touched Lizzy's forehead. Then she looked up, and a smile lightened her wrinkled face. Dawn relayed her words: "Be better soon."

Tears welled up in Pamela's eyes and trickled down her cheeks. "Thank you," she whispered.

John bowed his head. He covered his eyes with one hand, while the other dropped to Pamela's shoulder and squeezed.

Trying to remain composed, Elizabeth choked down a lump in her throat, to no avail. Her own tears of sympathy and hope blurred her vision.

Nick pulled her into his embrace. A quick glance at his face showed wetness in his eyes, clinging to his dark lashes. He rested his cheek on her head and held her tight. She snuggled against him, feeling so very grateful to have his strength to depend on when she needed solace and comfort—or when she needed love…

The weeks of worry slipped away from her, almost as if a protective screen had fallen between the pain of her long vigil over the sick child and this moment. Now, in her love for Nick, and his for her, she felt elevated above sorrow and worry, filled with triumph. The long numbness of the last few days—no, if she was honest with herself, the last eleven years, passed away. In its place arose a glorious feeling of belonging to this rugged land and to the man holding her.

❋ ❋ ❋

A sky-filling flash of lightning, closely followed by a clap of thunder, caused Elizabeth to gasp. Overhead and toward the south, the dark clouds had turned the sky pewter and the pine trees in the foothills to a gray-green color. But surprisingly, to the north, sun shone through patches of blue sky.

"It's fixin' to be a big storm," said Nick. "Best head back to the house." He looked down at his wet clothes, then grinned at her. "Although I don't think a little more water will bother us a bit."

No sooner had he spoken than the heavens opened up, as if releasing all the weeks of prayed-for rain. Fat drops pelted down.

Pamela snatched up Lizzy, wrapping her in the blanket while the medicine woman handed John the precious packet of herbs.

John clasped Good Earth Woman's hand. "I thank you."

Perhaps the old woman couldn't understand the English words, but John's tone and heartfelt look conveyed his gratitude.

From within her cocoon of blankets, Lizzy solemnly surveyed the old woman.

The herb woman waved a kind of salute and pronounced what seemed to be a blessing before turning toward her horse.

John immediately became businesslike. "Hand Lizzy to me. Put your shoes on, then mount Belle," he told Pamela, taking their daughter from her.

Elizabeth grabbed up the gun belt, already spotted by rain.

"That's an old one of John's," said Nick, his mouth quirked in amusement. "Did you actually wear it?"

Not caring about the rain, Elizabeth cocked an eyebrow in a signal for him to watch. Slowly extending the gun belt to the full length, she wrapped it twice around her waist before buckling the belt. Then she leaned down, scooped up the Colt, and jammed it in the holster.

"Well, I'll be." Nick laughed. Reaching out his arm, he pulled her to his side, and gave her a quick kiss. "I'll have one made for you."

Elizabeth sat on the log to put on her shoes. When she finished, Nick extended his hand to help her up.

"Come on, you two." John called to them.

Laughing, hand in hand, they ran to the horses.

"This time," said Nick, "you're riding Freckles. And when we're home and dry, I want to hear how you managed to handle Outlaw."

"Oh, a Sunday ride in the park."

Nick shook his head, but his eyes twinkled. "Rides my demon horse, shoots a grizzly—my, my, proper Miss Elizabeth Hamilton, who'd ever have thought it?"

Elizabeth blushed and looked down. Then she saw that her skirt was still tucked up. With all the excitement, she hadn't even noticed her dress. She shrugged, not caring.

Nick helped her into the saddle. "Freckles isn't familiar with a ladies skirt, but he's a steady one," he said, handing her the reins. "You'll be fine."

Looking around for his hat, which had somehow become dislodged in his earlier rush to Elizabeth, Nick picked up the Stetson and clapped it on his head. He mounted Outlaw, reined the horse toward the ranch, and motioned Elizabeth to follow.

At first Nick seemed to be watching her to make sure she wouldn't have problems with Freckles. Then he relaxed, giving her a grin of approval.

In the glowering sky, a splintering pitchfork sparked from cloud to ground, followed by a thunder shot from God's rifle.

No longer afraid, Elizabeth turned her face to the sky, relishing the coolness of the rain on her skin. She'd been hot and dry for so long! And not only on her skin, but in her soul. Inhaling the rich scent of dampened grass and wet earth, she breathed a prayer of thanksgiving.

As they neared the ranch, Elizabeth saw a buggy pulling up to the porch. *Caleb's buggy.*

Oh, no, she thought in dismay, keeping her face averted from Nick. Why, today of all days, had Caleb finally appeared at the ranch? Although she'd rehearsed what she'd say to him if he ever again showed up to court her, she'd planned to look her best. With one hand, she tried to tighten the loose hairpins in the wet knot of hair sagging at the back of her neck. She glanced down at the saddle that necessitated her riding astride, her sodden blue calico dress kilted up to her knees.

Elizabeth lifted her chin. She'd make the best of the situation. She was a blue-blooded Boston lady—no, Montana lady—and thus would present a genteel appearance regardless of her attire. At least that's what her mama had always said. Now, if only she could get off this horse in a relatively decent fashion…

Nick dismounted, looping Outlaw's reins around the porch rail, then strode around to her. Reaching up, he placed his hands on her waist and lifted her from the horse.

Elizabeth leaned down and untucked her dress.

As if freeing her to go to the banker, he quickly released her, but she squeezed his shoulder in a silent gesture of reassurance before she turned to Caleb. Behind her, she stayed aware of Nick leading the horses toward the barn. She sighed, wishing she were going with him.

"Elizabeth." Caleb touched his hat, his face expressionless.

"Caleb." Elizabeth didn't intend to make this easy for him. Nor was she going to invite him in—they could talk on the porch.

Caleb climbed out of the buggy, tossed the reins around the rail, and ran up the steps. Shaking the raindrops from his suit, he took off his hat and dropped it on a rocker. Up close she could see a bruise shadowing one cheek. He studied her. "You're thinner."

Under his scrutiny, heat had risen in her cheeks, but she refused to drop her eyes.

"Perhaps you should change out of your wet clothing."

"After the heat of the last weeks, being wet feels refreshing." Her voice sounded as cool as the rain.

He shifted his weight. "It is a welcome relief."

Elizabeth knew she was being a terrible hostess, but she didn't care.

"How's Lizzy?"

Elizabeth didn't mince words. "She almost died."

He winced. "But she's better?"

"We think so. Her fever's down. She's not completely out of the woods. An Indian herbal woman gave us a tea for Lizzy to drink to help her get better."

"An Indian herbal woman?" He lifted a skeptical eyebrow. "I doubt she'll be able to help."

Like the thunderstorm, anger overwhelmed Elizabeth. It took every ounce of ladylike discipline she possessed to restrain herself from shouting at him and pounding her fists on his chest. But she couldn't stop the fury from blazing from her eyes.

At the look on her face, Caleb stepped back a pace, and cleared his throat. "Bank business has kept me very busy these last few weeks—"

She chopped the air with her hand. "I'm well aware of why you haven't been around, Caleb. And I'm thankful for it. It's opened my eyes to your true character."

Caleb looked like he'd been struck by the lightning forking across the sky. He opened his mouth to reply.

Elizabeth's words raced out, preventing him from speaking. "You claimed to be fond of Lizzy, to be fond of me, but you were too afraid of catching Lizzy's illness to be here when we needed you. It wasn't business, and don't you dare pretend it was."

A shamed look crossed his face. "I'm sorry you feel that way. I do have responsibilities. Will you forgive me?"

The contrition in his voice softened her anger to a light rain cloud. "I believe in time I will."

"How much time?" He stepped closer and put his hands on her shoulders. "In time for a September wedding?"

Elizabeth gasped, too stunned by his suggestion to even twist out of his grasp.

He smiled, mistaking her reaction. "Why don't you go put on some dry clothes"—he looked her up and down—"and we'll discuss it."

"No, Caleb." She stepped back, out of his hands. "I meant it when I said I've awakened to your true character." She lifted her chin. "I want a husband who will stand by my side no matter what comes, and you've proven you're not that man."

"I see." Once again his face was expressionless, but anger flashed in his eyes.

Elizabeth knew she'd wounded his pride. *But not his heart.* She stood her ground.

He leaned over to pick up his hat and carefully placed it on his head. "Then I will take my leave of you."

❋ ❋ ❋

Elizabeth clutched the porch rail, watching Caleb's buggy recede into the distance. Her anger drained away, and with it her energy, leaving her as limp as a deflated hot-air balloon. Too much had happened today. Her mind whirled with thoughts, and she couldn't settle on what she felt.

Nick strode through the barn doors and looked around. Even at a distance, she could see the relief on his face when he saw Caleb's buggy headed out of the valley.

Suddenly her confused feelings crystallized. *I need Nick.* Gathering up her heavy wet skirt, Elizabeth leaped down the stairs and rushed toward him.

He ran to meet her. She flung herself into his arms, and, laughing, he picked her up and spun her around.

Overhead, the dark clouds parted, and a circle of blue sky appeared. The sun's rays burst through, enveloping them in light.

Nick slowed their spinning, and, as Elizabeth's toes touched the ground, he kissed her like he'd never let her go.

Elizabeth clung to him, returning his kisses with a passion not at all ladylike.

Breathlessly they pulled apart. Then Nick's palms cupped her cheeks, and he gave her a last soft kiss. Dropping an arm around her waist, he guided her toward the house.

"Look." Elizabeth pointed upward.

In the misty space between clouds, a rainbow soared across the sky. Nick stopped and pulled Elizabeth back against his chest. With her head resting on his shoulder, they stood and watched the heaven-sent omen of hope for their future.

CHAPTER TWENTY-FIVE

Elizabeth shifted her weight in the saddle and leaned over to pat Belle's neck, grateful to ride quietly with Nick. For the first day in weeks, the constant tension she'd lived with had vanished. Finally, Lizzy had regained enough strength to be allowed out of bed, enjoying a near full recovery. The long, dark period of her illness had finally ended.

As Elizabeth breathed in the brisk pine-scented air, she reveled in her contentment. She looked up at the afternoon sun, its rays no longer the enemy but a gentle friend, and enjoyed the warmth on her face. For this ride, she'd deliberately left behind the hat that matched her riding habit. Sometimes hats weren't very convenient...

She glanced sideways at Nick and caught him watching her, his green eyes warm and tender.

"Admiring the sky?" he asked.

"Those clouds look like upside-down sheep," she said pointing at a cluster of puffs in the cerulean sky. "Heavenly sheep grazing in a limitless blue pasture."

"Enjoy the sunshine and the blue sky. Winter will be here soon enough. Although you'll miss most of it, being in Boston."

"I received a letter from Sylvia today. She talked to Genia's doctor. Dr. Sherman told her that Genia's fine, just too high-strung and hysterical—hence the bed rest. Now I know I don't have to rush home because she's seriously ill. I'll be there for Genia's last month. That's enough time to be away from everyone…from you."

"More than enough time. I'm going to have to stay too busy to think about how much I miss you." A mischievous smile crossed his face, and his eyes shone with excitement. "Our destination is just over this last rise," he said, pulling ahead of her and guiding Outlaw around a towering pine tree.

Elizabeth took a moment to admire the broad set of his shoulders and the way his muscles moved under his shirt, then gave Belle a kick.

Together, they crested the rise. Reining in the horses, they looked down into a crescent-shaped amber valley. In the middle, a small lake sparkled like the sapphire jewel in the golden crown of grassland.

"What do you think?" Nick asked.

"Beautiful."

Pride flashed in his eyes. "It's mine."

"Yours?"

"Been buyin' pieces of it off Widow Thatcher for the last few years. Bought the last parcel just before Lizzy took sick."

"Oh, Nick." Elizabeth's heart swelled with happiness. She'd fallen in love with a ranch hand and planned to live a simple life with him. But to learn Nick was a landowner…what an extra blessing!

"This valley will only support a small herd of cattle…and, of course, my horses. But I'll be able to keep my family in comfort." His eyes searched her face for her reaction.

Elizabeth knew her smile radiated love and reassurance.

Nick smiled back in relief. "Come on." He kneed Outlaw into a canter.

Elizabeth urged Belle to follow him. They descended into the valley. Wheat-pale tufts of dried grass rustled and rippled in the breeze, undulating over the hillocks like waves of the sea—an earthen ocean of warm colors instead of cool greens and blues.

Nick headed to a hill overlooking the small lake. When they reached the top, he reined in. He waved his arm. "I think this site has the most beautiful view of the valley."

"Oh, yes. In fact, it would be perfect for a house." In her imagination, she could see a large white house with the inevitable Montana porch running across the front. She'd plant a large garden just like Pamela's and have—*Whoa, girl. He hasn't asked you yet.*

With a smile, he dismounted. Tying Outlaw's reins to a bush, he reached up for Elizabeth, waiting while she unlocked her leg from the saddle and slid into his arms.

He held her for a moment, resting his cheek against her hair, both of them enjoying a quiet minute together, free of the fears and dangers that had haunted them for the last few weeks.

Then he pulled away and looked at her. "No hat?"

Elizabeth tried for a demure simper, but playfulness widened her mouth into a flirtatious smile.

Running a featherlight finger over her lips, he said, "I'll have to take advantage of that freedom, but first there's something I want you to see."

He took her hand and led her to the highest part of the hill. "I was going to build a log cabin right here." He pointed ahead of them. "This was going to be the doorway," he said, dropping her hand and pacing it out. "We're standing on the porch."

"Was?"

"Instead, I've decided to build a frame house." He turned to face her and took both her hands in his. "It might take a while, but when I've finished it, will you marry me, Elizabeth?"

A shiver started deep in Elizabeth's body, and she trembled with excitement. She was too full of emotion to speak, and her eyes welled with tears of love.

But the apprehension in his gaze tugged the words from her. "Of course," she whispered.

Relief swept across his face. He reached into his pocket, pulled out a ring, and slid it on her finger.

At the sight of the sapphire stone surrounded by tiny diamonds, she gasped. "Nick, it's beautiful!"

"It was my mother's. My father mined that stone here in Montana. He spent an entire summer searching for the right sapphire for her ring."

Elizabeth inhaled a tremulous breath. Good thing she'd worn a corset. Otherwise, her joy might burst her heart entirely out of her body. She reined herself in enough to speak. "This ring is very special. I'll be proud to wear it."

"It'll probably be two years before I can afford to build a house fit for you to live in."

"We don't have to wait. I have some money. It's not a great fortune, but it's enough to help build and furnish a house and maybe buy more land or livestock."

A strange look crossed his face. He shook his head, released her hands and half turned away. "I didn't realize you had money, Elizabeth."

Her stomach knotted. Had she offended him? Surely she wouldn't lose her newfound happiness because she'd offered him her inheritance? She'd always thought her fortune wasn't large enough, and now Nick was rejecting it. "What's wrong, Nick?" she whispered.

"A man has his pride, Elizabeth. He wants to know he can take care of his family."

"Nick, you wouldn't let money come between us. Not after everything we've been through?"

"I don't want your money, Elizabeth. I just want you."

She stepped toward him. "Since I've come to Montana, I've learned what's really important to me, Nick. I want a family like Pamela's. I know you do too."

He nodded.

"Life is so fleeting. We've both lost people dear to us." Her voice faltered, and she blinked back tears. "What's important is that we love each other, not which of us has more money." She went to him and slipped her hand around his elbow. "I want babies, and I want you to be their father." She pulled at his arm. "I don't want to wait to start a family."

Nick turned to face her again and took a deep breath. "I guess you're right about the money." He shook his head. "We have lost too many we've loved. Pride's a fool thing when you're facin' a grave."

"So we don't have to wait?"

"Only till I get the house built."

"I'm sure we'll have a lot of help. It will go up in no time."

He tenderly brushed a stray strand of hair out of her face. "Would you give me a daughter with your beautiful blue eyes?" he whispered, his face near hers.

"First I want a son with your green ones."

Nick cupped her cheeks with his hands, leaned forward, and kissed her gently. Straightening, he smiled down at her.

Elizabeth touched his cheek. He captured her hand, turned his face, and planted a kiss on her palm. Warm tingles raced up her arm and spread throughout her body, making her light-headed.

Nick scooped her up in his arms.

She gasped and locked her arms around his neck.

"In that case, my dearest, let me carry you over our future threshold."

Nick took several steps with her before setting her down. He picked up one of her hands, turned it over, and kissed her palm again before placing it against his chest.

Her heart melted in response, and her knees threatened to follow.

He turned her so they could look out their imaginary doorway to the beautiful panorama spread before them. "I'll start building our home tomorrow."

About the Author

USA Today bestseller Debra Holland is a psychotherapist, corporate crisis counselor, and martial arts instructor, as well as an acclaimed author. It wasn't until she finished many years of grad school that she began her writing career in earnest. In addition to her historical westerns, Holland is also the author of the self-help book *The Essential Guide to Grief and Grieving* and two books of fantasy romance, *Sower of Dreams* and *Reaper of Dreams*. She lives in Southern California, where she was born and raised.

Don't miss the next heartwarming romance in Debra Holland's *USA Today* bestselling Montana Sky series, *Starry Montana Sky*!

After inheriting her uncle's property, a young widow moves to 1890s Montana and contends with a handsome rancher who wants her land for his own.

Available now!